KING TEES

KING
TEES

JOHN NICHOLSON

Nick Guymer Series
No.10

Published by Head Publishing
Copyright © John Nicholson 2016

Edition edit by Robert Marcum

Printed by CMP UK Ltd

ISBN 978-0-9933817-1-3

http://www.johnnicholsonwriter.com

Thanks to my editor Robert for his cool Woodstock generation advice and his help to make, both the story and the text, so much better.
An emotionally repressed northern hug to Janet for close scrutiny, quiet inspiration and good memories, some of which are woven through the pages of this and other books.
And a big cheers to Julie at WAEML for advice, knowledge and just as important, some lovely positivity: it is the water that feeds the growth.
Thanks also to Diane for specialist transgender help, which expanded both my mind and my vocabulary.
Who could want more?
I must also thank the very wonderful writer and duffle coat-wearer, Dan Gray, for inspiring the whole concept of our Inner Boro, which is so important to this story.
And last, but never least, some proper big love to Dawn, for all the laughter and ideas forged on our walks in Inverleith Park and the Botanic Gardens and out of the extraordinary up and down, in and out, higher than high, lower than low, diamonds and dirt life, that we've lived together.
What a long strange trip it's been. At some point, the wheel of karma will turn and all the pain will pay off.

This book is dedicated to being yourself

"When you look at me
You better look hard and look twice
Is that me baby
Or just a brilliant disguise?"

CHAPTER 1

'Are you going to carry your new, innocent and virginal wife over the threshold, then?' said Julie, jumping on Nick's back as he unlocked the huge, glossy black Georgian door.

He laughed, put his hands under her legs and carried her piggy back into the apartment.

'Here we are then, little Miss Innocent. Your honeymoon suite awaits, madam.'

She dismounted, made as though she was swooning and affected a posh voice. 'Oh, darling, I am pure of heart and untouched of front bottom, so please be gentle with me on the night after my wedding night.'

'I don't think there's much chance of that, do you?' he said, laughing.

She slapped him on the backside. 'I should bloody hope not, no. Eee, my god, this is a bit posh, isn't it?' she said, looking around the big reception area.

'Well, you're a Wells-Guymer now - that's about as aristocratic a name as you can get, I reckon. This is the sort of place a double-barrelled ponce would live in.'

'I'm plain old Julie Wells, me, and I always will be, but it's dead smart in here, though. I could get used to a bit of luxury.'

They walked into a huge, high-ceilinged, mid-Georgian living room. The walls were covered in expensive two-tone red striped wallpaper. Two large cream sofas faced each other. Queen Anne reproduction desks and tables were pushed against the walls. Two 12-pane Georgian sash windows were on the south side of the room and faced onto Edinburgh's famous Heriot Row; a third faced west onto Howe Street.

He stood, hands on hips, and looked around.

'When Big Fish said we could use his flat for our honeymoon, I never thought it'd be this big. This is massive and really posh. Too posh for him.'

He raised his arms high and wide. The roof was at least 10 feet above and featured a huge plaster rose with a large chandelier set into it.

Julie took hold of one of the floor-length curtains - about eight feet of heavy gold, red and blue brocade. 'This sort of material costs a fortune in John Lewis. There must be 1,000 quid in each curtain, if not more. There's at least six grand of curtains in here! Six! Christ, how the other half live, eh? Still, it'll suit us nicely for our honeymoon week at the Fringe.'

1

Nick nodded and looked down at the cobbles of Howe Street in Edinburgh's New Town, just north of the famous Princes Street. It all seemed so grand and so very not Teesside. For all that it's not a big place, Edinburgh is a capital city and as such, full of history, culture and, crucially, money. Big money. And here in the New Town, a lot of it was invested in the streets of Georgian buildings.

There was a firm, rapid knock on the door.

He walked back into the hallway and pulled open the big door. A short, stocky woman, probably in her early 30s, stood there with a lopsided, ruffled up, dyed red, quirky haircut. She wore a tight petrol-blue suit, pointy black boots, a white shirt buttoned right up, ornate metal tips on the collar. No tie.

'Alright, mate,' she said, with a little burst of infectious energy, holding out her hand. It was only two words but the second one gave her away immediately as a Teessider. She pronounced it "maaayt" and only people from Teesside did that; most likely she was from Middlesbrough. Given a bit longer, Nick reckoned he could probably hone it down to a specific area of the Boro. Teessiders know each other in an instant. To the outside world, the subtle differences of an accent which only exists within a few miles either side of the Tees are undetectable, but to locally attuned ears, they are very obvious. When you're not on home territory, meeting someone from back home is always a little thrilling. Teessiders are quite a rare and exotic breed, so when they do meet each other, it feels like meeting a member of your extended family, somehow.

'I'm Jo King'. She elongated the "oh" in Jo, also in a classic Teesside fashion and pointed both index fingers at him. 'Don't bother making the joke, mate. I've 'eard it all before, me, like.'

Nick grinned and gripped her hand, noticing that she had long slim, pointy fingers. She shook with a firm, strong grip. The back of her hand and wrist was covered in little nicks, scars, grazes and dark bruises.

Julie came out of the room and peered at their visitor. 'Hiya,' she said, also holding out her hand and giving Jo's a quick shake, 'I'm Julie.'

Jo King nodded. 'Now then. Big Fish's agent texted me and said you'd be arriving today. I'm doing a show up here - my first one, like. I'm renting the top flat. He owns that one as well as this, y'see.'

'Does he? Bloody hell, he's so rich. Owee in then,' said Nick, gesturing for her to step into the flat.

She held up her hands. The palms were as blotchy and marked as the other side. On her right wrist was a long, diagonal dark pink scar. It looked very like she had slashed her wrist as some point in the last couple of years. 'Sorry, no, I can't. I've got to get up to Pleasance Courtyard, my show's on at seven and I've got to stand outside and hand flyers out just to try and drum up 50 people to sit in a roasting hot attic room for an hour. I just wanted to say hello and give you a couple of tickets for my show.' She handed over two strips of light card. 'I need bodies in the room to make me look successful, like.' She grinned again.

'What sort of show do you do?' asked Julie.

'Illusion and comedy...but mostly illusion.'

Nick glanced at the tickets. "King Tees!" was the title of the show. He grinned.

'Is that King Tees as in, "...'king Tees?" Or are you King Tees, or King Tease?'

'It means whatever you think it means,' she said with a cryptic grin, revealing wonky, misshapen teeth.

'Well, we'll come up later and see you, won't we, Jules?'

'Yeah, we always like to support local acts. Can we get a drink up there?'

'Oh, aye, the place is full of bars. Is this the first time you've been up here?'

'Yeah, we've both always meant to come for years and never have,' she said.

'Wow, well it's a bit manic, but it's mint, as long as you don't mind sweating a lot in hot little rooms. I'll see you later, then. Oh, and congrats on youse gerrin' wed, like.' She turned and sprinted off down the stone steps to the front door of the building. Nick shut the door.

'She was a funny lass, wasn't she?' said Julie as they walked around the rest of the apartment. 'Like a little rooster in a suit. Did you see the big bum on her?'

'Yeah, I noticed that. Did you see all the scars on her hand?'

Julie shook her head. 'Scars?'

'Her hands were covered in marks and her right wrist had been slashed at some point. There was a big red mark across it.'

'Fizz me. Is she a cutter, do you reckon?'

'You never know, do you? She might have been.'

They walked into one of the two bedrooms.

'Eee, god, look at the size of this bed!' said Julie, jumping onto it and thrashing around with her arms and legs, laughing.

'That's gotta to be a Jumbo King,' said Nick. 'It's big enough to have its own gravitational pull.'

'Aye, well, the BF needs a big bed to support his vast bulk, doesn't he? It'll make a change to have some room and not have you right up my arse all night.'

Nick laughed. 'Jules, man, you've always said you liked that!'

'Aye, but only when I'm awake.' She laughed, rolled over and stuck her backside up at him, comically.

He glanced at his watch.

His heart leapt.

Normally, being left-handed, it was on his right wrist. But it was gone. Stupidly, he looked at his left wrist to see if it was there. No.

'Hey, did I take my watch off in the living room, Jules?' He looked around the room.

She got off the bed and looked at him with her sapphire blue eyes. 'No. Why would you have done that?'

He held up his bare wrists. 'It's gone. How has it gone? I'm sure I was wearing it when we came in.'

She stared at him, then a thought occurred to her. 'Eee, the little lass must have robbed it off you. Magicians do that sort of stuff, don't they? What was her name, again?'

'Jo King.'

'Jo King? Joking? Are you sure?'

'That's what she said. Jo. King. Told me not to make a joke of it - which I was about to do, an' all. The cheeky sod. That thing cost me £10, 15 years ago...it's virtually an antique. I've only changed the battery once.'

'It'll just be a joke, man. She knew she'd see us later, didn't she?'

Nick shrugged. It didn't matter, really, but it was a bloody cheeky thing to do.

The apartment had a big bathroom with a sunken bath, a spacious shower, a large, well-appointed kitchen and a massive dining room with a long table which could have seated 16. Nick went into the kitchen, put the kettle on and made some Sencha green tea with some teabags he'd brought.

'Not entirely sure I've sobered up from last night, yet,' he said, handing her a mug, as she stood looking out of the bedroom window at the street below.

She sighed and stroked his bare arm. 'Yeah, it was a lovely day and a really good night. Pity the Boro couldn't have crowned our wedding day off with a win. Losing 3-1 to Ipswich at home was a rubbish start to a new season.'

'Aye, but I totally expected that. If you get married at the Boro, of course they're not going to win on your big, happy day. That'd be entirely out of character for the club and for Teesside. In a way, it was comforting. If we'd won 6-0 we'd have been under pressure to live up to such heights.'

She sipped at the tea and nodded. 'Yeah, I know what you mean...oooh, look, second window along, across the road. I spy with my little eye, a relaxed male penis with added testicles on display.'

He followed her gaze. Across the road, a man, probably in his 20s, was standing back from the window, naked and getting dry with a towel.

'That is definitely a male penis. Hopefully we'll see a female penis as well,' said Nick with a snort. 'You can see right into all the windows opposite; no-one has any net curtains, do they?'

'No. It's odd, that. I like it. Nets are very claustrophobic. I never liked them, but mam wouldn't have dreamed of not having them. Everyone on the estate seemed to. Ours were stained yellow from all the smoke. Oh, look, he's giving himself a little rub with the towel. Aw, bless him. He's nice looking, though, isn't he? Ha ha. I'm all in favour of a naked freebie. Nothing too vulgar, just a quick flash. Mind, he must've had a very cold shower, by the look of him. Eee, talk about a button mushroom.' She chuckled to herself.

'Yeah, these big Georgian terraces offer plenty of peeping opportunities.' He looked around. 'When you're in these big rooms, they do feel sort of private, don't they? You're so small in the room that you feel quite insignificant. I don't mind, anyway. If someone wants to see me naked that badly, I see no reason to deprive them of the opportunity.'

He put his tea down, pulled off his clothes and went for a shower. The cubicle was huge and the jet of water twice as powerful as he was used to.

'Does your first day as a married woman feel any different?' he said, emerging with a big bath towel around him.

She turned around from looking out of the window. 'Nah. Not in the slightest. Sorry. Should it?'

5

'No. It doesn't feel any different to me, either, except that I can refer to you as "my wife" now, that's the only big difference. But we had Don's blessing and that was nice. It felt like it was good thing to have.'

She grinned. 'Yeah, Don did a nice job for us. Mam was just about sober for the duration, too, which was something of a surprise.'

'And she and your dad got on well - another bonus.'

'Aye. It was lovely to have him there. Still feels very weird when I see him. Not really adjusted to having a dad again.'

'When he moves back permanently, you'll have more chance to get to know each other.'

She unzipped a small case and took out a change of clothes. 'You like him, don't you?'

'Yeah. From the few times we've met, he's got something about him that I like.'

She cast a glance out of the window. 'Is it going to rain this evening, do you reckon?'

'Forecast was for showers, but it's quite warm. A lot of the shows are on in tiny venues, so we'll get roasting.'

'Shall I go out in my bikini then?' she said as she unzipped her jeans and pulled them off, followed by her t-shirt.

'I'm certainly going out in Speedos.'

She yelped a laugh. 'Is the lad with the little willy watching me across the way?' she said, as she quickly took off her black underwear.

'Do you want him to be?'

'I'm not fussed. He can if he wants. I've seen what he's got, haven't I?' She made a rolling woody laugh.

He looked out. 'No, he's not there. He might have a hidden telescope, in which case he's putting in a lot of effort and it'd be shame not to at least briefly reward him with a glimpse of your nipples.'

She put her arms around his waist and pecked him on the lips. 'Oh, we can put on a better show than that. Do you fancy a quickie? We've got about an hour before the first show,' she said, 'and we've not consummated our marriage yet, due to being utterly wankered last night. Technically, that means we're not married, I think...'

'...only if it's still the 18th century and we're both witches, but you're right, we don't want to risk being illegally wed, do we?' He wrapped his arms around her tightly and whispered something obscene into her ear.

She looked him in the eyes. 'You're such a dirty boy, full of such dirty words, aren't you?' She pulled the towel off him and lay down on the big bed, beckoning him onto her, laughing loudly. 'Come on then, darlin', make a decent woman of me!'

'I can't do decent, but I can do indecent, if that helps.'

She gurgled a rolling laugh. 'Go on, then. Give me every inch of your indecency.'

An hour later, as they left the flat to get a cab, a woman, was coming down the stairs. She wore a smart, dark green linen suit with an expensive-looking silk scarf tied around her neck. Her hair was shoulder length and white. She stopped briefly and raised her eyebrows in acknowledgment of them, a look of surprise in her hazel brown eyes.

'Oh, hello. I thought I heard someone below.' She spoke in a light, slightly hoarse-sounding voice.

'Hi. I'm Nick, this is my *wife*, Julie.' He grinned at Julie. 'Stevie Salmon is letting us use the flat for our honeymoon.'

The woman nodded at them both. 'I'm Barbara Stewart. How nice. Congratulations. And you're going to the Fringe?'

Julie nodded. 'We're just on our way to see Jo King from upstairs, actually. Do you live upstairs, too?'

'Yes. We've been here for a few years now. We're the only people who actually live full-time in the building these days. It's sad really. It'd be nice to have some neighbours.'

'Are you from Edinburgh?' said Nick.

'No. We're from Yorkshire originally. Frank - that's my husband - he loves it here, especially all the galleries. We're both interested in art, you see. Anyway, nice to see you. I hope you have a nice stay.'

She trotted down the stairs, a leather bag over her shoulder.

Nick closed the door and locked it.

'She seemed nice,' said Julie, 'quite a sophisticated sort.'

'Yeah, I thought that. Classic arty middle-class type, if you ask me.'

They hailed a black cab to Pleasance Courtyard. It was jam packed with people, with queues outside of each building where up to a dozen gigs were happening at any one time, from the morning until after midnight. Some were big enough to get 750 people in, others were literally a metal container wagon with seats in for 50 people. The cobbled courtyard with a long bar at one end, covered in tables and seats, acted as giant bar-cum-meeting place and holding area. It was noisy.

'This is a genuinely incredible place,' said Nick, as they went to the bar and stood in line for two double vodkas and fizzy water.

Julie looked through a bunch of flyers that had been handed to them outside the venue.

'Amazing, I don't know how you decide who to see. There are thousands of shows.'

'Just lucky dip, isn't it?'

'I don't mind as long as we don't get some sexist pig male comedian, or a whiny lass going on about her boyfriend.' She held a leaflet up with a woman pulling a face on; it said, 'Why I killed my boyfriend and ate him.'

'I'm not feeling the love for that one,' said Nick, as she looked through them.

'How about "a musical celebration of non-sexist trousers"? I'm all for celebrating non-sexist trousers, though quite how many songs you can sing about them, I'm not sure,' said Julie.

'Well, we're both wearing decidedly non-sexist troos. Mind, I've always fancied you in those baggy black linen pants. Your arse is great in them, especially now you've put a bit of flesh back on you.'

She laughed. 'Got a fatter bum, you mean.' She shook her head and looked at him with a wry smile. 'It's all in your head, y'know. Mine is just a normal blotchy, dimpled, pimpled, very farty arse. You'd probably think it was great even if I was wearing a barrel held up with braces! You're just an arse man, that's your trouble.'

'You're right. It's hard-wired into my libido. The weird thing is, I don't know how or why that happened, 'cos I'm sure I've not made a definite decision to be arse focused, but since puberty, it's always been my thing. I'll tell you now, every lass I ever went out with had a great arse, or at least, I thought so. I can still see most of them in my mind's eye, even though I couldn't tell you the colour of their eyes. That's not by accident. It must be driven by something.'

'Hmm, well, you might not want to look into it too much, lad, and you can stop dreaming about your old girlfriend's arses now, if you like, you dirty sod.' She pushed at him, a little.

'I bet you still think about the lower portions of old boyfriends.'

She looked at him in mock horror. 'Me? I'd *never* do that.' She gave him a wicked grin. 'Not unless I'm conscious, anyway.'

He rubbed his forehead as though to wipe away the memories. 'Yeah, see, you don't have a fixation like me. Not really.'

She cocked an arched eyebrow. 'Maybe not quite so single-minded as your bum fascination, but I'm sure there's something similar in my psyche somewhere. I always dated men with nice eyes, even when they were bastards.'

'How do you have nice eyes if you're a bastard?'

'Oh, that thing about the eyes being the gateway to the soul, that's all bullshit. I once went out with a man with dreamy, watery blue eyes, who looked like a poet or a painter. He seemed so sensitive.'

'But he wasn't?'

She shook her head. 'He was a twat. He was selfish and controlling and...' she stopped and flexed her lips a little '...he wasn't a nice man at all. He was angry. He behaved...' she stopped again, looking into the middle distance. 'Let's just say, he behaved very badly and I got in the way of his rage.' She sighed. 'So don't psychoanalyse yourself too much. We're all a mess, one way or another, especially by our age.'

'Aye, but as a writer...'

She interrupted him. '...as a writer?! You never say that. You never believe in yourself enough to call yourself a writer.'

'I'm trying to self-identify as one, now that I'm writing a novel and not just writing about football.'

'Good. If *you're* not a writer, I don't know who is. Go on...'

'...as a writer, it interests me how we construct the interior world of our mind and how something, to one person, looks really attractive, but to another it just doesn't.'

She gave him a slack-jawed dumb look. 'Eh, 'ow you do what, like? I don't like books, I like telly, me, like.'

He got their drinks and handed the plastic glass to her. 'Cheers, Jules. Here's to being a married couple.'

'Cheers, hubby.' She gave him a big toothy grin. 'You know what we need here? We need a wet bar.'

'A wet bar?' he said.

'Aye, a bottle of water and vodka or gin, so we can avoid these big queues. Just booze it up while we stand in line. I fancy that. Me and you, pissed up all over town. It'll be fun.'

He put his thumb up. 'Now you're talking. We should put vodka in IrnBru as we're in Scotland - not to stereotype the place much, but it is the only country on earth where Coca Cola isn't the best-selling pop.'

'I think that's brilliant, meself. Scotland holding out against the imperial culture of Coke. God bless the Jocks.'

He went to look for his watch. 'Bugger. I forgot Jo King had nicked my watch. What time is it, Jules?'

She glanced at hers. 'Six forty-five. You know, it's always annoyed me that women's watches are smaller than men's. Do women want a smaller display of time for any reason? Is time smaller for women? No. Some of us want a big watch and some want a small one - same as blokes. So why do they sell them as women's and men's watches? It's sexist shite, is that.'

Nick held up a fist. 'Right on, sister. Come the revolution, all watches shall be of equal size for all sexes, especially for chicks with nice arses.'

She gave him a sharp rabbit punch to the stomach. 'Careful, son. I'll withdraw your marital privileges.'

He laughed. 'We should get in line for Jo King's show. It's over there in the Attic,' he said, pointing at the yellow and black sign beside a doorway, which stated the venue's name, along with all the shows and times they were due to be performed. 'We'll get tickets for a couple of other shows after we've seen her.'

They wove through the crowds of people, many of whom looked like students in their early 20s, and found a line of people outside the venue. A young woman in a black fleece, smiling broadly, tore their ticket stubs and thanked them for coming.

'I love this. It's organised chaos,' said Nick, feeling light and happy. 'It's so much better than going to something where it's run like a military operation - all neat and tidy. By the look of it, everything is running on time, but it's really messy and sort of tight but loose.'

'Like all the best vaginas,' said Julie, nodding, sucking her lips in and casting a wide-eyed innocent look at him. 'What, like?!'

He laughed and rested his left arm around her shoulder, smiling at her. 'What?' she said, again, a little smirk on her pink lips.

'I love you.'

'Just because I said the word *vaginas*. You're so easily pleased with dirty words, you. An arse and a vagina, that's all you need to be happy.'

He bellowed out a laugh. He doubted he'd ever been more happy on any of his days on earth, or not since he'd been a small boy, anyway. Here he was with his wife, a woman who was beautiful in spirit and body. For a fucked-up kid from Fairfield, maybe he'd done alright, after all. 'There are a few deeper reasons that I love you, too.'

'Deeper? Deeper than my vagina? I think you'll find that is impossible! Ha. Well, you'd better love me 'cos you're stuck with me, now we're legally shackled.'

He drained his glass and pointed to it. 'If we had your wet bar, I could get a top up now. But there's not time to get to the bar and back.'

'Totally. We'll deffo sort that out tomorrow, 'cos I've got a right thirst on us and I fancy a proper drink-up. That voddy is hitting the spot good and proper.'

The line began to file upstairs and into a small, dark, hot room on the top floor of what looked and felt like a medieval building. Standing on the door as they filed in was Jo King herself, still in her tight electric-blue suit and pointy shoes. She greeted each audience member with a handshake as they entered.

'Alright there, maaayt, 'allo darlin', thanks for comin', like...mint that, like...from the Boro, are ya? Brill that...Mind, it's proper maftin' in there, son.' It was like listening to Teesside's greatest hits. Wonderful.

'Now then, Jo,' said Nick, holding out his hand.

She grinned up at him.

'Ah, there youse are. Alright, fella. Thanks for coming over. Hello, Ju-lie.' She even said it as "Jou-lee" the way it really should be pronounced if you're a working-class Teessider.

But there was no time to chat about his missing watch as they filed in. There were three rows of benches against one wall and on two sides. On the right was the open floor and at the back of it was a black curtain which presumably hid props, chairs and such.

Nick and Julie sat up on the middle of the back row. The microphone was about 15 feet away from them. No stage, just an empty space, a small sound desk to the right. It was very intimate and a bit nerve wracking. The act was so close to you, what if she was no good? There was no hiding place.

'I hope she's good,' said Julie, in a whisper. 'It's so hot in here, I might fall asleep.'

'It's not like we can walk out, is it?' said Nick into her ear. 'This is why we should be more drunk!'

She gurgled a rolling laugh and squeezed his hand.

Nick looked around and counted 31 people. Not bad, considering it was still early in the month-long run.

'I've never heard of this lass, y'know, and you usually do if they start around Teesside. Have you heard of her?'

She shook her head. 'Maybe she's based in London. That's where the money is.'

Instinctively, Nick glanced at his watch. It was bang on 7pm. The lights went down.

He did a double take and his heart leapt up into his throat.

The watch. He had his watch on!

It had reappeared on his right wrist.

He nudged Julie and pointed at it, a look of total shock on his face.

'What?' she said and then realised what he was showing her. 'Bloody hell. Did she put that back on you when she shook your hand?'

'She must have. How come I never noticed?'

Julie flashed her eyes at him.

'Because she's obviously really good,' she said and shook her head in amazement, biting down on her bottom lip. 'This kid is special, if you ask me. She's got some balls to do that.'

A disembodied Teesside voice boomed out of the PA.

'Ladies and gentlemen, thanks for comin'. I'm Jo King. No, I'm not *joking*. I *am* Jo King. Shit, that sounded like I was saying I was joking and I'm not. Jo King is my name, right?' Her Teesside voice got broader in its accent, as she got more frustrated trying to explain herself. 'So, I'll start again, eh. I'm Jo King, anyone got a problem? No. Smashin', right. Joking apart...oh, I'm not starting that bloody shit again...I'll just come out, eh...hang on...I'm only just behind this black curtain at the back here, I was tryin' to do a big entrance an' 'all...and it's all gone tits up...sorry, this usually goes smoothly.'

There was a flapping and tugging at the curtain, as though she was trapped behind it. 'Bugger it, I'm...I'm bloody stuck...' the microphone picked up her cursing. Everyone was laughing now. 'I'll be right with youse lot in a minute. I'm sorry about this. George. George, man, give us a hand, me pants are stuck on the bloody hook here...'

More laughter...surely it was actually all part of the act...but it had gone on for several minutes, now.

'I think she's really got stuck back there,' said Julie, into Nick's ear.

There was a tearing noise from behind the curtain now. 'Oh, no! Me fuckin' good pants!'

That got a massive laugh.

The curtain moved again, everyone's eyes were focused on it, almost willing her to get free, come out and do her show. A common mood often grips an audience and they become as one. This was one of those moments.

Then, suddenly, the spotlight that had been on the back curtain went out, the room was thrown into total darkness, a white spot light came on, and as though out of nowhere, there she was in front of them. Not standing on the black floor, but suspended in midair, apparently hanging by the neck from a rope slung over a beam. They all saw her at the same time. As one, the audience let out a shocked gasp. Three girls on the front row screamed loudly out of genuine fright. How had that happened?

Nick's heart missed a couple of beats as a spotlight picked her out, hanging there, staring out blank eyed, apparently dead. Then there was a loud bang and the room filled quickly with dense smoke. The lights went out again.

More screams from the audience, some laughs, but not many now, more murmurs of confusion.

For a moment, Nick wondered if she had somehow been murdered. This would be a good moment to kill someone, because everyone would think it was part of the act.

The lights came back up and a new voice said, 'Ladies and gentlemen. Jo King.'

This time she came out from behind the curtain, through the now-clearing smoke, laughing and clapping in her blue suit. As alive as anyone. While it had obviously been a stunt, it was somehow still quite a relief that she was free and not hanging dead from that noose. You could hear the palpable sigh of tension groan out of people. Now, everyone was ready to laugh at anything, as much out of relief as anything else. They all applauded.

Nick turned to Julie. 'That was very weird.'

'I proper shat meself,' she said in a hissed whisper.

Jo King was smiling, as though she hadn't just been hanging from a rope. Maybe, somehow, she hadn't.

She took a bow.

'Hello hello, thanks for coming to my show. Sorry if I scared you, there. That was just a little introduction to my world. Remember, what your eyes see tonight might be real, or might not be real. I have one message for youse all. This is it, right? Question all realities. Knoworramean? Is what you think real, *actually* real? And what the hell does *real* mean, anyway? Am I real? Am I a woman called Jo King? Is my big fat arse real?' She bent over and pointed at her buttocks. Everyone laughed. She slapped herself. 'Yeah actually, that is all too real, but is this tie real? Sir, front row, is it real?'

A student with a big beard nodded. 'Yeah. It's real.'

She looked down at where the tie had been.

'Is what real, son? What tie are you talking about, eh?'

The tie was no longer there.

'The tie...' said the man on the front row, laughing and pointing where it had been.

Jo's attitude was now one of faux puzzlement. 'I'm sorry. I don't know what you're talking about. Is what real?' She was more insistent now.

'You had a tie on,' said the man.

Jo King shook her head. 'No I didn't. I just said I did, so you believed me.'

'You did!' said the man, incredulous that she could claim such a thing.

Nick tried to recall. Did she have a tie on? No, she didn't. Not when they met her outside on the stairs and not outside the flat. Did she when she started the gig, though? He wasn't sure. And that was what she was playing on.

'I had a tie on? Where is it, then? What could I have done with it?'

She struck a confrontational tone and the man began to doubt what he'd seen. Nick decided that she had been wearing a tie. But Jo was somehow able to undermine your belief in what you had seen. People applauded, feeling like they'd seen a trick, but not sure if they had or they hadn't.

Jo opened her arms wide. 'Was the tie ever there? Or did you imagine it? You don't know for sure, do you? Only I know, and I'm not telling and even if I did tell you, would I be right? Maybe I'm delusional. Remember, question all realities. Y'see, life worries me. I'll be honest, I'm not coping well. Doing this for a living is a lot of pressure and there really are times when I wish my eyes couldn't see what is happening all around us. The inequality, the poverty, the abuse...who wants to see that? Not me.'

In a seamlessly swift, smooth move, she took out a long nail from her pocket and, momentarily held it parallel to her right eye, with her right hand. Then, at speed, she drew it back and jammed it into her eye, dropping the nail to the ground after doing it. A squirt of blood came from somewhere and she bent over with a groan, blood running through her fingers.

Someone screamed and shouted out, 'Are you alright?'

But, now, prepared for an illusion, Nick saw what she'd done this time. As she'd dug the nail into the corner of her eye, she'd let go of it for half a second, but had kept it contained within her clenched fist, thus there was no pressure on it to drive it into her eye, as her fist banged into the side of her head, letting it go as she did so.

Jo looked up and grinned, fake blood running down her cheek. 'Don't worry. I'm OK. That was a just a trick, a sleight of hand, if you like...whereas this isn't. I'm *really* going to fucking do this.'

She pulled out a large hunting knife, a huge blade with one side of it serrated, for not just cutting flesh, but sawing bone. Without she hesitation, hacked into her wrist with a gruesome violence, first stabbing the point of the blade in to pierce the skin and then carving through the flesh, sawing for a few moments at the bone and soon cutting off her entire hand. As it became detached from the wrist, it fell to the floor with a heavy thud. Two women and man on the front ran for the door, making distressed noises. Jo looked at them go, like they were in the distance, her eyes spaced out as though she was in a trance.

She'd now lost about a third of her audience. Some hardier souls, knowing it simply had to be an illusion and that no-one cuts off their own hand and survives, laughed heartily. A couple of fat, boozy student lads alongside Nick loved the gore, and as blood dripped from the stump, they started clapping. The hand began to twitch and crawl, seemingly independently, across the floor.

'Fuck off!' yelled Jo King belligerently, and kicked at it as though it was a small dog that was annoying her. Then she stared bewildered at the wound she'd apparently inflicted on herself and in a tone which suggested light-hearted amusement said, 'Bloody hell. Bit of a flesh wound. I'd better go and get this sorted, eh? Hold on.'

She walked behind the black curtain. This was all very punky and uncomfortable.

Nick's heart was pounding hard in his chest. He was scared and amused in equal measure. He felt like he'd been totally manipulated into being like this and that only someone who understood the human psyche could do it to you. She played with your emotions, making you scared and then amused and then comfortable and then offended.

Julie looked at Nick. 'That was so sick,' she said, in a low whisper, 'I don't get what's going on. It was really gross, but I knew it wasn't real.'

It was sick and certainly macabre, but it was really interesting and seemed to be in service to a greater, bigger idea. King returned, now with hand intact. Obviously, it had been a prosthetic hand that she had masterfully cut off. She nodded and bowed, now needing to ingratiate herself with the audience after being so confrontational. She began a little bit of regular stand-up, chatting and making jokes about her life on the road. Just inconsequential but human stuff. It relaxed her audience a little.

'I'm an illusionist or a magician, if you like. Perhaps nothing you see in this room is actually happening. So don't worry about any of this, right? I mean seriously, nothing bad is happening. So when I do this...' she began digging at her throat with her fingers, as though tearing open the flesh '...I mean, I won't lie to you, it does sting a bit...' she made a choking noise and coughed and pulled out what appeared to be a bloody organ '...but the important thing to realise...is that...this isn't really a bit of my lung or any other bit of me.'

She looked at it and laughed and placed it in a plastic bowl, wiping the blood from her hands and neck on a white towel. For all the world it looked like she had pulled it out of her own throat by tearing open the flesh.

'See? Not so much as a scratch.' She wiped away the blood to reveal an untouched neck.

Everyone applauded, still as much out of relief as anything else.

'OK, that's enough of the shock tactics...what I'm doing here is making you question the nature of reality and stop believing so much in what your eyes appear to be telling you. The trouble is, humans are very suggestible. We all are. It doesn't take much to shake our faith in what we think is the truth.'

She turned to a balding man in his 40s who was wearing a checked shirt and jeans and was sitting at the end of the front row.

'For example, you sir, what's your name?'

The man sat upright and respectable. 'I'm Robert.'

'OK, Robert. We've never met, have we?'

Robert shook his head and looked a bit sheepish at being caught up in the show.

'No...so if I do this...' she took two steps over to the man, pulled her arm back and hit him hard in the face. The wet slapping noise of her fist against Robert's cheek seemed real enough. The man groaned and fell off his chair holding his face, really shocked. Was this for real? Jesus Christ, she'd hit him...no come on...she hadn't. It was fake. Was it? It looked too real.

But there was a stunned silence in the room.

A man who'd been sitting beside Robert got up and kneeled next to him and kindly asked if he was OK.

'He's alright,' said Jo King, sneeringly dismissive of her act of violence.

Jo stood arms outstretched and defiant. 'C'mon, people. Think about it. Do you really think I'd do that to a stranger? I'd be arrested, wouldn't I?'

Robert stood up and saluted. They'd faked it. It was a set-up.

Question all realities.

It was almost offensive to be fooled like this. But even though it was a sort of insult, it was also quite brilliant. In a short space of time, she had completely subverted their sense of what was real and what wasn't. It was now impossible to know if anything was faked or was real and that was clearly the whole point she was making. The way she kept getting you to relax, get you on her side and then used that to shock you once more, was supremely manipulative.

'And now, right at the moment that you've stopped believing anything I do on this stage might be for real, I could do almost anything, couldn't I? If I killed a man now, killed him for real, you would totally assume I'd performed an illusion, because of what you've just seen. Think about that. I could kill someone now and you would think I hadn't. So you see how easy it is to be fooled? I'm just a chunky Teesside lass in a cheap suit, in a sweat box of a room and I had most of you going at some point, tonight. We're all vulnerable to it. I'm not taking the piss out of you, I'm saying something bigger, right? We get conditioned to how we think things are. If I can pull the wool over your eyes here and now, how easy is it for a government, or a corporation, to do the same thing? They create realities for us that are actually fiction, they set us up, just as I set you people up, and they make us believe shit that isn't true, in order to provide solutions to problems that don't even exist and to make profit from that. They control us like this. We need to wake up. So, when you go back to your normal life, ask yourself, what's real and what's false? Question all realities. Have I been Jo King, or have I been joking? I'll let you decide. Thank you and goodnight.'

She took a bow and received a lot of applause from those still in the room. There were a few whistles and calls for more. The two fat student lads gave her a standing ovation. But these places were on a tight schedule and a new show was due in the space in 20 minutes.

Julie laughed a little. 'Well, I don't know what to make of her. Parts of that were quite upsetting but then, I quickly got used to the idea that anything might happen. It wasn't funny but it made a big impression.'

'I thought it was ace. Her little speech at the end was spot on, I thought. I feel a bit emotionally drained, though.'

17

They were both sweating heavily as they got downstairs into the cooler air.

'Owee, let's get a good drink on us,' said Nick, taking her damp hand. They went through the courtyard to a large tent which housed seating and another big bar.

Julie got them both double vodka and tonics.

'What I loved was, she was saying, y'know, don't trust me, don't trust your own eyes, necessarily. She totally set us up to believe something, time after time. That's a really profound thing. It makes you realise that everything is subjective and that you can easily be led into believing things that aren't true,' said Nick, taking a drink from her.

Julie nodded. 'I do totally get that, it made sense, especially after she did her speech, but at the time it was just gross. Hacking her hand off - I mean, I knew it was fake, because no-one would do that in those circumstances, but it was still awful to see.'

'It was, but you can't strip out one element, it's the whole show that you've got to judge. I tell you what, Jeff would bloody love it. Right up his strasse. He likes a bit of gore.'

'Well, he's got the record fair on Saturday and that market thing in the Grassmarket from Wednesday, hasn't he? So he can come and see it one night.'

'Yeah, of course. It'll be a nice break for him from looking after Argie.'

Julie nodded, but was distracted by Jo King, who was walking across the courtyard. Jo spotted them and gave a wave and a big smile. She looked smaller and chunkier when not under the spotlight.

Nick squinted a little at her as she approached, noticing for the first time that she walked in an unusual way - a sort of cocky, swaggering, rolling gait. It was the walk of someone who thought they were in some way special. The sort of walk someone who was going to be famous might have. Apart. Different.

'Now then, how are we?' she said, clapping her hands together.

'Great, ta,' said Julie. 'Your show was quite something, Jo. Amazing.'

'Thanks for giving me my watch back,' said Nick holding up his wrist.

She made a face. 'Sorry. Force of habit. It was loose and a total gift. I was a pick-pocket for years.'

She seemed very pleased with herself, presumably pumped up on the post-gig adrenalin.

'Eee, were you really a pick-pocket?' said Julie, with a snort.

'Yeah. The best in the Boro - not that the competition set a high bar. Most crimes of robbery in Middlesbrough consist of stealing razor blades from Boots, shoplifting knickers from Marksies or putting a brick through a shop window. Smack heads are rubbish thieves. Ha ha.'

She shifted her weight from one leg to the other and back again, as though dancing briefly to a beat no-one else could hear.

'So you liked me show?'

'It was *really* shocking,' said Nick. 'I nearly shat meself at least twice.'

Jo laughed a little. 'Bowel loosening is deffo one of the reactions I want.'

'How did you get from being behind the curtain to being in the noose and back again, so quickly?' asked Julie.

'Ha ha. That would be telling. All I'll say, is that it's about distraction and not trusting what you see. I want people to realise how we're being set up to think certain things all the time. All I do is shape your conditioning in that room, so that you're not the same when you come out as when you go in. Get me?'

Julie nodded firmly. 'How long have you been doing this? I've not heard of you on Teesside - we live in Stockton.'

'Yeah the Big Fish's man said you were from good old Stockton, like. I don't live on Teesside any more. I live in London. Work the London clubs - it's the only way to make a living. That's where I met Big Fish. He was down south and saw my act in a club in Islington. He's been really good, actually. Supportive, like. I know everyone says he's a bit of twat, but he's always been alright with me.'

'He's actually my best mate's brother. He gave us his flat rent free for a week while we're on our honeymoon.'

'Ha, well, he's charging me rent! I should've got wed to someone, eh? This is my first Edinburgh show, though. Hoping to get a big break, but it's hard work getting people in when no-one has heard of you. Not had a full house yet and it only holds 55 people at most.'

'God, that's tough economics,' said Julie.

'Yeah, I'll lose money, even if I sell it out for the rest of the month. But you've got to get seen, haven't you? All the TV people are here at some point and there's no-one out there like me...so, we'll see what happens.' She looked at her watch. 'I've got to go and do two 10-minute bits on some *Best of the Fest* shows.'

'What will you do?' asked Nick.

'I'll just tell a few gags and put the nail in my eye and then bleed heavily.' She grinned and held a small soft ball between thumb and forefinger. 'Look, I'd better go. I'll probably catch you later, eh.' She tossed the little ball into Nick's hand and left with a little wave, running to catch up another performer she knew. Nick looked at the small, soft sphere. It was a blood capsule. He slipped it into his pocket as they watched her walk out of the courtyard.

'Impressive buttocks on her. Big, but firm,' said Julie.

'Maybe it's a prosthetic arse and she'll detach it and...I dunno...vomit into it, as part of her act.'

'Ha ha, that wouldn't surprise me at all, actually. Come on, let's get tickets for another show,' she said.

They went to the box office and picked up a 2 for 1 deal on a show performed by drama students who did spoofs of Sherlock Holmes stories, performed in a damp old building in the courtyard. It was entertaining, just because it was done with so much energy and enthusiasm. If you'd seen it on TV it'd have probably seemed like a lot of posh kids mucking around, but the energy and commitment of a live show drove past that.

After that was over, they went across to the Cabaret Bar to see a young stand-up comedian. He'd attracted an audience in their early 20s, making Nick and Julie feel old. All of his cultural references were to things that had significance for his own age group, but much less so for people in their late 40s.

As they filed out, Nick took Julie's hand. 'I have a feeling he was good - everyone in here loved him - but I couldn't care about anything he said - y'know what I mean?'

She nodded. 'We were definitely the wrong demographic.' She yawned. 'God, I'm ready for my bed and it's only 11.30. Look at all these studenty types. They're so wide awake.'

'I remember what that was like. You just didn't get tired, did you? Not at 20. And if you did, you soon recovered. Of all the things I miss about being young, the limitless energy is definitely one of the biggest.'

They walked out of Pleasance Courtyard and down the hill, back towards the Royal Mile.

'I'm not even a bit drunk. I think I must have sweated out all the booze,' said Nick as they sauntered.

'Aye, we need to get that wet bar together. Jo King was the best of the shows, I reckon. Did you think so?'

'I did, yeah. Easily. It was really original and had a point to it. It wasn't just fluffy. She's very confident, almost to the point of arrogance, but then you need that as a performer, don't you? Do you think she's gay?'

'I have to say that I assumed she was, but that's being very clichéd. Just because she wasn't a girly girl and had that tomboy aspect to her. Shouldn't be so quick to stereotype people.'

He shrugged. 'Yeah, but we all do that about people, don't we? It's a form of cultural shorthand. I don't think it's wrong, really. We're not judging her harshly. We all dress to give off some sense of who we are and she gave off a strong, modern kind of lesbian vibe to me.'

'Hmm. Maybe. Not sure what vibe I'm giving off in baggy black pants and black t-shirt.'

'That the lady loves Milk Tray?'

'Ha ha...I bloody did, as well.'

They walked up the Royal Mile and crossed over North Bridge, then along Princes Street, turning up Frederick Street and heading north to the New Town. Despite being nearly midnight, the streets were really busy with people, out and about at various Fringe events.

'God, this is all a bit different from Stockton, isn't it?' said Julie as they walked. 'The High Street is dead after five. That's the one thing I really don't like about back home. That feeling that all the life and energy is drained out of the place at the end of the work day and all that's left is a few junkies and drunks hanging around and getting up to no good. Being in a big city is so vibrant, isn't it? When I first went to London that's what I loved about it. You felt like something was always going on and anything could happen. It's a bit like that here.'

She hooked into his arm as they walked. 'I've never lived in a big city. Harrogate is quite a size, but it's definitely a town and not a city. It shut down at chucking-out time. Mind, the Fringe has got over 3,000 shows and I was reading that half a million people come here over August, so it's going to be extra busy here, right now. It's probably less vibrant in a February hailstorm.'

'Yeah. I suppose so. God, I really love it, though. It's such a beautiful place. The castle all lit up, the Georgian streets, it's just so grand.'

They walked happily back to the flat on the corner of Howe Street and Heriot Row with the imposing St. Stephen's church lit up at the bottom of the hill.

It was all quiet on the stairwell as they let themselves in. Nick went to put the kettle on, while Julie got changed into pyjamas. She came padding into the kitchen wearing her red and white striped cotton bedwear and carrying a dressing gown. She took a mug of Sencha tea from him.

'Thanks, luv. I feel proper posh in this flat. There's so much room to do everything. How much do you think it cost the BF?'

'I was looking on Zoopla at houses in this area. Flats like this go for half a million or more.'

'Bloody hell. Mind, if it was in London, Kensington, say, it'd be a million and a half or more.'

They went into the living room and sat opposite each other on the sofas.

'You almost have to shout at each other across this cavernous room, don't you?' she said, pulling her bare feet up under her.

'Aye, you could never call a place like this cosy. It's grand, but it's not snug the way our flat is.'

'Snug? Small, you mean. You could get our whole flat into this room.' She yawned and sniffed at herself. 'I should've had a shower after all that sweating. Can't be arsed, though.'

'I like you all sweaty, anyway.'

'Just as well, lad. Ha ha.'

A blue light from a police car flashed outside. Nick got up and looked down to the street. 'It's parked outside. Wonder what's going on?'

As he spoke, there was a knock at the door. He went and pulled it open. Two police officers stood there. It immediately threw him back to the evening he'd learned his dad had died and two coppers had turned up at his flat in Harrogate. These two looked just the same. One tall, one thick set, with radios bleeping, except these two both spoke with Edinburgh accents.

'Sorry to bother you so late, sir,' said Tall.

'No worries. Do you want to come in?' said Nick.

'Aye. Thanks,' said Thick Set.

Julie looked up as they all trooped into the room. She pulled on the white towelling dressing gown and fastened it around her waist.

'What's up?' she said.

The coppers stood there in that uniquely heavy, oversized and awkward way that absolutely all of them seem to have; at least all of the men, anyway. Maybe they pick them for their awkwardness? They looked around the lavishly appointed room.

'Do you live here, sir?' said Tall.

Nick explained the situation.

Julie stood up. 'Can I ask what's happened?'

'Have you met the woman who lives upstairs?' said Tall.

'Barbara Stewart? We saw Barbara just briefly, before we went out,' she said.

'What does she look like?' said Tall.

'Err...she had shoulder-length white hair, and had on a dark green linen suit and silk scarf,' said Nick.

'And she had a leather shoulder bag,' added Julie. 'Is she alright?'

'In that case, I think we need to ask her a few questions.' The copper took out a print of a photo from a file he was carrying. 'Is this her?'

Nick took it from him. It was clearly taken from a CCTV camera and showed the woman, exactly as they'd seen her on the stairwell. Julie looked over his shoulder.

'That's her,' she said. 'Is...is that a gun she's got in her hand?!'

Nick held it close to his eyes and squinted. 'Yeah, it's a small pistol. I don't understand.'

'Has there been a robbery or something?' said Julie. 'She's not...'

'It's much more serious than that, madam. There's been a murder.'

Nick looked blankly at him. Julie put her hand to her mouth. 'She's been murdered? Oh, my god.'

The policeman shook his head, a little impatiently, like Julie was a bit thick. 'No. Not her. She's the one with the gun, isn't she?' He pointed at the photo.

Nick and Julie looked at each other in shock. That woman had shot someone? Really? It just did not seem possible. A less likely murderer you couldn't have met. No. Surely not. She couldn't have shot someone...or could she?

But then, if life had taught Nick anything, it was that one of the most likely things to happen, was something you had previously thought to be the least likely. And, as Jo King's show had earlier so well expressed, sometimes your brain tricked you into thinking about things in the wrong way. Barbara had appeared to be a perfectly respectable middle-class woman. But here she was with a gun, coming out of what looked like an office or shop door, having apparently just killed someone. Question all realities.

Bloody hell. They'd met a killer.

CHAPTER 2

The next morning, the shooting was all over the local television news programme. It had happened at an office, five minutes' walk away on George Street, one of the poshest streets in Edinburgh. Details were few and far between. All that was known, or at least all that was being released to the media, was that she'd walked in and shot a man in the head. Just like that. No robbery, nothing. They said that she was not to be approached by the public. She was now presumed to be on the run, armed and dangerous. There were no other details about her or any motivation for the murder. They showed the same CCTV picture that the police had shown them, but didn't give her name. The reports didn't say what she was called. It seemed very hard to believe what that woman had done.

Nick and Julie walked down into nearby Stockbridge to get a fried breakfast of bacon, sausages, egg and black pudding. Nick bought a local newspaper. The CCTV freeze frame was on the front page. Nick read the article, such as it was, headlined 'Murder On George Street.' It didn't give her name, either.

'We told them it was Barbara Stewart, didn't we?' said Nick. 'Last night, when the police came. We did tell them her name, didn't we?'

Julie poured them some tea from a pot. 'Yeah, so why haven't they released her name to the media?'

'I don't know. Does seem a bit odd. Maybe they're still checking her out, or there's some procedural reason that they can't say.'

'Of all the social demographics, the elderly, middle-class woman must be the least suspected of any crime of violence,' said Julie, sipping at her tea. 'They must make up the smallest percentage of criminals.'

Nick bit into a sausage. 'I've got to say, I'm proper shocked. I wonder what on earth her husband - what did she say he was called - Frank, was it? I wonder what he makes of it?'

'Maybe he put her up to it,' said Julie. 'And he's now on the run with her.'

'Who just shoots someone like that? I feel totally shocked cold about it.'

'Tip of an iceberg. Has to be. Maybe she had some sort of breakdown,' she said.

'Maybe, but, reading the account in the paper, it only happened about 15 minutes after we saw her. We got a cab and she was already walking up to George Street to do the shooting. She didn't seem disturbed in any way when we saw her. She was so calm and erudite. I know that outward appearances can be deceptive but she seemed very in control of herself.'

'She did. I totally agree. But then people who have made a terrible choice often do. Suicides are often said to be happy after they've made the decision to end it all. It's all been put to bed and somehow, the future seems brighter.'

Nick took a drink of coffee and thought about his own suicide bid. It was true. The moment you have made your mind up to do it, however fleeting, is a moment of sweet release, when you can finally let go of all the pain, knowing that you are ridding yourself of your torture.

Julie continued. 'But where's she gone now? How long can a woman of that age go on the run for?'

'They'll stop her bank accounts and credit cards, so she'll need cash.' He shook his head. 'Surely, she'll get picked up soon enough. She seemed so normal, though. I don't get it. It's disturbing. I want lunatic murderers to have a spider's web tattooed on their face. I don't want them to be po-lite, well-educated, well-dressed pensioners.'

'Oooh, look!' Julie pointed out of the window. Walking past the cafe window was Jo King. Julie tapped on the glass and waved at her. The chunky lass stopped and waved, pushed the door and came into the cafe.

'Now then, newlyweds. How are we?'

She pulled out a chair and sat down, looking from one to another, her lopsided hair all spiky on the crown.

'We're fine, but what about the woman upstairs - or rather, downstairs, from you?' said Nick.

'What are you on about?' She ordered some tea, toast and scrambled eggs from the waitress who came up immediately.

'Don't you know what happened?' said Julie.

'I've been out all night - I did "Late 'n' Live" until 4am and I've been in a pub on Rose Street since then. I was just going for a walk in the park before getting some kip. What's been going on, then?'

Julie explained everything they knew. Jo looked at her with a sneer.

'She shot him? Old Babs? Gettaway with you. She never,' said Jo, dis-missively. Almost laughing.

'You've met her?' asked Julie.

'Yeah, I met her on the stairs, the day I moved in. End of July. And once since. She was really nice. And her husband Frank was a frail sort of old fella. Poor old lad. I only met him once but he was nice and polite, y'know? Hang on, I can't get my head around this at all...I'm just not hav-

ing that she's shot someone in the head. That's insane. She's not a gang-
ster, she's just a regular old lady who likes knitting and drawing.'

'It's not just a rumour,' said Nick. 'It definitely happened and she's gone
on the run.'

The waitress put her food in front of her and Jo began eating her eggs
so hungrily that it suggested she hadn't eaten for some time. 'Something's
not right about that. I don't think that's for real.'

'What do you mean?' said Julie.

Jo winced and shook her head, put her fork down and jabbed a finger
in the air.

'I don't believe she was capable of shooting someone. So, if she didn't
do it, why do the police think she did?'

'Because the CCTV picture shows her coming out of the office with a
gun,' said Nick, flatly. 'And they came to our flat and asked us. We told
them it was her.'

Jo ate all her eggs quickly and then bit into the toast with an exaggerated chewing action. She was obviously high on something and not just
drunk.

'Alright. There are questions to ask. How do you know the CCTV
printout they showed you, really was of her? How do you know it was
taken at that time and not on a different day? How do you...'

'...I see what you're doing,' interrupted Nick, 'you're building some sort
of conspiracy theory...'

Jo stopped eating and jabbed a finger at him aggressively. 'No. I'm
not.' She was curt and definite. 'I am not doing that at all. All I'm saying
is you've built a picture out of evidence that may or may not be an accu-
rate representation of reality.'

Nick felt a bit narked by that. Her attitude reminded him of Jeff's worst
conspiracy theory days in Harrogate, when he had become convinced
that everything and anything was some sort of plot. It got wearying, after
a bit. Experience had taught him that cock-up rather than conspiracy was
the human default.

'How could all of that not be true? Someone was shot in the head in
that office,' said Julie, who hated conspiracy theories even more than he
did. They went against her practical nature.

'Were they? How do you know that?' said Jo.

'It's in the paper,' said Julie.

'Means nothing. Obviously. Could be black propaganda.'

'It means something,' said Nick, firmly.

'OK, so who was shot? Why them? Were they really shot? Do you know that for sure, or have you just been told that?'

'Well, obviously, we've been told that - we didn't see it happen - and I don't know who it was, the paper said it was a man in his late 60s, that's all,' said Julie.

'Well, there you go, then. All I'm saying is there are variables in any situation and you can't just accept them at face value. All you've seen is a photo of someone who looked like someone you met who called herself Barbara Stewart. You don't know when that was taken, or under what circumstances. You can't know for sure it is her, anyway. You've not seen a body, you don't even know who was shot, or anything about them, yet you think you know what happened. Think about it. You don't.' She probably didn't mean to sound so flippant and arrogant, but that's exactly what she did sound like.

Nick just didn't feel like arguing and it almost felt disrespectful to the dead man to do so. This wasn't a game. Jo King just had a mindset in place from doing her show, that reality was all just a constructed fiction of some sort and that facts might be lies. But the reality was they had been visited by two police officers, the picture they'd shown them was now in the paper, and the story of the shooting all over the media. If it was all made up then...well...it couldn't be all made up, not least because Barbara Stewart wouldn't be missing, she'd be protesting her innocence. Then again, Barbara Stewart hadn't been officially named, so maybe she wouldn't.

Jo stood up. 'I'd better go and get some sleep. Nice to see youse two.'

They watched her go.

'Well, that was rather annoying,' said Julie, arched eyebrows raised, sucking air into her nostrils in an indignant manner.

'I think she might have been coked-up, or something,' said Nick.

'Yeah, she did have that sort of coked-up, cocky vibe thing going on. Didn't like it. It felt like she was accusing us of being stupid when, you know, obviously what happened happened. We didn't dream it. They weren't people dressed up as coppers, in a fake police car, with a fake photo, of a fake person, committing a fake shooting, were they?'

'No, obviously not,' he rubbed his forearm, contemplatively. 'But it is a very odd situation, all the same.'

'You can take an idea too far. I'm not sure what Jo is trying to prove, really.'

'Oh, she's just caught up in her own thing. Come on, let's go back to the flat and get ready for today's shows.'

They walked through Stockbridge and up to Howe Street, climbing uphill as they did so.

'Christ, this city would keep you fit. My hamstrings are feeling tight already,' said Julie, panting a little.

Rain began to fall from a disturbed sky.

'Crackin' summer weather,' said Nick, looking upwards, as they got to the steps up to the flat.

They'd just unlocked the front door to the building when an old man came around the corner and walked up the steps. Nick held the door as he walked up towards them. Christ. It had to be Frank Stewart. He looked exhausted. As Jo had said, he seemed frail, walking with a slight stoop.

'Hello, there,' said Nick, not knowing what sort of tone to adopt in this situation. 'We're Nick and Julie.'

He held out his hand but Frank didn't even look at it; walking straight past them, he mumbled, 'Sorry if I don't stop to talk, I'm really not in the mood.'

The poor old bloke looked totally washed out. Deathly pale, dusty, papery skin. His wife had killed someone and disappeared. Maybe she'd even taken her own life. What an utterly appalling turn of events for him.

'If there's anything we can do to help...err...just ask,' said Julie. He didn't reply.

They stood outside the door to the flat. Nick turned the key in the Yale. 'We'll be here until Sunday, so do let us know if we can be of any help,' he said to Frank, as he went up the next flight. But the old man didn't say anything else.

'My heart goes out to him,' said Julie as she packed a shoulder bag and got a few things together. 'But I don't know what we can do. I mean, you wouldn't want strangers poking around in your life, would you?'

'No. I wonder if they've got kids that can come and sit with him. He shouldn't be on his own up there.'

They took a walk down to the Dean Gallery to see the modern art collection, then got a cab back into town to the Assembly Rooms on George Street to see a really good, if sparse, performance of *Midnight Cowboy* put on by a theatre group from York. The far end of the street was where the murder had happened, near Charlotte Square, home to the book festival, which was just about to begin its two-week run. The central gardens were full of tents and marquees. George Street was closed off to the public and was causing traffic chaos.

They dropped into a restaurant on Hanover Street called the Dogs, ate some delicious lamb chops and roasted root veg, then picked up a bottle of vodka, two bottles of tonic water and a metal flask. Sitting on a bench on Rose Street, like a couple of alcoholics, they mixed the liquids up in the flask.

'We are now with wet bar,' said Nick holding it aloft, happily triumphant.

Julie applauded. 'Owee then, we've got to get over to Pleasance Courtyard again for a stand-up act. It's a ventriloquist woman with an obscene puppet. Sounds class that, like. Exactly the sort of highbrow stuff two people with three degrees between them should be stimulating their intellect with.'

'One of Jeff's favorite sayings used to be, "Only the truly clever can be properly stupid", and I like to think we're living up to that by going to see a filthy glove puppet.'

'When is Jeff getting up here, again?'

'Tomorrow afternoon.'

'I hope the weather picks up for him, then.' She looked at the leaden skies. 'It's started raining again and I wish I'd put a jumper on. How is it both hot and cold within the same hour of one August afternoon?'

'Because it's Scotland. No other explanation is needed.'

The show was in a basement room, which was hotter than hell, so hot even the glove puppet was sweating. The cool rainy afternoon felt like a wonderful balm to hot skin as they emerged.

'That was so funny,' said Julie, taking a big hit of vodka and tonic from the bottle and narrowing her eyes in a wince, as the alcohol burn hit her throat. 'If I'd seen it on telly, it wouldn't have been half as good, but having it right there in front of you in the room, the energy of the live performance really made it.'

'I've thought that about all the shows. You know what? I think I just like seeing people having a go at making people laugh, because it's quite noble really - cheering people up and giving them something to chuckle about. There can't be a much more generous thing to do than that.'

She smiled and nodded. 'The dirty puppet was ace. Eff-ing and c-ing about the woman's body and the bloke in the front row...ha ha...it really did seem like it was the puppet that was saying it and not the ventriloquist woman with her hand up its arse.'

'I think I'd like to communicate with the world exclusively through the medium of glove puppetry. It'd be easier to be honest with people, if you could pass everything off as the words of a small woolly creature on the end of your hand. Actually, I was thinking how, in a way, it was a similar show to Jo King's in that they both created an alternative reality and made you believe in a fiction. Jo did it through illusion and this last woman did it through ventriloquism.'

'Eee, you're quite the theatre critic you, eh,' laughed Julie, enjoying herself and handing him the drink. 'Mind, that's dead strong, so don't go necking it all at once.'

He took a swig. 'Bloody hell, that's like a quadruple or a...whatever comes after quadruple - a fivetuple.'

The day passed quickly into night, the way that it does when you're drunk and having a great time with someone you love. They walked across town from one show to another. Some were great, others boring, but the city was alive with people right into the small hours and, driven on by the booze and the excitement of it all, it was after 2am when Nick and Julie finally rolled into bed, drunk to the point of passing out.

They woke up with hangovers. Nick put some tea down on the bedside table and got back into bed, feeling a bit rough.

'My god, I'm not sure that wet bar was a good idea, at all,' he said, eyes closed, head hurting.

'I'm still pissed, I think,' said Julie, her face buried into a pillow.

'My legs hurt. What were we doing last night?' he said, flexing his calf.

She turned over and made a noise with her bone-dry tongue. 'I have no idea. None. Can't even remember how we got back from the Gilded Balloon after that late show.' She let out a low moan. 'Did we see what I think we saw last night? Or was that a sick dream I've just had?' she said.

'I don't know what sick dream you've just had, but I'm afraid we really did see Puppetry of the Penis.'

She groaned again. 'I thought I might have just imagined two men folding and shaping their toilet parts, like a pervy sort of origami.'

'On the whole, it's probably best we were too drunk to remember much,' said Nick.

'How on earth do you end up doing that for a living? How do you even discover it's a talent that you've got?' she said, sitting up and pushing her hair out of her eyes.

'I dunno, Jules, we mess around with those things so much from an early age, all men can probably make a good fist of it - so to speak. At least you can never leave the house without being equipped to do a show.'

It was after 10am. Only two hours of the morning were left. He hated being in bed late, as it felt like you never caught up with yourself all day long. His phone buzzed with a text. Nick squinted at it.

'Jeff. He's getting ready to leave. Will be here at 3pm.'

'I might just have sobered up by then, but only if I have a big bloody vodka,' said Julie, sliding out of bed to go to the bathroom. She stopped, farted loudly and then looked down at herself with a confused frown. 'How come I've got nowt on? Where's my pyjamas or my underwear?'

Nick propped himself up. 'I think I'm wearing them.' He held up an arm to show the stripey red and white cotton.

She looked at him with bleary eyes. 'Have you got my knickers on as well?'

'Hold on...' He felt down below. 'No. I'm underwear-less.'

'Well, that's a relief. You'd stretch them right out of shape with your doo-dah.' She snorted, went to the toilet and returned, laughing to herself. 'This is like being a student again. Getting ratted, waking up in a strange bedroom with no clothes on and no real memory of how you got there, or even if you had it off the night before. We didn't, did we?'

Nick sipped at the tea. 'I don't remember. I doubt it, somehow. Not sure I was capable of even starting, let alone finishing.'

Returning from the toilet, she got back into bed and began sipping at the tea. 'Oh, god, that's lovely. I'm so dehydrated from all the booze.'

Cars rumbled past noisily on the cobbles below. They sat quietly until they'd finished drinking.

'I feel much better for that,' said Julie, putting the big mug down. 'How's thee?'

'I'll live.' He turned to look at her and let out a sigh as he saw the look in her eyes. 'Aw, no, Jules. Do I have to?'

'What?' she gave him her best wide-eyed, innocent look and curled the tip of her tongue up to touch her top lip.

'You've got hangover horn, haven't you? I can tell by the look in your eyes, but I still feel a bit sick.'

She gurgled a laugh and nuzzled into him. 'Aw, go on. I admit it, I do have massive hangover horn.'

'You made the idea of "hangover horn" up. You often feel randy in the morning, even when you've not been drinking,' he said.

31

'No, no, no, there's deffo such a thing as hangover horn. It's a hormonal thing brought on by booze or something. Anyway, as Jeff will be in the next-door bedroom from tonight onwards, this will be our last chance to have noisy sex.'

'He'll not hear us in there. These rooms are so big and the walls so thick, you could detonate a small, tactical nuclear weapon and you'd not hear it next door.'

'Well, why don't you detonate your small tactical nuclear weapon in me then! Ha ha, come on...don't be a spoilsport.' She slung her left leg over him and lay flat on top of him, so they were nose to nose, gurgling a laugh again. 'I'm just going to lie on top of you until you firm up. Don't try and act so cool and disinterested...ha ha...you know you can't resist.' She began whispering obscenities in his ear, about what she'd like to do to certain parts of his anatomy, something he totally loved and wasn't in either a psychological or physical position to resist, as her hip bones rested on his.

She put her lips on his. 'I shouldn't even be kissing you, my lips are sore.'

She rolled off him and picked up a vanilla chap stick from the bedside table, applying it to her lips. He took off his pyjamas as she rolled back on top of him, and she wriggled around, pressing herself into him. 'Ah, so you're interested now. I knew you would be.'

'I can't help but feel you're exploiting my inbuilt priapic response to having a naked woman lying on top of me and talking dirty,' he said, running his hands over her smooth, bare backside and then squeezing her hips.

'Of course I am, darlin'. Come on, I'll do all the work on top. You just have to lie there like a randy animal and let me do it to you. Anyway, it's now part of your married man's duties to keep your little wife well serviced.'

She took hold of him, raised her hips a little and pushed herself onto him, wrinkling her nose up as she did so. 'Ooh, now, isn't that nice? You're not going to be sick, are you? Ha ha. Vomiting on your naked wife is bad manners when you're *in flagrante*.'

'Weirdly, the thought of having it off has made my nausea disappear to be replaced by raging hangover horn.'

'You're not kidding, lad.' She let out a little pant of air. 'Ouch, hold on, you're poking into me at a funny angle. It'll be like straddling a wonky spin-dryer if I don't move you.' He lay still while she raised herself up, wriggled herself into a comfortable position and then put her hands either side of his shoulders, looking down at him, her hair spilling into his face and groaned slowly. 'You remember what to do, don't you? In and then out, and repeat until desired effect is achieved.'

He burst out laughing. Sex was always a mixture of laughter and lust, because it always seemed to be a vaguely ludicrous thing to be doing to each other and as soon as you caught yourself doing it, it seemed just very silly and odd. They often just broke off half way through, after making some daft dirty joke and collapsing into laughter. Maybe it was just proof that being able to make each other laugh was actually a sexy thing in itself. Certainly, taking sex too seriously is one of the least sexy things you can do.

Just after 3pm, Jeff's white van rolled to a halt outside the steps up to the building. Nick waved at him from the door.

'Hey, big man!'

Dressed in his regulation blue-and-red plaid shirt, army pants and big boots, with his long, greying hair half way down his back, Jeff came up the eight steps two at a time. They hi-fived.

'Now then, Mr Julie Wells. How's your first week of married life going?'

'A case of meet the new boss, same as the old boss. But it's all good. Jules is in town buying gifts for her family, so I thought we'd go and get a burger and a drink.'

'You is talking my language, brother. Where do I park the Mystery Machine? I need a spot populated by thieving Joan Armatrading and Leo Sayer fans, 'cos I'm hoping to get rid of a lot of rubbish stock.'

Nick pointed to a metered area. 'It costs a fortune, like, but only for another couple of hours, then it's free till 8am.'

'OK. Have you seen the motors parked up on Heriot Row? There are five Range Rovers, two Aston Martins and a Maserati.'

'Yeah, a 75 grand Mercedes estate is the entry level round here.'

Jeff parked up, checked the doors and then saluted Nick. 'Right, I'm all yours. Mind, it's bloody lovely here, isn't it?' He stood looking around at the grand Georgian terraces. 'What's your flat like?'

'Huge. Big Fish size.'

'It would be, wouldn't it?'

'Mind, we've had something really odd happen, though...'

'Is this what you were talking about in your text? Someone got shot?'

Nick explained about Barbara Stewart and the murder as they walked up the street towards the Cambridge pub.

'So let me get this straight. She's this respectable middle-class woman in her 60s, she chats to you, walks up the street, shoots an old bloke in the head in an office and then disappears.'

'That's as much as we know, yeah. We've not heard anything else. Her name still hasn't been in the paper.'

Jeff flicked at his long curtain of hair as they pushed open the pub door.

'See - right away, that seems weird. I mean, it *all* seems weird - but one thing, especially. What are you drinking?'

'Just water for me. We were heavily on the lash last night. Got hammered.'

They took a table and ordered a cheeseburger each, wrapped in lettuce rather than in a bun. Jeff cleared his throat. 'If you want to shoot someone and not get caught - and as she's disappeared and not just hung around to get arrested, we can assume she doesn't want to get caught - then you wouldn't do the deed in a public space, where you know you'll be on CCTV. You'd go around to your victim's house, or somewhere quiet and out of the way, wouldn't you?'

'I guess so. I never thought of that. So what are you saying?'

Jeff took a drink of white wine. 'I'm saying that she did it in the office in order to be seen...'

Nick crossed his arms and chewed on his bottom lip. Jeff was right. He was good at this stuff - at seeing the line of logic through an apparently insane act.

'...and there's only one reason anyone wants to be seen doing a crime and that is so everyone, or someone specific, knows they've done it,' said Jeff.

'But she was such a normal, well-spoken woman...'

Jeff held up an index finger. 'Whatever she was like is irrelevant - she still did it. There is conclusive proof, by the sounds of this picture they showed you.'

Nick thought for a minute as their food arrived. 'So she wants to be seen doing it, but she wants to get away with it, all the same? Weird.'

'Yeah. Deffo.' He bit into the meat. 'Maybe she was working for someone. Working as a hit man. Or hit woman, as the case may be. So had to be seen doing the job in order to pick up the money for the job.' Jeff jabbed his middle finger on the table. 'That's spot on, that is. She's popped him for someone.'

'You should be a detective, not a second-hand record salesman.'

'Maybe I am, but I'm just deep, deep, deep undercover.' He flashed his eyes at him. 'Have they said who the dead guy was, or anything about him?'

Nick put his burger down and did a search on his phone for the *Edinburgh Evening News* website. It had just been updated.

'The victim is believed to be John Grayson-Thomas, 71, of Royal Crescent, Edinburgh.'

'Seventy-one and he was still working?'

Nick read on. 'Ah, he owns a letting agency. There are thousands of flats to rent in Edinburgh all the time. It's a big business. That was his office where he was working.' He scanned the rest of the piece, reading it out loud. ' "Mr Grayson-Thomas was chairman of Kid's Planet - an orphan charity - and held other public roles, including positions on Edinburgh City Council". He was quite a dude for the public-spirited work. He set up JGT letting agency in 2001, after a career as a Latin teacher.'

Jeff jabbed the table. 'He could have made a lot of enemies in his civic life. Those sorts of things are always a hotbed of political intrigue and rivalry. Maybe Babs Stewart was acting on behalf of a group of disgruntled people who our man had double-crossed.'

Nick winced. 'Possibly. It's a hell of a thing to do, though, if you're right. Shooting someone in the head in cold blood isn't the sort of thing you do on a whim, over a dispute about height of hedges or pot holes in the road. I'm sure the police will be going through his past in detail.'

Jeff sat back. 'Yeah, actually, that's a good point. If there are a load of people who wanted him dead, the cops will soon dig that out. One person can keep a secret, but it's much harder if there are a lot of people involved. And if there's a dispute that's been festering, then it'll likely be a matter of public record. They'll round up everyone concerned and it'll all come out.'

'Well, maybe that's what will happen. It's only about 40 hours since she killed him. I still can't work out why they haven't named her, though.'

'Maybe because the name she gave you isn't actually her name and they've found that out. In other words, they don't know who she is, or they do but want to keep it quiet for a while.'

'Again, that's good thinking, Jeff. That hadn't occurred to me.'

'You need a logical brain for this stuff, not a warped creative one, son. Anyway, apart from running into a murderer, what else has been going on?'

Nick went over some of the shows they'd seen and also brought him up to speed with Jo King.

'I'd like to see her, yeah. It won't be the same for me, now I know what's going on. Sounds good, though. Anyone who removes a limb gets my vote. I'll get a ticket for tonight, if it's not sold out.'

'She's a really good illusionist and I liked the point she was making, I think it'll chime with you. She's very into the idea that everything is a conspiracy; or at least, you shouldn't take anything for granted.'

'Ah, my days as a conspiracy theorist are over. I'm no longer a believer. It's all too mainstream these days. Back when I was consuming alternative media, everyone believed what people in power said about everything. Now, no-one does and everyone thinks the world is run by a secret cabal of bankers and industrialists, who may or may not be aliens. It's lost its appeal. And UFOs are all clearly a load of rubbish now that everyone has got a camera on them at all times. If they really existed there'd be some definite proof and no need to Photoshop videos. Nope, it's all over for me. The world is mad enough as it is, without having to invent more shit to explain it all. Argie has made me grow up a bit, I think, albeit very late on in life.'

'Shocking, that, Jeff. You'll be missing the wee man.'

Jeff finished his glass of wine. 'Aye, I am. He's never off my mind, really. It's the first time I've been away from him for any length of time, since he was born. In the five days I'm away he'll probably grow and change. Every day he seems to develop a bit more. Amazing to watch. Now he's crawling it won't be long before he's walking, talking, swearing, drinking lager and shagging lasses...or indeed, lads...or, if he's got any sense, both. Bisexuality surely increases your odds of pulling on a Friday night. Variety is the spice of life. I always wished I'd been bisexual...well not *always*.'

'Ha ha...yeah, it must...but you've got a few years before any of that kicks off.'

'He's a Teessider, remember? So probably not that many, trust me.'

After eating, they walked up onto George Street to meet Julie at the bar in the Hard Rock Cafe. The Charlotte Street end of the road was clear now and traffic was moving through.

'Was the shooting up there, then?' said Jeff.

'Yeah. It was all closed off yesterday, but it was knackering the traffic, so they've got it open as soon as possible. God forbid traffic gets held up for long by a brutal slaying.'

Jeff laughed. 'God no, losing your brains to a bullet is one thing, but slow-moving traffic is much more important. Owee, let's go and have a look at the crime scene.'

They walked past Waterstones and some posh bars. The office where it had happened was set on the corner of North Castle Street. Barriers had been erected and taped off. It was entirely glazed on one side, though screens had been erected so nothing inside was visible.

'There's no hiding place here,' said Jeff. 'Two big plate-glass windows reveal everything that is going on inside and look,' he pointed up at a CCTV camera mounted on a wall, facing up the street. 'That was probably where the police got the picture from. The one that they showed you.'

'It showed her coming out with the gun in her hand.'

Jeff frowned. 'Have you got the picture on your phone?'

Nick found it on the newspaper website and showed it to him.

Jeff peered at it. 'Hmm, well, you've just shot someone and you're coming out with the gun on display. I mean, why not just put it in your bag or pocket? She wasn't carrying it in her hand when you saw her, so she must have had it in the bag or a pocket at that point. But she comes out with it on display, so to me, that's just as I said earlier - she's presenting evidence to prove *she's* done it.'

'Maybe she just panicked and legged it, forgetting to hide the gun.'

Jeff winced and shook his head. 'Nah, she's gone up here and coolly dispatched this man - it's not a crime of passion, it's malice aforethought. She's thought it through at length. No, she's definitely letting the CCTV camera see the weapon.' He tapped at the screen.

'It's possible she didn't know there was a CCTV camera there, though, isn't it?'

Jeff pulled a face at him. 'Stop spoiling my otherwise watertight theories, Guymer. Like I say, I think this is well planned, she'll have known, alright. Maybe she had to prove it was her that had done it, or else *she'd* get whacked,' said Jeff.

Nick shook his head. 'Oh, come on, man, you're just making rubbish up now. I thought you were over the mad theories?'

They walked back along George Street and into the Hard Rock. Julie was leaning on the bar looking at her phone with a very tall vodka, lime and soda in front of her. She was wearing dark glasses, a fitted white shirt and tight white jeans and black boots. Her blonde hair spilled down her back in long, loose curls. Her black leather biker jacket hung on a peg under the table.

'Here she is, Teesside's Stevie Nicks,' said Jeff, patting her on the back. 'You're looking cool, lady. Whatcha drinking?'

'I'll have another vod 'n' lime when you're ready. Now then, Jeff. Good trip up?' She took off her shades and grinned up at him.

'Smoother than our Argie's arse, aye. And look at you, is this your big city look? Impressive.'

'Yeah, well, I like to make an effort, sometimes,' she said.

They sat around a high table on stools.

'Did you get prezzies for your mam and auntie?' said Nick.

'Yeah. I just dropped them off at the flat. Just a bottle of single malt and some tartan shite - well, it's what they expect. If I didn't come back with whisky, shortbread and a Nessie tea towel, they'd not even believe I'd been up here.'

'We've just been along to the office where the shooting happened,' said Nick, as Jeff went to the bar. 'It's all screened off.' He explained about Jeff's theory that she wanted to prove she'd shot him.

Julie turned around and patted Jeff on the back as he was paying for the drinks. 'That's very good thinking, Jeffrey,' she said.

He put glasses down in front of them. 'I thought so. Right, don't disturb me for a minute while I buy some tickets for tonight. What are you seeing?'

Nick pushed their itinerary in front of him.

'Right, I'm going to see this Jo King lass.'

'He'll like her, won't he, Jules?'

She nodded. 'She's got a big bum an' all. You like a big bum on a lass, you, Jeff. You're always saying.'

'I do. It's comforting, is a well-padded arse. Suggests generosity and an ability to sit still for long periods of time - which I take as a much under-rated quality in a human.'

'Does my arse not suggest generosity, then?' she said, laughing.

Jeff pulled a face and held a finger up. 'Ah, I can feel I am at one of those moments in a conversation when anything I say will be a terrible social faux pas and gain me at least two enemies. Now shut up whilst I try and work this technology on me phone and get some tickets. What the hell is an app, anyway?'

They laughed. Nick clinked Julie's glass. 'You look very glamorous. When you said you were going to get changed, I didn't realise you were going for the full rock chick. I like it, baby.' He leaned into her ear and whispered something dirty.

She gave him a wicked grin, put the flat of her hand on his belly and gave him a quick kiss. 'I think we might get arrested if we did that here, darlin'. Actually, this was my London Look for years. A bit rock, a bit posh, a bit slutty. Ha ha...don't say it's not true, I know fine well it is. I've got 25 per cent of these jeans up me fanny and another 25 per cent up me colon, they're that tight,' she said, adding as an afterthought, 'just as well I didn't bother with underwear.' She pulled a shocked face at him and put her hand over her mouth, as though she'd accidentally said something she shouldn't have.

'I heard that,' said Jeff, not looking up from his phone. 'And for the record, I'm disgusted, worried about possible chafing and, no disrespect, Jules, I'm also concerned about unsightly staining. Believe me, a single father with an incontinent human animal to look after knows how difficult some human expulsions are to remove from clothing.'

They laughed. Julie slapped at him playfully. 'I know, I know, one wet fart away from disaster, as mam would poetically put it.'

Nick looked at the walls, which were hung with guitars signed by famous musicians, along with various pictures and record sleeves. 'Some of the guitars in here have just been signed by a guitarist, they didn't necessarily own them. That seems a bit of a cheat. And others are just photos in a frame or reproduction posters, like that Woodstock one. That's not an original, you can just buy them.'

Julie wandered around, looking at things and then came back. 'I know what you mean, but I like it. I'm happy just being around rock music stuff. I'm not bothered about its authenticity.'

'Yeah, but there's a special thrill when you know someone legendary played or wore it.'

'True. Remember that Hendrix white Flying V at the Hard Rock near Hyde Park? That really gave me shivers when I first saw it in the 80s,' she said, sitting down.

'Yeah, I saw Clapton's psychedelic painted SG in Newport Beach in California, I think it was. I genuinely felt like it was a holy relic. And I'm not exaggerating at all. Also saw a Todd Rundgren SG in the same place...'

'...Oh, god, don't. I'd have rubbed that all over my naked body, given half the chance.' She threw her head back and made an ecstatic face.

'I hate to interrupt your guitar-based sex games, but I'm sorted. I've got tix for your big bum lass, and then for the other two shows you're going to. Just need to pick them up at a box office. Cheers!' he raised his glass and sank half of it.

Julie pulled out the metal flask. 'I've loaded the wet bar, so we can at least have a drink during the shows.'

'A wet bar, you say...what is this magic of which you speak?' said Jeff, wafting his hair up and down like a giant pair of ears.

'We overdid it yesterday. Got righteously fuck faced on vodka. It's just so you don't have to queue for drink,' said Julie.

'Righteously fuck faced, you say? I like this thinking. Drink on the move. Makes sense. So we're on a bender, are we?' He rubbed his hands together. 'I've not had a good drink for ages due to being a responsible dad.'

'We had one last night. We can't have another,' said Nick. In the back of his mind he knew that the highs that drinking brought him could later drive him to very deep, very black lows. It was why he'd stopped drinking for a long time. But then, drinking in a situation like this was exciting, it was fun, and he couldn't do it with better people, and who knew about the future anyway? The future would have to take care of itself. It's impossible to worry all the time about the existential threats of possible future moods.

'Yer bollocks, we can't. I'm up for it,' said Julie. 'I've got a proper thirst on us - all we need to do is get a decent volume of food in us tonight. We didn't eat enough yesterday. There's a burger stand at the Pleasance. We should have a couple of those.'

'This is why we all love you,' said Jeff. 'Drink, no knickers and knowledge of easy meat-based dining. No more perfect woman has been created.' He put his big arm around her shoulder and squeezed her affectionately.

'You wouldn't say that when she's puking her ring into the toilet,' said Nick.

'Vomiting a good night into a toilet is every working-class rocker's right,' said Jeff, looking out of the big plate glass window, as tourists, locals, drinkers and festival goers poured past. 'You know what? It is bloody great to be somewhere where there's a lot going on.'

'I totally agree. It's fantastic,' said Julie, excited. 'I mean, when you're working, it doesn't make any difference - but when you want to go out and it's not just old men's pubs full of gadgees, I just love it. Stockton's got its own thing but...I dunno...there are times when I miss proper city life. Y'know, the art and music and nightlife. I'm a city lass, at heart, always was, really.'

Nick didn't say anything, but he felt exactly the same way. Yet they were tied to Teesside for work. They couldn't live here. They couldn't afford it, for a start. But looking at Julie, she was so energised, a real spark in her eyes that she didn't have when trying to find a parking space in the Cleveland Centre or getting wolf whistled at by drunks outside the Pound Pub in Stockton.

She grinned at him and in one of those transcendent, slow-motion, and yet defining moments of life, where everything falls into focus, time slows to a crawl and your brain works overtime, a shaft of sunshine skimmed in through the big windows and picked up the yellows and platinum blonde in her hair, she was all iridescent blue eyes, curved hips and full pink lips. And now she was his wife. Sometimes he felt like he didn't deserve her; most of the time, in fact. She was the sort of woman you saw with someone else and not with you. He was nothing special, he knew that, but she really was. She was the one in the room that *everyone* wanted, but she was *his* girl. She was looking so right, it was giving him chills. Yeah. In his head, he said a quick prayer of thanks.

'Are you alright?' she said, nudging him, her eyes looking into his with a little puzzlement.

He smiled. 'Yeah, just got some dust or something in my eye,' he said, clearing his throat, rubbing at the moisture in his eyes, and taking a drink. He didn't want her to know how he was feeling. It was too much pressure to put on someone to tell them they were like an angel in your life. No-one wants to hear that. It's too much. Even if it is true.

'Right, so we'll have a couple in here then up to the Pleasance for large-buttock-based illusion. Tell me this though, O wise married love-lies, how do you know Jo King's buttocks are not, in themselves, an illusion?' said Jeff, wobbling his eyebrows up and down while wafting his beard. 'Illusory buttocks will not keep a man warm at night.'

'We were saying the other day that they were possibly prosthetic, strap-on buttocks,' said Nick.

'Of course. You can actually buy a fake arse, but then, I've been making an arse out of myself for years,' said Jeff, pulling a puzzled face then breaking into a crazy grin. They hi-fived.

Time spent with friends, when you don't have to worry about the workaday practicalities of life, are such a blessing. The days when you put some velvet between your vertebrae are some of your best days. For the too many of us who work too hard, for too long, for not enough, such days are too few and far between.

While Jeff went to Jo King's show, Nick and Julie saw a supposedly topical news sketch troupe who seemed to amuse posh students like the performers themselves, but left everyone else cold. They came out of the room pulling faces at each other and stood against a wall, enjoying a big hit from the wet bar.

'I'm sorry, but I couldn't help hating all the well-to-do kids who performed that,' said Julie. 'I know that's entirely my issue - but people like them have such an easy life. It just gets on my wick. I lose empathy because they're too confident of their own great future. And you just know they're born into an easy life. Their parents have got a big house that they'll inherit and they'll be alright. When you're an old bitch like me, you can just see how their lives will go and everything will be so easy for them. I hate it. It's jealousy, I suppose, but it's also political outrage that the fruit machine of life paid out for them, but leaves so many behind.'

'Yeah, I know it shows I'm shallow and pathetic, but anyone who pronounces "bath" as "barth" and has been educated at Eton, is gonna be fighting to get me on their side from the start. The thing is, they'd probably say that just showed how chippy we are, but I don't think we should be ashamed of it. When you've got the money and the power, you're in no position to critique those who don't have either. I hate being told I should be more broad-minded by people like that. Fuck you. We're arsy, Northern and we fucking like it. Because if we don't have that, we have nothing. We have to fight, somehow. We're chippy because we can see how we've been screwed over forever.'

'Amen, fizzin' brother Nick. Here comes Jeff,' said Julie. 'Jo's show must be kicking out.'

Jeff came across the courtyard. Nick held out the wet bar to him.

'Need a hit of the hard stuff after all that?'

He took it off him and took a long drink.

'That was the most amazing thing I've ever seen,' said Jeff. 'She's something, that one. What a ride!!! Whoo!'

'We thought you'd like her,' said Nick.

'I know you'd told me what she was all about, but even so - when she was hanging from that beam I *proper* shat meself. I was laughing so much at her behind the curtain, that I wasn't ready for such a shocking thing.'

'Yeah, she's so good at sucking you in and then messing you up,' said Nick.

'How old is she, do you reckon?'

'Early 30s,' said Julie.

'Is she gay?' asked Jeff, with an unusual curiosity.

'We thought she might be, but then we felt bad for making such an assumption, just because she's not girly,' said Julie.

Jeff tutted. 'Trust you two to beat yourselves up about such PC bollocks.' He took another big drink. 'She looks classic lesbian material to me. You were right about her arse, mind.'

Julie looked at him quizzically. 'You fancy her, don't you? Eee, you do. Ha ha...I can tell...ha ha!'

Jeff shrugged awkwardly. 'Nowt wrong with fancying an illusionist. In my line of work, the ability to cut your own hand off could be invaluable for scaring away shoplifters,' said Jeff. 'And if she can make all the Cliff Richard records disappear, she'd be worth her weight in gold.'

Nick grinned at him. Jeff had always had unusual taste in women, right since they'd gone through puberty together. But whereas Nick had, from an early age, liked intelligent, attractive, quietly passionate women, Jeff tended to favour noisy, quirky lasses with odd hair cuts or an unusual fashion sense. Arty women, bikers and general outcasts seemed to be who he was drawn to, with the exception of his short and tragic relationship with Rita, who had been as straight as a die. So in that regard, Jo King was very much in his ballpark, though she was a lot younger.

'She'll be out in a minute - I'll keep an eye open for her. Was it full in there?' said Julie.

'Still a few seats available. A couple of people walked out when she started hacking her arm...I bet she gets a lot of that. I thought one bloke was going to faint when she started digging her fingers into her own flesh. Ha ha...was ace, that. All the blood reminded me of Saturday nights drinking in the Talbot in the 70s! Yes!' He punched the air.

Julie spotted Jo coming out, trotted over to her and brought her back to Nick and Jeff, fancying a spot of match-making.

'This is our old pal, Jeff, he's staying with us for the rest of the week.'

'I've got to shake your hand Jo,' said Jeff, eagerly. 'I thought your show was just brilliant, absolute class from start to finish. I've never seen anything like it in my life. You deserve to go right to the top with it. Honest, it's brilliant and the message behind it is right on the money for me,' said Jeff, shaking her hand as he spoke, towering over her by about a foot.

'It is good, isn't it? Thanks, Jeff.' There was her arrogance, again. But she was obviously pleased to hear it. 'Did you see those two who walked out? Ha ha...fuck 'em...they're my best publicity. I'm the show most people have walked out of, they reckon.'

'So did you train as a butcher?' said Jeff. 'Excellent knife skills, lady.'

'As it happens, I can actually gut a pig, me,' she said. She made a stabbing gesture.

'I can see you're an expert. Slice me off a piece of that. That could be your next show!' said Jeff.

She laughed and patted him on the arm. 'Roasting a hog and serving hot delicious meat would probably make me a lot more money.'

'Who doesn't like hot hog? I speak as one myself,' said Jeff.

'God, your hair is amazing,' said Jo, going behind Jeff, picking it off his back and letting it fall like a greying curtain. 'When was the last time you had it cut?'

'When was it, Nick?' said Jeff.

'Err...incredibly, it was 1972, I think. Your mam made you have it cut for the first day at Stockton Grammar. Don't remember it being cut since then, though it should be much longer by now, really.'

'It just snaps off. Actually, I think I had it cut in 1981, like all the long-haired rockers who briefly tried to not look really out of fashion. It didn't take, though. We were in the second year at Newcastle Poly, remember?'

'Oh, yeah. It didn't suit you. You just looked like a long-haired bloke with short hair. Like the missing foot of hair was a ghost that lived on.'

'1981! Bloody hell. You old get. I was two back then,' said Jo, laughing, combing her fingers through Jeff's hair like he was a long-haired dog. 'And your beard must have taken a lot of work. How long is it?' She gave it a tug.

'It's bad form to measure a gentleman's beard and indeed, any other part of his anatomy,' said Jeff. Jo laughed and stroked it a bit more. 'Keep looking and you'll find the Little Owl that lives in there.'

'Aw, I love a Little Owl, me. It's me favourite bird. God, man, You're one big hairy muthafucker, you, Jeff. I really like it,' said Jo. Jeff grinned.

'Hey, Jo, did you get to see Frank Stewart?' said Nick.

Jo shook her head. 'No, I knocked, but there was no-one in. Have they told you about this murder, Jeff?'

'Yeah, shocking stuff. Nick was saying you've got some good conspiracy theories about the murder.'

'I just mistrust what I'm told on principle. That's all. That's what my show is all about, like. Don't believe your eyes. All of us are so easy to trick. Me included. We're all prone to seeing what we want to see, or formulating a scenario that we understand, regardless of what is actually happening.'

Jeff nodded. 'My theory is that Barbara Stewart wanted to get seen committing the crime. She could have done it somewhere much less public and without CCTV cameras present.'

'Yeah. Good thinking.' Jo looked at her watch. 'Aw, bugger, I've gotta go. I've got three appearances on compilation shows to do, then I'm doing "Late 'n' Live" at the Gilded Balloon, again. I'll catch you lot later. Nice to meet you, big hairy fella. I'll see you around the flat, I suppose.' She slapped Jeff on the arm and walked away with her distinctive cocky strut, buttocks shuddering a little with every step.

'It's funny watching you in chat up mode,' said Nick. 'I'd forgotten what it was like.'

'I wasn't chatting her up. I was just enjoying talking to her. She's gay, isn't she? She's got to be gay. She looks gay. Everything about her is gay. How do I even fancy a gay woman? Is that sexist? Or even legal?' He fastened his hair back into a long ponytail.

'Are you going to say "gay" any more?' said Nick.

'No, that's me empty of gay now.'

'Of course it's not sexist. She might be straight, or do a bit of both - you don't know, Jeff,' said Julie. 'You just think she's gay because of how she looks.'

Jeff looked at her in astonishment.

'Well, duh, aye, of course I do. How people look is how I tell what they're like, man,' said Jeff, like she was stupid.

'Yeah, but you heard what she said - "question all realities, don't believe your own eyes," ' said Julie, who was rarely outsmarted in any argument. 'She looks like some lesbians look, but that doesn't mean she is. She might be the living embodiment of her own philosophy.'

'She might, or she might just be what, in the 70s, we used to enjoy calling a "muff diver",' said Jeff, shrugging.

Julie raised an eyebrow. 'Well, there's nothing uniquely gay about that. He's a top-notch muff diver, aren't you, luv?' She nudged Nick and cackled.

'What? Now?' said Nick, cartoonishly. 'Alright, if you insist.' He got onto his knees and grabbed her around the thighs and started nuzzling into her crotch, like a snuffling dog.

'Ha ha, gerroff...stop making a show of us.'

'He does look like a professional, though,' said Jeff, laughing. 'I should be taking notes, just in case I get lucky.'

Nick got to his feet. 'A professional? I'm not charging for it. It's a service performed free of charge in return for other intimate favours.'

'And at that point I must put my fingers in my ears,' said Jeff, scrunching his eyes up tight. 'C'mon, we better start queuing for the next show.'

They stood in line beside the entrance to the Pleasance One, a bigger room which could hold up to 750. The courtyard was jam packed.

'I've never seen anything like this,' said Jeff, taking it all in. 'It's almost as though it shouldn't all work. Twenty or more little venues all in one place, policed by students in waterproof jackets. But it does. It looks like it's falling apart, but it's actually all working. Much like my shops.'

'That's what we were saying. It feels chaotic, yet it all knits together well,' said Julie.

Just as she ended her sentence, a big, red-faced, chubby woman with ragged brown curls poking out from under a baseball cap, and a bustling gait, gave them a silly little wave, bending at the knee slightly as she did so. She wore a blue fleece and jeans. ' 'Ello there! I thought I recognised you.' She spoke in a broad, almost silly, Yorkshire accent.

Nick didn't know who she was, but thought she was a bit like the sort of bluff and slightly daft character Victoria Wood might play.

'Hello, Mandy. Fancy seeing you here, what brings you to Edinburgh?' Jeff said, patting her on the back a little.

'I come every year for a few days. Love the Fringe, me. Been comin' for 20 years.'

'Mandy is Colin Harcombe's number two,' said Jeff, pointing to her. 'We've met a couple of times, haven't we, Mandy?'

'Aye, but only because you're a shit robber,' she said, quick as a flash. Jeff laughed.

'Oh, yeah, Mandy Beale, isn't it?' said Nick, remembering him having mentioned her.

'Aye. Always sounds a bit dodgy being called a number two,' said Mandy. Unusually for a Yorkshire person, her broad accent had a laugh installed into it as a default.

They chatted about what they'd seen. A woman in her early 50s, she seemed very down to earth and was there on her own, staying in a cheap hostel, which suggested that she was quite an independent, free spirit. Completely different to her boss in that regard, who was as straight up and down as they come.

'Did you hear about the shooting?' said Julie. 'The woman who did it lives in the flat above where we're staying. We met her on the way out - right before she must have done it.'

'Really? Aye, I did read about it in the paper. The perp has disappeared, apparently. I'm sure Lothian and Borders plod will find her. Who was the victim, any idea?'

'It was a John Grayson-Thomas. He ran a letting agency,' said Jeff.

'Now then, why does that name ring a bell?' she said, pulling a red-cheeked, gurning, quizzical face, making little popping noises with her lips as she thought.

'He was a local Edinburgh dignitary - involved in lots of charitable works. The sort who's on every committee. Probably how he made an enemy of Barbara Stewart,' said Jeff.

Mandy Beale shrugged. 'Well, I've got three days off, so I want nowt to do wi' scumbags for a change. Right, I'll gerroff, pick meself up two pints and then on to me next show. Bloody love it. Have a nice time, eh, kids.'

She left them with a wave and wandered off towards a bar.

'I like her. She's a proper human,' said Julie, watching her go.

'Yeah, if someone told me that Colin Harcombe was actually a robot, I'd not be at all shocked,' said Nick, 'as much as I like him, but Mandy is almost the exact opposite. Good to think someone in her position is a nice person.'

'When I first met her, I thought right away that she was a comedy Yorkshire woman. All gurning, big vowels, tits and belly. You can see her in a flowery housecoat hitting a bloke with a broom in a 70s situation comedy,' said Jeff. 'But, this may just be the wet bar talking, but I reckon she's really sexy, y'know. I thought that when I first met her. There's something about her.'

'Gettaway, she is not,' said Nick, incredulous.

'She is, man. She's got that thing about her...' said Jeff, staring in the direction she'd gone.

'*I* know what you mean. She's got that physical, passionate thing,' said Julie. 'You're right, Jeff.'

'Aye, you can really imagine her doing it, can't you, Jules?' said Jeff. 'I can, anyway. Big wobbly lass going for it, like a blancmange on a roller-coaster. I bet she loves a bit of...'

'...Jeff!' she interrupted him, pushing at his chest. 'Fizz me, you're a dirty get. Keep your lustful thoughts to yourself, thank you very much. You're right, though. You're not going to try and chat her up when we get home, are you?'

'She must be a couple of years older than you,' said Nick, surprised by this confession from Jeff.

'I don't care about that. Save on contraception, won't it?'

Julie slapped him on the side of the arm in a comedy fashion, laughing.

'I know she's long divorced. Must be on good money now, cracking pension. You could do a lot worse than feel the warm embrace of a cop-per's thighs, let me tell you,' said Jeff. 'Not Colin Harcombe's, obviously. That'd be like being embraced by a stick insect.'

Nick laughed. 'What's happened to you, Jeff Evans? You're a sex machine, these days. Chatting up coppers and lesbians. It's like you're a player.'

'A long player. Boom and indeed, boom.' He held his big arms out wide and pulled a daft face.

After their last comedy show finished at midnight, they made their way back to the flat in the New Town. As they walked down the slope and stood on Heriot Row, lights were on in the flat above theirs.

'Frank Stewart must be in again, or maybe Barbara has returned,' said Nick, pointing at the yellow light in the windows. He looked up as they stood at the crossing point in the road. A woman appeared at the window briefly. She had dark, curly hair. It shocked Nick to see her. It wasn't Barbara...but who was it?

'Did you see her?!' said Nick, excitedly.

'Was it the killer woman?' said Jeff, nodding.

'No, it wasn't her. She had longish white hair. That woman at the window looked younger with short curly hair. Maybe she's Frank's sister, or something,' said Nick.

He opened the front door and they climbed the two flights of stairs to their flat door. As they did so, the flat door above closed and footsteps came down the stairs. It was Frank Stewart.

'Hello again,' said Julie cheerfully. 'Is everything OK? Err...' she didn't know what to say and halted mid-sentence.

'Fine, thank you,' he said in a slightly hoarse, light voice.

'Have you got a visitor?' said Nick. 'Good to have some company at a time like this.' But he knew right away he'd said the wrong thing because Frank paused briefly, looked at Nick with a frown and shook his head.

'No. No visitor.'

He hurried off, shuffling along like an old invalid.

Nick let them into the flat.

'Can anyone come up with a reason why he just lied to us about having a visitor?' he said, pointing towards where Frank had been standing, as he closed the door behind them and kicked his shoes off.

'Oh, I'm sure we can come up with something outlandish. Let's have a night cap and think about it,' said Jeff, looking around and cracking his knuckles. 'By the 'eck, as Mandy Beale would say, this place is grand. Big Fish must have bought it already looking like this because he'd never do it up so classy. There's nothing at all which says 1970s bachelor, for a start. No smoked glass, black leather, leopard skin print or tasteful pictures of naked women with yoghurt on their breasts.'

'You don't want yoghurt on your breasts, you want it on your downstairs lady cave to relive your cystitis,' said Julie, pouring them all a glass of whisky. They sat on the sofas in the living room, the big table lamps casting a low orange light.

'Cheers, Jules. Here's to you both, now chained together by law,' said Jeff, raising his glass a little. 'I enjoyed your wedding and I really bloody enjoyed tonight, it was a proper good laugh. It's almost like we're old friends or something. Nice to be out and about around younger people, people who aren't fucked out their heads on cheap vodka from the Pound Pub, or gaunt-faced smackheads.'

'Yeah. Being around younger people does make you feel younger, there's no doubt about it,' said Nick. 'I've noticed that. As you get older, when you don't have kids, it's so easy to get locked into a grumpy old man frame of mind, but coming to something like this, it's really reconnected me to my youth, in a way. It's all really bloody positive.' He relished the lovely, smooth whisky.

'So what about upstairs, then?' said Julie, pulling her feet up under her, undoing the top button on her tight white jeans and letting out a groan. 'Oh, that's better. I wonder why he said he didn't have a visitor. I wonder who she is?'

Jeff sipped at his whisky and then flashed his eyes at them. 'Why don't we go and ask her?'

'What?' said Nick.

'Why don't we go and ask her? Why not?'

'Well, it's nothing to do with us, is it?' said Julie. 'And it's well after midnight.'

'She's still up. I'll go up and ask. This is my brother's flat - I'm just making sure everything is safe and secure for him...or whatever...basically I'm just nosy, right? You stay here. Leave this to the big hairy man.'

He left the room, put the door on the latch and went upstairs. They heard him knock a couple of times.

'She's not opening the door. That's odd,' said Julie, ear cocked to hear movement.

Then they heard Jeff's voice, shouting through the letterbox. 'Hello, there. I'm Jeff Evans, my brother owns the flat below, I was just wondering if I could have a quick word.' He was even modifying his voice, so it sounded less Teesside and more well-spoken.

Still no reply.

There were voices on the stairwell. Nick got up and looked out the door. Jeff was talking to Jo King, who had obviously just got home.

'Alright, Jo,' said Nick. 'I thought you were working late.'

She shrugged and rubbed at her hair. 'Oh, I couldn't be arsed. There's only so much abuse you can take in one day.'

'Tough crowds?'

She rubbed her forehead with her fingertips and scrunched up her eyes. 'You could say that. Freaked a couple of people out, who then decided that to shout abuse at us was the right way to behave. Twats. What are you up to, then?'

Jeff explained about the woman they'd seen. As he did so Julie came out onto the stairs with a grin and nod to Jo.

'Why's she not answering, then?' said Jo. 'That's just rude. Come on, I'll have a go.'

She rapped on the door. 'Hello. It's Jo from upstairs.'

'A thought has just occurred to me,' said Jeff. 'We saw Frank come out. Maybe he's murdered that woman in the time it took us to cross the road and come in.'

They looked at each other, all thinking it was not the least likely reason that no-one was coming to the door.

'Frank's not a murderer, though, is he? He's a harmless old bloke,' said Jo.

'Well, why is she not answering, then?' said Nick.

'Shall we get the police?' said Julie.

'She might be bleeding to death in there, for all we know. We can't wait for them,' said Jo, inspecting the Yale lock on the door and then pushing open the big, wide brass letterbox and peering inside. 'Hello?' she called out.

Still no reply.

'Right, I'll have us in 'ere.' She took out a telescopic rod from her inside pocket, pulled it out to its fullest length, stuck some gum she'd been chewing onto the end, stuck her arm through the letterbox and wriggled so she could reach right up towards the latch.

'I love a woman who carries around her own telescopic rod, just in case of emergencies. This is quality housebreaking,' said Jeff. 'And Jules has, in the past, set a high entry level.'

'This is a piece of piss. Right. Push on the door when I tell you.' She jabbed at the knob on the Yale, briefly releasing the sneck in the lock. 'Right, push it.' Nick leaned on it and the door opened.

Jo dropped her telescopic pen and grinned up at them. 'Not that I've ever done that before, you understand.'

Julie clapped a little.

'Question is - did you do that for real, or do we just think you did it?' said Jeff, pulling her to her feet, with his hands under her armpits. 'I for one am always open to the possibility that I'm hallucinating.'

Jo gave him a withering, but friendly look. Jeff ruffled her spiky hair and she leaned into him a little, almost affectionately.

Nick went into the flat with some degree of trepidation, expecting to see a body at every turn. He called out again, but still no-one replied. Somehow, there was no-one there. No-one alive, anyway.

He flicked a light switch by the door. The flat was laid out exactly as the one below.

'Which window did you see her at?' said Jo, skipping past him.

'The one facing out onto Heriot Row,' said Nick, pushing open the living room door and putting the lights on in both main rooms. Two big chandeliers of bulbs filled the room with bright light. No-one was there.

'If you ask me, this flat is quite obviously empty,' said Jeff, looking into the dining room and finding nothing. 'Let's check the bedrooms.'

They were both empty, as was the bathroom and kitchen. The flat was deserted. But there was no way out, apart from through the front door and if she'd come out that way, they'd have seen her.

'Could she have left while you were getting your drinks?' said Jo.

'No, we'd have heard her. You can hear people walking around up here and you can feel a judder as the door closes. We could even feel Jeff knocking on the door.'

'Well, at the risk of saying the obvious thing, she must have left via a window,' said Jo, 'probably out of here.' She looked out of the 12-pane kitchen window, below which were the back gardens of the Georgian terrace of Heriot Row. It was very dark down there.

Jeff undid the catch, pointed at it and pulled the window up. 'Well if she did, she miraculously locked it after her. Or Frank let her out and then locked it and I can't see for the life of me why he'd do that. What's wrong with leaving via the door?'

He leaned right out and looked from side to side.

'Is there any way down to the ground?' said Julie.

Jeff closed the window again and shook his head, dusting off his hands. 'Nah. Not even a drainpipe. She'd have had to jump and it's a long way down. The back gardens are set below the pavement level. It's probably a 30-foot drop, at least. You'd break your feet if you jumped from here.'

They walked back to the living room and looked out of the windows at the front, but aside from being at the junction of two main roads and thus making being seen leaving via a window almost inevitable, there was simply no way down other than to jump and if you jumped, you'd break a leg at the very least, or impale yourself on the black, spiked iron railings below.

'You're the illusionist, Jo. How did she get out of here?' said Jeff, putting his hands on her shoulders from behind and drumming out a little beat.

As though to better think about it, she put her hands over his and followed his rhythm. Her eyes flicked from side to side. 'She's either *still* here, or she was *never* here. Take your pick.'

'Well, she's not here,' said Nick. 'We've looked everywhere, even in the cupboards and wardrobes.'

'Could be a false wall somewhere,' said Jo.

'The only false wall is the one used to make the kitchen. The rest are part of the old Georgian structure,' said Nick, walking back to the kitchen and tapping on the walls. The plasterboard was solid.

'Well that means she was never here - but she was - we saw her. All three of us saw her,' said Jeff. 'A collective hallucination of the exact same person seems unlikely.'

Nick walked around the flat again, going into a bedroom where a large double bed was in the same position as in their flat. Two large double door wardrobes stood opposite. He pulled the left-hand one open. It was full of what had to be Barbara's clothes. A range of dresses and suits, all quite expensive looking. The other wardrobe was shirts and ties: Frank's stuff, presumably.

Julie came in. 'Found anything?'

'Just clothes.'

She took out a linen jacket from Barbara's wardrobe and looked at the label. 'Karen Millen. Expensive.' She skimmed through a few other pieces. It was all designer stuff.

'Well, Frank isn't so flamboyant. This is all standard plain, sensible Marks and Spencer gear,' said Nick. 'Come on, let's get out of here.'

Julie reached down to the foot of the wardrobe and picked out a pair of brown leather court shoes with a low heel. 'Jimmy Choos. I used to want a pair of these when I lived in London. I don't know why...but they were very desirable.' She held them up to her foot. 'Bloody hell, she's got big feet.'

Nick looked at them. 'Your feet are sevens, aren't they?'

She inspected the inside of the footwear. 'Aye, my Auntie Pat has nines but these are a ten. I didn't know they made them that big.'

She put them back and they followed Jeff and Jo out of the flat, closing the door behind them. No-one would even know they'd been in.

They stood on the great concrete landing. 'Well, that was a bit weird. Are you coming down for a drink, Jo? See if we can come up with a conspiracy theory that doesn't involve lizard people or a man opening and closing an umbrella?' said Jeff.

She wrinkled her small nose and patted him on the belly. 'I tell you what, I've got a bottle of good vodka upstairs. Do you want some?'

Jeff bowed a little. 'Me and vodka are old friends and have never been known to deny ourselves to each other. Aye, go on, then.' She put both thumbs up. He put a hand on the small of her back and they went upstairs, Jeff turned around briefly and gave Nick the eyebrows. Nick and Julie went downstairs and left the door on the latch.

'Fizz me. How about that?' said Julie as she closed the flat door.

'Amazing. She was quite touchy-feely with him right from the start, did you notice?'

'Oh, yeah. There was a proper connection between them from the first moment.'

'Yeah, I think it's great.'

'Yeah, sometimes you just click with someone. Aw, I'm dead chuffed for him. He won't be down here tonight. I reckon they'll be shagging or some variant thereof,' said Julie.

'Variant thereof, eh? Ha, I thought I was the one with a degree in English. I've left the door on the latch so he can come in when he wants.'

Once in their bedroom, they washed in the en-suite bathroom.

'Those jeans are just too tight on me. They're a 10 and I'm a 12 again,' she said, rubbing at deep red marks left around her hips by the waistband. 'They fitted fine when I'd lost all that weight after the miscarriage, but I've put on half a stone since then and they dig in summat rotten.'

'You looked bloody good in them, though,' said Nick, patting her warm, bare backside and kissing her neck, inhaling her Calvin Klein perfume as he did so.

'Actually, I felt a bit mutton dressed as lamb,' she said, dismissively, running her hands over her hips again, pinching at the red skin.

'I don't understand that concept at all.'

'Yes, you do.' She filled the circular glass sink with warm water and took off her bra, throwing it onto a wash basket and rolling a bar of soap around her hands.

'I know what it means, but who says what's young and what's old, Jules? You're 46, why shouldn't you wear tight white jeans? Who said it was wrong and what are their credentials for this job as a fashion critic?'

She laughed a little as she soaped her arms and washed her face and then her armpits. 'God, I'm so sweaty. Well, I know what you mean. I didn't say it was wrong. But I just felt a bit like I was dressed as though I was a younger woman.'

'Yeah, I get that, but who sets that standard? I see women aged 25 who dress like much older women. Are they lamb dressed as mutton? No-one ever says that, do they? I'm not having this. It's silly. It's another way to oppress women, if you ask me. I'm not saying I don't think it, like you think it, but that doesn't mean it's right. Question all realities, Jo said. Well, I'm questioning the mutton dressed as lamb reality.'

She rinsed off the soap and took a towel from the rail to dry herself with. 'That's all very good in theory, but people are very judgmental if an older woman is dressed too sexily - and I hate that word because it brings in so many other things - but you know what I mean.'

'Oh, yeah, they are - but, y'know...sod 'em. We're all inventing our own future. Why live by someone else's rules of what is or isn't acceptable? I'm 49, I wear quite close-fitting jeans, just like I always have. Should I not do that? Should I dress in a lambswool V-necked golf club sweater and Farah slacks? I mean, I'm not a fashion dude but rock music is my culture, so I'm dressing to align myself to that in some vague way. I want people to know that I'm not some middle-aged boring twat, like my dad. God rest his soul.' He put his fingers together and looked upwards, briefly.

She cooed at him a little. 'Alright, alright, don't get over-excited. I do agree with you. It's complex, though. Like you were saying about Jo upstairs. We all make judgements about people from how they look and I don't want people getting the wrong idea about me, do I? I don't want to look like some sort of tart. I mean like I said, my London Look was, quite deliberately mind, a little bit posh, a little bit rock and a little bit slutty and that was for the same reasons you just said. I wanted to say I'm a rock lass, I'm not boring and I like a good time. But some people think that is tarty. They just do.'

He shook his head and crossed his arms. 'See, I don't even know what that means, either. What *does* it mean?'

She looked at him with incredulity as she pulled on a baggy bed t-shirt. 'You know what being tarty means.'

Nick paused and thought about his words for a few seconds. 'I *think* I do. Obviously there's the prostitute thing. But women who are called tarty are usually not being accused of actually being prostitutes. They're actually being accused of being a woman who has sex a lot, or even just being a woman who wants to have sex a lot. Is that right, Jules? If it is, what's wrong with that? Why can't a woman have a lot of sex, without being judged harshly? A man would never be judged harshly for having a lot of sex. There's no male equivalent for tart. It's a female-only word, which in itself shows it's inherently sexist.'

She rubbed some moisturiser into her forehead and cheeks. 'Darlin', you know you going all Germaine Greer on me makes me fancy the arse off you, but life is lived in the real world and in the real world a lass with jeans right up her vulva, with tits out, looks like a slag to a lot of people. You know it, I know it. Don't be naïve.'

He groaned and rubbed his eyes. 'I know, I know, but I still feel like it's some form of cultural bullying to say one type of clothing equates to a certain set of morals and then judge someone on that basis. What it's saying is a woman who's judged to be a tart or a slag because of how she dresses is of less worth and to be disregarded or condemned, and I just don't see how that's right, at all. It's one step from that to the whole "she was asking for it" mindset. Obviously, a woman who has a lot of sex isn't of less worth. No man would expect to be thought less of because of how sexually active he was or wasn't. In fact, if he was very sexually active, he'd expect to be respected, at least by other men.'

She raised her eyebrows. 'Yeah, that's obviously true, but this is still women's lot in life. It's basically unequal and unfair. And it's not right and it drives me nuts, especially when you hear other women push it as the orthodoxy, too.'

'Seriously, though, Jules. Don't get hung up on that mutton dressed as lamb thing, right? I genuinely thought you looked fantastic. You were you and that's as much as anyone can want to be.'

Her expression relaxed into a nice smile. 'Aw, thanks luv. Alright. I won't. I've not so far, have I? Tell us this, though. If we're getting to the sexual politics of clothes, why do you like me so much in those tight white jeans?'

He didn't even have to think. 'Easy, because it shows off your figure and I think your shape is really attractive. It's my thing, isn't it...like we were talking about the other day. And because it's you. In fact, it's mostly because it's you. My lass. My Jules. And I love you.'

She looked almost embarrassed. 'You soppy get. You never used to be so connected to your feelings like that.'

He rubbed his nose. 'It's probably all the therapy with Marc Lewis. That and the drink. And I also think you're expressing your cultural leanings. You're a rocker. You always have been. You should have ownership of it. Plus I'm weird about white jeans. I have no idea why. Always have been. I think I even like blokes more if they wear white jeans.'

'Have you ever worn them?'

'Good god, no. Do you want me to?'

She shook her head. 'Not if you don't want to. It's all a bit too Mod for me, white jeans on blokes. That or faux spiritual, New Age bollocks.'

He used the water she'd run into the sink to get washed.

'I think we're the first generation to have to really deal with this stuff,' he said. 'You're aligning yourself with the rock 'n' roll culture of tight pants and being...I know you hate the word and I do, too - but sexy *is* that word. I suppose I am, too - though I know I am not in any way sexy.'

She picked up the towel and rubbed at his wet chest, arms and neck. 'Gettaway with you. 'Course you are. To me, anyway,' she said. She nibbled a little at his shoulder blade. 'It's when you put the physical and mental together, that's when the really big fireworks go off, I think.'

'I do know what you mean. Would I fancy you as much if you had a fat arse like Jo King's and not a small, firm, pert peachy one?'

She passed an old t-shirt to him. 'I'll answer that for you. No, you wouldn't. Like we said the other day, it plugs into something in your psyche.'

He leaned over and pecked her on the lips.

'Maybe, as usual, I'm just thinking too much about it. We are what we are. We like what we like. We lust what we lust. It's part mental, part physical. Who knows how or why it happens? Self-identity is such a complex thing. It doesn't yield much to analysis and god knows, I've had a long old go at analysing it. About 49 years, at the last count.'

They got into bed and turned out the lights. The noise of cars driving up the cobbled streets seemed very loud in the otherwise quiet late night. She rested into him and put her left arm across and under his t-shirt, fiddling a little with his chest hair, as he put his arm around her and held her close, her honey and straw smell filling his nostrils. Her breath crept across him like warm mist. These were the most enriching, quiet moments and were the moments that he loved the most. Since his deep, crushing depressions had lifted, he felt open to these times as battery-charging experiences. They made him feel whole and not diminished. They were about love and trust and beauty and had become a kind of psychic scaffolding for his life to be built on. No matter what happened, they returned to their intimate, quiet selves at the end of the day.

Just being close to someone in bed is such a lovely thing. It's easy to take it for granted and to forget what sleeping alone is really like. The fact that he knew she wanted to make love, simply because of the pace of her breathing and how she touched him was, even now, after all this time, such a beautiful thing. Intimacy can never be taken for granted, because you spend so much time in life without it. There are so many times when you don't connect with anyone and other times when your relationship isn't so strong, and it feels embarrassing, unwanted, or just alien to be intimate. It was in these instances when their relationship with each other was rebonded.

He kissed her head. 'I love you so much.'

She leaned over him and, pushing up his t-shirt, kissed his left nipple, her tongue licking at it briefly.

'I love you, too.'

He rolled onto his left side so that they faced each other, breathing each other's breath, just kissing a little.

'Jules...?'

'What, darlin'?' Her breath was quickened with her lust for him, as she lightly rubbed him from his chest to his thighs with the flat of her hand. Just barely touching him. He closed his eyes to better worship the feeling. As he did so, his mind opened and realised something important. Maybe the chemicals that are released into your brain when your body is getting ready for sex improve your thought processes, or maybe they wipe away everything else, leaving a blank canvas for new thoughts to paint themselves on. Certainly the male mind tends to be utterly subjugated to the sex drive in such moments, but suddenly it was all so clear to Nick. Several disparate things knitted together to form one reality.

'...I've just realised who that woman we saw at the window was,' he said, even as his hand explored her pubic hair, his fingertips twizzling some into a small knot.

With the fingers of her left hand still wrapped around his erection, she propped herself up on her right elbow and looked at him in the darkness and said, 'Who the fizz was she, then?'

'It was Frank. That woman was Frank, and so was Barbara. They're both him.'

CHAPTER 3

She let go of him.

'Eh?! Frank is a woman? You're saying Frank Stewart is a woman?!' He put the bedside light on and sat up.

'No. He's a man who dresses as a woman. It's the shoes that gave it away,' said Nick. 'You saw them, they were big for a woman. You measured them against your trotters.'

She sat up and brushed her hair off her face, licking her dry lips and shook her head. 'I think you're mad.'

'Jo said that either the curly-haired woman was still in there or was never there. She didn't know it, but in a way, she was right on both counts - she'd been there, but she was Frank and it was Frank that had gone. He walked past us. And if he can be her, he could have been Barbara, too.'

'Some women do have big feet, y'know. It's not unheard of. Like I said, my auntie Pat has nines and so does my cousin Janet.'

'I know, but he had two separate wardrobes in there. One for him and one for her. We have all our clothes mixed up in the same wardrobe.'

'Yeah, but that's because we don't have much room and we share so many things, like t-shirts and sweat tops. Plenty of women keep their clothes well apart from their fella's, I'm sure.'

'When we saw that woman at the window - what did she look like?'

Julie closed her eyes in recollection. 'Brown curly hair, is all I remember.'

'Exactly. He could easily have just been wearing a wig. We saw him, or her, for no more than three seconds. When he passed us he had a big leather bag with him, probably with his wig and clothes in.'

She got up and got a glass of water and then got back into bed. 'Nope, I still don't believe it. What you're suggesting is bonkers. You're saying he's been living a double life as a man and as two different women...'

'...that's not so hard to believe, is it? All sorts of people lead double lives, in one way or another.'

She frowned, her expression part tired and part drunk. 'I'm too exhausted to work all this out. Come on, let's get some sleep and then we'll see what Jeff says in the morning.'

She put the light out and turned over. Nick spooned into her and kissed her on the neck, passing his hands over her hips, thighs and buttocks.

'Don't go making a rod for my back. You've missed your chance, lad. I'm too tired now. You can have a go if you want, but I'll be asleep.' She was dozing off even as she said it and within a minute they were both in the arms of Morpheus.

Even as he began to wake at 7am, still tucked into Julie, his mind was still filled with men dressed as women.

He got up and made tea, taking in a strong Yorkshire Tea brew for Jeff, who must have come down at some point and was snoring at a volume that made the floorboards vibrate slightly.

'Here you go, big man,' he said, giving him a shake. 'Tea.'

Jeff grunted.

Nick took Sencha green tea back in for him and Julie.

'I think I might have been going off on one last night, Jules,' he said as he got back into bed.

She looked up at him with bleary eyes. 'Eh? I went straight to sleep - aw, you didn't go and make a mess on me, did you?' She patted at herself for damp patches.

He laughed a little. 'No, you daft bugger. I wasn't talking about that. You've got a one-track mind, you have.'

She rolled onto her back and coughed. 'Hmm, you're forgetting I know what you're like, lad. But amazingly I appear to be dry. Remarkable restraint.' She sat up and drank some tea and then made a daft grin at him. 'Morning, husband.'

'Morning, wife.'

Nick had started frying bacon and sausages when Jeff came into the kitchen in a hoodie and camouflage army-style pants.

'Ah, there you are. What time did you come down?'

'I was only up there an hour and a half. Nowt happened, if that's what you're fishing for. Just had a couple of drinks and a few laughs. Was really good. I really like her.'

'Yeah and she likes you. Hey man, those trousers have more pockets than strictly necessary, don't they?' said Nick, looking him up and down.

'I once counted them, there are 14! 14! There are even pockets inside some of the pockets. Seems excessive.' He looked over Nick's shoulder at the frying bacon. 'My, that smells good. No man should be able to sleep through the smell of hot lard.'

'I had a mad idea in bed. It seems a bit more nonsensical, in the cold, sober light of day.'

'If it involves vegetables pushed into a body cavity for pleasure, I don't want to hear it.' Jeff closed his eyes and put his fingers in his ears.

'You daft get.' Nick explained about his idea of Frank being the woman they'd seen and also Barbara.

Jeff perched on a stool at the breakfast table and listened intently, his fingers together in a pyramid. When Nick had finished, Jeff held a finger in the air. 'What I like about this is that it does explain everything. Well, almost everything.'

'It does, doesn't it? It explains everything, except why.'

Jeff was looking at his phone. 'Not quite everything. I've just put her name and Edinburgh into Google and there's someone called Barbara Stewart who works at an art school on Great King Street. She's listed as a tutor. Didn't you say she said to you she liked art?'

'Yeah, she did. Well, that totally knackers my theory. Bugger. I'm totally wrong. I must be. If that's the same person and she really worked there, it couldn't have been Frank dressed up. They'd have known he was a bloke.'

Jeff raised a bushy eyebrow. 'Ah. Not necessarily. It's not always that clear cut. You didn't think she was a bloke, did you? You see a lot of older women who could pass for older blokes.'

'Aye, you do, but up close in a work environment? I'm not so sure.'

'I'm just saying it's not impossible. We can't rule it out. What actually made you think he was a she or she was a he?'

'Ah, well, y'see I remembered that she was wearing a silk scarf around her neck when we met her on the stairs and...'

'...to hide the Adam's apple?' said Jeff, pointing at him and nodding. 'Yes, I like it. Good thinking, Guymer.'

'And we only saw the curly-haired woman at the window briefly and at a distance. I couldn't say it *wasn't* Frank in a wig and where did she go? And then there was a wardrobe of women's clothes and big shoes.'

Jeff went with this idea, nodding vigorously.

'So, he's just trying a wig on in the house before leaving, maybe to go to somewhere else to be this other woman? Yeah, it works. I think you're onto it. And, think about this, my large bicepped sex-monster, it's also the perfect disguise to kill someone in. The police are looking for a woman. She even posed with the gun so that everyone could see it was a woman who had shot this bloke. Now, all he has to do is never dress up as Barbara again and the police can never find her. It's perfect.'

'Jeff, you're brilliant. That could be exactly right.'

'Aye and plenty of blokes like to get up as a woman, don't they? I sort of understand why, an' all. If you're a woman you can wear men's clothes but men are far more limited as to what's acceptable. Dunno why. I mean, what's the difference between a kilt and a skirt? Nothing.'

'Yeah, I totally get why men want to do it. I mean, I know there are other sexual identity issues going on sometimes, but when you think about it, half the rock bands we loved in the 70s wore women's clothes. Robert Plant wore those little silk blouses.'

'Exactly, and no-one thought he wasn't a red-blooded male of the species. I might get one meself!'

'You've got the locks for it, darlin',' said Julie, coming in combing her hair. 'Is he giving you his theory?'

Jeff saluted her. 'Morning, Jules. Yeah, I don't think it's that mad. I like it. The question we need to answer is has anyone seen Frank and Barbara together? If yes, then it's all over as a theory. But no-one else lives in this building to ask. The Big Fish just has the two flats as investment properties and rents them out on short-term leases. People come and go all the time, so it's not like there's a community who all know each other.'

'We should go to the place where she worked, then. The Edinburgh Art School,' said Nick.

'Good idea, but I've got to do the stall in the Grassmarket all week, haven't I?'

'Me and Jules will go. We've not got any shows until late afternoon.'

'Hold on...what's it to do with us?' said Julie. 'I don't want to spend my honeymoon looking for a cross-dressing killer. I'd quite like to go and have a few drinks in the Hard Rock, instead.' She strummed an air guitar. 'I may wear slightly less-tight jeans this time, though. My hips actually feel bruised from wearing those white ones.'

'Spoilsport. Anyway, we can do both. It won't take us long,' said Nick. 'We'll just find out how long she'd worked there.'

'On what pretext?' she said, arched eyebrows raised.

'I'm a journalist, just getting a bit of background to the story.'

Jeff tapped on the table with his finger. 'And technically it's true. You are a journo, albeit a football journo which is one of the lowest forms of life.'

She sighed. 'Oh, alright then. It can't harm, I suppose.'

The Edinburgh Art School was a little overstated. Its title suggested a grand organisation, whereas it was, in fact, rather a modest place, housed in a Georgian basement on Great King Street.

Nick opened a glass porch door and then pushed open a big wooden Georgian door and went in, with Julie behind him. A woman with a silk bandana on looked up from a desk.

'Hello, there,' she said, in a lilting middle-class Edinburgh accent. 'How can I help?'

Nick gave her his best smile, though he always felt it made him look as though he might be feeling sick, so he stopped. 'Hello, there. I'm Nick Guymer. Can you tell me if Barbara Stewart works here?'

Her face dropped into an expression that was somewhere between shock and fear.

'Did you see the photo in the paper, by any chance?' asked Nick.

'I can't believe it. I mean, I literally can't believe it.' She shook her head and seemed dazed.

'Had she worked here long?'

She nodded. 'About a year. She was very nice. I can't help but think some terrible mistake has been made. It wasn't her who did that...it can't have been. They didn't give out her name, did they?'

'No, they haven't. Have you seen her since?' said Nick. The woman shook her head. 'Can I ask what she did here?' he said, sitting down opposite the woman. Julie took another chair and pulled it up to the desk. Noise from other rooms suggested there were classes being taken.

'She was very good at drawing. Like all our teachers, she was part-time. She took three classes a week. Everyone liked her.'

'Have you told anyone that you think that that she's the person in the photo?'

She shook her head again.

'So the police haven't asked you anything?'

'A man, a detective, came from the police, the next day, and asked me who she was and all sorts of other questions. I tried to help but he was horribly aggressive. I mean, I worked with her but I didn't know anything about her life.'

'Right. I know this might sound odd, err...' he looked at her name tag '...Joyce. But did you think there was something quite...err...well, masculine about her?'

Joyce looked at him as though he was insane. 'What...what do you mean?'

The question had made her suspicious and tense. Julie tried to diffuse it a little. 'Did you meet her husband, Frank?'

'Oh, he would often pick her up from here in the year she's worked here. He was very interested in art as well, apparently. What did you mean about her seeming masculine?'

'Oh, it's just one of those silly rumours that's been going around the media.'

She stared at him with sagging eyes and deep crow's feet.

'What? That Barbara was...was a man?!'

'Yeah. It's not so shocking, it happens a lot these days,' said Nick, as casually as possible.

'Does it indeed? Well, I'm certain Barbara is a woman.' She said it indignantly. Maybe she took offence at being accused of being unable to tell the difference.

'You're positive?' said Nick. 'Never had any doubts?'

That was the wrong thing to say. Joyce stood up. 'I'm sorry, I must ask you to leave. This is all too...it's *very* strange. It's all just a big mistake, I'm sure. I shouldn't have said anything.'

'Sorry, I didn't mean to upset you. We'll be on our way,' said Nick, standing up, realising she was now too defensive to be of any more help.

Julie pulled open the wide wooden door and they stepped into the porch area. Rain was splattering the pavement outside at eye level.

He hadn't noticed when they'd walked in that on the white plaster wall of the porch was a collection of seven photographs, one for each of the teachers and of Joyce, too. In the top right-hand corner was a headshot of Barbara Stewart. Nick quickly took out his phone and snapped a photo, then joined Julie outside on the pavement.

'Did you see the portraits by the door?' He held up the picture on his phone. There she was. Shoulder-length white hair, a paisley silk scarf around her neck, pearl earring in each lobe. She wore a little make-up; some dark pink lipstick, a little blue eyeshadow and some rouge.

'Is that a woman, or is it Frank?' he said.

She grabbed the phone off him.

'I'd say that was a woman, 100 times out 100, if asked. I would have no doubt at all it was a female. And it doesn't really look like Frank. Or does it? Put it this way, if you'd never suggested it, I'd never have thought it was.'

They walked along to Dundas Street. Nick couldn't stop looking at the photo. She was right. If he hadn't any reason to think it wasn't a woman, he would have unquestioningly assumed the person was female. She did have a fairly square jaw. She wasn't pretty or delicate, but then you could say that of a lot of women. Without a picture of Frank to hold alongside it was impossible to say if it was or wasn't him.

They walked up the hill to George Street and the Hard Rock Cafe.

Julie spoke as they walked. 'If you looked at a lot of photos of older women, a lot of them would be traditionally unfeminine. Take my Auntie Sandra. She's got a face like a bulldog chewing a wasp. She's got the makings of a moustache and she could easily pass for a bloke, in the same way Les Dawson could pass for an old woman.'

'Aye, but she's got big breasts on her.'

'Yeah, but they're the easiest thing to fake, aren't they?'

He nodded. 'True. Did you notice what colour Frank's eyes were, by any chance? I didn't.'

'I did. They were hazel brown.'

'Are you sure?'

'Yeah. I always notice eye colour.'

'Well, that does it. Barbara's eyes are blue in this.'

She stopped and took the phone off him again. 'Oh, yeah. So they are. Well, what are we even doubting her for? That Joyce woman said she'd met Frank, so that's that.'

Nick tugged at his bottom lip. 'She didn't *quite* say that.'

'She did. She said he often picked her up from work.'

'That's right. Which isn't the same thing as meeting him. Maybe he was outside, but he never came in.'

She looked at him wearily. 'Oh man, don't be daft. The implication was clear. You don't say someone has been picked up from work by their husband if you never see them. She'd been there for over a year. That's a long time to potentially get found out as being a man. And now we know their eye colours are different, too...'

'...Frank could have worn coloured contacts when he was Barbara,' interrupted Nick. 'All part of the role play. And she's only there to do three classes a week. She's not doing eight hours a day. She's there for one or maybe two hours at most. But even so, I am definitely clutching at straws here, I know.'

'Yeah, you are.' She shook her head in frustration, pushed open the door to the Hard Rock and hopped up onto a bar stool. 'Can I get a cocktail? It's still our honeymoon, remember?'

Selecting the Tequila Sunrise from the menu, Nick ordered them both one.

'OK, so let's just go over the facts, as we think know them,' he said. 'Barbara did the shooting and has since gone on the run, possibly aided by Frank, possibly because she *was* Frank.'

Julie shook her head at that. 'I think you should forget that idea.'

'OK, regardless of the Barbara situation, there *was* a woman in their flat who disappeared into thin air. The only credible explanation of that is that she was Frank. What seems odd to me is that the police don't seem to be overly interested in him, even though we gave them her name and said she lived upstairs. Which seems strange, all things considered. I'd have thought they'd have been all over the flat by now, especially since they'd gone straight upstairs after talking to us but didn't get an answer.'

'It does, but who knows what they know? There could easily be a good reason for that.'

They clinked glasses. Julie let out a heavy sigh. 'So is that us done with all of this nonsense? It's our honeymoon and we're supposed to be having a good time all the time. Mind, I'm loving it so far.'

Nick nodded. 'Totally, yeah. We're done. I'm enjoying it, too. And we've had an excellent amount of top-notch naughty, by the way. You're on very good form, Jules.' He kissed her on the lips and leaned on the bar.

'You're not doing so bad, yourself, kidda, especially for someone who doesn't believe in hangover horn. Dear me. Feels like I've been riding in the Grand National.' She touched him on the arm. 'Not that I'm complaining, luv.' She chortled a woody laugh.

'Ha, I might have to revise my view of the old H.H. So what do you reckon about Jeff and Jo? Their names actually go together really well. They sound like a couple. Any chance for them at all, do you think?'

She winced. 'There's a big age difference. There's a connection between them, though. There definitely is.'

'Yeah, you'd have to be blind not to see that. And he was up in her flat for a couple of hours. He said nothing happened. But don't forget, she is gay.'

'Ha, yeah. She does look gay. I'll give you that. Whatever, I bet she's a good shag.'

'You reckon? Why?'

'It's like what Jeff said about Mandy Beale. She's got access to her passions and she seems quite uninhibited. I genuinely think there are some lasses you can imagine having orgasms and there are some you just can't.'

'Yeah, I agree. I used to think I could spot it in a woman's eyes.'

'You? Are you sure?' She looked a little incredulously at him. 'Being perceptive about humans hasn't always been your strong suit, not until recently, anyway.'

'I'm not saying I could do it successfully, but I was fortunate to go out with some passionate lasses in my teens, so I think I got a good early education. There's a spark in the eye, I reckon. A connection to their passion.'

'So what you're saying is that you could spot a woman who was a go-er?'

'I wouldn't go that far. I think it was more that I was attracted to women who were passionate, partly because they'd not be backwards at coming forwards and I always loved that. It was hard being a nice bloke...'

'...knowing you, I bet it was very hard, indeed and for a long time, too. Ahem.' She made a snort into her drink.

'Well, yes, obviously...that...but I mean, we know that horrible blokes sometimes force their sexual desire on women and we nice blokes don't want to do that and worry that if we're too forward, it'll seem like we're one of *those* guys. Seriously, I used to worry much more about making sure women knew what I wasn't, rather than what I was.'

She shook her head and smiled affectionately. 'That is *so* typical of you. It's both thoughtful but also waaaay too self-conscious. Annoyingly so, in fact. It is possible to be who you are, by just being who you are and trust that people will realise you're a nice person.'

'Yeah, see, I could never trust that to be the case. Probably because I don't really know if it's true or not. Me and Jeff often used to say that we hated blokes who thought they were great. You know the sort...'

She hopped off the barstool and sank at the knees a little. 'Oh, god, yeah, I totally know what you mean. I used to call them...' she lapsed into a strong Teesside drawl and did a cocky little pose in front of him, swaggering at the hips '...the, "now then daaarlin' " blokes, 'cos that's how they always came up to you, giving it large, like you'd be impressed by it.'

'Some women are impressed by it.'

'Yeah, only damaged women, in my experience.'

'I wish I'd known this when I was 16. C'mon, let's drink these and go and see Jeff on his stall.'

They wandered up The Mound, along George IV Bridge to Victoria Street and from there down to the Grassmarket, feeling a bit drunk and feeling that it was entirely appropriate in Edinburgh, somehow. The

Grassmarket was just along from Cowgate where they had a show to see at the Underbelly. There was a long line of market stalls selling everything from fruit and veg to candles and jars of honey. At one end was Jeff's stall - six tables lined with boxes of hundreds of vinyl records. As usual, half a dozen men were looking through the records with a scrutiny and passion that suggested over-focus.

'Alright, big man,' said Nick. 'You got these unloaded OK, then?'

'Aye, no bother. Plenty of punters. Tourists, mostly.'

'Sold much?' said Julie.

'Yeah, it's been good. Did you go to the art school?'

Nick told him about their meeting and what they'd concluded.

Jeff tugged on his beard and drank from a big cup of coffee. 'I still wouldn't rule out your idea about Frank being Barbara. I think there's something in that, but I bet old Frank disappears now, as well.'

'Yeah, well, we're just going to enjoy our honeymoon. I'm done with playing detective,' said Nick.

'Jo is coming down in a bit,' said Jeff, holding up his phone and pointing to a text she'd sent him. 'Just to keep me company for a bit, like.' He grinned at them.

'We were just saying you two have really clicked,' said Julie. 'Look at you. You look like the cat that got the cream.'

Jeff flicked his hair over his shoulders and took £10 from a man for a couple of Thin Lizzy albums. 'Aye, we have, like. Funny, isn't it? Some people you just get on with right away. She'll be away down to London soon enough, though. So it'll not go anywhere, obviously.'

'You don't know that,' said Nick, who was coming round to the idea that Jo and Jeff would be a great couple, the one odd enough for the other. But then, she'd have to be OK with Argie. Maybe that was a lot to ask.

For the rest of the week, Nick and Julie saw shows, drank a lot of wet bars and partied with Jeff and Jo in bars and in the flat. No more was seen of Frank or any of the women he may or may not have been dressing up as. After seeing a total of 28 shows, they got the train home on Sunday morning.

'Eee, god, it's so small in here after that flat in Edinburgh,' said Julie, putting the kettle on, as soon as they got into their flat. 'We'd better go down to the allotment in a day or two and do a few hours' graft. Those courgettes will have gone daft - they'll be huge marrows by now and the whole plot will be choked with weeds.'

'Yeah, I suppose so. Funny how quickly you get used to living in those big rooms, isn't it? It does seem very cramped in here now. I counted it was 18 strides from the middle of the living room to the kitchen. Here it's three,' said Nick, feeling like the place was cramped and dark.

'We couldn't afford a place like that, even if we wanted to. They're over £1,200 a month,' she said.

'Yeah, but we pay £600 and that place is about five or six times bigger, so it's not five or six times more expensive and it's in the centre of the posh bit of the capital city of Scotland. Housing is so messed up in this country. If that flat was £1,200, ours should be £300 or less.'

Her phone buzzed. She peered at the screen. 'Martha from Teesside Women.' She read the text. Nick went into the living room and flopped down onto the sofa, feeling a bit low. Maybe it was the post-holiday blues. They'd been looking forward to the wedding and the honeymoon for a few months and now it was all behind them and life seemed to offer little sparkle compared to being in Edinburgh, but then that was a holiday, not everyday life. All they'd done was go to see shows, drink and mess around in bars and restaurants. You couldn't live your life like that, not least because the Fringe Festival was a unique three and a bit weeks in August.

Even so. He made a low growl in his throat and rubbed his eyes. This was the trouble with going on holiday - honeymoon, or not - it showed you a life that, in certain circumstances, you could live, if you had the money or opportunity. So rather than come home refreshed, you came home feeling that you were settling for a third-rate life, whereas, before you went, you were perfectly content with your daily routines.

Julie brought tea in.

'Have you heard of Northdean School?' she said.

He yawned. 'Yeah, it's a posh public school near...err...Bedale, I think it is.'

'Aye, that's the one.'

'I actually stayed there once.' He poked some wax out of his right ear.

'Oh, aye? How come?'

'Oh, I can't remember why, but when I was 15, I went with the school on some long weekend touring round abbeys and churches. I was always keen to get away from home for a day or two. We stayed one night at Ampleforth College and another at Northdean. It was a different world. We each got assigned a boy who let us sleep in their dorm room on a camp bed. The lad I stayed with was a Rolling Stones fan - that was the first time I heard the *Get Your Ya Ya's Out* live album. Didn't rate it, actually. He was a really nice boy, though. He was called Dev. His mam was Indian. Kind and thoughtful lad and he had soft brown eyes and lovely long black hair.'

Julie smiled. 'Aw. That sounds a bit like you had a teenage crush on him.'

He reflected for a moment. 'Yeah, in a way I did, I think. He seemed very exotic to me. The fact I can still remember him must mean something.'

'Tell me about your gay phase.' She drew her legs up under her as she sat down.

He rubbed his arms. 'It didn't last long. I was just curious around then, I think. I could have been persuaded to have a go with a nice lad, I think. But it soon passed and by the time I was 16 I was absolutely bloody obsessed with girls.'

'I think a lot of boys and girls go through that curious phase. I never did, but I know plenty who got all touchy feely aged 15.'

'Pity, I hoped you might have some lesbian confessions. I could do with cheering up.'

She laughed. 'Sorry to disappoint you. I've always been *very* heterosexual. A couple of lasses have had a go at turning me on to their Sapphic ways, but I just never fancied it, not even when drunk and randy.'

'Oh, well, I'm sure you're a loss to the lesbian community. I recall, Dev's room had wood panels and was like something from the 16th century. I had woodchip from the 1960s. Different worlds, eh. I was really jealous of him.'

'Single-sex environments always seem to end up messing with people's heads. Though, I suppose you could say the same of mixed schools. When I think back to school it seems to be 20 per cent learning and 80 per cent chasing or being chased by boys. The sexual tension of having a load of 15 and 16 year olds together was almost painful. I used to fall in and out of love every other week. It was very distracting and it put you off your school work.'

Nick nodded and then snorted. 'I'll tell you how distracting it was, right? In a 4th-year history class I actually had, what at the time we would have called a hand shandy, at the back of class, so distracted by the raging horn, was I. There was a girl I fancied so badly at the front of the class, I manipulated myself through my pockets while staring at her back.'

Julie yelped a laugh. 'Fizzin' hell, kidda. You dirty sod.'

'Nobody knew. I was good at hiding it under the desk.'

'But what about...err...leakage?'

'You forget, 70s underpants were big, heavy and absorbent.'

She turned away and pulled a face. 'Eurggh. Gross. You were walking around all day like that? God, teenage boys are *disgusting* creatures.'

'I know. I'd lay odds that you were the object of some kid's lust in the same way. The teenage boy is ridiculously distracted by sex. It was an almost minute-by-minute obsession. Horrible, in a way. I mean, it really did mess with your head.'

'Well girls aren't much different, I suppose. Mind, I never did *that* in class! I saved it for under the covers in bed or when I was having a bath and could lock the door. Anyway, you're distracting me with your sinful ways. To get back to Northdean, it's a mixed school now - girls and boys - some day kids and some boarders and Caroline Reed, who used to work at the TWC, works there as a kind of in-house social worker.'

'So she gives succour to weeping children whose rich parents have dumped them there for a few months at a time?'

'Something like that. In the old days she'd have been called a nanny or nurse. I think her job title is something like a Welfare and Support Officer. Anyway, she's swung it for TWC to have an away day there free of charge.'

'What's an away day?'

'It's all team building, isn't it? We get given tasks to encourage collective problem solving. We have to work as a team without the stresses and strains of personal relationships getting in the way.'

'So you're trained to stop co-workers getting on your wick? Is that it?'

'Sort of, yeah. When you've got a group of 10 women or more, they're not all going to get on with each other to an equal extent, but it's not good for the women who use our services if we're fighting with each other or treading on toes. These team-building days help you to develop strategies to deal with such things and train you to work collectively and not try to get one up on someone else, the way you might do in a competitive job.'

'God, I don't know how you go about doing that sort of stuff. I'm so used to working on my own, I'd struggle to be part of a group, I think.'

'I like it. You learn to take the pressure collectively and not so much on your own shoulders.'

That sounded very noble but was utterly alien to Nick. He took everything on himself and always had done. 'So when is this away day?'

'I go down there on Tuesday, we stay overnight and then do a full day before coming home, Wednesday evening.'

'If you get nice weather, it's lovely down there. It's just out of town, with views up to the Pennines.'

He folded his arms and sat in contemplation while she busied herself organising some paperwork. After half an hour she sat down next to him. 'Are you alright, luv? You seem a bit quiet.'

'Yeah. Just got the after-holiday blues. I do feel low.'

She pushed some wisps of hair off his forehead and tucked them behind his ear with her fingertips. 'I hope that's all it is. We did have a lot to drink all week, maybe you're getting a depressive reaction to that.'

'Yeah, I wouldn't be surprised. We did hammer it. I enjoyed it, though. It feels like our normal life here is a bit shit in comparison, to be honest.'

She chewed on her bottom lip. 'If you're feeling low, why don't you take the Phenibut again?'

He sighed. 'I think I'd better.' He made a growl in his throat, suddenly feeling the dark weight of depression falling over him like a lead curtain. 'I don't feel very good at all, Jules. Why can't I just feel good all the time without taking a drug? Why can't I just be a normal person?'

'Yeah, I hear you, but what's normal? Feeling depressed is quite normal for a lot of people. Don't get hung up on normal, luv.'

He growled in his throat again and got up to get his pills, taking two with some water and then returning to the sofa, sitting down with a groan.

'I just feel at a bit of a dead end, to be honest. I've done the same job writing about football for years. I'm just phoning it in most of the time. I don't really care much about it any more. Just feels like there's no future in it, anyway. Everything is geared towards sensationalist free content, written by gobshite people for no money. Paid writers are a dying breed. Everyone wants more and more for less. Then when I hear you talking about your job - something you've got a passion for, it only shows what a fucking dead end I'm stuck in.'

'Well, when you've got your novel written that'll be a whole new thing for you.'

'Yeah, but no-one makes a living from writing novels, even if it gets published, which it probably won't. It's hard to keep your enthusiasm for life up, sometimes. It all seems so difficult. I remember when it didn't. When I was a kid I thought life just happened. I didn't know it was all such hard work. I feel so crushed by it. And I really miss my mam. I wish she was still alive.' It was a random thought that was out of his mouth before he knew it.

'Aw. She's sort of with you in some important ways, though,' said Julie.

But it was no good. The world closed in on him quickly now, like someone was building a wall between him and everything else, isolating and trapping him into a claustrophobic isolation. Then the thought of his mother brought a huge sob of emotion up from his soul and out of his mouth. Out of nowhere, he started crying uncontrollable tears. Within minutes it had utterly overwhelmed him, like a madness. He put his head in his hands, leaned forward and howled like a baby, his mind feeling shattered into pieces.

There are times when just making it through the day is so hard, when being an adult seems like wading through quicksand and it feels like a battle you can never win. Times when the dice are loaded against you and the only way you can win is to lose a little more slowly. Of course, he'd felt like this before. It was all too horribly familiar. An almost physically painful sadness, it was jet black and smothered you like a heavy blanket or a hood placed over your head and tied around your neck. Julie tried to comfort him, putting her arm around his shoulder, but all he could do was go to bed, curl up into the foetal position and cry. It robbed you of your ability to empathise or feel positive about anything. Whether it would ever pass was hard to tell, even though what was left of his rational mind told him it *would* pass. All the same, it felt like an all-encompassing insanity had enveloped his mind. The scary thing was, it felt like a sane response to being alive. That was the thing which was most frightening. The inability to deal with being a grown-up didn't seem in any way, or to any degree, unreasonable or crazy.

Oh, fuck. It was so upsetting and so utterly debilitating. He'd thought these days were behind him. But no, they're never behind you. Learn the lesson, you fucking idiot. The black dog just hangs around, waiting for a gap in your defences. It's patient. It'll bide its time, keeping its eye on you, waiting, just waiting, just waiting and then when you're vulnerable, it'll rip your fucking throat out.

Now everything upset him and being upset, upset him even more. It was bloody horrible and exhausting. Drifting in and out of silent crying-induced dozing for the rest of the day was as much as he could do. Julie knew that it was no use just cooing over him, so she got on doing things, chatting to him as though he wasn't a depressed mess. It's probably the best thing anyone can do - you sure as hell don't want someone feeling sorry for you - understanding is all you want but, cruelly, even if someone does understand, it doesn't bloody well help and you don't even care that they do. In fact, sometimes, only death would help and though you try to resist that thought, the black dog keeps vomiting it up onto the carpet in front of you.

He lay in bed and tried praying to God to release him from the torment of his own dark thoughts, his hands clamped together in supplication. He prayed to his mother, talking to her in his head, trying to get some comfort from it, but it didn't really help. He fell to sleep at 9.30pm and didn't wake until 8am the next day. It was as though his body finally shut itself down as a safety measure, in order to prevent him feeling any more pain. When he did wake, Julie was already up and he could smell cooking bacon. It smelled lovely. And that in itself was an indication of his frame of mind. The sadness had lifted. For now. He took two more Phenibut capsules. It often took them time to build up in your system. They'd helped lift his dopamine levels. By the time these two kicked in, he'd surely be back to normal. Or maybe it was praying to God and his mother that had changed his brain chemistry.

CHAPTER 4

'Sorry about all of that, yesterday, Jules,' he said, walking into the kitchen in a t-shirt and shorts.

She was dressed for work in a white blouse and loose black trousers.

'Oh, you poor thing. You don't need to apologise. What a state you were in. You just suddenly fell off the cliff. I've not seen you like that for ages, it washed in like a tidal wave of depression. Give us a look at you. You're looking a bit brighter.'

'I think the dope is kicking in now. I felt so desperate yesterday.' He rubbed his fingertips into his forehead. 'It's like drowning. One minute you're OK, then next it's as though the ground has gone from under your feet and life is impossible to deal with and you just want to hide...or worse.'

She shook her head slowly, as she put a small pair of gold earrings in. 'I'm sure it was the drinking. We've not drank every day in that quantity for a long time. And since you don't take the drugs when you're drinking, you've suffered a backlash.'

'I know and very quickly I was right back in the zone where I wanted to drink every day. At first I was excited by the thought of doing it, but then by the end, I was agitated by the thought of not doing it. Once a drinker, always a drinker. It got its hooks in me again really quickly.'

She fussed around him, putting a hand to his cheek and then squeezing his fingers. 'I've got to go to work. Will you be OK?'

He nodded. 'Yeah. I've got some pieces to write and I'm going to work on the novel. Just have a nice quiet day.'

She stroked his cheek tenderly and searched his eyes with a worried look. 'Take care, mister.'

It was embarrassing. He felt like he'd let Julie down and let himself down - almost as though he'd done it on purpose. Every time it happened, it was as though it was connected to the last time, as though it was quite literally a place he revisited time and again. It had been several months since he'd had an episode that bad and it really left a scar; or rather, it tore open the wounds that had healed since that last time.

Once she'd gone, he went back into the bedroom and stripped off his t-shirt and began to lift his weights, first using two 20kg dumbbells and then doing curls and lifts with a 60kg barbell. Nine reps in groups of three until his muscles burned with lactic acid from the pressure of the weights. When he couldn't lift any more, he did sit ups until he couldn't manage another, breaking his previous record of 141 by four. His abs protruded with the exercise; his pecs, biceps, triceps and shoulders likewise.

Afterwards, he was sweating heavily, but felt much better, almost to the point of elation. The endorphins from half an hour's workout made him feel energised, bright and also peculiarly horny. It was probably the Phenibut kicking in, too. As all men know, feeling distractedly horny is not a matter that can go unaddressed for long. It interferes with your thought processes and generally gets in the way of your day. Every movement of your body seems to be informed by it. So he went into the bathroom, conjured himself and Julie doing very rude things in a hotel room in Laguna Beach and very quickly did what comes naturally. Some would have used the internet for these purposes, but not Nick, because everything about pornography bothered him, but every time he'd tried to broach this subject with other men, it was clear that he was in a minority of about one. In the 21st century, porn was such a common part of men's lives and a lot of women's too - though how willingly for them was less clear. For him, sex was obviously a union of physicality and mentality and couldn't be separated. If you felt mentally uncomfortable, stressed or ill at ease, it ruined the physical and how could you not be ill at ease about porn, given the exploitative nature of the whole thing? How could anyone just ignore that in favour of satiating their own libido? He certainly couldn't, even though he knew fine well that many had thought him to be merely prudish about it over the years.

Julie had often said that he was wired more like a woman than as a typical man, being stimulated more by words and emotions than by visuals, but he felt that was a cop out. Claiming it was all just gender seemed too easy. It let men off the hook for indulging their base emotions. And anyway, on a more prosaic level, after the initial transgressive thrill, surely watching people screwing is boring. Filming it reduces it to pure mechanics. We all know how it goes. The only thing that hardcore pornography on the internet has taught everyone is that, give or take a few physical differences and positions, we all do the same thing. It is, in that regard, unexceptional. What makes sex so great is the unique combination of shared intimacy and physicality. When it's just on a screen, you don't actually get either of those things. But he knew that he was totally out of step with the modern world in how he felt, so much so that he'd stopped even talking about it to anyone, including Jeff. It was not just the battle that was lost, it was the whole war.

After a shower, he weighed himself. 11 stone 8lbs. He had a small hand-held device which measured body fat, which had been given to him by a trainer at the Teesside International Health Club the previous year. It bleeped and flashed and said he was 11 per cent body fat. Was that good or bad? He shrugged. As he got dried, he looked at himself in the bathroom mirror. Now very lean and well-developed, more so than at any time in his life, every muscle on him seemed to have some definition. If it wasn't for the sadness in his eyes and all the introspection, depression and weeping, he could have passed for quite a macho bloke. The way he was physically, was totally at odds with how he was spiritually and mentally constructed. Ripped on the outside, but torn on the inside.

He passed his hands over his pecs and abs. They were firm and he had a six pack that you might see in a men's magazine, but 12 hours ago he'd been weeping helplessly and feeling like death wasn't such a bad thing. You can so easily trick people with appearances. Question all realities - that's what Jo King had said. And bloody hell, she was right.

But now he felt fine. In fact, now he felt really good. That was worrying, really. To be so low and then so high, isn't normal. It felt like he had veered from despair to happiness in such a short period of time. Trouble was, when you felt good, you felt disinclined to question why. You just enjoyed it while it lasted and in doing so, forgot to take preventative measures to stop yourself falling off the cliff again.

He was about to get dressed when a funny thought struck him. He made sure he was fully aroused again, set his phone camera on delay and then took a photo of himself naked from the knees upwards, pulling a corny muscle-man pose, and sent it to Julie's phone with a message saying, '*As you can see, I'm hard at work.*' Ha. That'd surprise her on her lunch hour. Selfies, let alone naked ones, were not something he normally felt comfortable with, not least because he seemed to look terrible in all photos, usually caught mid-blink or with his mouth open or just looking nervous. He looked at it again and laughed. He looked totally ridiculous, as men do, when in a naked priapic state.

As he made himself some scrambled eggs, Julie sent him a text. '*Shocked! I've always said you're a fine, upstanding man. Glad you're feeling so much better xxx.*'

He settled down to work. Once absorbed into writing, time passed quickly. He'd just stopped for some tea when his phone rang. He didn't recognise the number.

'Hello?'

'Nick?'

'Yeah.'

'It's Jo King.'

It was a surprise to hear her voice.

'Oh, hello, Jo. How's the show going?'

'OK. Getting a lot of interest due to the walkouts. Listen, I'm calling you because I was speaking to a copper. Met me after the show, last night, in fact. He was asking questions about Barbara Stewart. He wanted me to go over my meetings with her...'

'...OK, but you must have only met a few times.'

'...two times, to be exact and then just briefly on the stairs. Yeah. Anyway, he took some notes but as he did so, I got the feeling that something wasn't right.'

'What wasn't right?'

'I don't think he really was a policeman...'

'...so why did you think that?'

'His attitude was wrong. You know what coppers are like, they have a weird way of talking - half jargon, half uneducated idiot.'

Nick grinned to himself. She was totally right. Few members of society could mangle the English language more than a police officer having to explain something to the general public.

'And he wasn't like that at all.'

'What did he look like?'

'Nondescript. Dark but bright eyes. Typically Scottish, really. Then I thought, how did they know I was even staying there? You didn't tell them, did you?'

'No, we didn't. That does seem odd. Did he actually use her name, Barbara Stewart?'

'Yeah. He came up and said he wanted to ask me a few questions about Barbara Stewart. He knew she lived below where I was staying. I just thought I'd let you know in case someone from the pretend police turns up on your doorstep and asks about Barbara.'

Nick tugged on his bottom lip in contemplation. 'OK. Seems *really* odd, that...they've still not used her name in public at all, yet. Which seems weird.'

'It could have been a journalist, I suppose. Someone looking for a story. They were definitely trying to find out exactly what I knew about Barbara and what I thought of her. Obviously, I don't know her and that's all I said. She just seemed like a normal, middle-class, educated type of woman. Unexceptional, like.'

'Has Frank come back yet?'

'No, or I've not heard or seen him if he has and I don't think he will. He's with Barbara somewhere, if you ask me. But...look, Nick, I was looking at that CCTV photo of her and I'm not even sure it *is* her. You'll think I'm crazy, I know but I think it could be someone *pretending* to be her.'

He looked at his feet and frowned. 'Well, I thought she was Frank, didn't I? I'm still not really sure I was wrong about that. He's possibly been seen with Barbara at the art school, so it couldn't be, if that's the case. Why do you think someone is pretending to be her?'

'Just call it an illusionist's gut instinct. It doesn't look right, somehow. The picture could have been doctored to hide who it really is. How do we know that it hasn't been? We don't. We're trusting the police to release a genuine photo and no good comes from trusting the police. They're bent as fuck - we all know that.'

'OK, but why, though? That's the question to ask. Why would the police do that? If you've got a good reason, then it makes it much more likely to be true. Do you think she's being set up for some reason?'

'Yeah, deffo, and she knew it. That's why she's gone awol. She's not disappeared because she's guilty but because she's being framed. When you saw her, I reckon she was leaving, knowing that something was going to happen that would implicate her in a crime. She's made an enemy in high places.'

'And your evidence for this is what?'

'Like I say, it's just an instinct.'

Nick felt cynical. Just saying something was 'instinct' sounded more profound than saying you had made it up, or that it was a guess.

'Well, I'll look out for unconvincing coppers asking questions. I don't know what else I can do, Jo. It's nothing to do with us down here, is it? We were just on our honeymoon, that's all...we got caught up in something.'

'Yeah, I suppose so. Something isn't right, though, and a bloke was murdered, so if we can find out why...I dunno, I think the police are bent on this...something just isn't right. I'd better go...err...' she paused and just as she should have hung up, she didn't.

'Yeah?'

She cleared her throat. 'Err...I wanted to call Jeff, but I lost his number. Do you have it?'

Nick grinned to himself and gave her Jeff's mobile and the shop number as well.

After the phone call, he finished off his columns, emailed them to his editors and then took a walk for half an hour alongside the river, over the Infinity Bridge, staring into the slowly moving River Tees that wound its way from Cross Fell, high up in the North Pennines, 70 miles away, towards the North Sea. As he did so, a familiar figure came towards him.

'Hello, Josh,' said Nick, bending down to ruffle his dog, Stanley's, ears. 'I've not seen you for a few weeks. You on school holidays?'

Josh nodded as he spoke. 'Hello, Nick. Yes, everyone tells me I shall look back on these six-week breaks as some sort of golden time in my life, but they don't feel any different to me. They seem exactly like every other day.'

Nick grinned at him. The lad's Asperger's Syndrome gave him a pleasing bluntness. Sometimes there was nothing between Josh having a thought and him saying it. It meant he occasionally said inappropriate things - a fact which distressed him when he realised, or was told - but Nick found it sometimes amusing and usually easy to deal with. As someone who often struggled with the foggy layers of human behaviour, he found Josh's plain, unaffected way of going on a pleasure. When you knew someone had no side to them and were unable to hide their thoughts very well, you always knew where you were with them.

He kept in regular touch with Josh, mostly by email, and found himself to be very fond of him, partly because he saw something of himself in him, and partly because he was a funny and very intelligent lad. Now 15, he was turning from a boy into a young man, and had big almond eyes with dark eyelashes and a cheeky way about him that, if he'd been socially more functional, would have guaranteed he'd be popular with girls. He'd got rid of his floppy fringe in favour of a closer cropped haircut and his voice had broken. It was going through a phase of being deep and also squeaky. It is a challenging time in any boy's life. You don't know what the hell is going on, half of the time. But then, Nick felt that at the age of 49, too.

'Have you got anything planned? If not, we could go for a coffee, if you like,' said Nick.

'No, I am just walking with Stanley so that I don't have to be in the house all day long.'

'I used to do that all summer. I loved to be out of the house. I was out for 12 hours a day, mostly on my own, wrapped up in my own thoughts.'

'Are you sure you don't have Asperger's, Nick? Ha ha...no, you're just a loony. It's different, baby!'

Nick laughed and patted the lad on the back. 'Owee, kidda, let's get ourselves something to drink.'

They walked back over the bridge and towards a coffee shop on the High Street. He contemplated taking Josh into Jeff's, but Josh didn't like loud music. It seemed to scramble his brain a bit. Even a loud radio seemed to disrupt his peace of mind.

'How's your mother?' he said.

'Trying to be nice to me, so that I don't run off. I am not going to run off, I am *so* done with that, but she doesn't know that. I feel confused about her and dad divorcing. I wish they were just happy together, but they're not. They seem to actually rather hate each other now. It's odd. How did they go from loving each other to hating each other? Why does it change? It's two such different feelings. How can you feel both things towards someone? People say Asperger's kids are weird but going from love to hate seems very weird to me.'

Nick blew out air. 'Wow, that's a big question Josh. People grow apart, sometimes. As you get older you change or one person does something to alienate them from you. The way you feel isn't a constant thing. It evolves.'

'I don't understand that. How can you change? I don't change. I'll be like this forever, like it or not.'

'No, that's not true. You *are* changing.'

'No, I'm really not.' He nodded up and down, saying it like it was a badge of honour.

'You might not think you are, but you are. You develop new interests and passions, don't you? You used to collect stamps, but now you don't so much. Now you collect coins.'

Josh frowned. Nick knew that meant he was trying to work out the right thing to say; trying to second guess what was the appropriate response.

'But collecting stuff - that's just things. Feelings aren't things. Parents are supposed to be more than just things. It's supposed to be bigger than that, isn't it?'

'Yeah. It is. But sometimes it just doesn't work out. Human relations aren't rational things, Josh. They're all wrapped up in emotions.' He patted him on the arm. 'Now, what do you want to drink?'

'Green tea please, Nick. I'm not allowed coffee due to the fact it makes me go extra loopy!' He laughed his boyish giggle and made a silly face at him by crossing his eyes and sticking his tongue out. Nick laughed.

He got one for himself too and they sat down at a table.

'Did you enjoy your wedding?' said Josh, fussing with the lovely, placid dog a little.

'We did, yeah. Thanks.'

Josh nodded again, as was his way. 'I bet Julie looked lovely.'

'She did. Yeah.'

'What did she wear?' he said, leaning forward, eagerly.

Nick was well aware that, like any 15-year-old boy, Josh had an almost permanent interest in girls and women and was a bit smitten with Julie, even though she was 31 years older than him, possibly exactly because of that.

'She wore a cream-coloured suit that she got from a charity shop and then had tailored to fit her.'

Josh nodded. 'And have you consummated the marriage yet?' He rolled his tongue around the word *consummated* with relish.

Nick looked at him, thinking he was trying to make a joke, but he wasn't. It was just one of Josh's slightly inappropriate questions. It was hard to know whether to correct him and tell him he shouldn't ask things like that, or whether to let it slide. He could get upset with himself when he said or did something unacceptable, even though it was never done maliciously or nastily. It was just how he was. But he had to admonish him - if he didn't, non-friends would be less forgiving.

'If you think about it, that's a bit of a naughty question, isn't it, Josh? That's, like, private between me and Julie. Do you get me? I don't mind, I'm just saying it's one of those things you've got to think twice before saying.'

Josh looked blankly at him. 'Oh. Sorry.' He pointed at Nick. 'Because it's about sex. Oh, yeah. Sorry, Nick. You know what I'm like. I can't always understand you people and your strange, non-Asperger's ways.' He pulled his cross-eyed face again.

'I know. It's alright. But for your information, yes, we have. Several times. Fucking vigorously.' He raised an eyebrow at him, due to unusually using a swear word.

82

Josh giggled and flushed at the swear word. 'Aw, I bet that was *really* great.'

That made Nick laugh and that made Josh happy. 'We went up to Edinburgh for our honeymoon. The Fringe Festival is on. We saw a lot of shows. Had a great time. Drank too much, though.'

'Were you sick?'

'Not sick as in vomiting, no. I wasn't well yesterday, though.'

'What was the matter with you?'

Nick weighed up whether to tell him. He was only young, but in some ways was wise well beyond his years. 'I was depressed. Very down. You know I suffer from depression, right? It comes and goes. Yesterday I was crying a lot and in a dark place. I'm much better today, though.'

Josh couldn't do empathy, even though it often seemed like he wanted to. Sometimes he tried to fake it.

'I'm sorry to hear about that Nick,' he said, almost formally. He drank some tea and thought for a moment. 'I'm not being rude, but wouldn't having sex with Julie cheer you up?' He offered it up as though it was serious advice.

Nick patted him on the arm. 'It doesn't work like that, I'm afraid. When you're depressed you can't even think about anything like that.'

He looked genuinely concerned, 'That must be horrible. I'd hate not to be able to think about sex.' Nick coughed out a laugh. 'Oh, what have I said now?' The lad looked momentarily annoyed. Nick patted him again.

'Nothing. You're fine. You just have an unusual turn of phrase, sometimes. I like it.'

Josh did his big nodding gesture. 'I shall change the subject to make sure I don't say anything wrong. So what is Edinburgh like?'

'Oh, it's amazing. And something amazing happened while we were there.' Nick described the capital of Scotland to him and then went on to tell him about the shooting and how they'd met Barbara Stewart. Josh listened wide-eyed. Then Nick showed him the CCTV photo on his phone. Josh took it and stared with his big eyes.

'She looks weird,' he said.

'Does she? Why?'

Josh wrinkled his nose and squinted at it. 'She's dressed like she's going somewhere posh, after killing someone.'

'Maybe she was.'

'You can see the gun very clearly. It looks like she's holding it up for the camera,' said Josh.

Nick thought it was interesting that he said that.

'Yeah, we thought she would want to hide the fact she had a gun.'

'Yes. Who is she?'

'She's a teacher.'

'Where does this picture come from?'

'It was in the newspaper.'

Josh frowned. 'The newspaper took it?'

'No. I mean, they published it.'

'So where did it actually come from?'

'Oh, I see what you mean. I think it's from a CCTV camera.'

Josh was getting frustrated again.

'No. That's not what I mean.' He blew air out of his nose. 'I mean, who got it from the camera and into the newspaper?'

Nick folded his arms across his chest. It was a very good question.

'I don't know, Josh. But you've hit on something important there. That's good thinking. How did the paper get the photo? Was it from the police or from someone else?'

Josh nodded. 'Have they caught her?'

'No. She's disappeared.'

'How do you disappear?'

'Good question. I don't know.'

Josh finished his tea. 'If you ask me, the best way to disappear would to become invisible.' He made a 'pow!' sound and spread his long, slim fingers out like an exploding shell. He nodded and stroked the now-sleeping Stanley.

'What do you mean by that?' asked Nick.

'No-one can catch you if they can't see you, can they? God, being invisible would be great! You could go anywhere and no-one would know.'

Nick saw what he meant. 'When I was your age, I wanted to be invisible so that I could walk into the girl's changing room at Ian Ramsey School unseen and just sit there while they got ready for gym classes.' It was an old memory and one which had formed the narrative of many of his teenage night-time fantasies.

Josh thought that was hilarious. Maybe it was already in his mind. His whole body shuddered as he laughed, hand over his mouth. He didn't seem to get embarrassed really, but this was about as close as he came.

'I shall go home now for my dinner and I shall *imagine* being invisible at school.'

Nick knew what 'imagine' really meant and it was some progress that Josh hadn't actually spelt it out for him. He did learn things eventually, even if he didn't understand why it might be necessary to do so.

He put his arm around Josh's shoulder as they left the coffee shop.

'You take care of yourself, Josh. Come round to the flat for some dinner sometime. OK?'

Josh smiled at him in the pure, unaffected way, that only someone who couldn't do social niceties could manage.

'Guess what?' said Jeff, with bright eyes, as Nick walked into the shop, having waved Josh and Stanley off.

'Err...let's think. You've just had a phone call from Jo King.'

Jeff stopped and looked at him. 'How did you know that?'

'I'm psychic, aren't I? All these years, I've been listening to the thoughts in your head, and it's been a litany of sick perversion.'

Jeff made a 'whooo' noise at him and wiggled his fingers. 'What you actually mean is, she called you to get my number, because she'd lost it.'

'Aye. She actually called to tell me about this meeting she had with someone who said they were a policeman.'

'Yeah, she said about that. I agree with her, something is weird about it. I looked it up and they've still not said they want to interview Barbara Stewart, yet they obviously know it's her in the photo, not least because you told them.'

'Young Josh just came up with something interesting. He wondered how the picture got into the press. Was it released by the police or does it come from somewhere else?'

Jeff raised an eyebrow. 'Good old Josh. That is an important thing to know. Can you find out?'

'I was wondering that. I might.'

He perched on a tall stool by the counter and looked through his phonebook, calling Jeff Gooch, a football journalist at the local paper, the *Gazette*, and picked his brains to get a contact on the football desk at the *Edinburgh Evening News*. Middlesbrough FC often played a pre-season game against the Edinburgh club, Hibernian, especially when ex-Middlesbrough man Tony Mowbray was in charge, so Jeff knew some newspaper men up there and gave Nick a couple of numbers.

He called Jim Underwood on the sports desk and introduced himself.

'Jim, you know that shooting up there of John Grayson-Thomas, there was a photo in the paper of the woman who did it, wasn't there? Do you have any idea where the paper got that from?'

'It was probably released by the police, but I can find out, if you like,' said Jim. 'Just a minute.' He put him on hold while he spoke to another part of the paper. 'Nick?'

'Yeah?'

'My pal on the news desk says it was emailed to them from an anonymous source. It didn't come from the police. Apparently, the police are pissed off at us for publishing it. Words have been had at the top level. But that's stupid, there's no way we'd sit on a photo like that.'

'That's interesting. The police still haven't named her, I see.'

'They've not said anything about her officially. Gordon Smith is in charge though, so that's not a surprise. None of the crime beat boys like him and he doesn't like us. And he likes us even less, I'd guess, now that we published a photo of his killer.'

'Question is, where did it come from? Who got it from the CCTV cameras?'

'Whoever it is has been good at keeping it secret, that's for sure.'

Nick thanked him for his time.

A couple of people came in and went through to the cafe, which was already almost full. Matty and Emily were busy making coffee and clearing tables. They both waved at Nick as he sat down by the counter.

'Emily's supposed to be working in the shop, isn't she?'

Jeff nodded. 'Aye, it gets packed in there at lunchtimes, though, so I've asked her to give Matty a hand. We need another full-timer in there. I'll sort it at some point.' He waved a big sheaf of papers at him. 'Seen these? It's all the paperwork about turning the old church hall into a club. Half of a rainforest was chopped down just for this.'

'How's that going?'

'It's all approved, subject to alterations being made, such as the wiring and plumbing and inspections by men who have never known the loving hand of a woman. They could just have written that on one sheet of paper in purple crayon, but no, they have to turn it into *War and Peace*.'

'So when does the work start?'

'Couple of weeks. We have to get it open by Christmas, for obvious commercial reasons. It'll be tight, though. Starting to wonder what I've taken on. You have an idea and then you've got to wade through bureaucratic mud for months, instead of just being able to get on with making it happen.'

Nick picked up a copy of UFO's *Strangers in the Night* from the desk and held it up at Jeff. 'Best live album ever?'

'Got to be up there in the top five, hasn't it?'

Nick nodded. 'What else did Jo say to you?'

'Turns out the Evans charm is a powerfully addictive chemical.' He flexed his eyebrows at him.

'Are you sure?'

'Not really, no. She's coming down to Middlesbrough to see her mother, once her shows are done. We're going out for a drink and food.'

'Brilliant. You two are a good fit.'

'Yeah. She's different. She's interesting and quirky. When she was hanging around the stall on the Grassmarket, she was chatting away non-stop and doing little tricks with the punters, nicking their watches, making stuff disappear. She did this one thing with a bloke's two-quid change. She held two pound coins on the palm of her right hand and she says to the bloke, "If you guess which one your change is in, I'll give you a fiver". The bloke goes, "Alright, then". She closes her hands with the coins on her right palm, so the bloke goes for her right hand, as anyone would, but it's not there and it's not in her left hand. She points to the bag his records are in and they're in there. I have no idea how she did that. It was brilliant, man.'

'That's cool. So why I do I sense there's a problem?'

Jeff winced a little and made a face. 'Dunno. Nothing. Just want to be careful...Argie and that, you know? I might be a bit...you know...err...' He always struggled to articulate his emotions at the best of times, even when he wanted to.

'...be a bit vulnerable, like? After everything.'

'Aye.'

He nodded. And that was as much taking about his emotions as you'd get out of Jeff. He obviously just wanted to avoid falling head over heels and ending up getting hurt. He had Argie to think about.

'Well, just treat it like it's a bit of fun. She obviously likes you. You got on great, up north.'

'Yeah. We did. She's...I don't know, man...she's on my level or I'm on hers. It feels weird, though. I sort of fancy her, but I like her as a mate as well...don't know why. I've not had that before.'

'Well, I'm terrible at judging such things at the best of times. I was the one who still never asked Shawn Yeadon out at school, even though I was mad about her and all her friends told me she wanted to go out with me. Remember? That went on for about two bloody years. I just didn't believe it could be true. More women asked me out, than the other way round. So just go with how you feel.'

'It's not until next week, though. It'll just be a one-off thing, I reckon. She lives in London, anyway, so it's not really a goer, is it?'

'Aye, well, just play it as it comes. Hey, do you fancy coming round the flat for a music session tomorrow? Jules is going away overnight on some team-building gig.'

'They love a bit of bonding and building, that lot, don't they? Alright, then. Shall we crack a bottle of vodka?'

'You can - I'm off the drink for a bit. We necked so much up in Edinburgh. Also...' he let out a groan and kicked at the floor '...I was bad yesterday when we got back.'

'Bad?'

'Yeah, depressed, like, really badly. I think it was a reaction to all the boozing. That was why I gave up in Harrogate, if you remember.'

'You're alright now, though, aren't you? You look all pumped up like you're a gay bloke in a Calvin Klein underwear ad.' He squeezed Nick on the bicep.

'I'll take that as a compliment. Yeah, I'm alright today. But, I bloody hate feeling depressed much more than I like drinking, so it's for the best that I abstain for a bit.'

Jeff nodded, doing what he'd always done when it came to talking about depression - he largely ignored it and got on with talking about normal life and that was always exactly what Nick wanted. 'OK. Here's an idea. We'll have an evening of playing only EPs. That'll involve some good digging.'

'Best EP ever?'

Jeff responded in a heartbeat. '*Life's a Long Song* by Jethro Tull. No competition, whatsoever.'

'Correct answer, though I like the three *New Live and Rare* volumes from Deep Purple.'

Aye, they were good. Seen this *Dedicated Kinks* one? Just brought in by someone. It was their old dad's. Just snuffed it.'

Nick took it off the desk. It was in perfect condition. 'Sweet. How much?'

'It's worth at least £100.'

Nick whistled. 'Has Emily got it on eBay?'

'Aye, it'll be sold by the end of the week.'

'How much did you pay the punter?'

'Seventy-five.'

'Jeff man, you need to make a better margin than that. You should have paid 50 at most.'

'I know, but you don't like to when it's someone's dead dad, plus they were nice. Anyway, it might go for £150 yet. There's already an £80 bid on it. Kinks always do well. It's a tricky balance to strike between giving a fair price and being greedy.'

'No-one has to sell to you. They could put it on eBay themselves. You've got to pay Emily and for everything else.'

'I know, aye. There's been a lot of good stuff in recently. It doesn't hang around for long. All of old Fred Flynn's albums that I bought from Dot have gone, some for big money. The more rare it is, the faster it seems to sell. It's all the Joan Armatrading records that are impossible to shift except by throwing them in a skip.'

'Hiya, Nicky boy,' said Emily, trotting up to him, dressed in skin-tight red leather pants and a cropped, cap-sleeve Poison t-shirt showing off her tattooed arms, giving him a kiss on the cheek in an exaggerated manner. She poked her tongue into the gap between her front teeth, grinned and ruffled her 1973 Suzi Quatro hair. 'Did you have a passionate honeymoon?' She held her hands over her heart and gave him a swooning look.

'We had a good time.'

'I was looking at my photos of the wedding. You two looked really good. It was a great day,' she said.

'You looked good, too - I bet not many women have worn a black leather jumpsuit and stiletto heels to a wedding.'

'I always used to, but that was before the court order was served on me,' said Jeff, in an offhand manner, while putting a record into its sleeve.

Emily tutted at him. 'Jeff was telling me about the woman you met, who shot someone. What a terrible thing.'

'Hmm. It's all a bit odd, to say the least.'

'As the big chap here often says, the only really weird things in life, are things that aren't weird.'

Jeff tugged on his beard and grinned. 'I missed my vocation as the Dalai Lama...'

'...or just as a llama,' she added and laughed. Jeff made a bleating, goat-like noise. 'Aren't you going to try and find out why she shot this man?'

'Why should we?' said Nick.

'Well, you were involved in it,' she said.

'Not really. We just met her before she did it. It's for the police to sort out, not us, though they don't seem over active so far.'

'If you ask me, there's something weird about the police involvement, or lack of it,' said Jeff.

Nick shook his head. 'We don't know that.'

But Emily was her usual sparky self. 'You could write about it for a newspaper, or something. Make some money. You're always skint.'

'That's a good idea, Em. He doesn't have an eye for the main chance, this lad,' said Jeff, checking the float in the till.

'But there's nothing much to write,' said Nick, defensively.

'Well, find out more then,' said Emily, squeezing his hand, quickly rubbing his middle finger up and down in a very suggestive manner, as was her flirty way, before giving him a cheeky smile and going over to the cafe again.

CHAPTER 5

Julie left the following morning with an overnight bag, driving down to Bedale in the Porsche. Jeff turned up at seven that evening and they started to select records from Nick's collection to play. They'd just finished playing a clear vinyl UFO three-track EP from the live album, when Nick's phone went. It was Julie.

'Hiya, how's it going?' he said.

'It's all good. We're at Northdean, but my car isn't very well. She's not firing right. I need to reset the points and do a few other tweaks or she'll not make it home. Trouble is I've left my toolbox in the boot of your car 'cos I'm always having to fix your heap of junk. Are you doing anything tomorrow?'

'Nothing that won't wait. You want me to bring it down for you?'

'Could you? I know it's a drag.'

'No, it's fine. It's not far to Bedale. About 40 minutes, isn't it?'

'Yeah. You can just drop it off and then get back. You don't need to wait for me.'

'No worries.'

'Thanks, luv. Are you still feeling OK? I worry now if I don't get a naked picture of you in all your engorged glory.'

'Ha ha, I'll send you another one if you like. But, yeah, I'm fine.'

'Are you sure?'

'Yeah, really. Thanks for asking, though.'

'Don't be so polite, man. I'm your missus, remember? Love you.'

She rang off.

'Fancy a drive out into the country tomorrow morning?' said Nick.

Jeff looked up from the record player. 'Aye, go on. I'll have to bring Lord Argie, though. Mam's at work. Where's this place she's gone to, again?'

'Northdean School. It's a minor public school.'

'Oh, yeah. And they've rented it out to them?'

'Some deal with an ex-TWC worker. School's out just now, so they often rent out facilities in the summer holidays, I think.'

'That's the place we went to with the school, back in the day, isn't it?' he said, dropping the needle on a rare Yardbirds EP.

'Yeah, there and Ampleforth.'

Jeff threw a few shapes as the music came on.

'What a piss up that was. Dear me. Those monks at Ampleforth could really put it away.'

'Yeah, unholy amounts of cider, as I recall.'

'Didn't we each get assigned a boy to look after us?'

'That was at Northdean, yeah. I was telling Jules about my lad, Dev.'

'Mine was a toff. He fucking hated me and was obviously a bully. Imagine being trapped 24 hours a day in your school with someone who just wants to beat up on you. It'd send you crazy and probably traumatise you for life.'

'I know. At least at Ian Ramsey we could go home every day to avoid being beaten up by Smez and his gang of semi-psychotic thugs.'

After playing a pile of records, Jeff went to pick up Argie from his mother's house. Nick turned out the lights and got into bed. Turning to Julie's side of the bed, he put his face into her pillow and breathed in her smell, kissed the pillow and said goodnight to her.

He found himself just occupying the right side of the bed as usual, rather than sprawling over the whole space and was wide awake by 5.30am.

When we say 'sleeping together', it's often sex that expression brings to mind first, but it is the calm reassurance of being asleep with someone that is the really lovely thing about it. There you are, passed out, side by side, for eight hours a day, unconscious in the same space. You spend so long sleeping alone, often from childhood onwards and then one day there's someone else there. At first, it seems such an odd thing and quite invasive of your personal space.

As he lay there in the early morning light, he remembered the very first girlfriend he had ever actually slept with. It was after a party at a friend's house and they'd had some form of very safe sex in their underwear and had then fallen asleep in a very modestly sized double bed, pressed up to each other. It was a lovely memory and one he cherished. Waking up with her next to him, his arm around her waist, her soft, warm skin on his hand, was intimate in a way he hadn't felt until that point in life. He'd found it quietly very thrilling, because it was a both trusting and, in its own small way, a loving thing to do and a leap from everyday teenage life. Time passes so quickly, in some ways it felt like that night had only recently happened. They'd both been quite cool about it at the time, like it wasn't a big deal, but that's how you are at that age; you don't want to show how inexperienced or naive you really are. It seemed very likely that she didn't even remember it, all these years on, but he'd made a habit of storing pleasurable, warm memories as emotional bookmarks in his life because they gave him something to cling to when he was in a low mood. A small shaft of the light from them shone into those dark moments and that was an especially bright one. He smiled to himself and sent a quiet thought of affection into the universe. Some good stuff should never leave you.

There are people who don't get on in bed, they both want to sleep on the same side or can't stand the noise the other person makes, but he and Julie had just fitted together from the start, and more often than not, kept a hand or foot touching throughout the night, perhaps as some sort of mutual reassurance. So when she wasn't there, it really felt disturbing; like something was wrong with the world.

By 8.30am he'd cooked himself breakfast and was at Jeff's new house in Hartburn Village, taking Argie's carrycot to the car while the big man locked up.

Nick pulled away and set off towards the A1 on the A66.

'Who was the first woman you spent the night with?' said Nick, continuing the musing he'd started while lying in bed.

'The first to actually spend the night with, as opposed to have sex with?'

'Indeed.'

'Err...it was Kathryn Beard. Remember her?' said Jeff, taking Argie out of the carry cot.

'Oh, yeah. She was goofy, wasn't she?'

'Had the protruding teeth of a cartoon rabbit. Lovely lass, though.'

'I've not thought about her for 35 years.'

'We swore our love for each other in 5th year. When her parents were away, I stayed over. We never did anything - well - you know - the usual bit of hand jive. But we just snuggled up under the sheets in her bedroom.' He nuzzled at the little lad.

'Yeah, I remember you telling me about it. I was so jealous of you. I wonder what happened to her?'

'She was mega brainy. Went to Cambridge to do biological sciences. I'll look her up...can't be many Kathryn Beards.'

He poked at his phone.

'Here we go. She's on Facebook. Bloody hell.'

'Has she still got the teeth?'

'Err...no...she's got some new American-style white teeth. Look at her, Argie. She could've been your mam. Err...hang on, no, she couldn't...that was too weird. Ignore me, son.'

Nick grinned and glanced over. The woman in the profile picture looked really glamorous. A big pile of dark hair, full red lips and, it had to be said, a huge, rather intimidating set of teeth. She grinned out at them.

'She's really attractive, in a toothy sort of way,' said Nick.

Jeff looked at her public profile. 'By the heck, she could take a bite out of a side of beef with those. She's got four kids and lives in York. Husband is Maurice Goldberg. A lawyer. Wow. That's totally freaked me out. He's so straight. I was never straight and she said she loved me. Did she lie or has she married the wrong, if rich-looking bloke?'

'Nah. She did love you at the time, I'm sure. In some young sort of way, I loved the first girl I spent the night with. I know I'd never felt like that about anyone before. But I was as much in love with the idea of being in love, as actually being in love, I think. If you know what I mean.'

Jeff put Argie down to sleep and made a groaning noise. 'Oh, typical of you, that is. An 18 year old's emotions are simultaneously very deep and very shallow. I'd got over Kathryn by the 6th form largely due to Claire Dalby wanting to lose her virginity to me. I was more than happy to lose mine to her...or indeed to literally any other girl, anywhere, at any time. In fact, any reasonably sized female mammal would have done. She's some sort of high-up nurse in Newcastle now. Funny how life goes, isn't it?' He put his phone down and looked up at him. 'What's this all about? Are you off on one of your infamous dwelling-on-life's-mysteries trips?'

Nick sighed. 'Oh, it's nowt, I just couldn't sleep well last night with Jules not being there. So I was remembering that first girl I shared a bed with and what a great thing it was.'

Jeff pulled a face at him and shook his head.

'Good grief, you don't need much prompting to go all misty-eyed, you. Let it go, son. It's the past - everyone has got one.'

'I know, but it all goes to make us who we are and I don't like to forget nice things. That was a really nice thing. Having someone feel like that about you...'

'...aye, but even so...'

'...see, when you get depressed, everything is so dark and negative. The light of loveliness just can't reach you, so I think, when I don't feel like that - when I'm not depressed - I need to remind myself of the lovely moments in my life when I felt happy, or good, or proud. It's something for me to hang onto in the worst moments. I think that's the real reason I'm always dredging things up that most people would have long since forgotten. Just recalling a nice time with a girlfriend, or some huge laugh you shared...'

'...or some bed you shared...yeah, I can see what you mean. Never thought about it like that. But then I'm not cursed with the black dog. To me, tomorrow matters more than yesterday,' said Jeff.

'But without knowing about yesterday, how much can we know about tomorrow?'

'Ah, tomorrow never knows, Grasshopper, so turn off your mind, relax and float downstream.' Jeff rolled his eyes up into his head, so only the whites showed.

The Northdean School was an imposing Victorian building just to the west of the North Yorkshire market town of Bedale. Set in its own grounds behind tall hedges, it felt separated from the real world.

Julie's distinctive mid blue Porsche was parked up to one side of what had originally been a substantial country manor house.

'Here we go, old boy. Bloody hell, imagine going to school here?' said Nick.

'This is the sort of place I imagine a Prince from Rangoon would be locked in a tower. It's all a bit Enid Blyton, isn't it?' said Jeff. 'I'd hate for Argie to go here. It's too weird. It'll be full of boys called Tristram and girls called Jocasta.'

Nick parked up and went to the boot, taking out Julie's large toolkit. The Porsche's engine was in the back, so he popped the bonnet and put the toolbox inside, slamming it shut.

'Right, that's us done, Jeff.'

Jeff got out of the car, wound down the window so Argie had plenty of air, hitched up his army pants and looked around. 'No chance of a cup of tea?'

'Don't think so. We'll stop off in Bedale for refreshments.'

Nick sucked in some air and took a good look around. The land rose quickly up to the moors of the Pennines. The school felt like it was on the boundary between life in the town and the wilderness of open country.

'What age do kids come here?' said Jeff.

'Eight to eighteen.'

Jeff flicked his hair over his shoulders and scowled. 'Shit, imagine being here on your own, aged eight? Poor little mites. You'd totally crap yourself.'

'It was bad enough at Fairfield Juniors and Ian Ramsey...'

He was interrupted by a shout from the house. He turned and looked towards the main entrance. Julie was trotting out, waving at them, dressed in navy cargo pants, trainers and an untucked yellow-and-blue plaid shirt.

'Hey, Jules,' said Jeff, waving back.

'Thanks for bringing the toolkit. I've got something to show you two. Owee inside.' She gestured for them to follow her.

'I thought you were hard at work,' said Nick, going after her.

'We are. It's just a mid-morning coffee break. I've only got 15 minutes. There's something I've got to show you.'

They walked through a grand entrance onto an old wooden parquet floor which led down a hallway to a grand staircase. It smelled of polish and dust and privilege.

She gestured to them and pointed to a long wall, on which were various wooden plaques with hand-painted lists of headmasters going back to 1840.

'Look here, from 1975 to '80, the gaffer here was one Frank Stewart. Name ring a bell?' she said. 'And come this way...' she led them into the school's admin office. As school was out, it was empty, but it had a large wall of photos of teachers and headmasters going back to before the first war. She tapped on one from 1975. 'See, Frank Stewart. Barbara said they were from North Yorkshire originally, he was the Head here for five years. Look.'

Nick peered at the black-and-white photo closely. It was a much younger Frank, alright. He was, if anything, a little more gaunt here, with a receding hairline and delicate, bony features and a strong chin.

'How old would he be here?'

'Well, even if it was taken in 1980, that's 30 years ago and he looked well into his 60s when we met him. So he must be mid 30s here. He actually made it to the top at a really young age,' said Julie. 'I wonder why he left in 1980. Was he sacked? Did he quit?'

Jeff flicked at his hair. 'He looks almost underweight to me. He's got a big bony head.'

'I thought that, too,' said Julie. 'He's got a skeletal look about him.'

'We can probably find out what happened, if we do some research. I wonder if Barbara worked here, too? People often end up marrying work colleagues,' said Nick.

She shrugged and flapped her hands up and down. 'Well, that's all. I just thought it was a funny coincidence when I saw them earlier. I mean, what are the odds that we'd meet him...and then I come here.'

'It's a small world, Jules. Everyone is only a few degrees of separation from knowing everyone else,' said Jeff.

'Yeah, that seems so true, now more than ever,' said Nick.

'I once met my next-door neighbour on a small railway platform in rural France. Neither of us knew the other was going there, let alone at the same time. I walked on, he walked on, we stared at each other like we were ghosts. Now that's a coincidence!' said Jeff.

'I've got to go,' said Julie, looking at her watch. 'Thanks again for the toolbox. I'll see youse boys later.' She patted Nick on the backside and skipped off up the stairs.

They got back to the old BMW. Argie was awake and making a disgruntled noise which suggested he might be hungry. Nick turned over the engine, but Jeff raised his index finger.

'Don't drive away yet. Something has just come back to me. When we read that local newspaper report of the shooting, didn't it say that the victim had, at some point in the past, been a teacher?'

'Yeah, that's right. He was a Latin teacher.'

'Aye, it did. I wonder if he was a teacher here? Now we know Frank was headmaster, is that a coincidence? Maybe he and his wife had a long-running feud with him. How do you like them apples?' said Jeff, bouncing the baby on his knee to soothe him.

'Eh? What apples?'

'It's a saying.'

'Not on Teesside, it's not.'

'I think it's more a New York thing. Look, there can't be more than one John Grayson-Thomas who worked here.' He got his phone out and did a search for the name and the school.

'Nope. Nothing listed under Grayson-Thomas, Grayson or Thomas. Oh, well, it was just a long-shot idea. Let us away back to the glamour of Teesside's chimneys.'

'Maybe he worked here using a different name.'

'Why would he do that?' said Jeff.

Nick sat and thought about it. A stiff breeze was getting up, bringing rain over the Pennines from a bruised sky.

'I don't know. Maybe we shouldn't believe the reality we think we're being presented with. Just like Jo is always saying. Her words keep coming back to me, you know. She's so right, in so many ways. I was thinking the other day how appearances don't match realities.'

'I don't get you.'

Nick shrugged. 'I don't get me, either. That's my point. It's just I was looking at myself in the mirror, right?'

'Always a dangerous thing to do. What did you see?'

'I saw a well-developed bloke. I'm ripped, me, at least by my historically puny standards. I'm in the shape of my life. The weights and the low-carb eating have just...well...y'know...'

'Aye, I've noticed, like. If I was a member of a rugby club, and no greater crime against nature and all that is holy can I imagine, but if I was, I'd say you'd got "killer guns" on you. But I'm not, so obviously, I'd never say anything as crass, nor as homo-erotic as that.'

'I hate all of that V-necked Pringle wool sweater, macho shit. Always have. Blokes being all blokey is just awful.'

'Aye, I bloody hate the towel flickers, me.'

'You what?'

'Towel flickers. You remember. When we were kids, there were always the lads in the changing rooms who would flick you in the balls with a wet towel. Bloody hurt like hell. That was a very rugby-club bloke sort of thing to do. Me and you just wanted to get dressed, get our dinner and play some records. They were far too interested in inflicting pain and, if possible, a bit of humiliation. Ever since, I always think of that lot as towel flickers.'

'That's sheer poetry, big man. No-one likes them, apart from other towel flickers.'

Nick chewed at his lip, unsure just how much to say. He glanced at Argie, who was now settling down. 'The thing is, I'm not a body builder type, but I know I've got some muscle and I'm strong.'

Jeff nodded. 'I don't know anyone built like you.'

'But here's the thing, right? I'm weak as fuck.'

Jeff looked at him squarely but without expression. 'You mean the depression thing?'

'Yeah. People might look at me like I'm this quite powerfully built dude, but inside I'm the opposite. When Jo talks about the reality being different to what you think you see, I'm the living embodiment of that. The other day, I was curled up in a ball weeping, unable to cope with life and hating myself. I was a defenceless child, like Argie here. Do you get me? On the outside people would see me and think I was strong and just couldn't guess at the fucked-up human that lives inside this body.'

Jeff didn't reply immediately. A lifetime of friendship means you don't have to respond quickly or indeed, at all.

Nick drove them back to Teesside on the A1 and the A66. Finally, after fussing with Argie again, Jeff spoke, letting out a sigh first.

'I feel so bloody sorry for you, sometimes.'

That wasn't something he usually said. Nick glanced at him.

'Yeah? Why?'

'Well, I reckon you look like loads of blokes would like to look, but you're just not comfortable in your own skin. I don't know what to do about it, but I wish I could change it for you.'

Nick was pleasantly surprised by Jeff's words. 'Thanks, man. That's good of you.'

'I mean, by contrast, I'm a physical mess. I've got skin hanging off me from the fat days, but even so, I quite like myself, I've not had a day of depression in my life or at least not like you've had it. Even when I was a massive bloke on an almost endless bender, it was all just part of my happy-go-lucky life. At least think it was. Then I had the heart attack and that put an end to all of that. But somehow, I just keep on keeping own, quite cheerful, like. Even after Rita died - I just sort of got over it. Things don't crush me the way they sometimes crush you. I just got lucky like that. If we put your body with my temperament, we'd have the perfect man, eh.' He made a funny face at him.

The road was quiet, as they got to the outskirts of Stockton. 'Well, like I said, I can't stop thinking about what Jo said in her show, y'know. It has really resonated with me, about how things are not necessarily as they seem to be.'

'Yeah, she's on to something. She's got some wise in her, that lass.'

They went silent again.

'But we're not being conditioned to see that Edinburgh murder in a specific way, are we? It's not some sort of con by an illusionist, is it?' said Nick. 'I know that sounds mad.'

'Maybe it is and we just don't know it, because it's so good. Maybe no-one was shot and there's been a huge conspiracy by the police to make everyone think there has.' He flashed his eyes at Nick and pointed at him.

'Could be. You don't know they didn't covertly leak the photo to the press.'

Nick laughed a little. 'That's top-notch fantasy work. And I admire it. But it's not possible, is it?'

'Let's just forget logic for a bit and think outside of our, or at least my, capacious underpants,' said Jeff. 'If that is even possible.'

'Alright, then. Here's some made-up rubbish. Let's say the shooting didn't really happen. No-one died. Barbara Stewart is just photographed leaving there with a gun. The police turn up and pretend there's been a shooting and put up screens.'

'See - that doesn't sound massively unlikely, does it? Let's run with that. Say the police want to publicly make out that Grayson-Thomas is dead, so that he can disappear. This is a great way to do it. An apparently public shooting means no-one will question it. They even release a photo of the shooter carrying a gun and showing it to the camera, so we're all in no doubt. They convince Barbara to pretend to do it, then they pay her to disappear and live under an assumed name, followed a few days later by her husband.' Jeff coughed and cleared his throat. 'That isn't totally implausible, at all.'

It really didn't sound that unlikely. Not really. Not when you spelled it out like that. 'There's no doubt that MI-5 or someone in the security services could set all of that up. They'd just have to make sure that it happened when no member of the public was near enough to see that actually, no-one had been shot, at all. They'd also need the rest of the office to be in on it or given a good reason not to be there.'

'He runs the place - so he could easily have sent everyone home early or something. That would have been no problem. And this explains why that art school co-worker thought she wasn't capable of doing such a thing. She wasn't, because she didn't actually do it,' Jeff smoothed out his long beard in contemplation.

Nick nodded. 'Yeah, it's all making some sort of sense...but seriously, why? What's so special about Grayson-Thomas that he requires an elaborate set-up like this? I mean, if he's a spy or something, it's not going to come up on Google, is it?'

'OK, I'm just riffing on this. But, like we said earlier, what if that's not his real name? That's another part of the illusion,' said Jeff.

'Not sure that makes sense. Surely he needs to be the man he is known to be, in order for him to be declared dead. If he's got enemies, they need to know he's out of the way.'

'Not if those who want him dead know what his real identity is,' said Jeff.

'You're right, it doesn't seem that outlandish. That's not the same as it being true, though. And even if it was - I keep returning to this fact and it is that it's actually nothing to do with us, is it?' said Nick. 'We're not the police, we're just people who got caught up in it.'

Jeff thought about that a bit. 'Yeah, but we can't have people getting their head blown off with impunity. Also don't forget what Emily said about writing a story for money. Mind you, it's true that I've got other important matters to sort out, such as the price, quality and shape of toilets.'

'I'm glad you raised that. Can you just have stalls and not a big trough? It's very old school to just have a latrine to piss into. It's horrible. I don't want to stand beside other men just passing urine, even though now that I've been hypnotised I can actually perform. I reckon most decent blokes hate it or would just rather have some privacy.'

'Ha ha, you might be right. Though you might, with respect, crazy dude, be overthinking such a thing.'

'I would never overthink any one specific thing - I overthink everything. I'm an equal opportunity overthinker. So what are you going to call your club?'

'Ah. I have given it some thought.' He raised an index finger.

'And what obscure reference to a Uriah Heep song have you decided on as the name?'

'Naturally, I was inclined to go that way, but then I thought, no, it's part of my empire - so it's going to be Jeff's Rock Club. I'll get a JRC logo made for above the door.'

'JRC. Yeah, sensible. I like it.' It was a great thing that he was doing and he seemed so suited to it.

'Never underestimate the general public's indifference to what you call your business. It's not worth a lot of thought, if you ask me.'

Nick got home, parked up the car and suddenly, now being on his own, felt very like having a drink. It was an itch that was difficult not to scratch once you got the urge. He tried to do some work, but felt restless and the Phenibut was making him feel lustful, as per usual, but he wanted to save that for when Jules got back later that evening, feeling she deserved the best of him.

Just sitting and writing wasn't doing enough to take his mind off either sex or drinking, so he got up and marinated some lamb chops in garlic and herbs, peeled and prepared some vegetables for their dinner and then had yet another mug of tea. It was no good, though. He wanted a bloody drink and he hated himself a little bit for that. He had picked open the old drink wound and now it was demanding to be paid attention to.

He took a litre bottle of vodka out of the kitchen cupboard and poured a finger of it into a small glass. Maybe just one shot would knock back the desire. He added some lime juice to it and a splash of fizzy water, picked up the glass and was just about to down it in one when his phone buzzed. It was Julie.

Putting the glass down on the kitchen bench, he took the call.

'Hey lady, are you on your way home?'

'I am, but something weird has happened.'

'Eh? What? Are you alright?'

'Yeah, I'm fine. I'm following Barbara Stewart.'

'You're what?!' he said, shocked.

'She was in a Volvo in Bedale as I was leaving.'

'Are you sure, Jules?'

'Certain. She was even in that green linen suit and scarf that we saw her in.'

'Christ almighty - did she see you? Was she on her own?'

'No. She'd not know me from anyone else, anyway. She only met me for a couple of minutes. She's on her own, though.'

'She *is on her own*?'

'Yeah, I'm two cars behind her. I'm following her.'

'Bloody hell. Where are you?'

'I'm now on the A66 near Sadberge, so she must be going to some- where in our neck of the woods. I followed her up the A1.'

'I can't get my head around this, Jules.'

'It's not that difficult, lad. Her husband has connections with the school in Bedale - OK, he hasn't been Head for 30 years, but he's probably on the Board of Governors or something and maybe she is, too. These pri- vate schools have lots of advisory groups.'

'Can you take a photo of her?'

'I've tried already. I'm not sure I got a clear shot, though. I will if I can without her seeing me.'

'Be careful, Jules.'

'I'm just following a posh woman. I'm not chasing a thug.'

'Not a thug, but almost certainly a killer. Just watch out.'

She went quiet for a few seconds. 'She's turning off...'

'Where?'

'The Yarm exit. The 135.'

'She looked very Yarm. Leave me on speakerphone while you follow her.'

'Alright. Hold on, she's taking the right-hand lane at the roundabout. Deffo going to Yarm. It's busy, like. A lot of traffic on the road.'

Nick could hear the Porsche's deep rumble in the background, dropping revs as she approached the roundabout. He could see it in his mind's eye so clearly, because it was a road he'd been on thousands of times.

Then she screamed. 'Oh, my God! Oh, no!'

'What? What's happened? Are you alright?!'

'I don't believe it!'

'Jules! Jules! What's wrong?'

But she'd gone. The engine had been turned off and there was a slam of the car door.

The speaker phone was still on. He listened intently but the noise was too generalised to make out precisely. Sirens sounded in the distance.

He was worried. Very worried. And he couldn't hang around to wait for her. He ran down to the car and set off for the A135 roundabout. It was only 10 minutes away, south to the A66 and west for a junction. He kept his phone on throughout, hoping Julie would come back on the line, but it just hissed with background noise.

As soon as he got within a few hundred yards of the exit, the traffic jammed up and was not moving. The turn off had been blocked by police cars. Even the slightest disruption to the main routes through and around Teesside could bring the whole network to a halt. There were people who had spent approximately 29 per cent of their lives on the Teesside Flyover in traffic jams.

Bollocks to this.

He slung the BMW over onto the hard shoulder and jogged down the turn off, phone in hand. The two police cars blocking the turn off were both unoccupied. Straight away he could see what had happened. A Volvo had crashed into one of the concrete pillars that held up the A66 overhead. Cones and yellow police line tape had been put around the car. Away to the west he could see Julie's distinctive blue Porsche in a jam of cars.

There were four, five - no, seven - cop cars on the scene.

He sprinted down to the roundabout looking for Julie.

'Go back to your car please, sir,' said a copper, coming up to him, as soon as he got near to the roundabout.

'I'm looking for my girlf...for my wife,' It still seemed an odd thing to say. 'I'm worried she was involved in this smash. She was on the phone to me when it happened.'

As he was talking to him he saw Julie in the distance, walking back up the incline to her car, her distinctive yellow-blonde hair standing out against the black tarmac.

He waited until she'd got back into the vehicle.

'Jules! Jules! Can you hear me,' he shouted into his phone. 'I'm over on the other turn off. I've left the BMW on the A66 hard shoulder. It's jammed up. They've shut the road off. What happened?'

Her breath distorted the phone speaker and she spoke quickly and in short bursts. 'God, I don't know. Something...something weird. I'm not even sure what I saw. I'm confused. I might have been wrong...it's all weird.'

'Calm down, Jules. Take some deep breaths.'

He heard her suck air into her nostrils and then make a long slow exhalation.

'The Volvo Barbara Stewart was driving crashed, right? But the person who was driving it wasn't Barbara Stewart. It was her *before* she crashed, but it wasn't her *after* she'd crashed.'

He walked back up the exit to his car, his phone pressed to his ear.

'Are you OK?'

That made her indignant. 'Yes, of course I am. I'm just confused about what I've seen.'

Jo King's words came right back to Nick once again: 'Question all realities'.

CHAPTER 6

It took two hours for traffic to clear from the A66 and it was after 8pm before Nick got home. Julie didn't unlock the door and come in until nearly 9pm.

He gave her a hug. 'I was really worried about you.'

She groaned and shook her head. 'Can I have a massive fucking vodka?'

She followed him into the kitchen as he got a large, tall glass, filled it a third full of vodka and topped it up with fizzy water and lemon juice.

'There you go, I'll get the dinner on.' He put the lamb in the oven and a flame under the veg and poured away the vodka he'd got himself before she'd called, no longer feeling the urge to drink.

She perched on a stool and took a long drink.

'Oh, god, I needed that. What a terrible thing that was.'

'OK. Tell me about it.'

She shook her head slowly.

'The woman I followed from Bedale was Barbara Stewart, right?'

'Right.'

'But the woman driving the car when it crashed, wasn't her.'

Nick looked at her, trying to understand. Was this another reality that had to be questioned?

'Yeah, you said that on the phone. But how?'

'I don't know how. But the woman who was in the car in Bedale wasn't the woman at the wheel of the car that crashed.'

'Was she OK?'

'She'd hurt her head. There was blood on her face, but she seemed OK. They took her away in an ambulance.'

'Did you get to her car?'

'No. Police were there almost immediately. Like, it seemed within seconds. But I could see her from where they stopped me. She looked dazed. But it wasn't Barbara. She looked like her but it wasn't her.' She took another big drink. 'I'd like to talk to Jo about this. I feel exactly like I did in her show. It keeps coming back to me. Like something is happening that feels real, but I know is unreal. Like when she cut her hand off - I knew no-one cuts their hand off like that - but it looked so real it was hard to believe she wasn't doing it. And just like that, I know Barbara can't have got out of the car to be replaced by a lookalike, but it wasn't her in the crash. I saw the car go off the road. She just took the bend too fast and hit the pillar, maybe her brakes failed or something. She smashed into it really hard. The traffic came to a halt, when I got out of the car and began to run down to the crashed car, along with couple of other people, but within seconds a police car had arrived and immediately started cordoning off the scene and kept everyone well away. One of those coppers stopped me and these other two blokes before we got to the car. I wasn't far away - maybe 15 or 20 feet - but I could see the woman at the wheel wasn't Barbara. She was younger but had shoulder-length white hair and a green linen suit.'

'At the risk of stating the obvious, she can't have become a *different* person. It mustn't have been her to start with.'

That infuriated Julie.

'It *was*! It was her! I knew you'd think I'd made a mistake, but I didn't. It was definitely her in Bedale.' She snapped at him, suddenly looking very like her mother when she was narked.

'OK, then she must have been replaced at some point, though why, I can't imagine.'

'It feels like I've seen a ghost or something. I feel spooked to buggery about it.'

'But to take the Jo King analogy again, she presented a reality to us which wasn't real. It was all a trick. There was a way to explain it all. So it must be the same for this crash. There must be an explanation; even if it looks like the impossible has happened, it hasn't, it just looks that way. Did you take any photos?'

She took out her phone and pushed it across the counter at him. He plugged it into his laptop and downloaded the pictures from it.

'They're not very good. I took them from behind the wheel.'

There were seven shots. He arranged them on the screen by the time they were taken.

He tapped at the screen with a pen. 'This first one was taken nearly 30 minutes before the others...'

...that was just outside of Bedale, then we got onto the A1 and it was really busy. I couldn't take any because she was a few cars in front.'

'Cool...OK...then this first one is of the woman you're certain was Barbara.'

'It *was* her!' she thumped her fist down.

Nick made it as large as possible on the screen. It had been taken as the Volvo had been taking a sharp right-hand bend and showed her almost side on to Julie, who was two cars back. It was quite blurred, for obvious reasons. He made some adjustments in Photoshop to try and sharpen up the image.

'There. That looks better,' he said, increasing the contrast and reducing the colour saturation. 'That really does look like the woman we met on the stairs. The shoulder-length white hair is really distinctive.'

'And she's got the strong chin. Remember in that photo outside of the art school? We said she had a solid jaw. And look, she's wearing that paisley silk scarf and you can see the top of the green linen jacket. She was wearing those when we saw her.'

Nick nodded. It *was* very like Barbara Stewart.

He went to the next photos. 'These were taken on the A66?'

'Yeah, just before I called you.'

The first thing to notice about them was that they were certainly all of the same person because all six had been taken within two minutes of each other whilst on the road. Four were really no use, though, because all they captured was the back of the driver's' head. You could tell it was white but that was all.

'I pulled out into the middle lane to get those two,' she said, pointing to photos which had been taken from the right side of the Volvo. They both showed someone with shoulder-length white hair and a green jacket. Julie tapped at the screen. 'That looks superficially like the same person I photographed in Bedale, but when she'd crashed, she was a more slight woman, smaller than Barbara was when we met her on the stairs. So, given that I saw her car from this point to the point she crashed, this must be the woman who crashed, she's dressed exactly the same.'

'Did you lose sight of her car for any length of time?'

Julie shook her head. 'I had her in sight all the way up the A1, then she took the A66 turning, south of Darlo. There's a long curve in the road and she went round it ahead of me by about 9 or 10 seconds. I lost sight of her there, but there wasn't enough time to stop, get out and put someone else in the car, though. No way.'

Nick tugged on his stubble. 'No, but enough time for someone in a *different* car to replace her. You come around the bend and the Volvo is still up ahead, but it's a different one. The one with Barbara in has turned off and disappeared down a country lane.'

'But it hasn't, has it?' she pointed at the car in the first picture and then in the later ones. It's a navy blue Volvo 440. Look, it's the same.'

'It's the same colour and type of car, but we can't see the plate in the first shot. Here it's YK 545 TWD in all the later shots. YK is a York plate, by the way.'

She stared at the pictures as closely as possible, her brow furrowed deeply.

'The thing is, Jules, let's just assume some sort of identity swap has somehow been done. It's not been done for your benefit, has it? They weren't waiting to just fool you. That's impossible. So even if we accept what you're saying is true - which is a big leap of faith - exactly why was the switch done? Who was intended to be fooled by it, what is the point?'

'It's all insane. It makes me feel like I'm going mad.'

'Often, the easiest answer is the correct answer. And the easiest answer here is that it really was the same person all along - whoever that is.'

She scowled at him.

'It bloody was Barbara. I'm telling you and it *wasn't* her in the crashed car.' She was insistent.

Nick wasn't going to argue any more, but quietly felt that it was all one woman and very unlikely to be the same woman they'd seen in Edinburgh, no matter how like her it looked. The photos didn't disprove that. Maybe it was all just a coincidence that someone wearing apparently similar clothes to those Barbara Stewart had been wearing when they met her had lost control of her car and crashed. It was just a green linen suit and a scarf. There must be lots of variations of that type of outfit. Maybe they were too busy constructing a reality to see that it was just similar people in similar clothes, not the same person in the same clothes.

'Well, one thing for sure is that we'll not learn anything more just staring at these,' he said, getting up and taking the chops out of the oven. 'Come on, let's eat.'

He served up the food and got cutlery out.

'So were your team-building days any good?'

'Yeah, it was fine. And I got the car going quickly as well. She's running smoothly again.' She let out a tense sigh and took another drink. 'Jo's show has messed with my mind, y'know. I keep seeing everything as some sort of artifice. Like life is being played out for me, rather than just happening. That's just insane though, isn't it?'

He looked at her and made a skeptical face.

'Yeah, it's bonkers. Life happens to us. It's not being constructed specifically for us as individuals. It's not a play put on for our benefit. If it is I want my ticket money refunded because there have been too many mistakes in my play, half the cast don't know their lines and at times it's been obscene and X-rated!'

She snorted a half laugh, rubbed her eyes and pushed her plate away after eating. 'The X-rated bits are usually the best bits. Yeah, I'm totally going off on one about this.' She sighed and collected her thoughts. 'I suppose all that happened was I, along with lots of other people at that junction, witnessed a car crash. That's it. Whoever it was. The police were on the scene quickly because that's a busy junction and they were probably traffic cops watching the flow of traffic.'

She rubbed at her forehead.

'That's a good thought, Jules. They do often have patrol cars around there because there are often breakdowns on the hard shoulder and such to deal with. It jams up so easily, so they've got to be on the ball. But I agree with you about Jo's show. It keeps coming back to me, as well.'

He got back onto his laptop and did a search on the *Gazette* website for any report of the crash. It was now four hours since it had happened, so it would just have been updated. Nothing a local newspaper website likes more than traffic accident stories because they affect so many people and everyone can relate to them.

'If it's not been reported I'm going to go into paranoid mode, though,' said Julie, finishing her vodka. 'They were lovely chops, by the way. You do them just right, so they're still pink. Posh get. I dunno where you learned to do that, we were brought up to make sure all meat was well-done to the point of incineration.'

'It's on here, alright,' said Nick, clicking on a link. 'A *fatal* crash at the roundabout on A135 to Yarm. Cynthia Thorpe, 61, died as a result of her injuries.' He looked up, his heart beating a bit faster. 'So it really wasn't Barbara. Poor woman.'

But Julie wasn't having it. She stood up and jutted her jaw out, exactly as her mother did when in the middle of an argument. She wagged her finger in mid-air.

'No, no, no. Whoever she was, wasn't that badly hurt. It looked like she'd busted her nose, that's all.'

'But an ambulance came?'

'Yeah, within five minutes. They took her out of the car on a stretcher. There was some blood, but she wasn't fatally injured. Those Volvos are like tanks and the airbag went off. I'm sorry. That report is wrong. The police are making out she's died. She hasn't died. That's the truth of it and

I'm not having it any other way. It's some sort of deception. She was dressed as Barbara and they want to make out Barbara is dead.'

'But Jules, man, think about it, they - whoever "they" are - can't want to do that. They've given her name as Cynthia Thorpe,' said Nick, pointing to the article. 'If *they* wanted to make out Barbara was dead, they'd have used her name.'

'I don't care.' She was adamant. 'The whole point of this is to kill off Barbara, but no-one has actually died. There was a switch somewhere along the line and this Cynthia woman took her place and deliberately crashed the car. It's all a big deception to allow her to get away with the murder of Grayson-Thomas. This is the next stage in that plot.'

Just when it seemed like she was coming to her senses, this had thrown her back into conspiracy mode. Nick knew it was all nonsense but just wanted to diffuse her emotions. There was no point in arguing about it. After all, they didn't stand to gain or lose either way, whoever it was, but he was fairly sure that Julie was not just chasing the wrong dog up the wrong tree, but that it wasn't even a dog and there was no tree.

'Well, we can ask Jo what she thinks about it soon enough, because she's coming down to meet Jeff when she visits her parents next week.'

Julie tied up her hair into a ponytail with a hair band and finished her drink.

'Is she? How do you know that? Eee, is she seeing Jeff?'

'Oh, yeah, she called me to get Jeff's number and has since called him, and just to feed your paranoia a bit more, she also told me about what she thought was a fake policeman who interviewed her.' He explained what she'd said.

Julie put her hands on her hips, resting on one leg, giving her an almost indignant pose. 'Oh, well, that's it - there's definitely something going on. Listen, I've just remembered something. When we met Mandy Beale she said about John Grayson-Thomas, "Why is that name familiar?" Remember?'

'Yeah. I do. Yeah...it's a very distinctive, probably unique name.'

'That means she'd heard of him for some reason...and now the woman who shot him is dead on Teesside? Come on, that's not a coincidence.'

'Jules, wind it back - Barbara is *not* dead. It was a woman called Cynthia in the Volvo. You *know* that wasn't Barbara. That was the point you were making. It *wasn't* her who crashed. You're getting confused about your own conspiracy theory, which, even if you're right, means Barbara is actually alive.'

She knitted her eyebrows together in a frown and then slapped herself on the cheek. 'Shit, yeah. You're right. I'm getting so messed up about this. It's frying my mind.'

Nick was inclined to agree but was losing faith in his ability to discern what they were making up from what had actually happened. Reality seemed to exist on unreliable foundations, built on shifting sands.

They took a night cap of hot milk with a splash of whisky in to bed.

Nick sat and wrote some notes for his novel on his laptop.

'Have you felt OK all today?' she said, a hand on his back, tracing his spine with her index finger with a lovely, small, intimate touch that made him shiver a little. Life's biggest gestures are often the smallest.

'Yeah, fine. I was OK yesterday, as well. I think the depression was just a one-off response to the holiday and the drinking and everything.'

'Yeah. I think so, too. I think it was a byproduct of the emotional high from the wedding and the festival, coupled with exhaustion, equaling a major downer. Not the end of the world. Just inevitable.' She nuzzled his neck affectionately.

Nick saved his work and began to close windows on his computer, saving the photos from Julie's phone as he did so.

'So what was sleeping over at Northdean like?'

'Oh, I've not had chance to tell you, have I? It was ace. Like a posh country house hotel. We all got our own rooms. Wood-paneled walls and a lovely big queen-sized bed. Slept like a baby. It was so quiet. Reminded me of our old house south of Yarm out in the countryside. Owls were hooting outside.'

'Sounds good.'

She gave him a funny look. Almost bashful, which wasn't a regular look for her.

'What?' he said.

'I have a confession to make.'

'You didn't wet the bed, did you?'

'Ha...in a manner of speaking.' She made a wiggling gesture with the middle finger of her right hand and scrunched her face up.

He laughed. 'What does that mean when it's at home?'

'That was me last night.'

'Eh? Sorry, I'm not getting you.'

She frowned at him. 'C'mon lad, don't be so gauche. What does a girl do when she's on her own with a lovely naked picture of her husband on her phone?'

It dawned on him. 'Oh...ha ha...I see. Really?'

She raised an arched eyebrow. 'Yes. Really.'

'That's unusual for you.'

'Is it? Well that's as much as you know,' she said, only half-joking. 'I don't always tell you about what I get up to when I'm on my own, or when you're asleep, just like you don't always tell me. I like to have something private. I don't usually have such a vivid visual stimulus, though.'

He nodded and smiled. 'Any good?'

'Not as good as the real thing, but much quicker. Ha ha. Turns out I'm better than you!'

'Well, you should be an expert, you've had the equipment all your life - I only get occasional access to it. You'll have to give me a photo of you similarly compromised, for just such occasions.'

'You don't need pictures, your mind is full of filth as it is.'

'That's true, actually. While we're confessing to self-abuse, I had to relieve myself in the same manner while thinking of us in Laguna Beach. It was the pills.'

She tutted. 'I don't mind as long as you're hygienic and don't wipe your wotsit on a clean towel.'

'I wouldn't do that. I only ever use the curtains.'

'Good boy. You've got to have standards.' She turned over and put out the light out.

The crashed Volvo didn't even make it onto the local news in the morning. The website didn't update with any further news and by the end of the day, it was as if nothing had happened. That wasn't so unusual, though. If you want to have your death swept away and quickly dismissed, die in a traffic accident. It often seems as though the congestion it causes is treated with more importance than the life that is lost, with much more time spent on it than on who the person was killed. But maybe that's as it should be. The living have to get on with living, at least until it's their turn to hold up a major route with their own untimely, unexpected death. The story was over and held no more interest for the media.

Over the next few days, life fell back into its normal routine. Julie went to work, Nick stayed at home and wrote and dropped in to see Jeff, Emily and Matty for an hour every other afternoon. On the Saturday he and Julie went to see Hartlepool United play at home because the Boro were away.

Afterwards they went out for a meal at a country pub in Sadberge and then put some flowers on his mother's grave in Sadberge churchyard. Nick said a little prayer to her, asking, as he always did, that she be happy and at peace, whilst apologising to her for all the years when he hadn't been sympathetic enough towards her. He always came away feeling a little more at peace than when he'd arrived, though was never quite sure why. Perhaps it was his mother's soft, kind spirit infusing into him. He wished now that he had a grave where he could visit his dad. Just somewhere to go and think a little, because it was a positive thing. But his ashes had been scattered to the four winds at Acklam Crem. His mother was still in Sadberge, but who knew where his dad was? Come back to me, dad. Some day.

Julie drove them back home in the Porsche.

'You know how you were hypnotised so that you can have a piss in public? Is that still working, do you reckon?' she said.

'I assume so, yeah. I don't think it wears off. I certainly don't have the old trouble anymore.'

'That is so weird. Does it feel weird to you?'

'Not really. It just feels normal, even though logically, I know it's a big change.'

'And you've not dried up in the toilets under pressure once?'

'Nope, and I never will now. I know that. Why do you ask?'

She thought for a moment. 'Well, I was thinking how that just proves Jo is right. How you see things and how you feel about them is all intrinsically linked to how you've been conditioned, or how you've conditioned yourself. And actually, we learn that every day at work. Women arrive thinking how things is is how they'll always be, and can see no other life than the one they're suffering from at home. In a way, they've been brainwashed by the abusive partner to think this is how life must be. They've had their ego and self-respect broken down and down to make them controllable and we have to try and give them a perspective and make them believe that a way out is possible, at some point in the future. You can't force that sort of thinking, you've just got to be supportive and let them know that if they need us, we'll be there for them.'

'Everything is definitely relative and nothing is absolute. She's right about that. It's had a really massive effect on both of us. We must have referred to that show, literally, almost every day since we saw it.'

'Oh, totally. It has, yeah. I get echoes of it all the time. I wonder if we'll see her when she comes down to see Jeff?'

'Do you think it'll work between them?'

'You never know. He might give us a ring and rope us in for a drink if he feels like he needs support or a bail out.'

That call came at 8pm on Tuesday night.

'Now then big man, how goes it?' said Nick, feet up on the sofa, at the time.

'We're in the Masham. We've just had a great dinner in Big Meat.'

'What did you have?'

'We both had the Mega Mixed Grill. It's a thing of wonder and beauty. Have you had it?'

'Yeah, I'm drooling just thinking about it. Kidneys, liver, pork and beef sausage, err...what else is on it?'

'A little pork chop, steak medallion, slice of black pudding, tomatoes stewed with basil, onion rings in a tempura batter, a thick slice of smoked duck breast and, crucially, a very small amount of watercress...'

'...well, it's the watercress that makes it.'

'Totally, aye. I like how Mike the Meat is serving it - basically on a massive wooden chopping board. That place is the best restaurant I've ever been in. It's all top-rank nosh, but not at top-rank prices.'

'Did Jo dig it?'

'Very much. She's at the bar getting in the whisky.'

'Is it all going OK?'

'Great, yeah. Fancy coming down? Be nice to see youse two. She was asking after you.'

'Yeah, if you don't think we'll get in the way.'

'Not at all. I want you to hear Jo's new ideas about the Barbara Stewart business. She's got some interesting info.'

'Really? OK, man, we'll get a cab down to Hartburn Village. Shall I wear a rugby shirt, so that I look right in the Masham?'

'Aye, you'd better. Change your names to Tristram and Jocasta, as well, while you're at it. Make sure you join the Conservative Party before you arrive, an' all.'

Nick grinned to himself as he rang off.

'Was that Jeff?' said Julie, looking away from some football on the TV.

'Yeah. They went to Big Meat.'

'Wish we could afford to. Always nice to get a look at Mike the Meat.'

'I'm more interested in the Mega Mixed Grill.'

She gave him a lustful look. 'Oh, god, aye. It's to die for. I wish we had enough money to eat that amount of quality protein.'

'I said we'd go down and meet them in the Masham.'

She pulled a face. 'Aw, can't we go to the Stocky Arms?'

'Aye, well, we can have one in the Masham and then move on. Jeff sounded very relaxed. Said it was going well.'

She gave him a toothy smile. 'Do you think he's going to ask her to stay over?' She arched her eyebrows at him.

Nick nodded. 'Oh, aye. I reckon so. Especially as they're only a couple of minutes walk from his house.'

She made an excited little face. 'God. He's about a foot taller than she is. How does that work for sex?'

'In the normal way, I think.'

'Ha ha...I suppose so. It'd be like having a huge wardrobe lying on you, though.'

'Oh, I think she'd have to go on top...he'd crush the poor lass.'

She got up. 'Do I have to get changed?'

'You're just wearing old jeans and a Gram Parsons t-shirt. Do you think they'll chuck you out, like?'

'I could put a smart top on...and a bra...and knickers...no, ha ha...I've surprisingly got knickers on, which is unusual when we're at home and you're on a high dose of Phenibut. Might as well not bother, really, 'cos they're off more times than they're on.' She stuck her tongue out at him, playfully.

'Remember, this is Stockton, darlin' and thus, knickers are never need-ed. Knickers are a bourgeois self-indulgence on Teesside. Owee, let's go and get a cab.'

They walked across the High Street to the cab rank outside of what Nick still thought of as the Odeon, even though it hadn't been a cinema for decades and was now criminally derelict.

As Nick paid the driver, Julie got out and hitched up her old Levis.

'It's a lovely summer evening,' she said, looking around her at the leafy village, as the car drove off.

He put his arms around her and pulled her in, kissing her on the head.

'It is and you are a lovely woman.'

'Aw. Come here, you.' She kissed him on the lips. 'What a nice, happy man you are now. So pleased about that.'

'Drugs are a great thing, eh,' he said, putting his hand in her back pock-et as they walked up to the pub.

'Yeah, god bless drugs,' she said, pecking him on the lips again and pushing a strand of hair off his forehead.

Jeff and Jo were sitting in the corner where Nick had sat when he was a teenager, when he would drink lager and lime and read books.

'Now then, you two. Good to see you again, Jo,' said Julie, giving her a kiss on the cheek. Nick hated greeting people that you only knew a bit. How did you know what to say and do? Handshake? OK, but did you do an old-fashioned one or an upwards grip, or some sort of knuckle bump? Did you hug? If so, do you kiss on one cheek, or both, or not at all? It was all fraught with difficulty and little seemed gained by it.

He was glad to just go to the bar and gesture to Jeff to see if he wanted a drink.

'Two Bushmills,' he said.

Nick ordered them along with a double vodka for Julie and a tonic water for himself. As he did so he could hear all the chatter among Julie and Jo and Jeff, but he knew he didn't have to take part, which was exactly how he liked it. Groups of more than two were always a bit of challenge to him. The more people present, the less he could manage to say. Crowds intimidated him and made him clam up.

'So how was Edinburgh overall, then?' said Julie.

Jo was wearing a floral Hawaiian-style shirt in vivid primary colours, a pair of loose-fitting cerise cotton pants and green baseball boots. Her hair was dyed vivid, Ziggy Stardust orange and was spikey on top with her lop-sided fringe. A couple of the locals were already eying her with a degree of surprise, like this was still 1956 and they'd never seen such a thing.

'I sold out six nights. Only three of those weren't discounted. Basically, on each Saturday night, I pulled in enough casual punters to fill the room. It was OK for a first run but I've come out five grand down.'

'Ouch,' said Julie, pulling a face. 'But it was good exposure?'

'Yeah, and I got a five-minute spot on that big show they film for TV at the Festival Theatre, so who knows what will come from that? I mean, that show can make you a star when it airs, in the winter.'

'What did you do in just five minutes?' said Nick.

She made a sawing gesture across her wrist. 'It went down well. There were some proper screams 'cos I came out and just did it without saying much. I just made out I'd messed up a trick and had decided to cut my hand off in a fit of self-harm...as you do!'

Jeff laughed a little. 'What a way to make a living. Limb hacking every night. I dig it so much.'

'The important thing is to remember that your audience hasn't seen it before so it's a shock to almost all of them,' said Jo. 'Except for those who've seen me do it on You-bloody-Tube. Punters filming you is a killer to a show like mine. I won't be able to do it much longer. I'm going to have to come up with some new shit.'

'I bet it's a good feeling of power,' said Julie. 'Knowing that you're going to provoke a reaction.'

'It is, but the hard thing is to keep the element of surprise going. Once you've not died after stabbing yourself in the eye or cutting your hand off, how can you shock people one more time? They quickly become immune to the horror element. I'm still working on pacing and timing of the stunts. I moved the hand chop right to the end of the show because that's so gross that there's no way back from it.'

'I thought that at the time,' said Nick. 'It's so extreme that everything else after that seemed less shocking. Even when you hit the man in the face.'

'You should've told us, then!' She jabbed a finger at him in her strident way.

'Sorry.'

'So who was this so-called copper, do you think?' said Julie. 'The one you thought wasn't actually police?'

'Ah, yeah.' She held up a thumb and bent it right back.

'Ow, is that a trick?' said Nick.

'Nope, just double jointed.' She tapped on it with a finger. 'That was someone trying to find out what I knew about Barbara. As I've been telling Jeff over 50 kilos of fried meat, I've been doing some digging into Barbara and Frank.'

'Did you break in again?' said Julie.

'I tried but it's been locked with two mortice locks now, so there's no way I could get in.'

'So Frank has been back to do that, then?'

'Him or someone else. But I was out all day and night, so that was easy enough to do without me seeing them and there's no-one else in that building. I never heard or saw anyone there again, though.'

'So what did you do?'

'Well, sometimes the postie doesn't bring the mail up, he leaves it at the bottom of the stairs. Happens all the time in Edinburgh. And a few days ago, I noticed he'd left some with a rubber band around. Now, I'm not getting any mail up there and obviously the flat you stayed in is owned by Stevie Salmon so he doesn't get any mail at all. So it all had to be for Frank and Barbara, so I half-inched it. In amongst it was this - ' she took out a brown envelope. 'It's a voting form - you know, for the electoral register. They send them out every year to check that the same people are living at the address.'

Nick took it from her. 'What's so significant about this?' he said, passing it to Julie.

'It's only addressed to Frank Stewart,' said Julie, right away. 'Ours is to both of us. We're both on the electoral roll so everything is jointly addressed.'

'Well spotted,' said Jo. 'There's also something from HMRC to him along with a bank statement.'

'So there's nothing with her name on?' said Nick.

'No, and there should be.'

'Therefore, she doesn't actually exist?' said Jeff, his index finger raised.

'Well she does exist, in one sense - we talked to a woman who worked with her at the art school for a year,' said Nick. 'To them, she exists. And we both met her.'

Jo held up her right hand. 'Barbara is like my false hand. She's there to be disposed of when her job is done and her job was to kill John Grayson-Thomas. Now that's been done, has anyone seen her again? No. She's disappeared off the map.'

A thought came to Nick. 'My friend Josh said something interesting the other day. He said the best way to disappear would be to become invisible. And that's exactly what Barbara has done. She shot the man and since then, hasn't been seen. She's become invisible.'

'Ah. Not quite,' said Julie. 'Don't forget, I saw her in Bedale.' She explained the situation and about the crashed car.

Jo listened to the explanation with her fingertips pressed together, her eyes flicking from Julie's lips, to her eyes, to Nick, back to Julie. It was as though she was always taking things in. Weighing up a situation, her mind whirring at speed.

She pulled back her thumb again. 'There are only two explanations for that. One. It was never her at any point or, two, it *was* her and there was a switch. There are no other explanations. None.' She drew a line with a chop of her hand.

She was so certain of herself. Nick could never imagine having that much faith in his own perception of anything. He'd operated his whole life on the basis that he was probably misunderstanding things.

'It *was* her in Bedale,' said Julie, equally certain.

'No, what you mean is *you're* certain it was her - you don't *know* it actually was her - you don't have proof, it's all your perception. What makes me doubt you is that you'd been thinking about Frank and her, having found out he was a headmaster at that school, so your mind was preconditioned to see her.'

'I *did* see her and I'm sick of saying that. I did. It was her.' Julie was more frustrated than annoyed about it now.

'No. Stop saying that. Reconsider, Julie. You *think* you saw her. That's not the same thing.'

'That's like saying, that I only think I can see you here, whereas I *know* I can see you and I did see her,' said Julie.

'It isn't the same at all. For a start, two other people can confirm I'm here and I'm also able to confirm it too. Even so, that's still not 100 per cent proof.'

Julie looked at her in disbelief. Jo rapped on the table.

'OK, I know you don't believe me. So I'll prove it to you. I can make you see something that isn't there, just by suggesting it is. Your brain is trained to see things it thinks should be there and it can do that even when I've told you what I'm going to do, right?'

'With respect, you can't, Jo,' said Julie, crossing her arms.

Jeff glanced at Nick and twitched an eyebrow. Any sentence that begins with the words 'with respect' could be a prelude to a row, if you weren't careful.

'Aye, well, like I said, I know youse don't believe me, but I'll show you.' Jo took out a piece of paper and wrote out three sentences in a neat print and then pushed it across the table to Julie.

'Read that once and tell me how many words are missing from the sentences. Read it out loud carefully so that you've no doubt.'

She squinted a little and read out loud: ' "The world is a funny place, things you are real are not real. Things you have no doubt about, are false. Something is often missing".' She stopped and checked. 'There's one missing word in the first sentence. Things you *something* are real.'

Julie put it down and smiled at Jo, clearly thinking she had won the challenge.

'No. You're wrong. There are two. Check it again, make sure you've no *doubt* about it.'

Julie did as she said and read it out again. 'No, there's just one.'

Jo took the paper from her and held it up so both Nick and Julie could see it - Jeff peered around at it too. She put her finger under each word as she said them. 'I told you twice to have no *doubt*, didn't I? I did that on purpose so when you came to this sentence, "Things you have no *doubt* about, are false", you'd get it wrong.' Nick watched her point to each word and even as she did it slowly, he didn't see it at first. In fact, he had to do a double take to make sure the word *doubt* wasn't actually there, because he'd read it twice as though it was.

Julie let out a small yelp as she spotted it, putting her hand to her mouth in surprise. 'My god! The word *doubt* isn't there. I could have sworn it was. I was sure. I read that three times. Good grief.'

Jo grinned. 'I told you, your brain is trained to make sense of things. One word was obviously missing in the first sentence, and when your brain spotted that, it stopped being vigilant. My saying "doubt" filled in the gap for you. Your brain is always wanting to make patterns it understands. I said the word "doubt" and your brain hoovered it up and put it where it should have been in the sentence and did so without even telling you. See?'

Julie kept her hand over her mouth, a little shocked. 'That was just lucky though, surely,' she said. 'I was just in a hurry to get it right.'

Jo took a piece of paper out of her shoulder bag. It was a photo of a stately home.

'I'll prove it again for you. This is Riverside Manor in Richmond. Reputedly one of the most haunted houses in England. Look at the windows and tell me what you can see.'

Jeff got up and looked over Nick's shoulder again. Julie leaned and looked closely. 'I can see a girl standing at the upstairs window,' she said. 'She's got long fair hair.'

'And there's an old man with a grey beard down here in the corner,' said Nick. 'Can you see them both, Jeff?'

'Yep. Deffo,' said the big man, sitting back down, nodding, laughing a little to himself.

Jo nodded. 'Everyone can see those two figures, right? They've been used as evidence of the ghosts for years. Some say they even know who they are. They've tied it down to people in history who lived here. But the truth is this - there are no figures at any of the windows.' She looked at each of them.

'There are - you can see them clearly,' said Jeff, taking the printed sheet off her and looking at it again. 'Yeah, look there's the girl's hair and there's the old dude's beard.' He pointed with a thick forefinger.

Jo shook her head. 'That's what your brain wants you to see. I can see them as well. But they are not there. Here...look...'

She pulled out another printed sheet of the old manor.

'This was taken at a distance. The first picture is an enlargement of this one. When the blow-up was made, there was a flaw in the negative which allowed the parts you think are the girl's hair and the man's beard to be overexposed. What you think are their faces, are just indistinct shadows and light caused by that process. This is the original photo.'

Nick stared at it. The windows were clear, no-one was there, but it was the same photo because all the other factors - a bird on a fence, a gardener bending over a wheelbarrow and an array of garden tools lying on the gravel in front of the house were all exactly the same.

'It was assumed that the enlargement had somehow "caught" the ghost, but in fact, it was eventually, after many years, scientifically proven that it was just a flaw in the blow-up print. We can all see the girl and the old man and not just streaks of light on the negative, but that does not mean they were there. Moreover, you looked for them because I said, "look at the windows and tell me what you see". In doing that, I conditioned your mind to see *something*. See? You went into the exercise looking for something to see.'

Jeff laughed and patted Jo on the back. 'I've got to hand it to you, Jo, you're bloody good. I feel like my mind is a slug which has just had salt poured on it!'

Jo was pleased with herself, having made her point so categorically.

Julie pursed her lips together and folded her arms across her chest. 'I hate this.'

'Why?' said Jo, enjoying herself.

'Because it undermines everything.'

'Exactly! I told you that from day one!' She was triumphant and cocky, bouncing in her seat, a little.

'But what good does that do us?' said Julie. 'We need to believe our eyes or it might stop us from doing something that has to be done. We can't doubt everything, it makes life impossible.'

Jo was dismissive. 'Oh, owee man, but that's not what I'm saying. If you see someone crossing the road and stepping out in front of a car, I'm not saying you should stop and wonder if the car is real. I'm just saying that when someone tells you something is a fact and wants to prove something with this fact, you should always wonder who is telling you this, why and how they know this is the truth. And when you think you've seen something, but can't prove it, it's worth questioning if you could be wrong. You are sure you saw Barbara Stewart, but can't prove it. Your photos only prove someone who looked like her and was wearing similar clothes to clothes she once wore, was driving the car. We already know you are able to see a word that isn't there and two figures that were not there, either. So it's far from impossible that it wasn't Barbara at all, that you fooled yourself into thinking it was and the woman actually was Cynthia Thorpe all along.'

Julie had no comeback to her. Nick had never seen her so comprehensively beaten in an argument before. She was usually so clever that, even when in the wrong, she could often create a twist of logic in order to win an argument. But not this time. Jo had proven her point very well. It did eat away at what you thought you knew and it was disturbing, showing how we can all be manipulated by our own minds, or by someone else, into thinking something untrue was unquestionably a fact.

'So to go back to this shooting in Edinburgh,' said Jeff, tapping the table. '*Did* that really happen, do you reckon, Jo? *Are* we being fed a fiction?'

Jo shook her head.

'We just can't know. Maybe it did happen, but we can't take that as a fact. It's still all closed off in there. I took a look before I left. No-one has been allowed in to see the brains on the wall, have they? There have been no mentions of witnesses to the shooting and no public mention of Barbara Stewart's name. The only thing I will say is I am certain the scenario we're being presented with isn't the whole truth. How much the police know and are just not telling is impossible for us to tell. The only so-called proof of the murder is the picture that was in the paper.'

'But that very assumption could just be a fiction you've made up,' said Julie. 'Just like you say me seeing Barbara in Bedale is.'

'It could be, but I'd lay good odds that I'm definitely right. Too much about it is odd.' There was the arrogance again, very much part of her make-up.

Nick watched as Julie jutted her jaw out and was clearly going to start an argument, but then decided not to and took a drink instead.

'It's interesting all of this, but I tell you what I keep coming back to...' said Nick, spinning a beer mat around between forefinger and thumb

'...and that's that it isn't anything to do with me or Julie or Jeff or you, Jo. OK, we met the Stewarts, but that's all. We just stumbled into it. It hasn't all been done for our benefit, so why should we be bothered about it? Crimes happen all the time somewhere.'

But that wasn't good enough for Jo.

'Well, if there's a been a crime committed and if we can work out how or why, then we've a duty to do that. We stumbled into it accidentally, but we can't let people get away with shit like that,' she said, in an unexpected declaration of civic duty. 'I probably didn't make this point well enough in my show, but that's one of the inspirations behind it. That we, the people, like, should be responsible for one another. Society is a collective, isn't it? But the powerful divide and rule, don't they? And they do that most successfully by presenting warped versions of reality to turn us against each other. They tell us they've got solutions to the problems we face, but those solutions suit them, not us.'

Nick liked the sound of that and he knew for a fact Julie would. It played right to all her most passionately held political beliefs. And that aside, it was an intriguing mystery. Since they'd made a bit of a habit of stumbling into one problem or another, and had managed to find a way through them to the truth, maybe they could do the exact same thing here.

'I saw a good joke the other day,' said Jeff. 'There's a bloke with a huge bag of biscuits standing next to another with one biscuit, who, in turn, is standing next to an illegal immigrant. "Careful", the bloke with all the biscuits says to the other bloke, "that foreign bloke is going to steal your biscuit".'

They all laughed. 'That's exactly it, isn't it?' said Jo. 'Unless we wake up and see things as they really are, we'll keep being bossed around by the people with the power. I need to make that into a much bigger thing in the show. Make it more overtly political.'

'What you're saying is totally correct, as far as I'm concerned - but you're right - it didn't come over that much in your show. It's quite non-political and what you're saying is *very* political. Revolutionary, even,' said Julie.

'The thing is, Jules, if we're going to find out what really happened, we can't go to the police about it. They've done nothing so far. They may or may not have sent someone to talk to me and you two, as well, but what good has it done? I don't get the sense that they're very proactive. So we'll have to get the evidence and then go to the media about it.'

'None of us even live there,' said Julie.

'That shouldn't stop us. Anyway, it's only three hours on the train from here. Besides, it's not just doing what is right, it's got the making of a brilliant theme for a show. "Life: Delusion or Illusion?!" I can see it now and it'd make a great feature for you to write, Nick. Sell it to a Sunday paper for a fortune.'

'And Emily said the same thing,' added Jeff.

They were right, too. It was exactly the sort of exposé that a paper would love. If there was murder and a police cover-up, there had to be money in it.

'I reckon the key to this, is finding out about the man who was killed, John Grayson-Thomas,' said Jeff. 'If he *was* shot, then there has to be a grudge, if he wasn't and it is a big fake, then why him? Why is he involved in it? He's the one it revolves around and, whatever is going on with the police, they have at least named him.'

'Good point,' said Nick. 'Maybe we can research a lot about him without going back up there.'

'And we know Frank Stewart was a headmaster at Northdean School. So we should be able to dig up a lot more about him there. I'll ask my friend Caroline who works there, to see if there's a record of his time there,' said Julie.

'This is good, people,' said Jo, looking from one to the other of them with a happy grin on her face. 'I was hoping you'd be up for this.'

'If you get a big hit show out of it, can we all have a royalty?' asked Jeff.

Jo laughed. 'No, but you can have all my old prosthetic hands. Deal?'

'When I said I needed an extra pair of hands in the shop, that isn't exactly what I had in mind,' said Jeff.

'So, are you heading back to London tomorrow?' said Julie.

'Yeah, I've got gigs later this week.'

'Where do you live?'

'Hoxton.'

'Oh yeah. I lived around there in the early 90s when it was a shit hole and a long way from being an up-and-coming trendy place,' said Julie. 'I lived down there for nearly 10 years.'

'I've been down for two and I totally hate it. I'm ready to come back to the northeast. I hate the plastic bloody place. It's shit and it pretends it's sugar. People live in tiny little places which cost a fortune and they try and pretend like it's brilliant. It fucking isn't.'

'Do you find that they're often really culturally narrow but all think they're absolutely the most sophisticated people on earth?' said Julie.

'Oh, god, yeah. They think being in London gives them cultural superiority.'

'Totally right. I was always shouting the odds about that after a few drinks,' said Julie.

'Yeah, I know *exactly* what you mean. Did you find that you turn into a more gobby Northern bitch than you ever are normally?'

Julie laughed loudly. 'That's my whole 1990s life, right there, sister.'

Jo held up a hand for Julie to hi-five, something Julie never normally did but joined in with, anyway.

Nick cast a glance at Jeff, who was already looking at him. They both knew. Women sometimes think that men have no idea about how women relate to each other and they'd often be right, but it was obvious to both Nick and Jeff that Julie and Jo were created out of the same cultural DNA.

'I dunno man, the idea of moving back to the Boro hardly fills me with joy. But being back in the northeast in general, is great. You do feel like you're with friends and I never feel like that in that there Londinium. Where do you guys live?'

'Green Dragon Yard, off the High Street,' said Nick. 'It's small but cheap.'

'Oh, yeah, I know those places. You'd pay £5,000 a month for one of those flats in some toilet part of London. It's wrong, and I won't be told it's not. Y'know what I like best about being on Teesside? Knowing that I'm not standing next to some Tory wanker.'

'You're in the Masham, Jo. That's more likely here than anywhere else in the area,' said Jeff, tugging on his beard.

'Aye, I get you - and there's some right Tory bitches in here, did you see them, Jules? By the door. All big foreheads, golf club husbands and sensible Marksies knickers? Urgh! The sort of people who think being a bit alternative is changing which brand of olive oil they buy.'

Julie laughed. 'I'm not against sensible underwear, but I know just what you mean.'

They hi-fived each other again.

'Owee, let's go to the Stockton Arms,' said Jeff.

They walked through the village and up to the pub on Darlington Lane. Julie and Jo were deep in conversation as they went. Nick and Jeff walked slowly behind.

'Look at them, they're really getting on now,' said Nick. 'Is it just me, Jeff, or are they really alike in some ways? Not physically, but character-wise.'

'It's not just you. They're cut from the same cloth. Both sure of themselves. Jo is more arty than Jules but we're never going to win an argument with either of them, are we?'

'Yeah, they're totally the boss of us.'

'I don't mind that. When you see husbands or boyfriends who are the boss, they're always tossers. Have you noticed that? Always a bully or gobshite. Serious point ahoy!' He raised his index finger. 'I reckon being bossed around by a woman is probably good for us men. It takes the edge off the male instinct to be selfish and behave badly.'

Nick laughed. 'Yeah, I think you're right. They save us from ourselves. I have no interest in being the boss, anyway.'

'Me, neither. Far too much pressure. I'm happy to be nice and do what I'm told in return for regular sex and companionship and I think that's the only sensible position to take.'

'Where is she staying tonight, then?'

'Chez Jeffrey, I'm hoping. Mam has got Argie until tomorrow.'

'You fancy her, then?' Nick said it quietly.

'Well, she's different. I like different. She's passionate and I think she's got interesting ideas. We're on the same page, I reckon. Alright, she's a bit cocky - but I don't think she means any harm by it and she likes me. She's said as much. So we'll just see.'

After a couple of drinks in the Stockton Arms, it was chucking-out time.

'Well, that was a good night,' said Julie, hands in her jeans pockets, as they stood outside the pub.

'Nice to see you again, Jo,' said Nick.

'Stay in touch about the murder, I'm sure we can sort it out, y'know,' said Jo. 'And we should, if we can. It'd be amazing to do that. I'll have a think on and do some research of my own.'

He nodded and put his thumb up as Jeff and Jo walked back into the village.

'So they're deffo going to his house together,' he said, as he called a taxi.

'Of course they are.'

'What do you mean. Of course?'

'She told me,' Julie grinned at him. 'She said she'd made her mind up to stay over and "open up to him" as she said.'

'Open up? Is that a sexual term?'

'I don't know. Sounded like she wanted to move it up a level. She was asking me about him and what he was like and that.'

'Bloody hell, well, I'm really pleased for Jeff. He's had no action on that front since Rita.'

'I did tell her that...it's as well the girl is prepared. Ha ha!'

'And you got on well with her in the end; you were a bit prickly to start with.'

'She is a mouthy cow and full of herself - but I was the exact same at her age. Trying to cut yourself a place in the world. I realised that after a bit and also we're on the same page, politically.'

'So we've got a romance on our hands?' said Nick.

'I think we do, indeed.'

CHAPTER 7

Later, Nick sat in bed with his laptop while Julie took a quick shower. He entered John Grayson-Thomas into Google. There were a lot of links to news stories about his murder. He had been a local councillor on various education committees. Reports mentioned he'd been a Latin teacher. In 2001 he started his rental agency. The last decade had been spent doing public service and charity work of one sort or another, along with running his business. There was no mention of a family at all. His funeral had been set for Saturday at a crematorium in Edinburgh.

As he clicked various John Grayson-Thomas links, he kept coming up with the same information. There was even a small head shot of him on the rental agency website. It showed a man with a hooked beak of a nose but with attractive soft blue eyes and a full head of white hair.

Julie padded in, wrapped in a towel, and took out a long, baggy purple v-neck t-shirt from the chest of drawers.

'Found out anything about him?' she said, unwrapping herself from the towel and pulling on the top.

'Quite a lot. He seems like the classic elderly fella who gets involved in everything from Neighbourhood Watch to litter picking days, campaigns to keep post offices open, to helping out for kids charities.'

'Is he Scottish?'

'I've found nothing that says where he was born. There's a quote from someone who knew him on the council to say how shocked he is at his murder, but there's no weeping widow or kids.'

'Here's an idea I had while I was washing my arse. Look him up in Births, Marriages and Deaths.'

'Good thinking. It says he was 71, so he was born around 1939.'

He entered his name and '1939' into the search box. Julie got in bed beside him. He sniffed at her.

'You smell of melon.'

She laughed and pulled up the t-shirt and shook her breasts at him. 'Must be these melons then!'

He leaned over and kissed one of her pink nipples.

'God bless your melons.'

She looked at them and then pulled the t-shirt down again. 'They're more like a couple of grapefruits, really. I spent my teenage years wanting big tits, but now I'm 46 I'm glad they weren't. They'd be round me knees by now.'

'I've never understood why some men think bigger breasts are better. It just makes no difference to me at all - tiny, small, medium or extra large. The aesthetics of breast shapes and sizes, or anything at all to do with nipples has never pressed my buttons. I've always been happy to see or feel them, but whichever way they are, is the right way for me.'

'Just as well.'

'You've got a couple of lovely handfuls. If they were three times as big, what more would I do with them? I just don't get it.'

'Never mind what you'd do with them, what would I do with them? It'd be like carrying around a bag of cement on each shoulder.'

He went back to his research, stroking the stubble on his chin. The search didn't produce anyone called John Grayson-Thomas who was born in 1939. He widened the years in case they'd got it wrong in the paper, taking it back to 1930. Still nothing. He did a couple of spelling variations but still drew a blank. Finally, he did an open search for anyone with Grayson-Thomas as a surname. There wasn't a single one. Perhaps he'd been born abroad.

A Google search brought up a couple of companies, but no individual.

'You know what's odd?'

'You've found something odd?'

'Not as such. But there's nothing about his past beyond the last nine years and if there was anything at all, it'd stand out because there's no-one else with his name.'

'So what?'

'I don't know. Nothing...just seems odd that when he's being talked about, it's just for recent stuff. No-one says, oh, he was a teacher at this specific school for 30 years, or he was married in 1975, or whatever. There is a lot of info mentioning him - his name is present on council meeting documents, but there's no sense of him beyond that. And he's not on the Birth, Marriage and Deaths register either. Why's that?'

Julie sat and thought for a couple of minutes, rolling her wedding ring around the third finger of her left hand. 'You know what? I think I've got it. There can only be one reason.'

'What's that?'

'Because it's not his name.'

Nick turned to look at her as she twirled a long strand of hair around a finger. 'That's a great idea, Jules.'

'That's 'cos I'm a clever lass. I've got two degrees me, like,' she said in a willfully stupid version of the Teesside accent. 'His whole history was lived under a different name until 2001 and that's why you can't find out anything about him before that.'

The truth of that washed over Nick profoundly. A few locks dropped in the tightly closed door of John Grayson-Thomas's life. 'Brilliant. And that might well explain why Barbara Stewart shot him. She knew him from way back when he had a different name. Yes!' He clapped his hands together.

Julie nodded. 'And there's one other way to find out about him.'

'What's that?'

'Go to his funeral. There'll probably be someone there who knew him, family or whatever.'

He applauded. 'You've got nice grapefruit-sized breasts that smell of melons *and* you're clever. You're the perfect woman,' said Nick, patting her on the leg. 'That's two great ideas from you tonight.'

'I'm a quality old slapper, me, like.'

'So are you saying that Grayson-Thomas is just an assumed name?'

'Not assumed. He just changed his name for some reason.'

'Can you track that sort of info down and find out who they were before?' said Nick.

'No. Or, it's hard. It's not actually illegal to change your name at any time, if you want. Anyone can do it. I had to read up on this for a case years ago that I worked on with one of the Carlisle partners. Women often change their names to get away from an abusive man. I mean, make up a new name, not just go back to their maiden name. As I remember it, anyone can actually change their name and it's perfectly legal, unless you're doing it to evade the law. If you change your name and need a legal document, like a passport, you can get a lawyer to issue you a certificate to confirm it - but they're not obliged to keep them for more than five years, if at all, and there's no central database.'

'So you can become someone else, quite anonymously?'

'With careful planning, yeah. No-one need know, if you don't want them to and if you know what you're doing.'

'Cool. Hey, if you could change your name, what would you change it to?'

She didn't pause long. 'Stevie Benatar, obviously. My two fave rock chicks. I'd love to be a Stevie, but I'm just a massive Julie, me. Everything about me is a Julie. Even my tits are Julie tits. What about you?'

'Mam was going to call me Colin.'

'Oh, lord, you're not a Colin.'

'I used to want to be called Marty when I was a teenager.'

She laughed and gave him a flirtatious look. 'Hmm, you'd make a nice Marty. You've got a Marty body.'

'A Marty's got a specific body?'

'Marty is a snake-hips shagger and a sexy guy, but he's untrustworthy.'

'Is he full of self-doubt, self-loathing and insecurity? Does he weep like a small boy and feel like tomorrow is a black void?' Nick tilted his head and raised an eyebrow at her.

'No. Quite the opposite.'

'I'm not a Marty, then. I'm sticking with Colin. Colin has no ambition or ego. Any other preconceived ideas about names?'

She pouted a little. 'Melanies are the female Martys, but only the ones who abbreviate it to Mel. They're all shaggers, are Mels. Sex and drugs and rock 'n' roll types, to a woman.'

He paused for a moment. 'You know, I think you might be right about that. I've never known a Mel that wasn't up for a good time, one way or another. I went out with one at college. She couldn't get her pants off quick enough. I once had it off with her standing up against her halls of residence door.'

'Ha ha...very adventurous. The old knee trembler.'

'You're not kidding. I was about to go and see Rush at the City Hall and had about 15 minutes spare, so I was up against it.'

'So was she, by the sounds of it. Were you late for the gig?'

'No, I got there with 10 minutes to spare. I was a fast worker back then. Yeah, good old Mel and her yo-yo knickers. Eventually left me for a red-hot lead guitarist.'

'There you go, then. Mels are all shaggers. Your Johns and Janets, Janes and Jameses, they're respectable types, but with hot fires burning underneath a snowy roof.'

Nick laughed. 'I'm less sure about that, than the Melanies. There are too many of them to generalise.'

'People with plain names often kick against them in their own private ways. I did. You did.'

'True. So who is the most boring man? Name-wise?'

'Davids. There's no hope for them. Boring bastards. The only ones worth their salt are those who know being a David is a curse.'

'And women?'

'Margaret. They're not screamers, are they?'

'My mother was a Margaret.'

'Oh, yeah. Ha. Was she a screamer?'

'Not to my knowledge. Then again, dad might have had something to do with that. I find the idea of mam and dad having it off, vaguely bizarre and hard to believe. To think that I started out as an ejaculation one night in early November 1960 is too weird to think about. I genuinely can't conceive of it, ironically enough.'

'None of us like to think of our parents shagging the arse off each other. But it's funny how we become inseparable from our names, isn't it? I think I'm a totally typical Julie.'

'To be fair, I'm not sure I'm a typical anything.'

She smiled at him. 'Mmm, maybe not. I've never known anyone like you, of any name.' She took a pair of tweezers from the bedside table and plucked at an eyebrow hair.

He closed his computer and slid down the bed.

'You know when we met Barbara outside the flat?'

She took a sip of water and turned out her light, so they lay in the soft darkness.

'Uh huh.'

'What was your first impression of her?'

She thought for a moment.

'Middle-class. Arty. That's it.'

'You didn't think she was old?'

'Her age never entered my head.'

'No, me neither. But it should have done.'

She went quiet again. 'That is odd,' she said eventually.

'Isn't it? Even now I don't think of her as old.'

'I'm just thinking back to how we met her. You opened the door of the flat and I was right behind you and there she was.'

'So neither of us thought she was old?'

'But do we really think about people's age?'

'All I'm saying it that it wasn't a dominant impression. When I saw Frank Stewart I thought *he* was old. Y'know what I'm saying? He was slightly stooped and a bit frail. So you're immediately aware there's some age on him. I think when we met Barbara I must've just thought she was just generally middle-aged.'

'Some people just don't look their age. It's all genetics.'

'You don't look 46. I look 49.'

'What does 46 or 49 look like, though? When we were kids, people our age all just seemed very old - 40, 60, 80, it was all the same, somehow.'

They stopped talking. Nick felt her fall asleep, but his mind wouldn't stop working, restlessly turning over all the people related to the shooting. Frank Stewart was Head at Northdean in the 1970s. John Grayson-Thomas was also a teacher. Frank's wife shot him. Could there be a relationship between those three things? Was there a love triangle, maybe? It couldn't be a coincidence, could it?

He just could not sleep. Turning over on his side, he looked at the clock: 2.46am. He was wide awake and he needed a piss.

Quietly, he slipped out of bed and went to the toilet, aiming at the bowl so as not to disturb Julie. He tip-toed back into the bedroom, picked up his laptop and went into the living room.

He loaded the picture of Barbara coming out of the office, the small gun in her right hand. Her white hair to her shoulder, she was emerging from the doorway with two glass fronts either side, on which were notices advertising flats to rent. In the quiet dark of the night he tried to get inside her head and tried to imagine her actually being Frank.

Question all realities, Jo had said. OK. Let's do that, one thing at a time. When they saw the photo, they'd immediately thought it was the woman they'd met on the stairs. Was it, though? As he stared at the picture, it was impossible to separate his memories chronologically. They all became a porridge of recollection. This picture now looked like Barbara, mostly because they had thought it did when the police first showed it to them. You don't remember the person, per se, what you remember is that you *thought* it was them. You recall that thought. Not the actual person.

It was someone in a dark green jacket and trousers and with a patterned silk scarf on, just as the woman who had crashed the Volvo had been. The CCTV picture wasn't high-resolution enough to reveal the exact pattern. He was fairly sure the woman on the stairs had been wearing a paisley pattern and in the photo it was a small pattern of some sort.

Question all realities.

The woman on the stairs had *introduced* herself as Barbara. They'd taken *that* as the gospel truth. Why wouldn't you? But who's to say that was her? Who was to say that it was even the same person that Jo had met? They could be two different people using the name Barbara Stewart, both dressing alike. She'd introduced herself as that, but anyone can call themselves anything. The photo at the art school was of *a* Barbara Stewart, but was it the person they'd met? Jo said that your mind tries to make sense of everything. When a name is under a picture, you start from the assumption that it is that person. So if they look quite similar to the person you've met, you don't question that it is them. In fact, now he thought about it, Barbara existed so clearly in his mind and yet he'd met her for less than two minutes. Oh, man.

What questioning all realities did was make him realise that he knew nothing at all other than they'd met someone who said they were Barbara Stewart. Apart from that, he had nothing. What he needed was some hard facts.

The following morning, after just three hours sleep, he booked a ticket on the train to Edinburgh for Saturday.

'I wish I could go, I like a train journey,' said Julie, as she got dressed for work. 'But I'm on duty all weekend and it's not something I can get out of.'

'Well, it's just overnight. I'll go to that funeral, see who else is there. I'll check up on Frank Stewart, too. It'll probably all come to nothing and since we've still got the keys to Big Fish's flat, I might as well doss there for a night.'

She paused for a moment. 'I know what Jo said about public duty and helping put wrongs right and I do agree with her, but you don't have to go up there, you know. Not if you don't want to. It's not your responsibility.'

'I know. But...in a way it is. We were the last people to see Barbara, whoever she is or was, before she probably did a terrible thing, or at least before she disappeared. Also, you might hate me for this, but if I get to the bottom of this - frankly, it'll be worth a fortune as a freelance story.'

'You'd sell it?'

'Would that be wrong?'

'How much for?'

'Terrible to say it, but if it's something really juicy, it'd be a good four figures. Maybe five or six grand, depending on how much murder and corruption there is....I know, I know...but that's how these things work.'

She twisted her mouth in contemplation. 'I hadn't even thought of you selling it, till Jo said.'

'Well, it's worth thinking about. That could be a little nest egg for us. In a few years it could be enough for us to use for deposit on a flat or a house. Or just have a massive piss-up in Las Vegas.'

She nodded. 'Well, if it happens, it'd be nice. But don't put pressure on yourself. We're much better off now that I'm getting paid.'

His phone rang. 'It's Jeff,' he said, looking at it.

'Bugger, I can't wait to hear what happened last night. Tell us later.'
She blew him a kiss and rushed out of the door.

'Now then, fella. How's everything?'

Jeff just laughed. 'It was a *very* interesting night.'

Nick didn't know what that meant but assumed it was good.

'So it was...err...fun?'

'Obviously, I can't go into detail, but I'll tell you this. I've never had a night like it.'

'Well, that sounds good...so you're seeing her again.'

'Indeed I am. So any details of intimacies must remain undisclosed, as tradition demands. And...well...ha ha...yeah. What a woman she is.'

'Cool. OK. I'm really pleased for you, man. Good on you. So what's the plan?'

'She's off down to London this morning.'

'She's away already?'

'Aye. She's going to look into the idea of moving back north. Not sure it'll happen soon, though.'

'It's only a few hours down to London. You can still see a lot of each other.'

'Yeah, it's no sweat.'

'Is she any good with kids?'

'Well, I don't know, really. Argie is at mam's.'

'Nice having someone fancy you, though, eh,' said Nick.

'I don't mind telling you that women fancying me isn't something I ever expect.'

Nick paused a little. It was as though Jeff was being evasive.

'No. I know what you mean. I have never, not once in my life, thought of myself as fanciable. I've hoped I might be, I've tried to be, but I've never thought I was,' said Nick.

'Only wankers think they are fanciable. Involves too much self-regard, if you ask me.'

Nick told him about the Edinburgh trip.

'You can come up if you want.'

'I'd like to but I can't, man. Too much work on, plus I'll have Argie all weekend.'

'OK, not to worry. It's only overnight.'

'I wonder how the police investigation is doing? Is there no news on that front? Feels like there should be.'

'Nothing in the paper. No. It's all gone very quiet.'

'Maybe that's the way they want it,' said Jeff.
'Yeah, maybe it is.'

No amount of research in the following few days revealed anything more about Frank or Barbara Stewart. He'd been headmaster from 1975 to 1980, that was a matter of public record, but after that, things were less clear. He and his wife had such a common name, trying to find out which Frank or Barbara Stewart they were when searching for the names, was simply impossible. Similarly, the marriages register wasn't clear. Loads of Frank Stewarts had married a woman called Barbara over the years. So even as Nick looked over his notes as the train pulled into Waverley Station at 11am on Saturday morning, the leaden sky threatening rain, he was really no further forward in getting some hard facts.

The funeral was at 11 in Warriston Crematorium. He texted Julie to let her know he'd arrived and then got a cab down to Warriston Road on the north side of the city.

It was lovely, quiet area. Very well-to-do and respectable on the northern edge of the Georgian New Town. Full of respectable, square, symmetrical and very expensive Georgian terraced houses, it was exactly the sort of area that a respectable member of a respectable community would live in.

As Nick walked into the crematorium, a quiet old place with an imitation of cloisters, he couldn't help but be impressed by it. This felt like a religious place. It mimicked a church in that it had rows of seats set out in an old late Georgian stone building that you'd have to say was a kind of secular chapel. Stained glass windows depicting flying swans echoed a holy place, too. The coffin was set on a kind of altar under a green velvet drape. Like all churches, it had a cool and timeless stillness that was easy to call spirituality.

A man stepped up and greeted him.
'Hello, sir.'
'Hi. I think I'm a bit early. Are you the celebrant?'
'I am indeed.'
'It's lovely in here. Very peaceful. Is it to be a Christian service?'
'Yes. Catholic. But we deal with all faiths here.'
'What's the difference between a Catholic cremation and a Protestant one, then?'
That seemed to catch the man by surprise.

'I'm afraid that's a little too theological for me. We just have a range of services that we deliver.'

Nick nodded. He hadn't meant for it to be a difficult question. Typical. He'd misjudged what was the right thing to say. Sometimes he reminded himself of Josh. Or maybe it was the right question and the bloke was just a bit stupid. Nick had no way of telling.

'I'll just take a seat, then. Will there be many here?'

'Well, we don't know. It's not as if we sell tickets,' he said in a soft, middle-class Edinburgh accent.

Of course they didn't. Try and say the right thing, Guymer, for once in your life.

He sat at the back. There were seats for up to 200. Was John Grayson-Thomas that popular? A few people began to file in. All of them seemed over 60. There were no kids, no young people. By 11am just 12 people were in attendance. A younger man with tired bags under his eyes and an unshaven face sat at the end of the row, along from him and gave him a nod of acknowledgment. He didn't fit with the other mourners. As the service began, he took out a notepad and began writing shorthand. He had to be a journalist.

Nick wondered who had organised this, but it wasn't immediately obvious who, if anyone, was the next of kin. The celebrant said a few words, words he recognised in part from his own dad's funeral. Maybe there were generic secular services where they just inserted the name of the deceased into the blank spaces.

One thing was noticeable, however, there was no mention of a son and daughter and no mention of a wife or any other relations either. That was a bit odd for someone of his generation.

It was all over within 10 minutes. Some organ music played and it was time to file out. It was clearly the economy service.

Nick leaned over to the journalist and held out his hand. 'Hello mate, I'm a journalist as well - Nick Guymer. Who are you writing for?'

'Wally Givens. I'm a freelancer.' His grip was soft and unpleasantly sweaty. Nick wished he had a wet wipe after he released his hand. Try not to think about it. It'd be so easy to become a germophobe.

'Ah, right. Me, too.'

They stood up and headed towards the exit doors. 'Terrible thing, this shooting,' said Nick, as ever, hopeless at making small talk. 'Any idea why it happened?'

'That's what I'm trying to get to the bottom of. No-one seems to know why.'

'The police haven't released any information about the killer, have they?'

'No. Well, they haven't got anywhere with it - or if they have, they're keeping it very quiet. I think they're hitting a brick wall. That or...well...I don't know...'

They wandered outside.

'...go on. You were saying?' said Nick, hands in pockets.

'Well, I did go to the press conference that they held about this and I get the impression that they're not taking it seriously. The fact there's only been one presser is odd when it's a murder.'

Nick stopped and looked at the dishevelled Wally Givens. 'What does that mean, exactly?'

'It's just a feeling, but I've done countless murder pressers and this one was really different. They batted away every question and they've been doing that ever since. Normally, if they can't get anywhere, they'd be all over local TV making requests for sightings of the suspect, but not this time.'

'Have they given a name of the shooter, yet?'

Givens shook his head. 'Nothing. Unofficially, they've been making out that things are going well. Have you heard anything?'

Nick wasn't sure what to say to that, so he side-stepped it, saying, 'I thought she'd have been identified by now.'

'You would, wouldn't you? Maybe she has been, but the police are not saying, for some reason.'

'So what do you think is going on? Is there an issue with the police? Are they hiding something?'

'Could be. It's a bloke called Gordon Smith in charge. I've met him a couple of times on other stories. He's a sharp bloke, but he doesn't give much away at the best of times, and he definitely sees us as the enemy. He's never liked me.'

'What did you do to upset him?'

'Support Hibs. He's a Hearts man.'

'Ah, I see. I have heard about him. He's not popular with the *Evening News* journos. So what do you know about the victim? I've had a look into him, but can't dig much up before 2001,' said Nick.

'That's why I came down. He's a bit of a mystery; in fact, as murders go, the whole thing is totally untypical,' said Wally. 'It's like he didn't even exist before 2001. My view, for what it's worth, is that he was living abroad until then. I think he was born overseas, probably in an old British colony, because there's no record of him at all in the UK. I asked Smith about that, but he just brushed it off by saying they were more concerned with finding the woman in the picture that the *Evening News* published.'

'I heard that they were pissed off at the paper for publishing that.'

'Yeah, not pleased at all.'

'Where did the photo come from?'

Wally rubbed his eyes. 'Yeah, that's one more weird thing. It was sent anonymously to the paper.'

'Isn't that just a line the paper is spinning to cover their source?' said Nick.

Wally shook his head. 'No, I know a lot of the boys on the paper and it was definitely sent from an untraceable email address. It looks like a CCTV still to me, so how they got access to the CCTV camera footage, I don't know. I did wonder if it wasn't a ruse dreamed up by Gordon Smith to unofficially release a picture of the killer.'

'Why would he do that?'

'Because he wanted the picture out there, but wasn't allowed to publish it through official channels.' Wally shrugged again. 'It's just a guess.' He walked after one of the people who had been sitting at the front and asked him a couple of more questions.

Nick turned to face a small, elderly woman who had also been sitting on the front row of seats. He gave her a watery smile, or at least he hoped it was a smile and not a look of vague nausea. As he was doing so, in his peripheral vision he noticed someone sitting on the edge of a low wall, with a phone and looking as though he was taking a photo of Nick. Nick cast a glance at him. With a head of short ginger hair, he hadn't been at the service. Who was he?

'Hello, there. A sad day,' said the old lady. She nodded at him and spoke in a well-to-do Edinburgh accent. 'I can't believe such a thing can happen in this day and age. Can you?' Her lilting voice was pure Miss Jean Brodie territory. Almost so much so, that it felt like an accent she was putting on.

'No, it is very shocking,' said Nick, nodding. 'Did you know John well?'

'I worked with him as a local councillor.'

'Oh, right. Which ward did he represent?'

'Stockbridge.'

That was where he and Jules had breakfast.

'I didn't know that was where he lived.'

'Comely Bank Terrace. He had a lovely flat there opposite the bowling green. Did you know him well?

'No, not really. I knew someone who knew him. I just wanted to come along and pay my respects. There were not many here, though.'

'No. But he kept himself to himself outside of his work, so it doesn't surprise me.'

She walked away slowly.

What to do now? Wally had talked to a couple of others but everyone seemed quite tight lipped.

'Get anything?' said Nick, walking out to meet the journalist.

He shook his head and pushed his messy hair off his face. 'Not really. The impression you get is that no-one really knew him. I mean, even the few people who came here seemed to be work colleagues but none of them were friends, as such. He just didn't seem to mix outside of his work on the council and charities. No-one knows anything about his past, really. A real mystery man. And obviously, that might be the reason behind why he was murdered.'

'Some people are like that. They're very private. Have you got any info on him that dates further back than 2001?'

Wally looked at his notes. 'Nope. Nothing. Like I say, I reckon he was born abroad in the Commonwealth. OK, I'll get off. Nice to have met you, Nick. Here's my number if you hear of anything. Can I give you a lift anywhere?'

'Can you drop me on Queen Street?' said Nick.

Five minutes later, walking down towards the corner of Howe Street and Heriot Row, Nick looked up at the flat, turning the key over in his pocket. No-one at the window, male or female. He crossed over the road. As he did so, the big front door to the property at the top of the steps opened. Nick's heart leapt into his throat. He stopped in his tracks.

The figure coming down the steps was Frank Stewart. The same man they'd met on the stairs the morning after the killing had happened. He was dressed in a dark grey fleece and pair of walking trousers. Would he recognise Nick? No. Surely not. He'd only seen him briefly on the steps on two occasions. But Nick recognised him, so why not?

He took a chance as Frank walked across the pavement and waited to cross Howe Street.

'Hello, Frank Stewart, isn't it?' said Nick, head on one side, the way Julie did when she was being sympathetic.

'Yes...err...who are you?'

Nick held out his hand. 'I haven't seen you in ages. How have you been keeping?'

Making small talk, he found hard, but making up an extended fiction off the top of his head presented no problem. It came with being uncomfortable with his own reality. When you don't like yourself much, it's easy to pretend to be someone else; someone better and more interesting. Right away he could tell Frank hadn't a clue who he was. He didn't shake his hand.

'I'm sorry...err...do we know each other?' he said.

'Of course we do. Scott Mitchell?' He pointed to himself and laughed a little. 'You remember me?'

'Sorry. I'm afraid I don't.'

'I used to work with your wife, Barbara, at the art school, last year.'

Frank's face clouded over with a strange look. His skin looked oddly dry, almost powdery, and he was frightened. Clearly frightened. His blue eyes seemed to visibly darken and he swept his white hair from his brow with long, twiglet fingers.

'No, you didn't. You must be getting confused...'

'I don't think so,' said Nick.

Frank crossed the road as the green man lit up.

'Impossible. You didn't work with Barbara.'

'I don't understand. Why is it impossible?'

Frank turned and stopped.

'Because Barbara has been *dead* for three years.'

What?

Dead?

Nick caught up with Frank and walked alongside him.

'Dead? Are you sure?' Oh god, that was a stupid thing to say.

It clearly annoyed Frank, he stopped again and turned to Nick. 'What do you mean, am I sure? I think I know when my own wife died. Whoever you are, leave me alone.'

'But Frank, I saw her the other week,' said Nick, trotting in front of him. He wondered whether he should say he'd met her on the stairs and break his hastily constructed cover.

'For god's sake, man, have some respect. You can't have done. She's dead. Go and see her grave in Dean Cemetery, if you don't believe me. Please - this is very upsetting.'

'Well, someone is going round Edinburgh pretending to be Barbara,' said Nick. 'I've seen them. I've talked to them.'

'Really? I think that is a ludicrous thing to say. Are you well in the head?' He looked right into Nick's eyes. Was he scared? Yeah, he was. But he was also defiant and determined.

He got to a small Nissan car, unlocked it and got in. Nick's mind was in a whirl of confusion. Was he just lying? If she was dead, who was the woman they'd met on the stairs? Who had Jo King met? Who had been teaching at the art school? Oh, bloody hell. He stood and watched as Frank drove away. One thing he felt quite sure about, having stood so close to him, it seemed very hard to believe that he had been dressed as Barbara when they'd met her. In his mind, she was quite different. But then, that was just in his mind.

OK, take Jo's advice and challenge everything. That was a meeting with Frank Stewart. But was it really Frank Stewart? He stopped in his tracks again, standing on Heriot Row looking up at the impressive Georgian terrace. He hadn't a clue if there really was a man of that name. When they first met him, he didn't even say who he was, and just now, he didn't actually confirm it. He spoke of his wife Barbara, though. But anyone could do that. So actually, he had no independent evidence that it *was* Frank Stewart and not just someone who possibly wanted him to think he was. Shitting hell. God, how you assumed so much, based on little or nothing. That man could simply be anyone.

He rubbed his forehead, tracing the worry lines with his finger tips.

OK, so he could have been anyone just pretending to be Frank Stewart. What next? Nick had mentioned Barbara, his wife, and he'd said she was dead. So whoever he was, he was acknowledging that a Frank Stewart *was* married to a Barbara Stewart...but no...hold on...Nick had said, "I used to work with your wife, Barbara..." that was a giveaway. He'd allowed him to know who he was talking about and therefore who he assumed the man was, thus allowing him to play the role. So he hadn't even independently confirmed the existence of Barbara, Nick had effectively done that for him. Sod it!

He beat his fist against his leg. What else? He said she'd died three years ago and her grave was in Dean Cemetery. Now, that was at least verifiable, whoever he was. So if there was a grave there with her name on it, he, whoever he was, did at least know that.

Nick looked at his phone, found the cemetery on Google maps and headed towards it.

The 'challenge everything' principle was harder than it initially seemed, because there are so many things you take for granted in life. You have to. So it becomes second nature to trust in basic things. But as he walked, another important realisation flooded into his brain. Really important.

When the two policemen had called that first night they'd been in the flat, yes, they were dressed as policemen, and there was a blue flashing light on a car outside, but there was no way to know if they were for real. They'd just said they were the police. They didn't offer any proof and Nick hadn't thought to even ask them. You don't. You accept people in police uniforms *are* the police.

He stopped again and looked up the street, as he realised something serious. The whole reason they thought Barbara Stewart was the killer was because of *that* photo. And that was shown to them by the policemen. Nick thought they'd told the police who she was, but if they weren't the police, they hadn't told them at all. At the time it seemed impossible that they were not the police, but recent events made him doubt it now. What they'd done was confirm it was Barbara Stewart. Was that something the visitors wanted to know, or was it something that they wanted he and Julie to know she'd done? Where they showing them the photo to inform them or to be informed?

But who dresses as police to show a real or a fake photo to someone? And why to them, specifically? They were nobody. And was one of these also the presumably fake copper who had talked to Jo?

He walked on again. Hold on hold on...maybe they *were* the real police. Don't dismiss that idea. The 'challenge everything' principle didn't automatically mean everything was wrong, did it? Shit, it was all twisting his brain out of shape.

So, what else had to be challenged? The photo itself. Was is it really from the CCTV camera on George Street? Was it doctored?

He stopped in the shadow of the huge, dominant structure of St Stephen's church and looked at the CCTV picture on his phone again. Maybe it *was* a fake. Josh had said it looked weird. He was a perceptive lad. Maybe he'd spotted it was contrived, somehow.

Eventually he found the graveyard after getting a bit lost. He had such a terrible sense of direction even when holding a map. It was huge. How did you find a grave? Well it was only three years old, so it'd look quite new since most of them went back as far as 1790, 1706; bloody hell, there was even one from 1678. A man called James Slipper. Died aged 89. Well, he had a good innings and hadn't even needed lecturing about healthy eating.

Nick looked around. Graveyards were great places. He'd always loved them. They were history and nature and humanity all together. They spoke to him and synced in with his default mental state. A blackbird hacked away at some moss with a determined vigour. He sucked in the lovely damp, earthy air. Ashes to ashes, dust to dust. Yeah. Thank god for that. It was comforting. Sometimes it felt like death was a lovely big soft bed which you'd climb into and take the long final relaxing sleep to end all sleeps. Sometimes he almost committed that greatest of sins of the living: he looked forward to it. At least then, all the trouble would be done.

It took him nearly half an hour, but eventually he found it. *Barbara Stewart. Born York 1943, died Edinburgh 2007. Aged 64.*

Unless this was a fake burial plot, then Barbara really was dead.

She was dead.

Dead. So she couldn't have shot anyone. Not unless they'd buried someone else here and merely pretended it was Barbara. Or maybe this was just another Barbara Stewart altogether.

Frank had seemed upset and shocked by him saying he'd seen her. Maybe he was a good actor, but he did seem genuinely affected by it. As you would be if your wife had been dead for three years and some loony in the street is saying they'd met her recently. He looked at the photo of Barbara from the art school. There she was, with her name underneath her picture.

'Who are you?' he said out loud to the phone. She looked back at him, frozen in that microsecond of time.

Nick watched birds flitting around the graveyard. His early instinct that Frank was both Barbara and the other woman they'd seen, once again seemed more likely to be true. She was dead. He wasn't. So he was her. And, dressed up as his dead wife, for some reason, he shot Grayson-Thomas. Was that the truth?

After taking a photo of the gravestone, he walked back into town and up onto George Street, turning onto it from the Charlotte Square end.

John Grayson-Thomas's office was still fenced off with tape, the windows covered up with sheets of newspaper and orange barriers placed around the doorway.

He looked up at the CCTV camera that was on the top of the traffic lights at the junction. That had to be where it was taken from. It was maybe 25 feet away. Walking to the traffic lights pole, he stood behind it so he was directly underneath and then looked at the CCTV picture on his phone. Without getting up to where the camera was, it was hard to tell for sure, but the picture seemed to be taken from the correct angle, at least. If it hadn't been taken from the CCTV camera, it was easy to see where it had to have been taken from, but it'd have needed a zoom lens to be taken from the first floor of a building right across Charlotte Square. That had a clear view, but it was at least a hundred yards or more away. But it did look like a CCTV freeze frame.

As he stood looking at his phone. He noticed someone across the street looking at him. With a second quick glance, he realised it was the ginger man that had been at the crematorium who had taken a photo of him.

On impulse, or possibly a dangerous whim, he put his phone away and walked across the road right towards the man.

'Can I help you, mate?' said Nick, probably a little too aggressively, but then this was Scotland and aggression was a default mode of expression.

'You what, pal?' said the man, in a west of Scotland accent.

'I just saw you take a photo of me and you took one earlier at the crematorium.'

'You're crazy. Why would I be taking photos of you? What's so special about you?'

But Nick knew he had and that it was the same man.

'Are you with the police?'

'I'm a tourist, pal. Now back off, eh.'

The man looked at Nick belligerently. He was hard. Scottish hard. Not to be underestimated.

Nick sniffed and looked through narrowed eyes at him. 'What do you know about John Grayson-Thomas?'

'I've never heard of the man. Now jog on, pal. You're done talkin' t'me, now.'

There was no point in being more confrontational with him. Nick growled in his throat and walked away up George Street. He heard the man say 'Aye, go on, fuck off, ye prick' at him as he did so, but didn't rise to the bait; after all, he *was* behaving a bit suspiciously. But all the same. That man was up to something. Everything about this was bloody dodgy and it was annoying the hell out of him.

He decided to go back to the art school. Question all realities. If Barbara was dead, who was their Barbara?

He walked down Dundas Street, turning off at Great King Street and peering into the basement window. A different woman was sitting at the desk this time. She was younger and a more arty, student type.

She looked up at him and smiled as he walked in.

'Hello!' she said brightly, as though him being there made her very happy indeed, which surely can't have been true.

'Hi. I was told to come to see a teacher who works here. My friend said she was very good. Her name is Barbara Stewart. Have I come to the right place?'

She nodded enthusiastically. 'You have. Barbara works here.'

'Oh, cool. Can I sign up for her classes?'

He sat down opposite her. She shifted awkwardly.

'I'm afraid she's....she's not working at the moment.'

'Oh that's a shame. Why not?'

'Oh, she's taking some time off. We have other tutors who could help.' She said it with a straight face and fair play to her for that. Nick weighed up whether to ask her if she thought Barbara was a man, just as they'd asked the other woman, but it seemed pointless. If she looked like the picture by the door, she just didn't look male.

'I'll think about it,' he said, getting up again. Then he abruptly asked, 'Have the police been here to ask about Barbara, by any chance?'

She clearly was torn between admitting there was an issue around Barbara and saying nothing. Her eyes strayed from his and in doing so, told him that yes, they had. Probably Gordon Smith, if he was the chief investigating officer.

He looked at the picture of her again as he left. Was that who they'd met? Yes, definitely. It was. As far as it was possible to tell, it was.

As he walked along Great King Street, hands in his pockets, he wondered just what he should do next. He'd come back to Edinburgh to get some facts but had only got more confusion. He checked the local newspaper again just to see if there was any more news from the police, but there was nothing. Still they hadn't released Barbara Stewart's name. They didn't have to accuse her, they could just say she was of interest and wanted to speak to her. Was it possible that they just didn't know her name and that was because no-one at the art school had come forward to say it was her and because the police he and Julie had been interviewed by, and who had been to speak to Jo, were not police officers at all, but someone else with a different agenda? If that was the case, who had visited the art school? That woman had clearly thought it was the police, but maybe, like he and Julie, she'd been taken in by someone merely pretending to be the police.

Sitting on a wooden bench on Dundas Street, he texted Julie and briefly explained the situation. '*Maybe I should go and see this Gordon Smith bloke who is in charge of the investigation and tell him her name - just in case they don't know it. Then there's no doubt that they know*.' She texted back immediately.

'*I agree. 100 per cent the right thing to do. Then at least we know that they know. But it's still all a very weird business*.'

'*OK, I'll go now. The station is in Stockbridge*.'

She texted back. '*Be careful. Call me later at home. I'll send you a nice picture to keep you warm tonight!*'

He smiled to himself, checked the police station location on his phone and set off to walk there.

As he turned onto Saxe-Coburg Street, a smart quiet Georgian square, he checked the map again, wondering if he was still going the right way, as always fundamentally mistrusting his sense of direction.

Sometimes in life, you get a sixth sense of danger being near or imminent, as though your senses are able to slip their moorings and see into the future for a few seconds. Other times, you have absolutely no feeling that anything is going to happen to you. One moment everything is going along normally, as it does 99.9 per cent of the time, then it all changes in a second.

This was one of those moments.

Nick was just inspecting his phone screen and trying to work out which direction he was facing when someone ran across the road at a fast pace and attacked him. He did it so silently and Nick was so wrapped up in his own thoughts that the man was on him before he even realised he was there. His shock was total and absolute and his brain simply couldn't compute it for a few vital seconds. Caught off his guard, he was pushed down a flight of steps to a basement, below ground level. He cracked his head on the stone steps as he tumbled. Maybe he passed out briefly. Someone else was down there. They grabbed him, swore, pulled him by the shoulders and grappled him through an open door. Everything was a dizzy blur.

It was now five or six seconds into the attack and Nick, disorientated and groggy, drew on his inner Boro - that deep well of tough, arsy, right-eous indignation that is at every Teessider's core, even a semi-conscious Teessider. So he lashed out at one of the men, wrestling him to a wooden floor, hitting him somewhere in his chest, then raising an elbow and cracking the other assailant in the ribs, making him yell and release his grip. Nick got to his feet, everything blurred and fucked up, but knowing he just had to hit these people and hit them fucking hard. Someone with ginger hair came for him, and Nick swung a big and powerful right-hander into his face. It was a full blow, right from the shoulder with huge power. It'd have floored a Southerner, but this was a Scotsman and thus more used to pain, so he was just knocked backwards with a cry. He had him. Nick stepped forward and booted the man in the face as he stag-gered. Yeah, fucking take that. But then someone hit him so hard in the kidneys that it felt like something had exploded inside of him. It para-lysed him with a numb pain, robbing him of his energy and making him sink to his knees.

This wasn't going to end well.

The next blow to his head, delivered with something hard, rendered him unconscious in a black instant, so fast that he didn't even feel more than a moment of pain.

CHAPTER 8

Out of the void, he first heard voices, then smelled cigarette smoke and heard TV noise. His brain felt like it had been knocked out of his head. It didn't just hurt, it felt like it had been altered by the blow, probably from a baseball bat. Christ, maybe he had brain damage?

He was lying on his belly. Better not say or do anything for a bit. Get your shit together and work out what was going on. He tried to remember what had actually happened. He'd been knocked down some steps. There'd been a fight. He'd battered some bloke. What did he look like? Ginger. As he'd hit him, he'd thought there was something familiar about him. That guy. He was the bloke he'd confronted. The one who had taken photos.

So this *was* about the murder.

Had these people killed John Grayson-Thomas? Fuck. Why hadn't they killed him? Was this a warning? Were they stopping him going to the police?

A door opened, the noise from the other room grew in volume. It sounded like there were still just two people. Could he fight two off and get out? Yeah, he fucking could. There was often just one door in and out of these basement flats. They were a kind of subterranean cave, with a little yard in front of the door set right below the pavement.

'Is he still fuckin' oot?' said a voice he recognised as the ginger man.

'Aye.'

The man closed the door again. Nick raised his head and looked around. He was in the kitchen. The door he'd been pulled in through was behind him. A window let light in from up above. It looked like it was late in the day. He felt the side of his head. There was a swelling on his temple.

Fuckers. Again, he drew deep on that resilient, hard part of a Teessider that just really won't be pushed around by anyone; who refuses be intimidated.

Was the door unlocked? Didn't seem likely. They'd have to be very stupid to leave it unlocked. The place didn't seem occupied. It had the look of an unfurnished, unlived-in flat. He got to his knees quietly and moved his head from side to side. Remarkably, he didn't feel dizzy, though his head was splitting.

There had to be a weapon in a kitchen. He got to his feet and gingerly went to the door. There was no key in it. He pulled the black iron handle down but it was indeed locked. Looking around, there were no kitchen utensils on display. Where was a box of carving knives when you needed one?

A kitchen unit into which the sink was set, had a drawer. It was the sort of place he'd keep cutlery. Sliding it out carefully until it was fully extended, his heart sank, it was just full of old bills and bits of paper. He moved them to one side and there, at the bottom was something he recognised. A long, pointed metal skewer, the sort of thing you stick in a chicken to see if the juices run clear. He grabbed it and stuck it down his boot so it was parallel with his leg. He felt in his pockets for his phone. Gone. Shit. But...something else was in the coin pocket. He rolled it around his fingers. It was a small soft ball. He knew what it was. A plan formed in his mind.

The door was a big, heavy, wide Georgian one. There'd be no getting that open. The window was the best bet. Behind the sink, it was a Georgian sash but had a window lock on it. Fucking window locks. It was a tiny little thing. The key would be so easy to lose - in fact it probably had been lost. No. There it was. Pointlessly placed at the corner of the window sill.

It turned smoothly and released a catch. He'd have to pull the sash up and then vault over the sink and out of the window, but do it silently.

No time. There was noise in the other room. Laughing. The door opened. He turned his back to the window and rested on the sink unit.

The man was shocked to see him standing up and jumped slightly.

'Right. Fuckin' get in there!' he pointed to the other room.

'What the hell is going on, man? I don't know you - what's this all about?' said Nick, not moving.

'Don't fuckin' talk, just fuckin' walk.' The west of Scotland accent adds menace to even the most complimentary words, so when it came to actual threatening language, it wasn't to be argued with. But then, when you're a Teessider who is drawing deep on his inner Boro, you're not easily bullied, not by governments, not by Southerners and certainly not by Scotsmen. It's your secret weapon. The rest of the world doesn't even know it exists and they have no idea what a good weapon it is.

'I didn't realise I'd got assaulted and imprisoned by a bloody poet,' said Nick, arms crossed, determined not to show any fear.

'Do I have to fuckin' hit ye with that bat again?'

Nick scowled at him and walked through the door, two steps down a short hallway to a living room on the right.

As he walked in, the ginger man looked up. His nose was swollen and he had a bruise coming up around his eye from where Nick had hit him. He'd really messed him up. Nick gave him a bemused sneer.

'Want to take another photo, son?' he said, in his best Teesside accent, feeling decidedly indignant and belligerent, which is probably not the best emotion to feel when two Scottish nutters are holding you prisoner, but then, that's your inner Boro for you: bloody arsy.

The ginger man put a phone down and jabbed a finger at him. 'Shut up and sit down, ye prick.'

He pointed to a battered old armchair that looked like it had done significant time on a council tip. Nick knew it'd take 3 or 4 seconds to get to that kitchen window, a further 5 or 6 seconds to get that window open and get through it. But putting two men out of action for 10 seconds isn't easy, even if they were the kind of shortish, gaunt, underweight, bony men that Scotland's underclass specialises in producing.

So he sat down on the edge of the seat and laughed a little bitterly. He'd really fucking hurt Ginger. He was really swollen. Probably broke his cheekbone and eye socket. It was a superb hit. He'd put some power into it - must have hurt like hell. Ha.

'So what's it about, boys? Eh? What am I to you? I'm just some...'

'...fuckin shut yer yappin',' said the other man, who had a buzz cut and big ears.

'Why are you asking around town about Barbara Stewart and John Grayson-Thomas?' said Ginger. 'Why were you at that funeral?'

Nick glanced from one to the other.

'Why didn't you just ask me that, instead of assaulting me?'

'Dinnae be clever wi' me, pal,' said Ginger.

'Why is that being clever?' said Nick. 'Only a stupid person would think that was being clever.'

Buzz Cut hit him on the side of the head, right on the swelling. The pain fired through Nick like a bolt of molten lava. Bastard. He winced, but like Brian Close on a dodgy Headingley wicket in 1976 facing the West Indies fast bowlers and taking one on the side of the head from Andy Roberts, he wouldn't even rub it. Don't give them the pleasure in seeing they've hurt you. These things are where we draw our inspiration. These things are our emotional roots.

Instead, he ground his teeth together.

'Just fuckin' answer the question,' said Ginger. 'You'll get fuckin' badly hurt if ye don't.'

Nick was still determined not to show the pain that was surging through him. If it had been good enough for Stuart Boam and Graeme Souness, it was good enough for him. Slowly, he licked his dry lips and looked out of the top of his eyes.

'I met Barbara Stewart when I was on my honeymoon. I was then shown a photo of her after she'd apparently shot John Grayson-Thomas. She didn't seem like an obvious killer. I'm a journalist, I'm interested in the story. That's it. Why do you care, son?'

'Who are you writing for?' said Ginger.

'No-one. I'm a freelancer. Who are you? Why do you even care? Who paid you to get your fucking face pounded, son, eh?' He pulled back a bit; he was silently raging, ready to beat the snot out of him again.

'Where are you from?' said Buzz Cut.

'Teesside.'

'Teesside? Where's fuckin' Teesside?' said Ginger. Idiot.

Nick narrowed his eyes. 'It's the unfashionable but cool bit between North Yorkshire and Tyneside - basically wherever you're from, it's better than there and it's full of hard cunts.' In his head he immediately apologised to Julie for his language. She hated the word, but in his defence, he was under a lot of stress.

'What do you know about Frank Stewart?' said Buzz Cut.

'Nothing much. I'll ask you again, why does it matter to you?'

'Shut it. This is what you're going to do. You're going to go back home and you're going to forget all about this.'

'Am I, now? Why?'

'Do you ever stop fuckin' asking questions, prick?' said Ginger. 'I'll tell ye why, because if you don't, Julie, your wife, will receive a visit and she will be cut. Get me? Cut!' He picked up the phone from the floor and held it up at him. 'And I know exactly how much that would spoil her. She sent you a nice wee picture while you were spark oot.'

There was a sharp, well-lit photo on Nick's phone. It was Julie in very revealing white underwear, legs apart. He knew right away that she'd sent it to him that evening, as part of their mutual entertainment. Nick's guts felt instantly hot and leaden. This disgusting intrusion wouldn't stand.

'Fuckin' tasty bird, eh. Not so tasty with a fuckin' big scar on her face. Or maybe burn her cunt wi' acid, eh. Very nice.'

Nick's anger was instant and deep. He wanted to tear the phone from the evil little bastard's hand and stuff it down his throat. This violation into their private lives felt profound. He wasn't frightened, he was too angry now, but anger can cloud your brain. He knew that. You become blind to the consequences of your actions when you're properly furious and he was properly fucking furious. He also knew that when you're a depressive and you've seen the blackness of hell, you don't care about your own welfare as much as someone who hasn't. And that makes you dangerous. And he felt fucking dangerous. He just stared at the man, not blinking, unwavering in his gaze. Silent.

'Aye, you understand me now, eh,' Ginger said, feeling like he'd got the upper hand. How wrong he was.

Nick said nothing. Just stared. Hard. Inner. Fucking. Boro.

'So you know what you've got to do,' said Buzz Cut. 'Away home with you, right?'

Nick said nothing. Just kept staring at Ginger. Is that all this was? A warning? Someone had paid them to scare him. Well, they'd failed.

'Oh, playin' the hard man now, are we?' said Ginger, unimpressed.

Nick still said nothing, but flexed his right boot to feel the meat skewer still stuck down there.

'Thanks to your phone, we know where you live. Don't go thinking bad things won't happen to you if you don't just drop this investigation. Because they will. Right, stand up.'

As Nick did so, he made to scratch his ankle. A glance upwards told him the two men were gesturing at each other, deep in conversation and had turned away from him. This was his chance. All in one swift, smooth movement, he silently drew the foot-long skewer out of his boot, rolled the small soft ball in his other fingers then held it with the skewer, and with his other hand, picked up his phone and put it in his pocket. As he did so Ginger turned around and, seeing he was up to something made one stride towards him. As he did so, Nick elbowed him in the stomach as powerfully as he could, instantly winding him.

In a fast move, he sprang cat-like behind Ginger, got him in a choke hold around the neck and held the skewer to his right eye, the small soft ball now between his thumb and fingertip. The man was gasping for breath. It was poetry or dance, or something. Easy. Nick let go of his emotions, knowing that a bit of sodding crazy would only work in his favour.

As Buzz Cut advanced on him, Nick screamed, 'One more step and I'll stick this in his fucking eye!' Ginger properly yelled a weeping howl at that moment, terrified as he felt the point press hard into his flesh. Buzz

Cut stopped in his tracks and held his hands up as he saw the long, pointed skewer.

'OK, pal. OK. Take it easy, eh.'

'Take it easy?!' Nick yelled, his voice high-pitched and breaking with fury. 'You're telling me to take it easy? I should fucking gouge his fucking brain out, you fucking imbecile. Eh? Eh? Fuck you!' He gave it every mad sodding freak element he had in him. Gobs of foamy spittle spilled from his mouth.

Buzz Cut backed off from this tirade of hysterical screaming. There is joy in really letting go and letting all your shit out. He jabbed the skewer into Ginger's head again. Hard now.

Was he going to do it? Yeah. If he had to. He'd do it. The outrage at them having seen Julie like that was enough to make him. Nick leaned on the point so that it indented the skin at the side of Ginger's eye. Nick had him in an iron grip, his big biceps and shoulder muscles held him like a vice. He was half as big again as Ginger. He could crush a weedy fucker like this. Not so cocky now, eh, son?

'Now. Let me make myself very clear. If you turn up on Teesside I will kill both of you with my bare fucking hands. If you so much as breathe the air within 50 miles of Julie, I will torture you until you'll wish you would die. Get me? You fucking know I will. Now, what's the issue with this murder? What's it to do with you? Talk now! Or first he loses the right eye and then the left.'

Ginger made a little panting yelp of fear again, still trying to regain his breath after being winded.

'Alright...look...we're working for someone,' said Buzz Cut.

'Who?'

Ginger struggled and yelled out. 'Don't hurt me, please...please...tell him, Jocky.'

Nick pushed at the skewer a little more. It must have broken the skin but fuck it, he'd heal over.

'What are your instructions? Who paid you to scare me off?' he said.

'To stop investigations into that guy's murder. Some guy, man, honest, we don't know him, do we, Jocky?'

'Who's asked you to do this?'

'We don't know him!' yelled Ginger. 'Just some guy. We don't ask questions do we? Not our place to ask questions. We met him in the Iona bar in Leith.' He was clearly, totally in fear of losing an eye, at least without anaesthetic.

154

'When did you get told to do this?'

'Last night,' said Buzz Cut. 'Let him go, eh.' He was trying to be emollient now.

'I was told to take photos of everyone at the funeral. I saw you, took a photo and sent him it. He told us to scare you off. Honest!' gulped Ginger.

'Who is he?'

'We don't know. The guy who paid us was this bloke's mate. Said he wanted the funeral watched. Gave us a phone number to send the pictures to. Honest, man I dinnae know who it is,' said Buzz Cut. 'Let him go, eh, pal?'

'Nah, I really want to fucking hurt him,' said Nick, and he did, but he also realised this was his moment to really make an impression so that they'd leave him and by extension Julie, alone. 'No-one takes the piss out of my wife, you dirty bastards. You're not dealing with a normal guy here!'

'Aye, fair enough. I can see you're a big man. I get you. We didnae mean anything by it, pal. Crackin' lookin' bird ye got there,' said Ginger, still unable to move from Nick's grip. As though such a compliment would help their cause.

'A bird? You're calling my wife a bird? You know what, she could kick your fucking arse! What could she do?' He jerked at his neck to elicit a response.

'Kick my fucking arse,' said Ginger.

'You're pathetic.' Nick withdrew the skewer from the corner of his eye for a moment, knowing from seeing Jo's show, that fear is best delivered on the heels of relief. He could feel Ginger breathe a sigh to release his tension and just when he felt that, he squeezed the small pellet between his thumb and forefinger, then pulled back the piece of metal and jammed the point right into Ginger. Fast and hard. Right in the corner of his eye. Have that. You fucker. Bam!

Ginger screamed and promptly passed out in a faint.

Blood ran from his eye. A lot of blood. Dark, thick, sick blood.

Nick let the fainted body fall and looked up at Buzz Cut with a willfully manic stare that came easy to him. He went slack-mouthed, staring at him like he was crazy, making saliva dribble down his chin. 'Right, you're next, you dirty bastard. You want some, do you, son? Eh?' He held the bloody skewer aloft and moved towards him, like he was going to lobotomise him.

Buzz Cut was scared shitless. 'Fuckin' hell! You're a madman! Fuckin' hell!' He stared at his mate for a moment, then turned and ran for it. Nick heard him unlock the door and flee.

'C'mon, Boro!' he yelled, two fists aloft, because it was the only thing that made sense. His inner Boro had won.

Maybe he could have a career as an illusionist. Amazing what copying a simple trick and a blood capsule could achieve. As he'd jabbed the metal rod into Ginger's skin, he'd burst the blood capsule as he'd let his grip go so it slid backwards, but he'd gripped it again just before it had fallen to the floor. The effect had been to make it appear the skewer had gone right into his eye. Ginger must have felt the point jab into him and fainted at that point. That was a bit of a bonus.

Nick walked out of the flat, closed the door, skipped up the stairs and out onto the street. It was quiet, the sun was almost down. He was drenched in sweat, but he also felt weirdly elated. As he walked back to the flat, he called Julie.

'Hello?' she said, clearly suspicious.

'Jules. It's OK, it's me.'

She breathed a sigh of relief.

'What's been going on?'

He explained the situation. She yelped in shock when he told her about being hit.

'Oh, bloody hell. That's horrible. Oh, god. Are you alright?' she said, worried.

'I've got a lump on my head, but I must have a sodding thick skull or something 'cos even my headache has gone off.'

'Oh, for god's sake. And they saw that picture I sent to you, didn't they? Shit. I had my legs....oh, god!'

'I'm afraid so, luv.'

She made a frustrated noise.

'I knew something was up. I got a really vulgar reply to the photo, which just wasn't the sort of thing you'd ever say in a million years. I didn't reply. I thought maybe someone had picked up your phone in a pub.'

'Yeah, I was a tad cross, to say the least. I...err...I exacted a degree of revenge, if it's any comfort.'

'Oh, god, it's so embarrassing. Well, sort of. It's not like I'll ever meet the dirty bastards. Even so...urgh. Oh, god, your poor head.'

'I don't think the stupid fuckers were supposed to knock me out. They were supposed to scare me. They totally overdid it, which suggests they're hardly professionals. I overcame them, one way or another. I don't think they knew who had asked them to scare me off. It was done through an intermediary. I think the only person who might have known who I was had to be Frank Stewart, who I'd met earlier.'

'But he'd not go down to a pub in Leith and pay for some hard men to put the frighteners on you. He wouldn't have a clue how to do that, would he?'

'I know. It doesn't seem likely. But who else?'

'Someone at the art school?'

'I only went there after the funeral. They already knew about me by then. He'd taken the photo and sent it to someone and they'd said, go and get him. So I was known by someone once they got that picture.'

'Well, we're all easy enough to look up online these days. If I put your name into Google, loads of pictures of you come up.'

'Yeah, you're right. I'm going to have a kip in the flat. I'm exhausted. All the adrenalin in me has gone and I'm like a limp rag.'

'Alright, darlin'. Where are you now?'

'I'm just walking up Howe Street.'

'I bet it looks lovely.'

'Yeah, it's a nice evening.'

'I hate us being apart again.'

He unlocked the front door of the building and went up two flights of stairs to Big Fish's flat.

'Yeah, me, too. I miss your smell.'

'Ha ha...what do I smell of?'

'Honey and straw and muskiness.'

'Muskiness! What's that smell like?'

'It's a posh word for the smell of sex,' he said.

'Well, it's not surprising I smell of that in our bed, is it?'

He put the lights on and kicked off his shoes and laughed. 'I suppose not. Talking of which, I've not taken a close look at that photo you sent, yet.'

'Oh, you can't now. Not now those blokes saw it. Doesn't feel right. Delete it. Shall I send you another now?'

'No, Don't be daft. I'm going to bed. Not in the mood for that sort of thing after what's happened.'

'Of course. OK, luv. Sleep tight. I'll see you tomorrow. I'll pick you up at Darlo. When's your train get in?'

'Two pm. Alright, Jules. Love you.'

'Love you, too.'

His clothes stank of smoke and sweat, so he stripped them off and went for a shower. His body was covered in grazes and bruises from the fall down the steps. Looking in the mirror, he gingerly prodded the swelling on the side of his head. It felt a bit smaller. Most of the bruising was under his hair. He'd got lucky really. He must have been clipped with the bat rather than given the full meat of it otherwise he'd surely have had a serious injury or be dead.

After getting clean, he sat in the dark by the window looking out down the street as the clock ticked around to 11pm. A youngish woman got ready for bed in a flat opposite, walking around her bedroom with large breasts crammed into a black bra, a low light lamp illuminating her. He wasn't sure whether to look or not, given the intrusion both he and Julie had felt over the photo on his phone. Deciding that it would be intrusive to stare at her, he drew the big curtains shut.

But just as the thick, heavy curtains came together, he caught a glimpse of someone on the street below. After he'd closed them, who it was suddenly came to him. A woman, middle-aged, curly dark hair, coming up the steps to the front door.

Quietly, he hurried out of the bedroom and into the hallway with a towel wrapped around him. Without putting the light on, he stood by the big wooden door. There was frosted security glass, either side of it. The stairwell lights illuminated the hallway. The front door slammed shut and footsteps came up the stairs with a crisp clip clop. Closer. Closer.

Nick quietly turned the Yale lock to open the door.

'Hello!' he said, opening it, just as the curly-haired woman was at the top of the stairs, right in front of him.

She let out a yell. 'Jesus Christ! What the hell are you doing?!'

'Did I surprise you? Sorry.' He grinned at him.

Him.

Not her.

Up close, he could tell, having seen him only hours earlier. *She* was Frank Stewart. And Frank knew he'd met him earlier using a different name, but he couldn't say.

He made a pretty good woman.

Being fair and grey meant he didn't have much of a beard line to hide under make-up and the wig changed him significantly, but standing 18 inches away from him, there was no doubt who it was. Now he was standing tall and not stooped. That was his Frank act, to look older. Now he looked stronger and much younger.

Nick played it cool, as though he had no idea who it was, though clearly Frank must have known who he was. Maybe he had known when he'd met him in the street. If he'd paid those thugs to scare him off, this was going to be a bit of a shock for him.

'I'm sorry to shock you. I'm Nick. A friend of Stevie Salmon. He's letting me use the flat tonight. Just in case you heard someone moving around, it's just me.' He smiled again and pushed his wet hair off his forehead.

Frank spoke with a very light, slightly hoarse voice.

'Oh, that's alright, err, Nick. Thanks for letting me know.'

Nick watched him walk upstairs. He was wearing a loose pair of dark trousers and a blue blouse. Could easily have been a woman but was, in reality, a man.

Nick returned to the bedroom and looked at the notes he'd been writing on his phone. The last time he'd been in this bedroom with Julie, he'd briefly entertained the idea that Frank was dressed as the curly-haired woman and also as Barbara. But now it was a much less crazy idea. In fact, it felt like he'd discovered the truth.

He texted Jeff.

'Are you awake, big man?'

A reply came immediately. *'I have a baby crying with a voice as loud as Joe Cocker singing into a fog horn. Of course I'm awake.'*

Nick called him and explained what had happened.

'You know what this means?' said Jeff.

'I was hoping you'd tell me.'

'You knew it was him dressed in the curly wig right away, didn't you?'

'Right away, yeah.'

'But wouldn't you have guessed the woman you met as Barbara was actually a man as well? It's not like he's going to be rubbish at being a woman in a curly wig, but not in a long grey-haired wig.'

Nick tugged on his bottom lip in contemplation. 'I know it sounds mad, but it never occurred to me or to Jules that the person who said they were Barbara wasn't a woman, but then we hadn't met the man claiming to be Frank at that time, had we? So I had no comparison.'

'See, that's what worries me. OK, maybe he's a better Barbara than a...err...what shall we call the curly-haired woman? Who did he look like?'

'A bit like a mid 70s "I've Got the Music in Me" Kiki Dee, only older.'

'I loved Kiki Dee. Her first records came out on Motown, y'know...her real name is...'

'...Pauline Matthews and she's from Bradford. Yup, I know.'

'Aye, of course you do. OK, so maybe our Frank is a better, more convincing Barbara than he is a Kiki.'

'I just didn't think it was a man either on the stairs or in the photo.'

As he talked, Nick searched online on his laptop for any more news stories about the Grayson-Thomas shooting. The last was three days ago and was a short quote from Gordon Smith to say that it was still an active investigation; they were following leads. It was all a bit vague.

'Do you think I should go to the cops, Jeff? I was on my way there when I was jumped. When I got out I didn't know what to do. Maybe I should've reported it right away. I don't know if what we said to the police that night *was* actually said to the police.'

'I think you have to tell them what you know, just in case. Then we know for sure that they know her name. You don't have to tell them everything. Just give them her name. Look, I've got to go. I think Argie has laid an egg.'

The police station was a horrible 1960s building. All cheap yellowish brick and glass, it looked like it had come out of the same box as the poorly made secondary modern schools that were so typical of his youth. A desk sergeant with greying dark hair and dark eyes looked up as Nick walked in the next morning.

'Yes, sir?' he said.

'Err...I'm...err...it's a bit complicated. A man called John Grayson-Thomas was shot...and two police officers came around to ask me and my wife about it.'

'And what's your name?'

'Nick Guymer. And they showed us what they said was a CCTV photo of the woman who had shot him.'

The cop made some notes and was almost totally impassive, to the point of disinterest. 'And why have you decided to come and tell us this now, sir?'

'Well. Recently, I've begun to doubt that the people who came to the flat were actually the police. And I wanted to make sure it was you guys and that you actually know who I said she was. Maybe I could speak to Gordon Smith? I understand he's in charge of the investigation.'

Nick rubbed his fingertips across his forehead, knowing it sounded a bit odd, to say the least. He found himself wanting to say, 'I'm not mad, honest.' Which, he imagined, only mad people actually said.

'Just a minute, please, Mr Guymer.' The man turned away, opened a door and disappeared. Nick sat down on a chair and looked around. The weird thing about police stations is that they embodied the power of the state. Somewhere, not far away, were the holding cells. They could deprive you of your liberty, just like that and for a while, at least, there was nothing you could do about it. You like to think of the police as somehow a protector of your freedom but time and again, they had proven to be the exact opposite of that.

Nick felt nervous even being in there. What if they got hold of the wrong end of the stick and thought he was somehow involved in the murder? Don't be stupid. They weren't going to do that.

His hands were sweaty and he felt guilty, despite not having broken the law in any meaningful way in his whole life...well...apart from buying cannabis when he was younger. And he'd had a short but prolific shoplifting phase in Harrogate when he was very depressed, during which he managed to walk out of supermarkets with halloumi cheese and stuffed olives on a regular basis. Why those two things, he still didn't know, but he wasn't well in the head at the time. But if Edinburgh police knew about his brief period of cheese theft, he'd be very surprised.

Over five minutes passed before the desk sergeant came back.

'Someone will see you soon, Mr Guymer,' he said, still expressionless. How old was this bloke? It was hard to tell in Scotland, sometimes. People seemed to age quickly here. Perhaps it was the IrnBru. This fella could be anything from 30 to 60. He was impressively repressed. Not a flicker of any kind of emotion passed across his face. When it came to swallowing it down, drinking it off your mind and into an early grave, the Scots could teach everyone a few lessons, even Teessiders.

Eventually, a man in a bad suit emerged from a side door. He had to be some sort of detective. He might as well have had it tattooed on him.

'Mr Guymer?'

'That's me.'

He held the interview room door open for Nick. Nick sat down at a wooden desk and the detective sat opposite him.

'I'm Detective Gordon Smith. I'm working on the Grayson-Thomas murder. You have some information for us?' He spoke in a thick Edinburgh accent that Nick had to listen hard to, in order to understand. English people often thought the Glasgow accent was the least penetrable, but he'd always found the working-class accent of Edinburgh to be almost impossible to understand, as it was delivered at high speed and with a slur which ran all words into one, making it appear as though they were speaking words 169 letters long. Detective Smith almost expressed his sentence as though it was one long vowel noise.

This was who Wally had been talking about. He explained the situation again to him. Smith looked at him with dark, thoughtful eyes, arms folded across his chest as he listened.

'I just wanted to make sure you knew that the woman in that photo is Barbara Stewart. Or, at least, the person who told us she was called Barbara Stewart from the flat above.'

Smith nodded. 'Good. Thanks for coming in, Nick. Wish we had more concerned citizens to help us find criminals.' He gave Nick a quick half-smile. 'Can you tell me why do you think those people that came to see you were not police officers?' Straight away, Nick noticed he was careful to neither confirm nor deny anything. Keeping his cards close to his chest was probably an important requirement of the job.

'I realised that although they'd said they were police, and they were dressed as police officers, there was no proof they were. I accepted it as a fact. And I noticed you hadn't released her name to the press and I wondered if you even knew about her, so that's why I'm here.'

He was struggling to organise all of this into something cogent and now felt a bit stupid. It all made sense in his head, but from the outside, maybe it sounded like the ramblings of a madman or a conspiracy nut. And that was before trying to explain that Frank may well be Barbara. Sitting in the police station, that seemed too ludicrous to even say out loud, even though he was quite certain Frank was Kiki and therefore, quite possibly, Barbara too.

Smith opened up a file full of papers. You'd think it'd all be on computers.

'Was the photo you were shown, this one?'

He held up the printout of the image that was already so familiar to Nick.

'Yes, that's it. OK, so they *were* real policemen...I know it seemed odd of me to...'

'...I didnae say that, did I, Nick? Tell me exactly what these people looked like.'

'They weren't your people?'

He didn't exactly answer that. 'Until you came here, I had never heard of you, Nick Guymer.'

'Oh, shit.'

'Aye.' He looked impassively at Nick. 'Do you know where this photo came from, by any chance, Nick?' Smith flicked at the paper print.

'No. I've not got a clue. Sorry.'

Smith went quiet and seemed to be weighing up how much to tell him. He had dark and yet somehow bright eyes. The whites were porcelain-like, and not bloodshot like Nick's. He was an intense sort of bloke, yet quite attractive because of that.

'It was sent to us anonymously,' said Smith. That was what Wally Givens had said, too. 'I'd love to know who sent it. If you hear a name, will you let me know, Nick?'

'Yeah, of course.' In Nick's experience, Colin Harcombe excepted, the police were, by and large, quite stupid blokes. The women he'd met in law enforcement tended to be more bright. The blokes were a bizarre collective of often uneducated people, who had learned jargon in order to sound clever and others who were so emotionally traumatised that they were dead behind the eyes; thus ideal for a job which involved vile, evil tragedy, every single day. Gordon Smith wasn't like that, at all. He looked more like a university lecturer, but he was very reserved. Nick sat back and looked at him. He was tense, that was the overall impression he gave off. He had a habit of biting down on his bottom lip and his brow was constantly furrowed in a frown. It had to be high-pressure work, though. Everyone wants you to find a killer. All eyes are on you.

'Have you spoken to Frank Stewart?' asked Nick.

Smith was non-committal about that and blew out his cheeks, replying evasively, 'Women who look like that don't shoot people, but we've not been able to find any record of her. Do you know where she is?'

'That might be because she's dead. Frank told me she died of cancer. Her grave is in the Dean Cemetery.'

Smith seemed unmoved by that. 'So who is this in the photo?'

'The person we met on the stairs.'

'And who was that?'

Nick felt like he was being tested, somehow. Smith was far from stupid. It felt like he was being interviewed or even interrogated.

'I just said, she said she was Barbara Stewart, but she can't have been if she's dead from cancer...'

'OK, just a minute.' He got up and left the room.

Oh, god, the sitting around was interminable and claustrophobic. Nick felt edgy and wanted to leave.

Finally Smith returned, holding another sheet of paper and sat down, pointing at it, a look of slight surprise on his face.

'It says here that both Frank Stewart and Barbara Stewart died three years ago in a car crash. So whoever you met couldn't have been either of them.'

CHAPTER 9

Nick stared at him, doubting that the policeman was right. *Both* dead? Well, who the hell was pretending to be Frank, then?

'Are you sure?'

'Take a look for yourself.'

Nick glanced down at the piece of paper. It appeared to be a printout from the Police National Computer confirming that Frank and Barbara Stewart were killed in a head-on collision on the A9 over three years ago. How much could or should Nick trust this? Question all realities. After all, he wouldn't know a genuine PNC printout from any other official-looking document. He felt uncomfortable under Smith's intense gaze.

He looked up at Smith, who was drumming his fingers on the desk. Smith said, 'Hold on. I'm just going to check something again.'

He left the room again, taking the PNC printout with him. Nick placed his fingers together and thought about the news of the A9 crash. Both of them dead? Really? So where was Frank's grave? It wasn't alongside his wife's. Why had the 'Frank' he spoke with said she'd died of cancer? Who the hell had been working at the art school for a year? Who was the man dressed as Kiki Dee? Who'd paid the thugs to scare him away? How many more layers of illusion and deception did he have to dig through to get to the truth?

When Smith returned he cleared his throat and pulled out the chair, scraping the metal legs on the lino floor and letting out a gasp of air.

'Right, Nick. I want to thank you for coming in. I've cleared this up. It certainly *was* our boys who paid you a visit and showed you the picture. I now have the notes from that interview.'

Nick looked at him skeptically.

Smith looked at the back of his hands and sneered. 'I'll let you in on a secret, this place is on the verge of chaos most of the time, and information collation is in a mess. We sent out three teams of two to show that photo we were sent, to people in the New Town, because she looked like she was from around there - from the New Town.'

Nick thought that sounded ludicrous. That's not how policing works. Smith was surely lying to him. 'OK, but we told the two coppers who it was. We said it's the woman who lives upstairs and gave them her name. They went up and knocked on her door but got no reply. Is there no record of this? You're in charge, you should have known who I was.'

'Put it this way - it wasn't where it should have been. But everything is fine. It was acted on. You and Julie are in the system, so to speak. It just took me some time to put my hands on it.' He smiled again.

Nick narrowed his eyes and looked at Smith, feeling something was wrong about this. Was he lying, or maybe he was being lied to and that was making him look like he was lying. Surely the police were not so disorganised. Then again, maybe they were. Big organisations can easily get out of hand if not kept in check by good operational systems. He must have been unwittingly expressing his cynical disbelief because Smith held up his hands and sat back in his chair.

'I don't like it any more than you do, Nick. I wish I had everything at my fingertips but that's not always possible. So what we have here, in effect, is a murder being committed by someone dressed as a dead woman. It's a new one on me. You have no idea who they might be or where to find them?'

'No. None. Hadn't you better go round to that flat and find out who *is* living there? There is mail addressed to Frank Stewart there. Whoever he actually is, he was there yesterday morning. Someone calling themselves Barbara Stewart *has* been working at the art school, though she's disappeared now.'

Smith wrote that down and then stared at his own writing, as though digesting it.

'If you're already dead, no-one can arrest you for murder, can they?' he said.

'Exactly. I'm sure if you go over there and pull the man in who is living there, whatever clothes he's wearing, you'll get to the truth of this. The fact is, you should have pulled him in already. You should have been in that flat, found all his women's clothes and sorted it out. You had the info from me and Julie.'

He had the feeling that Smith wasn't listening to him. 'Yes. You're right. I want to thank you again for your help, Nick. Leave this with me now and I'll add this all into my work. We have been making good progress, actually.'

'Can I ask why you haven't publicly given out Barbara's name as someone you want to interview?'

Without hesitation he replied, 'That's all procedural, I'm afraid. I can't discuss that. There is a good reason though, I can tell you that.' He gave Nick a smile and held out his hand.

Nick stood up and shook his hand quickly.

'Here's my contact details, detective. If you need any more info, just call me. I'm going home now.'

'Of course. Thanks again for your help, Nick. We'll get to the bottom of this now, I'm sure. Leave it with us.'

As Nick sat on the train pulling out of Waverley Station heading south to Darlington, he found himself looking forward to getting back to Tees-side and leaving this weird shit behind. Nothing about it sat right and he now had little confidence in the police. The story he had so far uncovered was very commercial - but he couldn't make any of it stand up, yet. He still needed some hard facts and they were very hard to come by. Just when he thought he'd grasped a fact, it became unreliable.

The train journey south from Edinburgh is a magnificent one, with the wild North Sea on one side and rolling farmland on the other. In a country which is so often said to be overcrowded and even 'full', the miles and miles of empty rural Northumberland rather put the lie to that notion. The endless wide, romantic windswept beaches are easily the finest in the land. Nick stared out and not for the first time wondered what people coming from the narrow, cluttered world of London must think of this place. It must seem to them like they are miles from civilisation.

For part of the trip, his phone was off the network. Brilliant. Why should communication devices rule our lives so much? Sometimes it felt as though the future would be all about the places and spaces where you couldn't get a signal and had to rely on your own imagination instead. At some point, the new modern way would surely become what had previously been the old way.

Julie was standing on the platform as the train pulled into Darlington. She waved at him as he got out. His heart made a little leap as he saw her.

'Now then, you,' he said, wrapping his arms around her.

'You smell sweaty. How's your head?' She pushed his hair back a little. 'Oooh, that's nasty. It's going purple. You're lucky it hasn't blacked your eyes.'

'Actually, it's not been hurting. I took some Ibuprofen this morning before I went to the police station and it seems to have taken the swelling down.'

He took her hand. She look at him with a big smile. 'I don't know, you're always getting into trouble, you.'

On the ride home in the Porsche, he brought her up to date with everything.

'The fact the police might be a bit useless, doesn't surprise me,' said Julie as they got out in the car park at the back of Green Dragon Yard and went up to their flat. 'But when it's a murder investigation you'd think they'd be more careful. Do you think this Gordon Smith bloke is...I dunno...is he corrupt or something?'

'I couldn't work that out. It all may have been exactly as he said, or he could have been trying to muddy the waters for me,' said Nick. 'I'll tell you what, though, it's spooky meeting people who are pretending to be other people. It makes you feel like all of life is a play, or a film, and Smith just felt like another actor in the drama. Everything about it, from the moment we met Barbara, feels like it's been part of a fiction, but I just can't work out where the truth of it is and I'm not sure it's even possible to. One thing I do know is someone wants to scare me off finding out anything, which suggests I'm close to the truth, even if I don't know it.'

'Didn't you tell Smith about the attack?'

'No. Nor about Kiki Dee...'

'Why not?'

He shrugged. 'I just felt like I should keep it to myself. Instinct.'

'Well, as you did such a good job of playing the nutter with those two thugs, maybe we won't hear anything more about this.'

'In a way, I hope so. But it keeps nagging at me, like a stone in my shoe. The fact remains a man was murdered and someone doesn't want us to find out why or who by.'

The working week fell back into its normal patterns. Nick got the first draft of his first novel done and began to work on rewriting parts of it, unsure if it was any good. The events in Edinburgh fell back into the churning sea of life and they heard nothing more about the murder. Nick wrote everything they knew about the murder into a piece, just in case it was resolved and he could fill in the gaps and then sell it. Every day he checked the *Edinburgh Evening News* website in case there was any new information. But there was nothing. Jo emailed him and Jeff with some more of her conspiratorial ideas, but there was no way to prove any of them. Despite wanting to know who the murderer was and who the deceased was, it just seemed impossible to find out anything more.

The August bank holiday came and went and the feeling was palpable that the summer, such as it ever was in the northeast of England, had gone, as a cool and rainy September arrived.

Humans tend to live in the now, largely because we have no choice. We're mostly obsessed with what is happening in the moment and not what has happened or indeed, what will happen. So although the shooting of John Grayson-Thomas had been a big thing in mid-August, a couple of weeks into September, it simply wasn't any more. Uneventful ordinary life took over.

Nick was standing behind Jeff's counter early one evening, looking through a pile of records that had just come in.

'This is another dead hippy collection, Jeff. Top-notch gear. It still excites me when I see stuff like this.' He held up a copy of Cream's *Disraeli Gears.* 'First pressing, by the look of it.'

'Yeah, that's a £100 record. Nothing in there recorded after 1975. There's some spiral Vertigo stuff and some finger-in-the-ear folk on Transatlantic. The bloke used to live on Fairfield Road, actually. His daughter brought it all in. It's funny how a lot of people just hate these big heavy piles of cardboard and vinyl. I mean, I gave her a fair price, but I could have given her a tenner, just for her to get rid and she'd have been happy. They can't conceive that to some people, these are highly desirable items.'

'Rather them than those who think because they've got a copy of *Beatles for Sale* they're going to be minted.'

Jeff filed some papers into a box binder. 'Nearly there with the club, y'know. I reckon we'll be open for Christmas. Still a lot of men with thin moustaches and pencils behind their ears have to approve all the work we get done - but that's about it.'

'I admire your patience in dealing with it,' said Nick, looking up as Julie walked in.

'Alright, Jules,' said Jeff. 'What brings you to my Emporium for Dysfunctional Men?'

'Dysfunctional women buy records, too,' she said, running a finger down her centre parting.

'This is true. In the same way that some men like going shopping for shoes. They do exist, but they're an exotic elite.'

She coughed out a laugh. 'I hate shopping for shoes, too. In fact, I don't much like shopping for anything much, except bottles of vodka and gin.'

'Are you finished work for the day, then?' said Nick.

'Aye. I came straight here 'cos I've just had some odd news.'

'What's that, like?' said Nick, tidying up the record pile into a neat, even stack.

'Remember Caroline?'

'Sorry, no. Who was she?'

'She's the woman at Northdean School who set up that team-building away day we did down there.'

'I should have a team-building away day,' said Jeff.

'You do. You just call it drinking in the Royal Oak,' said Nick.

'Oh, yeah. That's right. I should claim back the cost of the vodka against tax. It's a business expense. Mind, calling the 20-foot walk to the Royal Oak "away" might be stretching it a bit. More traditionally it'd be called "here".'

'Actually, "Stay Days" *are* a business thing. When I was a legal PA we used to have them. They're basically a budget version of away days,' said Julie.

She perched herself on a high stool by the counter and adjusted her bra strap under her blouse. 'Anyway, I'd asked her weeks ago to look up Frank Stewart when he was headmaster and find out, if possible, why he left in 1980. Remember?'

'Oh, yeah. Has she found out something?' said Nick.

'Oh, god, not that business again? I've been enjoying not having to think about all that stuff,' said Jeff, pulling a face.

She raised her long, thin right index finger. 'She's found out one rather important thing, yes.' Her sapphire blue eyes looked at Nick and then looked over to Jeff. 'He didn't *quit* as headmaster.'

'He didn't? He was sacked? What did he do to get sacked?' said Jeff, putting his box file onto a shelf.

She shook her head. A loosely curled strand of blond hair fell over her shoulder. 'He wasn't sacked.'

'He wasn't sacked and he didn't quit. So what happened?' said Nick, puzzled.

'He died.'

The two old friends looked at her and then at each other, both as blankly confused as the other.

'He died?' said Jeff. 'He didn't die in 1980, he died in 2007. That copper told Nick. It was on the PNC.'

'They lied or were just plain wrong. He definitely died in 1980. Caroline eventually looked it up on the microfiche of old newspapers in

Northallerton library. Frank Stewart, headmaster of Northdean School, died in 1980. He fell downstairs while actually at the school and broke his neck.' She took a piece of paper out of her back pocket and flattened it on the counter. 'She sent me a scan from a newspaper. I printed it out. This is Barbara, interviewed a year later in the Harrogate *Advertiser*. She was raising money for a charity and even mentions the death of her husband Frank in the piece.'

Nick took hold of it and squinted at it. It was dated October 21, 1981. Jeff came and stood behind him then went to his big computer and found the murder picture to compare the two images.

There she was.

Jeff raised his index finger and looked at them. 'Well, I'll say it first. These two are the same person. Now, I know technically, the dead can't be murderers, but Babs here seems to have found a way around that. There isn't even one per cent of doubt about this being her. Not in my mind. This is the proof we've needed all along, as to her identity. Despite what you thought, she wasn't Frank, or someone pretending to be Frank, dressed up, it really was a woman called Barbara Stewart. She told you the truth when she told you that.'

'I agree,' said Julie, nodding. 'They're too similar to say otherwise.'

Nick looked at the picture. He wasn't so sure at all. They were similar, but 30 years can make someone change a lot and the CCTV shot wasn't super sharp. He recalled what Jo had showed them - how your mind can make connections and see things that are not true. 'But it's bizarre,' said Nick feeling incredulous. 'She's dead. I've seen her gravestone.'

'You've seen *a* gravestone, not a body,' said Jeff. 'And didn't you say that Smith said she'd died in a car crash but the faux Frank said it was cancer?'

'Yes.'

Jeff tugged on his beard. 'Can't both be right.'

'Hold on, does this mean that I really could have seen her in Bedale, then? She's from North Yorkshire so she probably fled down here. I knew it was her! I said, didn't I? You talked me out of being sure about that but I was sure. If she's not dead, it could have been her.'

'The woman who crashed the car wasn't her, but we have nothing to disprove that you saw her in Bedale,' said Jeff. 'Curiouser and curiouser. This is so whacked out that even if I made up my best conspiracy theory, it wouldn't be extreme enough. It's totally twisting my melon. Frank and

Barbara have, apparently, both died. Frank in 1980 and 2007, Barbara also in 2007, apparently from two different causes.'

Nick thought about it and cracked his knuckles one at a time in contemplation.

'I can almost hear the gears and pistons working in your brain,' said Jeff. 'Do you want me to throw some more coal into your boiler?'

'Shut up man, I'm thinking,' said Nick, taking out a notepad and writing ideas down as they flooded into his brain. Sometimes, the fog lifts and you're full, albeit briefly, of insight and original thought.

Julie looked over at his notes as he stopped writing and held up a hand. Nick spoke.

'Here's what I think, right? First, that PNC printout that Gordon Smith showed me was obviously wrong. I think someone is dressing as both Frank and Barbara. They've assumed their identities and hit upon this idea of killing Grayson-Thomas dressed as Barbara, for the reason we've always said - that if she doesn't exist, she can't be caught for murder. But creating a convincing, well-rounded, believable identity is hard and takes time. You need to know a lot about someone to pass yourself off as them over a long period. Now, we know that Frank is on the electoral register and that Barbara worked at the art school. But both are dead so it seems logical to assume the same person is being both Frank and Barbara. If that's true, the person doing that must have known them very well or at least had access to all the details about their life needed to pass themselves off convincingly. Now, the picture of Barbara in 1981 looks like the CCTV picture, but if it's not her, it must be a family member who looks like her. A sister, brother, daughter or son, seems most likely...'

'...and if they're doing this, then they're very messed up. And a messed-up person might come from a messed-up family and a messed-up family means only one thing...' interrupted Julie.

Yes. It all made perfect sense.

'...abuse of some sort, be it physical, mental or both,' said Nick, nodding. 'The dead man is anonymous before 2001. Odds on, he was the shooter's abuser and changed his name at some point in 2001, which is why we can't find him before that.'

Jeff began to lock up and turn off the lights. 'That all makes a lot of sense. You just need to prove it now and you've got yourself that tabloid story to sell. Cross-dressing, murder and child abuse. That's a golden ticket.'

'That's just what I'm going to do,' said Nick.

He got to the smart little market town of Northallerton just before 9am the next day. It fancied itself, did Northallerton. Always had. It was the capital of North Yorkshire, after all. Not that such a title meant a lot to anyone, except some people from Northallerton, possibly. North Yorkshire is easily the most snobby of all the Yorkshires. It elects Tory MPs and it thinks it's a cut above. Not for them the industry and the labouring classes to the north and south of the county. Here, they're more about rural pursuits and wearing quilted clothing.

Sitting down at the microfiche reader in the library, he soon found the reference to Frank's death in the Harrogate *Advertiser*:

Northdean School headmaster Frank Stewart, 33, was found dead yesterday at 4.30pm. It is believed he had slipped and fallen down stairs at the school. He was found by his wife, Barbara, 30. A doctor was called but he was pronounced dead at the scene. 'This was a terrible accident and has left the school utterly devastated,' said deputy headmaster Sean Michaels. Stewart leaves his wife Barbara and a 14-year old son.

Nick's heart flew up into his mouth. A son!

Yes. Get in!

And where was he now? Up in Edinburgh, pretending to be his parents, maybe.

Hold on, though. Barbara was 30 in 1980. That meant in 2007, she'd have been 66 or 67 and not 64, as it had said on the headstone. Nick took a deep breath and looked out of the library window at the autumnal weather blowing leaves from the trees swirling into the air. That headstone was another fiction; another plot twist in the story that was being woven for them. The man pretending to be Frank Stewart had lied. He'd not only lied, he'd had the lie ready to use. But the chances of finding a grave of someone with the right name, born in the same year, was too unlikely. He'd found one that looked about right, as long as you didn't know her exact year of birth.

He went back to his phone and looked for a photo he'd taken of the headmasters board at the school. Sean Michaels had taken over from Frank Stewart. He'd been Head until 1997, in fact. A good stint. He'd done well out of Frank's death. Had he not died, Frank could have been *in situ* for at least 30 years; in fact he could still have been in position in 2010.

He began looking back through newspapers from 1975 onwards for stories about the school, but there was nothing outside details of sports teams and choirs. Looking for other news about the school was going to be a task that would take weeks and months because you had to just plough through thousands of pages of scans. He went up to the woman working on the reference library desk.

'Hiya. I'm researching the history of Northdean School and would like a list of all the teachers who worked there from 1960 to 1980. I don't suppose there's any documentation of that sort of information?'

'Have you tried the school website?' she said with a smile. She was a washed out sort of middle-aged woman, who put Nick in mind of his own mother. Tired, but with kind eyes and yet quite timid.

Nick looked back at her. No. No, he hadn't. Stupid idiot. He'd be a shite investigative reporter. Better stick to reporting on the Boro's lack of a decent striker.

'Good idea. Thanks.'

He went to a computer. There it was. Northdean School archives going back to 1785 when it was founded. Sometimes you think life is going to be harder than it really is.

There were details of every pupil and master that had ever graduated or worked at the school. Public schools are nothing if not thorough in documenting themselves. Perhaps it's because they're very pleased with themselves, so proud of their history of promulgating elitism and privilege in the name of an education based only on ability to pay.

He did a search for the surname Stewart. There were a lot down the centuries. Seven masters in the last two hundred years, including Frank. There were 83 pupils who had that name, too. He scrolled down the list until he came to the 1970s. Their son was 14 in 1980, so would presumably have also attended the school. Barbara had him very young, she'd just have been 16. He grimaced inwardly. Are you ready to be a mother at 16? Frank must have knocked her up accidently, he was only 19 at the time.

There was only one from the mid 70s and his name was Charles. He had arrived in 1975 and left in 1980. That had to be their boy. He'd be in his mid-40s now. He left in 1980, presumably with his mother, after his father had died. She must have moved away.

He went to search the teachers. No Grayson-Thomases. So which, if any, might have later become John Grayson-Thomas? The report in the *Edinburgh Evening News* had said he was a retired Latin teacher. That narrowed it. He flicked through the pages to the Latin masters. Well, it wasn't difficult. There had only been three Latin masters since the war up to 1980. Bryce Scott-Rodgers 1935-1973. He sounded like a crusty old bugger. He'd been replaced by Rupert W. Sullivan up until 1995. From then until now, Leonard Pillinger had done the job. Who needed to learn Latin in the 21st century?

So was Sullivan their man? Was Sullivan, Grayson-Thomas?

He clicked on the link for a biography synopsis. 'Came to Northdean from Greenfield Grammar, Darlington. Retired 1995.'

Not much there. He typed the name into Google along with 'Greenfield Grammar'.

At the top of the results was a forum called 'Greenfield Survivors'.

Survivors?

Oh, god.

Oh, no. He knew what that meant in modern parlance. You're not a victim, you're a survivor. And you're a survivor of abuse.

Mouth dry and hands sweaty, he entered his email address and name and clicked on the button to be granted entry to the locked forum. Sitting back in the seat, he rubbed his eyes. This wasn't going to be pretty.

His login and password was auto-mail emailed to him within minutes. With trepidation he logged into the forum.

Within a second he flinched, scrunched his eyes up and had to look away from the screen, as though to stop himself seeing the words and what they meant. He just didn't want to read what he already knew he was going to have to read. He flinched away from horrible stuff like this, turning off TV reports about rape and torture and abuse. He never felt it did any good for him to know about it. He knew it happened, but he didn't want to know the details. You had to be strong to be able to deal with it and he wasn't sure he was strong enough, at all. He even asked Julie to shield him from her worst cases. It was too much for him to take and rather than empowering him, it made him feel weaker and more helpless. Evil sometimes seemed such a huge malevolent force that fighting it was an impossible task.

The forum stated it had been set up for people to document their abuse at the hands of a group of teachers across County Durham going back decades. There were names of people who were accused of being abusers and detailed descriptions of what that abuse had been.

It made gruesome reading.

He did a search for Rupert Sullivan's name. There were many entries. One post summed up several dozen.

He was my Latin teacher for five years. Unfortunately, I was one of his 'favourites'. In that time he anally raped me three times after school. It was so violent that I had to go to hospital and pretend I'd been injured in rugby. Though how would I have been injured like that? They must have known what had happened. But no-one said anything or did anything about abuse back then. It was all swept under the carpet. When I was 13 he forced me to perform oral sex on him three times in his office and on many other occasions he held me by the hair while he masturbated into my face. He liked to do that. He said he'd kill me if I ever told anyone and I believed him. I think he would have. He was pure evil and I lived in fear of him, as did every other boy. He was also occasionally brutally violent and would pick up boys by their hair in class. No-one seemed to suspect him. He was thought a strict disciplinarian and that was ap-plauded by parents and governors. When he left in 1973 for Northdean, I had never felt so happy. We never found out if he'd been sacked. Nobody talked about this sort of thing back then. Why hasn't he been arrested since? Everyone knew about him. And he wasn't the only one, there was at least six of them that I heard of at schools across the region. They all knew each other. There was obviously a cover-up.

Former pupils at other county schools all reported the same sort of ex-periences. These men had a pattern of behaviour and things they liked to do to defenceless boys from the age of 8 to 14 or 15. Sullivan had been a monster. There were pages of accusations and detailed descriptions. Some were anonymous, but others were fully attributed. Several dared him and the others to come forward and sue them for saying they were vicious paedophiles. Yet more challenged the police to arrest them for their crimes and were incredulous that no investigation had ever been carried out. It was also clear that no-one had seen or heard of him since 1995.

Presumably Sullivan's transfer to Northdean hadn't brought about a change in him, but perhaps because it was a wealthy public school, it had been able to suppress the information about him while he worked there, in just the same way the church had with so many priests. Even so, he'd been there for over 20 years. Christ, how did these men get away with this for so long? Looking back on his own childhood, he now knew for certain that children all around him were suffering one form of abuse or another; in hindsight, the tell-tale signs were often there, but he couldn't have guessed that at the time. At the time he didn't know this behaviour even existed as a thing that humans did. He wished he still didn't.

Relieved to be able to click away from the forum, he went in search of Rupert W. Sullivan. His tenure at Northdean had ended in 1995 and that was about all there was to be found. He searched Facebook in case he was on there, but to no avail. He seemed to have disappeared after 1995. A search of births, marriages and deaths didn't produce a death date.

Getting proof that Rupert Sullivan was John Grayson-Thomas was going to require a photograph to compare the two. You couldn't be in public life in the 21st century without having your photo taken at least once or twice. He already knew from previous searches that Grayson-Thomas had been captured at various council meetings and charity events. He searched again and soon found him in the *Edinburgh Evening News*.

There he stood, next to people who were also apparently respectable. 2008. At the opening of a new swimming pool for kids in Edinburgh. And another as leader of a charity which took underprivileged kids abroad on holidays. Nick closed his eyes, hoping that what he was thinking wasn't true, but knew it was more than likely exactly right. These people just never stopped scheming to get vulnerable children into vulnerable positions and then abuse them. The urge didn't seem to stop. Not even, in this case, into their late 60s.

He opened his eyes again to see the man himself. White haired. A slightly oversized hook nose. Nice eyes. Too nice. You want the evil to look evil. He didn't. He looked like any old man. Distinguishing features? Nothing really. You'd pass him in the street and never for a moment contemplate he was an absolute fucking beast of a man...and that was being unkind to beasts.

Eventually, after a lot of searching, he found an old school photo from Northdean in 1976, one of those where a camera takes a huge sweeping shot of the entire school of pupils and teachers. He increased the magnification. He had to be here somewhere. It was nearly 40 years ago, but even so. Where are you, you evil fucker?

Frozen in time, boys stared back. Nick could easily have indulged his imagination to consider what some of them had just that day gone through at his hands. Who knows how many similarly inclined bastards were on this photo? But, no, that would be a waste of emotion.

He looked at each teacher and had looked at all but three of them when he saw a man with big sideburns and dark hair.

Going back to the forum and looking for physical descriptions of the man, two people had mentioned the big sideburns in 1972 at Greenfields. He looked back across the rest of the staff. He was the only one you could say had big sideburns. It had to be him. He was tall and slim. His features were a little less pronounced than in 2008, perhaps.

He turned off the computer and sat deep in thought for a while, then went outside and called Geoff Jones, an old work colleague on the *Northern Echo*, based in Darlington, who had since retired. They'd worked together in the 80s and had seen each other occasionally since, usually at the football.

'Hello, mate. It's Nick Guymer.'

'Bloody hell. There's a blast from the past. How are you, Nick?' He spoke in a deep, tarry Durham voice.

'I'm OK.'

'What are you up to these days?'

Nick outlined what had happened in the approximately nine years since he'd last spoken to Geoff.

'I'm working on a story at the moment about a teacher that was at Greenfields Grammar. I don't even remember the school, myself.'

'Oh, it was the posh grammar school for boys. Always got great results.'

'There was a teacher there called Rupert Sullivan. Turns out he was a vicious child abuser.'

'Oh. Him.' Geoff's voice had a horrified tone to it. 'There's a name I've not heard for a long time.'

'You remember him?'

'I never met him, but his name cropped up a lot in the early 70s. There was always talk. The fact I can still recall his name suggests how serious the rumours were.'

'Well, he was an utter bastard to kids. He raped and abused them in every heinous way imaginable. But then he went to another school. A private school.'

'Where he continued on the warpath, I suppose?'

'That's my assumption. Do you remember anything about him at all?'

'Not really. You've got to remember, we had no idea how these men operated. We literally knew nothing and if it was talked about at all, it was almost done light-heartedly. I do remember there was talk of a few men like this being involved in what we'd think of today a being a paedophile ring. And Sullivan was mentioned as being one of them. How much was true or not, you never knew. It was always supposed to be High Court judges involved and such...but like I say, it was all pub gossip, really. One thing I will say is, if it was true, they got away with it because of the involvement of powerful people in the police, politics or the judiciary.'

'Yeah, I'm beginning to wonder if that's how he got away with it. These forums go back years and there was no sign of him being picked up. I'm certain now that he changed his identity.'

'Well, that'd make sense. Let me make some calls. So, you're doing a piece, Nick?'

'Yeah. A rare bit of investigative journalism. I sort of accidentally ended up in the middle of something, really.'

Geoff groaned and distorted the phone speaker as he did so. 'I still find it shocking how little we knew about this business. I was a hard-bitten Northern press man. If you'd asked me in the 70s, I'd have said I was a man of the world, a man who had been around and knew the book of sins from A to Z. But I never thought there was systematic, routine abuse of kids going on in every single town, in every kid's home, in schools, in church, in the police and everywhere in between. Never. You heard about the occasional perv or weirdo, but the degree and extent of it is mind-boggling. I don't mind telling you that I still feel guilty we didn't uncover it when it was right on our doorstep. It was our job as journalists and we failed the public.'

'Well, I look at it like this - it was like a colour that we couldn't see because we just were not on that frequency. We didn't ignore it, we just couldn't conceive of it happening. We had no understanding or thought processes that would allow us to see it, except in the most obvious cases. Yes, kids weren't believed or were hushed up, but there was no way we could have guessed at the extent of the problem. And these blokes seemed to think they were above the law and could do what they wanted. Well, actually, I don't think they thought it was even wrong. Sullivan must have been at the extreme end of the spectrum to get moved on in the 70s. You had to be really bad to get it even acknowledged.'

'Well, I hope you nail the bastard.'

'I think someone has already done that. In fact, I hope someone has.'

He got home feeling very introspective. This was the trouble with letting the details of abuse into your brain. Once they were in there, you couldn't get rid of them. They polluted you forever and, in a way, were an extended, albeit removed form of abuse, in themselves. The description in the forum post about the boy being held by the hair while Sullivan did...did...*that* to him...that was an image that hadn't ever been in his mind, but now it was and it would never leave. God knows what images still stained the poor kid's, now middle-aged man's, brain.

You need to try and preserve some part of your soul as childlike and innocent, or he felt he did, anyway. That was so often where any goodness you can put into the world is sourced from. But this sort of stuff robbed you of it.

Yet, in complete contradiction to that, it being hidden from squeamish eyes like his, had only protected Sullivan. Being concerned for your own psychic welfare didn't help the victims and it was they who deserved help and retribution. Maybe you just had to bear it. Somehow. It was the right thing to do.

He set about making their evening meal, rolling some haddock in a fine rice crumb, ready to fry and preparing some vegetables.

As she usually did, Julie came through the door with a big smile on her face. Having someone who is pleased to see you when they walk through the door should never be taken for granted. There are so many lonely times in life when you just want to see a friendly face, let alone a loving one.

'Aw, hey, it's Fanny Craddock. Look at you in your pinny,' she said, laughing a little. She kissed him on the cheek and went to wash her hands.

'I was always frightened of Fanny. I liked Johnny, better,' said Nick, putting large spoon of ghee into a frying pan.

'I feel obliged to try and shoehorn in a johnny and fanny joke into a sentence, somehow,' said Julie, an eyebrow raised.

'You should never have to shoehorn a johnny, Jules, let alone a fanny,' said Nick, poking his tongue out at her.

She laughed. 'I knew you wouldn't let me down, Mr Double Entendre. So what did you find out down in Northallerton?'

He groaned and went over the grisly details, while he cooked. 'I know you hear about this sort of stuff at work and you're good enough not to clutter my mind with too much of it...but how do you deal with all the heinous stories and the imagery they produce in your brain?'

She sat down and poured herself a glass of white wine.

'I deal with it by persistent heavy drinking! No, I suppose everyone deals with it in a different way. I try to keep some degree of detachment because if you gave everything of yourself to it, you'd be good for nothing by the end of the week. You'd be a wreck.'

'But isn't detachment just a fancy word for being cold or not caring?'

She winced a little at that.

'Not at all, man. All I mean is I try not to get too wrapped up in the emotional traumas people are going through. Or at least, I try to leave it at work and not bring it home. No-one is going to benefit from me breaking down and weeping, are they? Women come to us for support and help. They're having a bad time, one way or another, so it's down to me to be understanding and strong and, if I can, provide options to achieve a better outcome for them, or to help them understand how strong they really are. The fact I won't be judgmental is a given, but it's really all about making things better in the future, if possible. Changing things for the better and empowering women.'

It was a typically practical Julie-ish way of seeing things. She went on.

'That's what is so brilliant about it. Yeah, you hear some terrible things, but you have the power to effect change and help to improve things for someone. But it does get under your skin, sometimes. I won't say it doesn't. I do have to have a quiet moment after an especially gruesome case. Not letting it crush you, doesn't mean you don't care, though. Quite the opposite. It's caring that makes you want to keep your shit together. And anyway, I won't let it overwhelm me because, in a way, that's what the abusers want. They want us to give up and let them have their way, but we won't. Good beats bad. That's really how I see it.'

Nick nodded. She was so tough, so mentally strong and even now, after so many years, it still sometimes caught him by surprise. He admired it massively and wished he could tap into it more, but where did she get it from? How do you have mental strength when you feel quite mentally fragile, almost by nature? It was something he was going to have to learn if he was going to deal with this. He stuck a fork into the broccoli to see if it was done.

'So do you reckon that since working there, it's made you mistrust men more in everyday life? After this research on child abuse - which I've just done for an afternoon - it makes me see these evil men on every corner. Like, it's not just one or two people, it's bloody loads of sick bastards. They're everywhere. I must be meeting them all the time, y'know, serving me in pubs or shops, cutting my hair or whatever.'

She shrugged. 'It does affect how you see blokes, yeah. How can it not, when every day you meet women who have been through hell at the hands of men who the rest of the world think are good people? He's got one face in the house and another face outside the house. Once you get your head around even just that one fact, even if someone seems decent, you do wonder, yeah well, what are you like when you get home? Or after a drink? Or when your football team loses? Well, I do, anyway. I've become well attuned to the warning signs. You get aware of how controlling men go about their business. But I think I'm good at the job partly because life had made me kind of suspicious of men, anyway...' she paused and wagged a finger in the air '...no, not suspicious..."aware" is probably a better word. Growing up on a rough estate around violent men does that to you. But because I got out and went to university, I got a perspective on it. And I tried to learn from bad relationship decisions and from when things went...you know...bad...so that when I met you, I was pretty sure you were one of the good ones. It wasn't a surprise to me that some men are a big problem; I grew up knowing it and because of all of the above, I'm fairly unshockable. So what you've just told me about what this bastard was doing to boys, I know it's vile, but it's genuinely nothing I've not heard before. I mean, you've got a good imagination - whatever abuse you can think up, that's pretty much been done. And I do mean anything.'

Nick turned off the gas and drained the vegetables.

'Yeah, you are unshockable, aren't you? Much more than me. That's really what all of this is about, I think, I'm shocked by what I've learned. I shouldn't be, at my age, but I am.'

'When one in three women suffer domestic abuse at some point in their life, law of averages dictates that you're meeting men most days who are being, or have been, abusive, probably more. There's no point in sticking your head in the sand about it though, kidda.'

Nick served the fish onto hot plates and ran some butter through the broccoli and carrots.

'See, that's what I can't handle. I don't want to think that, even though statistically it must be true. I want to have faith in people, not feel like they're malevolent, evil swine who have just come from doing something terrible to someone.'

She raised an eyebrow. 'I totally understand that, nobody wants to think it, but not thinking it doesn't help, does it? That's what we're fighting against. I'm not letting the bad guys win. No way. You've got to keep a perspective, though. It's not *everyone*. I know people often think those of us who work in Women's Aid and organisations like ours are man haters. It's a bloody annoying cliché and it's never been true. I just hate the men who are bastards, same as you do. Not unreasonable, really.'

He put the plates down and got some mayonnaise out of the fridge. She sniffed at the fish, appreciatively.

'This looks crackin', luv. I love the smell of frying fish. Takes me right back to childhood and going up the chippy on a Saturday after the football.'

'Aye, back to a time when you could punch your wife in the face and people would think she'd done something to deserve it, or you could rape a child with impunity, or put your hands up a girl's skirt. See, it totally robs you of nostalgia. We can't even look back on "the good old days", now we know what was really going on. It's like when you think back to TV when we were kids. It was hosted by a bunch of rapists and...' he sighed and shook his head '...I just don't know how to deal with it, that's all.'

She put a hand on his arm and tilted her head at him, sympathetically. 'It's worth bearing in mind that not everyone is an evil sod and back then, as well as now, loads of good people did good things. We can't let the abusive twats define our life for us, can we? There's always been good amongst the bad, even in 1970s TV. I loved the Wombles. They were nice. Mind, it always annoyed me that they were almost all male Wombles. We need gender equality for Wombles, if you ask me. Madame bloody Cholet slaved in that kitchen. Typical. Womble society was too bloody patriarchal. Now, the Clangers was more progressive. The Soup Dragon didn't even appear to have a gender. See, I told you it wasn't all bad in the 70s.' She grinned at him.

Nick smiled and blew out air. 'I liked the metal chicken, myself.'

'Aye, that was a cool bird, that. I always thought Metal Chicken was a great name for an all-girl rock band.' She laughed to herself as they continued to eat.

'I totally understand what you're saying, but...I'm struggling, Jules. The stuff I read about today...and it was only the tip of the iceberg...where do I put that info and not let the poison from it leak out over the rest of my life? The images of it just flash in my brain and pollute me.'

She didn't say anything for a minute while she ate.

'So you thought the world was perfect before you read about that man, Sullivan?'

'No, of course not.' He could sense Julie was constructing one of her infamously watertight arguments.

'You knew that abuse, violence, rape and torture existed, didn't you?'

'Sadly, yeah.'

'So really, all you're getting your knickers in a twist about is knowing some details, some specifics.'

'But life is all detail and knowing the detail makes it live more strongly in the mind; it makes it more powerful.'

She finished her meal and pushed the plate away from her. 'That was ace. Thanks, luv. Look, it boils down to this: bad things have always happened. Humans can be shits. We know this. We make the world better or we let it get worse. We either give in or we fight. That's the only choice good people have: give in or fight. So do you want to give in, or do you want to fight?'

'Well, when you put it like that...'

She interrupted him. '...you're an arsy Teessider, so you'll bloody well fight. Exactly. And rightly bloody so.' She rolled a long strand of hair around her right index finger. 'See, it's not *that* hard to deal with, is it? You just need to learn not to be such a soft get.'

'Aye, well, that's always been my trouble, hasn't it? Too sensitive by half. I'm not sure I can deal with this, Jules. Uncovering and then documenting this story is going to be really painful and upsetting.'

She smiled a little at him and shook her head. 'Being sensitive is all well and good, but that doesn't mean you can't also be strong. Sensitive and strong is the thing. In this line of work, that's the twin pillars you've got to straddle. You can do it. I know you can. It needs doing. It'll help all of those people who suffered in silence or were never believed. Underneath it all, you're a tough, ornery sod with a strong sense of justice. If you weren't, I wouldn't love you, would I? No matter how well you fry fish. Not even if you were a Soup Dragon. You need to draw on your inner Boro. Isn't that what you call it?'

He snorted a half laugh, nodded and folded his arms across his chest. 'Yeah. You're right. My inner Boro will need to be set on 10.' He bit his bottom lip and resolved to be more like her. If life was teaching him anything at all, it was to listen to women and she was, even now, much more grown up, much more experienced and much more understanding of how life is, than he was. He'd got through being a dreamer and a faux philosopher, full of elaborate expressions and long-winded ways to say simple things. He knew now that it had been a way to hide from the world, it was how he dealt with things; it was a sort of psychic padding to insulate himself. But Julie had never been like that. She dealt with things head on and sorted them out. Always had done. She made him want to live up to her and the fact she was there to support him, made him feel like he was capable. Maybe that's what the people she helped at work felt, too. We all need someone on our side in life. Those abused kids had needed someone, but there was no-one there for them. He had to make it right, somehow. He felt so sorry for them and there was no unknowing this now.

When they'd lost Joni after 18 weeks of the pregnancy, he'd been forced to confront not just their own child's death but how he felt towards kids in general now, knowing they'd never have their own. It had made him feel very protective, very defensive on children's behalf. Maybe it was some degree of raised empathy born out of a sense of loss. Or maybe he'd just grown up and realised that life is not all about you and what you want. Yeah, he could do this.

'On my way home, I remembered what Mandy said. She said Grayson-Thomas was a familiar name,' said Julie.

He put the dirty plates in the dishwasher.

'Yeah. What about it?'

'Might be worth going to see her to find out why.'

'Geoff on the *Echo* thinks that Sullivan was protected from prosecution by the police for some reason.'

'Wouldn't surprise me in the slightest,' she said, taking her glass into the living room.

Nick sat with his laptop, typed up all of his research so far and built it into his existing piece, as Julie skimmed through TV channels looking for football, finding a Conference league game from Burton Albion. She lay full length on the sofa.

'I bet not many women are currently watching Conference football,' said Nick.

'I bet not many men are, either,' she said, sipping at her drink.

Nick read over everything he'd written. As he did so, he got a phone call.

'Hello, Nick, it's Geoff.'

'Now then. Have you got anything for me?'

'Oh, yes. I bloody do, Nick. I bloody well do.'

CHAPTER 10

'Do you remember a man called Gerald Starr? He was chief of police on Teesside in the 70s and 80s.'

Nick thought for a moment. It was a long time ago.

'Oh, yeah, I do. Wasn't he one of those Evangelical Christians who seemed to see the law as an extension of God's wrath? He was always on local TV shouting off about the sins of the youth of today. Big fat bloke with a beard. Absolute twat, if I remember, rightly.'

'That's him, yeah...'

'Are you going to tell me that man, who was forever being judgmental about people and their lifestyle, was a vicious child abuser? That would be almost a cliché.'

'I can tell you this. He and Rupert Sullivan were on a committee called the Youth Offenders Board whose self-appointed role was to report on children's homes...'

'...Oh, the fucking bastard!!' shouted Nick immediately, throwing his head back. 'The absolute fucking twat. If Sullivan was involved in that, it was for one reason only. To get access to isolated and vulnerable children.'

Julie looked over at him and put her finger to her lips and frowned a little, just to tell him to watch his language.

'Exactly. Fits the bill, doesn't it? Classically so. I just unearthed that from my own records. But it doesn't stop there, right. That board was six people. Let's say your man who was shot really was Sullivan. Starr was stabbed in a knife attack in Middlesbrough in 2006, remember? He was long retired by then, of course. He later died from his injuries, but they never caught his attacker and there were no witnesses.'

'I don't remember that.'

'You were still down in Harrogate at the time, I think. So that's two dead. A third, James Ancelloti, lost control of his car and drove into a barrier on the A1 at 80mph.'

'Dead?'

'Dead. Later they found his brake cables had been cut just enough that they'd snap when he really needed them. No case was brought over it.'

'Are the other three also dead?'

'All of them and all in what, if we were being a bit cynical, we could call suspicious circumstances. Poisoned, run over and drowned. Before the Edinburgh shooting, Ancelloti's death in 2009 was the last one. They died over a 12-year period.'

Nick whistled. 'So it's an extended vendetta?'

'Well, absolutely no-one is calling it that, because the deaths happened across so many years. But everyone on that board is now dead and none by natural causes. I looked them all up. The chances of that being the case seem very small, as they were of varied ages. But no-one has connected those deaths. And, of course, it *might* just be a coincidence. But I thought you should know - it might be useful for your story.'

'It is. Thanks Geoff.'

'No worries. Let me know if I can be of any help again. Like I said before, I feel guilty that we let all of this get by us, back in the day.'

Nick lifted Julie's legs up and put them over his lap, rubbing her feet as he did so and told her what Geoff had said. She patted at him with her foot, gently, as though to comfort him while he talked.

'I think anything which involved touring around children's homes should raise our suspicions,' she said. 'But you know what I'm going to say, don't you?'

He looked at her. He simply didn't.

'No, what?'

'That it's not up to any member of the public to kill these abusers. They should have been brought to justice and made to pay for their wickedness.'

Nick flexed his lips, and made a gesture with his head. 'They've pretty much already done that, Jules. Death is the ultimate justice, isn't it?'

'Justice isn't death; it's being publicly held accountable for your actions. Whoever killed Grayson-Thomas and all these other people, is in the wrong. It is not their right to do that. It's vigilantism. We need the rule of law to stop mob rule. And you should know that "if you listen to fools, the mob rules".'

He smiled at the reference to the Black Sabbath lyric.

'But what if that was the only way to get justice? What if every other way had failed?' he said. 'And let's be clear here, it had failed. Sullivan had got away with raping children with virtual impunity. Do I feel like he deserved a bullet in the head? Yes, I bloody do, Jules. If anyone deserves a bullet in the head it's someone who behaved like he did.'

'Even so. The principle stands.'

'Are you sure? What if he just couldn't be stopped any other way? He can't masturbate into the faces of any more children now. Can he?'

187

Julie winced at his words and looked back at him, a degree of uncertainty in her eyes.

'Think about it. It's kill them or they keep abusing. That's a hell of a choice.' He paused. 'I know which side I'm on here, Jules. I'm on the side of whoever pulled the trigger. Sullivan raped young, weeping boys for at least 30 years, some so violently that they had to go to hospital. He forced boys as young as eight to put his penis in their mouths. He thrashed boys with a leather belt until their buttocks bled. He...he...he...did things so unspeakable that I can't even bring myself to say the words. I've read the first-hand reports of it. God knows what other atrocities he indulged his evil with, that the victims have been unable to ever tell anyone about. We've lost nothing by someone putting that bullet in his head. He deserved it. And it stopped him. And if the rest were just like him, sod it. Who cares? If they'd been killed years ago, a lot of people would have suffered a lot less. That's a better outcome.'

She shook her head. 'Vigilantism can't be allowed, though. We can't conduct society like that.'

'What if vigilantism is the only way, though? What then? You would break the law to protect a child. I know you would. You would shoot a man in the head to stop him hurting a child. We all would. You would do it in a heartbeat. I would and I know you would. That's all this particular vigilantism has done. It's been specifically targeted.'

She turned off the TV and rubbed her eyes, groaning as she did so. 'This is all speculation. It's all theoretical.'

But Nick knew it wasn't. The shooting, whoever had done it, wasn't just a random murder. It was part of a bigger, longer story. He'd uncovered something very illegal and yet, weirdly, also very moral.

The next morning, he walked down to the police station and asked to speak to Mandy Beale.

She put her head around the secure door. ' 'Ello, you!' she said in her slightly daft way. She grinned at him in a cartoonish style. 'Ow are you, then?'

'I'm good. Nice to see you again, Mandy.'

'I'm just ready for a coffee break. You fancy some caffeine and a chit-chat?'

'Great, yeah.'

'Come on, then.'

She was dressed in a light grey suit with a red blouse. About two stone overweight, she bustled along with a pleasingly open body language, a thick roll of fat flopping over her trousers and big, fatty breasts wobbling with every step. Full of little touches on the arm, and big, red cheeked smiles, she reminded him of a Blackpool postcard of a fat, bosom-heavy, saucy woman with red cheeks.

'How was the 'oneymoon, then?' she said as they walked up Silver Street.

'We had a great time.'

'I bet you did. I bloody love the Fringe, me. It's all so vibrant. I love the energy of it.'

'Yeah, creativity is very attractive. Even when shows are rubbish, I like that someone made the effort.'

'That's right i'n't it? You can tell you're a fella who likes words. Nice way of putting it, that.' She smiled at him again as they walked across the High Street to a coffee shop.

'Eee, what did we all do before coffee shops?' she said, as they stood in line.

'We made our own instant coffee out of jars.'

She laughed in a coarse sort of way. 'Yeah, we did, didn't we? I can't drink it now. It tastes funny. My mother won't drink owt else. She thinks proper coffee is like medicine or something.'

'Medicine? Why medicine?'

'She reckons it's too bitter and nasty. She thinks it's a poison. She's a martyr to her jar of Mellow Birds.'

'Does that still exist? Very 1970s.'

She ordered them both black coffee. Nick took a seat in the corner.

She sipped at the hot drink. 'Oh, that's smart, is that. What a busy morning. Who knew there were so many lawbreakers, eh?' She laughed. 'So what can I do you for then, Mr Guymer? You've obviously got summat for us.'

'Remember when we met in Edinburgh, I mentioned a man called John Grayson-Thomas had just been murdered?'

'I do, aye.'

'Have you kept up to date with the murder, by any chance?'

' 'Ave I 'ell, as like! I've got enough to do on Teesside keeping on top of our local scumbags.'

Nick smiled. He liked her blunt Yorkshire way. There was almost a pride in it, with her. And she knew she was being funny, as well. He liked that degree of self-awareness. Jeff's words about her looking like she'd be passionate in bed, came back to him. He was right. He could see it now.

'But you said the name was familiar. Do you know why?'

'Why are you asking?' She scratched her mop of dyed-brown ragged curls.

Nick quickly explained about Sullivan and what Geoff had unearthed.

'You reckon all them deaths are linked?' she said with a little incredulity.

'Yeah. I'm certain. So why was the name familiar?'

She looked back at him. 'You're onto summat 'ere, but I'm bustin' for a slash. Hold on.' She got up and went to the toilet.

Nick looked at the photos on his phone of Barbara Stewart holding the gun while he waited.

'Oh, god, that were like a garden 'ose,' said Mandy as she sat back down. Nick put the phone down and turned it to her.

'That's the woman who shot him.' She picked it up and looked at the image.

'Posh sort, is she?'

'Middle class, yeah.'

She flicked the screen. Her eyebrows shot up. 'Bloody hell.'

'What?'

'I don't think you meant for me to see that.' She pushed the phone over the table to him with a laugh and began fanning herself with her right hand. He glanced at it. It was one he'd taken of himself naked. Shit.

'That's so embarrassing, I'm sorry, Mandy,' said Nick, covering his face with his hands. 'The only thing that comes close to that on my embarrassment index was my dad knocking on my bedroom door and warning me not to have sex with a girlfriend, while I was having sex with her.'

She laughed uproariously. 'Dear me. Never seen the like. Ha ha...no wonder your Julie has always got a smile on her face. Ha ha...the look on your face. Oh, that's made me day, that 'as.' She dabbed the corners of her eyes with a tissue as she laughed. 'Eee, lad. I'll not forget that in a long while.' She went off on another rolling laugh.

'It was just a daft laugh for Julie, that's all. Can we get back to talking about murder? I'm more comfortable with that.'

'Ha ha...OK.' She cleared her throat and settled herself down. 'Alright. Change of mood. Grayson-Thomas was arrested here about six months ago. That's why I remembered the name. It came back to me later in the day, actually.'

'What had he done?'

'I couldn't recall at the time but I looked him up when I got back from Scotland. He was just arrested and cautioned for public indecency.'

'Forgive me for asking, but what does that actually mean?'

'He were wankin' in a public toilet,' she said, with a look of sneering disgust.

'Is that actually illegal?'

'It is if you do it in front of a 13-year-old boy who has just gone in for a wee. Luckily the kid's father was outside; he ran in and gave 'im a bit of a Teesside twatting. We were called. The father didn't want to press charges, reasoning that the whole thing would just upset the boy more. Which were good thinkin', I reckon.'

'Does that sort of thing happen a lot around here?'

She shook her head. 'Nah. We get a few flashers - it's a grand old tradition, is flashing. You might want to give it a go from the look of that picture.' She laughed her coarse laugh again. 'But I reckon it all goes to suggest that he's your man. He's this Sullivan beast. He were still at it.'

'Can you find out if Sullivan did change his name to Grayson-Thomas?'

She puffed out her soft pink cheeks. 'Probably not officially. Which doesn't mean I can't find out. I think you can take it as read that he did. Given he's dead, what interests me more is if there's been a conspiracy to murder these members of the Youth Offenders Board across the years.'

'Would it matter if there had been?'

'Oh, bloody hell, aye, 'course it bloody would. We can't have punters killing people. That's our job. It might be a team of killers that's done them. Can't be 'avin' that.'

He ignored her quip. 'There's a forum detailing what people like Rupert Sullivan did to them in the 70s and 80s. Why wasn't he investigated?'

'How do you know he wasn't?'

'Well, he wasn't arrested for it.'

'He might have been. You don't know if he was collared, but they couldn't make it stick. Might have been no evidence. Hard to convict someone of something which happened 30 years or more ago with just anecdotal evidence taken off a website.'

'The weight of opinion should have counted, though. There are dozens of accounts of his abuse on that website. Not everyone is going to make up stories.'

'Possibly. Crown Prosecution Service might have thought it was too chancey and too expensive to risk a punt on it and anyway, they've only got serious about this sort of stuff very recently. I mean, when I were comin' up in the force, all sorts of disgustin' shite was laughed off. You could rape your wife and expect the police to be on your side. Bloody disgrace, it were. Can't tell you the times I attended a domestic and 'eard about that sort of business.'

'Yeah, Jules had a bloke take her room door off its hinges when she was in halls of residence. He ripped it off 'cos he thought she was in there with another lad. She wasn't even there. Police were called, and she gets it in the neck from them for "leading him on". Disgusting. They took one look at her and said in so many words, well you're very fuckable, what do you expect? You'll drive some bloke wild from time to time. If you don't like it, don't wear tight jeans. I mean, they really did say that.'

Mandy pulled a face. 'Aye, that sounds like the bloody 1980s.'

'This Sullivan man, he was a proper vicious bastard, it was known about even in the dirty dark 1970s. The lives that man has ruined, the people he has hurt, it doesn't bear thinking about. Eventually someone took it into their own hands to sort it out.'

'That's what I'm afraid of.'

'Yeah, but you shouldn't be looking for that murderer, you should be looking for those people who let it happen for so many years. Maybe they're involved in abuse as well. I refuse to believe that this was not known about. Even before he was shot, he was still on committees in Edinburgh whose job was to inspect swimming baths and other places kids might be vulnerable. Given what you arrested him for down here, it's clear he was still active.'

'That's what they're like, i'n't it?' She finished her coffee.

'How long have you been on the force?' he said.

'I'm coming up to 35 years. Joined when I was 18. When Colin decides to spend more time with his roses, I'll be top dog, I hope. It's been a long climb up the greasy pole.'

'Did you work under the Chief of Police, Gerald Starr, back then?'

'Oh, yeah. For two years. Horrible bloke. Classic bully. I mean, knowing what I know now, he totally fits the bill for an abuser. Nobody liked him, but everyone was scared of him. There were rumours back then that he liked young boys. But you heard that sort of gossip a lot. And he did have a lot of enemies, so it sort of got discounted as general slander. Also he was the boss, and where did you go back then to report the boss?

There was nowhere. When he retired there was general relief just because he weren't really a good boss. He was of that school which reckons shouting is the best way to get things done.' She looked at her watch. 'Eee, god, I'm late. Nice to meet up with you properly, Nick. Colin's often sung your praises. I can see why; though 'e's never seen you in the buff. Ha ha! Leave this with me and I'll see what I can do.'

'I'd rather you don't say anything to this Gordon Smith bloke up in Edinburgh, not just yet, Mandy.'

'I won't. Not good politics to poke your nose into other copper's business, anyway. I'll see if I can get confirmation that Sullivan changed his name, then at least we'll know who he was for sure.' She bent at the knee and wafted a hand at him. 'Ta ra then, luv.'

He liked Mandy a lot. And again saw just what Jeff had meant. She did have passion and she was attractive. She was a messy, generous, big woman, but beyond that, she was solid, plain-speaking and had whatever the Yorkshire equivalent of Inner Boro was. Despite her jokey way of going on, she also had innate authority and that wasn't something you could fake. He felt that right to her core, just like her boss Colin Harcombe, she knew, quite profoundly, right from wrong.

Nick spent the rest of the day on the forum, noting names down, forcing himself to read the litany of horrific acts. He noticed that after a couple of hours, the initial shock wore off. Once you'd read about one disgusting act, you've read about them all. In a way, it all becomes the one, same act. Perhaps it's a chemical mechanism in the brain to allow you to cope with stress and tragedy, it goes into an automatic mode where it refuses to keep being hurt. If you did this sort of thing for a living, it was easy to see how you could become numb to it all and indeed see some of the so-called lesser acts of depravity in a far kinder light than they deserved, because you'd seen acts of the blackest evil to contrast them against.

Finally he went back to the article about Barbara Stewart from the Harrogate *Advertiser* a year after Frank's death and sat reading the printout of it. She was very fresh-faced, smiley and expressive. Not conventionally good looking, but attractive all the same. She hadn't been like that when he'd met her. She wasn't open like that. She was reserved. But then, life can change you.

The thing was, that PNC printout that Gordon Smith had showed him was wrong about Frank Stewart dying in 2007, so it was almost certainly wrong about his wife dying in that accident, too. And he knew that the gravestone was also not the same woman, because the age was wrong. That meant, in effect, Barbara could still be alive. He pinched at his lips in contemplation. After all the to and fro over who the person really was that had said to them that she was Barbara Stewart, how ironic would it be if it actually *was* Barbara Stewart?

Nick chewed his cheek. No matter how much he searched, he couldn't find anything more about Barbara apart from her work at the art school. The news clipping said she was raising money for a hospice for people with terminal cancer. St Jude's on Forest Road, Harrogate. It sounded very familiar. He went to Google maps and found it. Yes, it wasn't far from where he'd lived. It had been on his regular walking routines. He must have gone past it hundreds of times.

It was an outside chance that anyone remembered her, it was a long time ago, but she had raised a lot of cash. He found their number and called them.

'Hello. St Jude's,' said a bright female voice.

Nick introduced himself. 'I'm looking for information on a woman called Barbara Stewart. She raised a lot of money for the hospice when it first opened in the early 80s.'

'Oh, well, I've only been here three years.'

'Right. I see. It's quite important. You see, she's due to inherit something valuable from a relation and I have been unable to track her down. I was wondering if you knew where she was these days.'

'Let me ask someone.'

The line went quiet.

'Hello, who's this?' said an older woman's voice.

He introduced himself again and said why he was calling. She seemed to believe him. Why wouldn't she?

'Do you know Barbara?' said Nick.

'As a matter of fact, I did. She was a very kind lady.'

'Do you know where she might be now, by any chance?'

'As a matter of fact, I do. In a manner of speaking.'

Nick's heart jumped hard into his throat.

'Oh, that's, err...that's good.'

'Yes, she lived off Cold Bath Road.'

'I know that very well. I lived in Harrogate for many years.'

'Oh, well, you'll know the graveyard she's buried in, then. It's on Forest Road.'

Nick took in a tight gasp of air.

'Oh, I'm sorry to hear that. I did hear she might have died in a car crash in 2007.'

The woman was confused. 'She's been dead since 1985, dear. Not 2007.'

CHAPTER 11

Nick wrote the year down and put a big circle around it.

'And...and...and how did she die?'

'It was a hit and run accident. Terrible. Poor lady. The car didn't even stop. It happened on Ripon Road. They never caught the driver, either.'

This was hurting Nick's head.

'Oh, good god. That's terrible. Do you, by any chance, know what happened to her son, Charles?'

'He was at University when it happened. I'm afraid I don't know what became of him. It was all such a tragedy.'

After putting the phone down, he began drawing lines from one fact to another, on a sheet of paper, to represent connections. Once done he looked at it. It was just like the sheets of paper he'd worked on to create the plot in his novel.

Hmm.

Yes.

That is what all of this was: a carefully created fiction. From the very start, it had felt like he and Julie and Jeff and Jo had been involved in a story. And that was right. It had been planned and executed over a long period of time and with great attention to detail in order to guarantee that all the members of the Youth Offenders Board were murdered with impunity. The killing of Grayson-Thomas was the final act in the drama.

But this wasn't the work of a normal person, this was surely the work of a psychopath. And, after a long look at all the names on the sheet of paper, it was finally obvious who that psychopath had to be. Frank Stewart was dead. Barbara Stewart was dead and only one person could pass themselves off as either of those people.

Charles Stewart.

He was the killer. He dressed as Barbara. He dressed as Frank. He, unsurprisingly, looked like both his parents. And he dressed as Kiki, so that he never had to be himself. He'd been at the school with Sullivan. Sullivan was a prolific abuser in a ring of prolific abusers. This was one long act of revenge by Charles. Maybe he'd done it all himself, or as part of a revenge group. He'd got away with it. So far. But for how much longer? And was that morally right or was it morally wrong? And now that he knew, what should he do about it? It was a wonderful newspaper story. But what was his duty legally and, perhaps more importantly, morally?

'Do you fancy a trip back to Edinburgh at the weekend, Jules?' he said, as he made their evening meal. 'I think I've had a breakthrough.'

She looked up from reading the new copy of *Classic Rock*. 'Yeah, OK. Well that breakthrough happens when you wear such threadbare underpants. I'll buy you some nice new ones in that shark-skin fabric.'

He wrinkled his nose up. 'Actual shark skin? Are you sure?'

'Well it's not *actual* shark skin. That's just what they call it. I've had my eye on them for a while. They're all soft and smooth and clingy. Trust me, you'll like them, probably a little too much, knowing your predilections.' She raised an eyebrow at him.

With a short laugh he said, 'I can't help feeling that you've selected these pants for purposes other than...whatever the purpose of underwear actually is.'

She made a face. 'I couldn't possibly comment on the idea that I might want to make mad, passionate love to you while you're wearing them, darlin'. Anyway, what's sauce for the gander is sauce for the goose - is that actually an expression?'

'They're definitely words; whether it's an expression, I'm not so sure.' She snorted and gave him a wry but admiring look.

The door buzzer went. 'That'll be Jeff.'

Nick let him in.

'Now then, big man.'

'Yo, crazy dude.'

He stepped in and put his shoulder bag full of records down. 'I smell hot animal fat. Hopefully, it's dinner and not you in a lather.'

'What's the point of underpants, Jeff?' said Julie as he came into the kitchen. 'Hello, by the way.'

'Hello, Jules. Underpants? They're human gravy absorbers, aren't they?'

'Aw, Jeff!' she pulled a face at him in disgust.

'Well, you did ask. You know it's true. They must be. The modern underwear offers little protection from a stiff northeasterly and nature has ensured the male floppy bits will still work even if not nestled in heavyweight cotton. So they're blotting paper. Plain and simple.'

'Any views on shark skin underpants?' said Nick, pulling the leg of pork out of the oven and inspecting it.

'I'm in favour, as long as the shark doesn't want them back, though the overpowering stench of rotting fish may be a passion killer. Talking of passion, Jo is coming up from London tomorrow.'

He made a goofy face and put both thumbs up.

'Eee, fizz me, are you two starting some sort of relationship? I hope so, I like the idea of you two.'

Jeff reached in the fridge and got himself some wine. 'Nah, as I've said, before, I don't think that's going to happen. She's just coming up to get out of London for a couple of days. She's not your normal lass, though, I'll say that and I like being round not normal people - which is why I'm here, of course.'

'In that case, do you two fancy coming with me and Jules to Edinburgh?'

'Could do, if she's up for it. Why the trip north again?'

Nick explained what he'd found out and his idea about Charles Stewart being the killer.

'He's made a life for himself up there, he must have, because he worked, albeit dressed as Barbara, at the art school for a year. So he must live around there somewhere. See, I think he's been working on this for years,' said Nick.

'I tell you what, that's some heavy duty psychological screw-uppage. Dressing as your parents to kill your abuser? Bloody hell. Where do you start with that?' said Jeff, wafting his beard at them.

'Oh, I mean, I think he's in trouble, myself. I don't see how you can be mentally healthy if you're pursuing a murderous vendetta for 12 years,' said Nick. 'Let alone splattering someone's brains all over an office, but if you think about it, we don't actually know what Charles looks like. We've never seen him when he's not pretending to be someone else.'

'Well, he must look really like his mother and/or father, mustn't he?' said Julie. 'When he's Frank, he's just made himself look older and more frail.'

'Yeah. When I last met him, his skin was pale and I thought it was almost powdery. That was probably true, he used make-up to age himself,' said Nick.

'Why do you say that?' said Jeff, as Nick carved the meat. 'When I was looking at a couple of old girlfriends on Facebook, with one I knew it was her right away, but another, I had no clue. She looked so different. Age seems to change some people totally, but others, not at all.'

Nick dished out the food, while Jeff topped up their drinks. 'It was all going to plan for him. He made sure he'd met us before the shooting, so that we could identify him as Barbara, and then he was photographed as his mother, so the police would try and find her. He got a job as her, that flat's council tax bill had his dad's name on it. No-one had any reason to think either she, or he, wasn't a real person.'

'Hold on...' Jeff stared into the middle-distance, in thought. 'If Charlie-boy was dressed as his mother, shoots chummy in the head, here's the million-dollar question, who took the photo and then sent it to the police and the papers? He can't have access to the CCTV camera. How could he?'

They all stared at each other.

'Fizzin' hell, that means he's got an accomplice.'

'Yeah, someone took the photo from across Charlotte Square with a long lens,' said Nick. 'Then they sent it to the paper. When I was there I could see the angle it had to be taken from. In fact, I bet we could easily work out which window it was taken from if we went up there.'

'For Sullivan to get away with his abuse for so long requires information being suppressed, deleted, disposed of and closed down at every turn. The only people who can do that are high-ranking coppers,' said Julie. 'The sort of men who have a lot of power and a lot to lose. We've got to be careful here - these people might not take kindly to four Tees-siders sniffing around their den of iniquity.'

'Whose side are we on, then?' said Jeff. 'If we side with Charlie, we're siding with a serial killer, effectively. But if we're on the side of the police, they're corrupt.'

'This has been my point all along,' said Julie. 'We can't defend a killer, no matter what was done to him. To do that is to just give licence to anarchy. We need a straight copper to sweep it all up.'

Jeff made a wobbling gesture with his hand. 'I don't know Jules, here's how I look at it. If some bloke did to Argie what we think Sullivan did to Charlie, and I'd tried to get him prosecuted but got fobbed off at every turn, I'm not saying I'd go on a murderous rampage, but I'd do something. I wouldn't just let it slide. I'd probably hunt the twat down and kick the crap out of him, to be honest. Yeah, I'd do that. Or...' he paused and thought about it for a moment '...or...if I had a gun, I can easily imagine shooting him. Seriously. I'm not joking. It's such a violation. My preference would be for the law to take its course but there comes a time when, if that's not worked out, you want to take things into your own hands. Whether it's right or wrong is, to a degree, irrelevant. He's there, you've got a gun, all you have to do is squeeze the trigger...hard to be judgemental against him, in my view.'

'I do understand...' she stopped and rubbed her eyes. 'But violence begets violence. It's been categorically proven. One violent act makes another far more likely.'

'This is the core issue, y'know?' said Nick. 'What we have here is a weird situation where something horrible has been done to horrible people, not at random, but because the law had failed the victims. Now, given, according to the forums I've been reading, they tried for the best part of 30 years to get Sullivan and the others busted, and got nowhere, I reckon Charles Stewart, possibly on behalf of all his contemporaries, took it upon himself to sort it out, to dish out revenge but also stop these men from doing any more harm. I'm struggling to see that as a bad thing.'

'Me too,' said Jeff.

'Well...I don't, either,' added Julie, 'but that still doesn't mean it's right. And it might not just be him. There could be a whole team of killers who took out the Youth Offenders Board members and others, for all we know.'

Jeff nodded. 'There are no easy answers here, but I'm not going to lie to you, my sympathies lie entirely with Charles Stewart and almost not at all with the bloody law.'

'I'm not sure I approve of first-class travel,' said Julie as she, Nick, Jeff and Jo settled into their seats on the Edinburgh-bound train early on Saturday morning. 'It's pointlessly elitist and divisive.'

'But on the upside, you don't have to sit next to any scumbags,' said Jeff. Jo laughed and hi-fived him.

'That's debatable,' said Julie, looking around at some business people settling into their seats.

'It's crazy. The first-class tickets were only three quid more than the regular ones. I don't understand the railways. The prices seem to be made up on the spot,' said Nick.

'They should be renationalised and run centrally on a not-for-profit basis. It makes total sense. Sickens me that politicians are so scared of doing it,' said Julie.

'Right on, comrade Julie,' said Jeff. 'It is a total mess, like. You get a train at one time of day and it's £15 and at another its £75. Wear a hat, that's £9.32 extra but odd socks give you a discount of 17.9 per cent, except on the third Thursday in any month with a "y" in it and only then if you stand on one leg and blow a trumpet, while interfering with a Yorkshire Terrier!'

They all laughed. Jo patted him on the back while chuckling. 'That's a form of poetry, that is, Jeff.'

'I've got to say, Jo. Your "question all realities" mantra has been messing with our minds ever since we got home last month,' said Nick. 'Once you mistrust one thing, you start mistrusting everything. I can't tell you how often I've gone back to it.'

She grinned and nodded. 'From what Jeff told me last night, I was, to some degree, right. I hope you get this story tied up and earn some decent money off it and I hope we can get the murder solved, as well. That'd be a bonus and just a brilliant thing to base my next show around.'

'I'm surprised you want to do a gig while we're up there overnight,' said Julie.

'Have prosthetic limbs, smoke bombs and fake blood, will travel. That's my motto. Also, a paying gig is a paying gig. I've got the second slot at the Stand, so I'll be done by 10pm. It won't be the full show. Just edited highlights. Maybe just a bit of pulling out of internal organs.'

'Sounds like a typical Friday night on Teesside, or Saturday night in Greggs in Newcastle at chucking out time,' said Jeff as they sped up the northeast coast.

'So what's your plan, Nick?' said Jo.

'Speak to Gordon Smith first, try and find out what he knows.'

'Why would he tell you?' said Jo.

'I'm going to pretend I've got some info for him. Me and Jules will meet him. I want to see what you think of him, Jules. I might be missing something about him. You can usually read people better than me.'

Julie nodded. 'Then hopefully, as we'll be staying in the flat underneath him again, we should see if we can track down Charles. He has to be living in or around Edinburgh. So if he's not going to that flat, which seems likely, he must have some other home, possibly under his Kiki Dee persona.'

'Won't the police have raided the flat for evidence?' said Jo. 'You told them who it was, surely they'll have been in there? If they haven't, then that's another example of the police pulling back on the investigation.'

'Yeah, if they haven't it's deffo because there's some sort of conspiracy of silence with the police,' said Jeff.

'And I'm sure that's exactly what's going on,' said Nick. 'The more I've thought about it, the less their behaviour adds up.'

'Have you checked to see if there's any connection between Sullivan and anyone high up in Edinburgh police?' said Jo, getting out her phone. 'Say, someone who worked on Teesside with that Starr fella.'

The three of them looked at each other. Then Jeff spoke up. 'That silence means no and also, bloody hell, why didn't we think of that?'

'We can't think of everything,' said Julie. 'And this whole business is so confusing and complicated that it muddles my fizzin' brain.'

'Well, you're all old people, aren't you? You need some young brains on the job,' said Jo.

'Hey, I'm three years younger than the old men, here,' said Julie.

Jo began doing searches on her phone. 'Yeah, that still seems old. It was Northdean School, wasn't it?'

Nick watched as she tapped at the screen, amazed at the fast dexterity of her fingers. He poked at his phone with blunt fingers; hers danced over the screen, her eyes flicking around with a rapidity which looked a like a speeded-up film.

'You've got super-fast fingers, you have, Jo,' he said.

'I was just thinking that,' pitched in Jeff. 'You'd be very good shredder, with fingers that fast.'

'What's a shredder?' she said.

'It's guitarist who plays very fast, whilst pulling silly faces,' said Julie. 'Usually, but not exclusively, male.'

'Err...right...is that good or bad?' said Jo, still staring at the screen.

'Oh, you have so much to learn,' said Jeff.

She sighed. 'There's so much to go through here. I'll have a proper look on the iPad later.'

As they approached Edinburgh, Nick called Gordon Smith and left a message.

'This is Nick Guymer, I might have some information with regard to the Grayson-Thomas murder. Give me a call so we can meet up.'

They were just pulling into Waverley Station when Smith rang back. He was obviously keen.

'Mr Guymer? Gordon Smith.'

Nick stepped down from the train onto the platform. 'I'm just in Edinburgh now. Can we meet up?'

'We can. What information do you have?'

Nick ignored that. 'Are you still working on the case?'

Smith ignored *his* question. 'We always need information, Mr Guymer.'

'So is that a yes?'

'Like I said, information is always useful.'

He arranged to meet the policeman outside the Hard Rock Cafe on George Street within half an hour. Clearly Smith either saw meeting him as important or he had nothing else better to do - both seemed equally plausible.

Jo and Jeff left them to go down to the comedy club to set things up for the show, agreeing to call to meet up later for something to eat.

Nick put his arm around Julie's shoulder as she rested on one hip, hands thrust into her torn, old leather bike jacket.

'They seem to get on well, don't they? Jeff and Jo?'

She pulled her hair over her shoulders and ran an index finger down her centre parting to detangle her hair.

'Yeah, nothing forced about it, which is good. They're very matey and quite touchy-feely with each other, but it doesn't feel like they're a couple, to me.'

'I thought that. No obvious sexual frisson between them, is there?'

'Not really, but she's stayed over with him and they're sharing that second bed in the flat tonight, so there must be, mustn't there? Hasn't Jeff divulged any details, then,' she said, 'in that annoying way men have when talking about sex?'

'No. He's not said anything. And I'm not one to pry. Also, it's a sign he thinks it might be a long-term thing.'

'Oh, yeah, this is part of your male code of not talking about sex with the missus, but sex with one-night stands is fine. Those things between your legs make you guys so weird.'

Nick grinned. They had to wait fifteen minutes before they saw the policeman. As he approached them, Gordon Smith looked like a copper, even though he was in plain clothes. It's something to do with the highly polished, but over-worn, black leather shoes and the black slacks which no-one would wear, unless it was part of some semi-official uniform.

He grabbed Nick's hand far too tightly, as though it was a crushing competition, and then shook with Julie and nodded. Nick saw his eyes quickly look her up and down and then smile. They began walking down George Street.

'So what have you got for me?' he said.

'Where are you up to in your investigations?' said Nick.

'They're going well. What brings you back up here?'

'Oh, just a day trip to do some shopping,' said Nick, lying instinctively. 'I thought you'd like to know a couple of things that we discovered. Do you know any more about Frank and Barbara Stewart?'

'A little.' He was being cagey again.

'Did you find out that actually Barbara and Frank Stewart didn't die in the car crash on the A9?' Smith stopped dead in his tracks.

'What?'

Nick repeated himself. Smith had his mouth open, like he was shocked, but Nick was fairly sure he wasn't really shocked at all. He was exaggerating the emotion, in the way a bad actor does.

'They died in 1980 and 1985.'

'Are you sure?'

'Very.'

'Well that's embarrassing. I didn't know that.'

They started walking again.

'Have you heard of Charles, their son?' said Nick, making sure to look him in the eyes as he said it. He was expressionless.

'No.' His tone was raised a little, slightly higher in pitch. 'What do you know about him?' He swallowed and cleared his throat.

Julie looked at him a little incredulously and then frowned at Nick. Smith was trying to be cool and in control but something was going on under the surface. He looked stressed out, the way someone who is waiting for the result of a biopsy looks stressed.

'Well, actually, it's six and two threes really. Dead is dead. We had ruled out Barbara Stewart as being involved, regardless,' said Smith. The policeman pointed at a Starbucks. 'Let's go in here,' he said.

'Regardless of thinking she was dead, you mean? That doesn't make sense. Why wouldn't you have done that, a long time ago? You thought she was dead anyway, in the 2009 A9 crash, remember?' said Nick.

'Oh, yeah. Err...yeah, of course.' He faked a smile at Nick and bought three black coffees and took them to a table in a quiet corner. It was almost as though Smith was struggling to remember the story he was trying to maintain. Very contemplatively, he put his finger tips together and looked up at them out of the top of his eyes. He twitched his eyelids a couple of times, the stress he was under showing in deep lines on his forehead and dark bags under his eyes.

'We've had a few breakthroughs. I've not explored the Stewarts at all, for that reason. And that's why I don't know about Charles. I'd like to know about him, though. Every piece in the jigsaw and all that. Does he live up here? What does he look like?'

He was quick and intelligent, but Nick thought he could tell a good liar when he saw one, largely because he'd spent years making stuff up, going right back to his childhood when he'd maintained a lie about playing for the junior school football team for three months before being caught out by his mother. Smith was making some of this up on the hoof, in response to what Nick was saying. He could almost see him constructing it in his mind as he spoke. He was a little too quick to respond; a little too keen to be dismissive and a little too keen to be agreeable.

'So, who did we meet that afternoon outside the flat, Mister Smith?' said Julie, sitting back, eyes slightly narrowed.

He shook his head. 'I dinnae know who that was. Strange, really. Why would they pretend to be a dead woman?'

'Did you ever meet the man claiming to be Frank Stewart?' asked Nick.

'No, no. There was no need. Like I say, once we knew he'd died in 2007...'

'...he died in 1980.'

'Did he?...yeah, you said, well, whatever, err...err...yeah, well, there was no need to even look at that flat. I mean it was all irrelevant. The woman we think did it is, y'know...someone he had a dispute with on a planning committee and not the woman you met, whoever she was. Just a coincidence that they looked similar. The one you met was nothing at all to do with this. The woman we suspect has left the country, so it'll be an Interpol thing soon and out of my hands.'

Nick licked his lips and took a drink of coffee, certain that Smith had just made all of that up off the cuff. He glanced at Julie. She was silent, but clearly sceptical.

Smith went on. 'The car crash thing on the A9 must just be a PNC error. We get them all the time.' He leaned forward once again and made a dismissive gesture with his hands, his mouth turned down in a 'what can you do about it?' sort of expression. 'Information gets corrupted or the wrong details get put in the wrong place. I swear the whole thing is held together with Sellotape and string.' He tried to laugh at his own joke, but couldn't quite do it. 'Oh and, ha ha...as if to prove that fact, you know I said the CCTV photo was anonymously emailed in. I also got that wrong. We recovered it from the camera and then it was emailed around the station. I thought it'd come from outside, but it hadn't. I told you infor-

205

mation collation was in a mess, didn't I, Nick?' He delivered it in such a casual manner that it screamed 'I'm making this up and trying to just be relaxed about it so you don't suspect'.

'Huh. That is bad organisation,' said Nick.

'Aye. Embarrassing is the word, I'd use,' said Smith. 'But do tell me about Charles Stewart anyway. What have you got on him? How did you find out they had a son? Have you been researching this murder?' He leaned towards Nick, again, robbing him of his personal space. Nick turned away from him a little.

'That's a lot of questions. I'm a journalist, so I was just writing it up and did a bit of research in a local newspaper.'

His phone vibrated in his pocket.

A text. Taking it out and giving it a quick glance, he saw it was from Jo. '*Just found out that Gordon Smith used to work for North Yorkshire police in the 80s and 90s. Northdean was on his patch. Be careful.*'

Nick turned it off and chewed on his cheek, now not just deeply suspicious of Smith but certain he was part of a cover-up. He could see from Julie's heavy frown that she was feeling the same way. His instinct was obviously to tell Smith nothing else at all.

Smith smiled at him.

'So you're happy with the way it's all going?' said Julie.

'Yes, Julie. I'm sure an arrest will be made soon, aye. So, about this Charles Stewart guy. What do you know about him? Where can I find him? I'll have him interviewed - just to rule him out.'

Nick drank his coffee. Smith knew him, or he knew of him. And he wanted him. No, not just wanted him, was desperate to get hold of him. He'd kept returning to Charles Stewart since they'd met. 'Well, if you're sure it's nothing to do with the Stewart family, it doesn't matter, does it?'

'Yeah, we just wanted to clear up the mistake about the dates they had died,' added Julie.

Smith looked awkward. 'Well, it's always good to get as full a picture as possible. I appreciate your making the effort. Both of you. Very good of you.'

Julie finished her coffee and got to her feet. 'We've got to get going. We're meeting friends in a bit. Nice to have met you, Mr Smith.'

She turned and left quickly and without hesitation. Nick shook Smith's hand, feeling like he was holding onto something dirty, then followed her out. He hadn't wanted them to leave, Nick was sure of that. They were going without telling him anything about Charles.

'Drop me an email about Charles Stewart, if you like, eh, pal,' said Smith as Nick got up to follow Julie.

'Yeah, no worries,' said Nick. 'Good luck with the case.' He nodded at him and walked out.

As soon as they were a good distance from the coffee shop, Julie puffed out her cheeks and groaned. 'What a bunch of bullshit that all was. Everything he said in there was a lie and I'll tell you what, he's a desperate man. He was so tense and he obviously wants to find Charles Stewart. He nearly shit himself when you first said his name.'

Nick showed her the text Jo had sent. Her mouth dropped open.

'Bloody hell. He's...'

'...he's a fucking wrong 'un, one way or another.'

She sneered like she was tasting something both sour and bitter.

Nick turned and looked back at the Starbucks. Gordon Smith was walking out of the door with a phone to his ear. Nick raised his phone and quickly took a couple of shots of him. He seemed deeply engrossed in his phone call and didn't even look at them.

Nick emailed the photo of him to Jo, along with a message: *'This is Gordon Smith. If you see him, watch out. He's a lying fecker.'*

They walked down to the bottom of George Street and stood underneath the CCTV camera set on the traffic lights that had apparently taken the infamous photo.

Julie turned around so her back was towards the offices where the murder had happened.

'I think we can safely assume everything Smith told us was a lie. Which means that the photo wasn't from this camera and *was* emailed to them by someone, as he told you originally.'

'I think he's had trouble keeping up with his own lies. When I was a kid, I lied to my parents all the time - usually just for the fun of it and to make life more interesting. And the hardest part was knowing what you'd said to whom and keeping your story consistent. I think that explains this whole attempt to change his story now on the camera.'

'Well, Charlie must have had an accomplice and to get a photo at the same angle, they'd have to be on the first floor of that building on Charlotte Square,' said Julie, pointing in a direct line behind the traffic light. 'Top floor would be too high, first floor is just right.'

They walked towards the huge Georgian terraces of Charlotte Square.

'Is this residential?' said Nick, looking around.

'No. I think it's mostly offices. Such a waste of nice homes to put offices in them. Hate the way that happens.' As she spoke Nick's phone vibrated. It was a text from Jo.

'That's the copper who interviewed me after my show. The one I thought wasn't like a copper. Fuck it. I was wrong. I'm never wrong.'

She still had her arrogant streak.

They got to the correct angle and leaned against some black wrought-iron railings. A plaque on the wall said it was a recruitment agency on the first floor.

'Yup, this is in direct line with the lights. A photo taken from up there, when blown up, would match the angle of the photo sent to press and police,' said Nick.

'I think they doctored it to look like a CCTV freeze frame,' said Julie. 'Because they'd want to hide the fact it was taken from here.'

'Possibly. Let's nip up and take a look around.'

He walked up some thickly carpeted stairs. The building had been sliced and diced inside to make smaller offices out of the big Georgian rooms. It was a terrible way to treat these lovely old houses. Some even had false ceilings put in as though wanting to turn the place into an anonymous breezeblock place.

The first floor landing was separated from the stairs by a fire door. Nick pulled it open and turned right, walking towards the front wall of the building and another fire door.

'Look, Jules.' He pointed at a window which was at the end of the corridor.

'Eee, fizz me, that's where it was taken from, isn't it?'

They walked up and looked out across Charlotte Square towards George Street.

'Yeah, brilliant. And it's quiet here. No-one would notice if you came in off the street just like we've done.'

They went back out onto the street. He put his arm around Julie and was about to suggest they get a bite to eat when someone came down the steps from the building. He glanced to his left as they did so, just instinctively on seeing the movement.

It took perhaps four or five seconds for the face to register with him, but as soon as it did, he let out a bark of exclamation.

'Hey!' He called out.

But the man had set off running.

'Who was it?' said Julie, grabbing Nick's arm.

'It was Frank Stewart.'

'It can't be, Nick, he's dead!'

Nick took off. 'I mean, it was Charles, dressed as Frank,' he said, shouting over his shoulder. 'Stay here!'

The man in front was fleet of foot as he rounded the corner heading towards Princes Street and easily kept his distance from Nick. Nick settled into his stride for a long chase.

Charles was wearing a blue light waterproof, the sort you wear for golf, so he stood out 20 yards in the distance. As he reached Princes Street he ran across the road and down into Princes Street Gardens. Nick put a sprint on so he didn't lose sight of him for long.

Standing at the gates he looked down into what had been a loch until 150 years previously. The beautifully landscaped flower beds were full of colour and pattern. There he was in the distance. Thirty yards away now.

Nick took off again. Charles had to be tiring now. He'd gone full pelt and it's impossible to maintain that for long. He'd need a rest. The paths are long and straight through the gardens, which are set down from the road. Nick had an idea. He sprinted back up through the gate on Princes Street and took off at top speed, running down the edge of the road to keep out of the way of tourists. Half way along was another entrance to the gardens. He took that and, as he had hoped, came out just in front of Charles, who had stopped to get his breath and was looking behind him, now unable to see Nick.

'Hello, Charles,' said Nick, walking up to him and grabbing him by his slim arm.

The man visibly jumped. Nick could feel the energy of the shock he'd inflicted reverberate through the man's body. Nick held him tightly and was bigger and stronger by far. This man had no muscle on him at all.

'Excuse me!' the man said, with breathless indignation. 'Get your hands off me.'

'That's not going to happen, Charles. Let's just sit down on this bench.'

There was fear in the man's eyes.

'I beg your pardon. I shall call the police if you don't let me go this minute.'

'Why were you running from me?'

'I go running in these gardens every lunchtime. I wasn't running from anyone. I've never seen you before in my life. Are you mad, man?' He tugged at Nick's fingers to get him to release his grip.

Suddenly, Nick doubted his initial judgment. Who was this man? Was it really that man who had come out of the flat that morning? Jesus Christ, it wasn't. He was just imagining it. He looked at the man's feet. He was wearing trainers. The black trousers he thought he was wearing, were athletic wear. Shitting hell, he *was* just a runner.

Fuck.

He'd got the wrong man. His brain had just made a similar type of man into the one he wanted to see.

This was just some random bloke going out for a run on his lunch hour. He'd never seen him before in his bloody life. Shitting hell. What was he doing? He was going mad.

Nick stared at him in the eyes, searching for the truth of who this person was.

'What's your name?' he said.

'I'm not telling you anything. Get off me, you're hurting me. Please. I'm frightened of you.'

And he obviously was. Nick could see it in his eyes.

He let his grip loosen.

'I'm sorry. I didn't mean to hurt you. I've made a terrible mistake.'

'Well, OK. I'm going. Don't follow me. I'll have to get the police, if you do.'

The man got up and jogged away from him without a backwards glance.

Nick took out his phone and called Julie.

'Where are you?' she said, breathless.

'Princes Street Gardens.'

She gasped for breath and was now clearly running. 'You've gone after the wrong man.'

'I know...I freaked out...where are you?'

All he could hear was her breath panting. 'Jules! Where are you?!

There was a scream and roaring noise and the phone went dead.

Was she chasing someone, or was she being chased? Shit. His heart was gripped by cold fear. What the hell had happened to her? He retraced his steps, running flat out on the road, his heart pounding hard up into his throat, his brain producing all sorts of horrible images.

She'd been run over.

She'd been attacked.

She'd been killed.

CHAPTER 12

A bus came up behind him, honking its horn. He swerved onto the pavement, dodging people while trying to maintain his pace. The last time he'd seen her was on Charlotte Square.

Sprinting over the road and running fast, he reached where they'd been standing and began looking around for any sign of her, pain in his lungs, his leg muscles howling out in lactic acid hurt. Roadworks were being done. A team of three workmen in hi-viz clothing were blocking off a lane of traffic, probably to allow trucks to take away the tents and other paraphernalia from the remnants of the book festival which had been held in the Charlotte Square gardens.

Nick ran up to a man with a pickaxe and spat out a congealed gob of saliva.

'Hey, man...did you see a blonde woman here with me a few minutes ago?'

The man said something in an Edinburgh accent that appeared to be one long single word. He was incomprehensible.

'Sorry I couldn't catch that,' said Nick, bending over, hands on knees, gasping for breath. 'Did she run after someone?'

Another of the workmen turned to him. He was obviously Polish but was easier to understand than the Scotsman. A rough-looking man in his 20s, he was unshaven and covered in dust and muck.

'Was she...?' he made an in and out curved shape with each hand. '...old jeans...blonde?'

'That's her, yeah. Did you see her?' said Nick, still trying to get his breath back.

He pointed down towards Queen Street, a main thoroughfare which runs parallel with George Street. 'She went that way, running fast...'

'Was she chasing someone?'

The man made an exaggerated shrug. 'A woman came out there.' He pointed at the offices that he'd seen the man he thought was Charles Stewart come out from.

'What did she look like?'

'Err...you know...how to say...curly hair. Smart. She had a...' he made a cycling gesture.

'A bike? The blonde woman chased after a woman on a bike?'

'Yeah, that way.' He pointed to Queen Street.

Nick had his phone to his ear dialing Julie's number but without any reply. It just went to voicemail.

'OK, thanks, mate.'

He ran down towards Queen Street and stood looking the full length of it. To the right and a long way in the distance was the National Portrait Gallery, to the left a cobbled street that led around to the main road out of Edinburgh. Straight ahead led down Forres Street to Moray Place, one of the poshest, most expensive parts of the city.

Spitting out another gob of phlegm, he had to make a decision. He couldn't see her along the length of the street to the right.

Bollocks.

He crossed the road and ran down to Moray Place. It was, in essence, a circle of huge, three-storey, imposing Georgian terraced properties. Grand entrances with classic pillars either side of the door were commonplace here. In the centre was a mini-park, surrounded by black iron railings. Everything was cobbled.

It was impossible to know which way to go, there were four exits from Moray Place. At random he took the one at 12 o'clock, running down a hill. A sign on a wall said Doune Terrace.

Still no sign of her.

His back was running with rivulets of sweat. This was pointless. She could be anywhere.

Stopping at the bottom of India Street, he walked up to some tall black railings and looked down to the main street through to Stockbridge below, which was busy with traffic. He tried her phone again. Nothing.

We get so used to being available. We feel like we should be able to talk to anyone we want to talk to, at almost any moment, and on demand. The absence of communication is a worrying thing now, in a way it never used to be. We used to be much more self-contained.

You feel so helpless when you lose someone. What do you do? Where do you wait? There is nowhere to wait. You have to wander around aimlessly looking for them, your eyes desperately searching, almost hurting to see the missing person. It's a vicious torture. His stomach twisted into tight, worried knots as he walked back toward Charlotte Square. At least her body wasn't lying in the road and that was a relief, despite it being a horrible thought.

As he stood by the traffic lights, hands on hips, he tried to imagine the scene. Julie was fit and light on her feet. She wasn't as fast in a sprint as he was, but she had great endurance, probably better than he did. She could outrun most women her own age and she'd been wearing trainers. But chasing someone on a bike was a race she was always going to lose. But as she wasn't around, she must have fancied her chances of keeping her in sight and following her at long distance. The road here was long and straight. You could keep people in sight for a long while. The Polish guy had said it was a curly-haired woman. It had to be Kiki Dee.

So where was she? Why hadn't she called?

He crossed the road and stood on a traffic island in the centre of Queen Street.

Then he saw it.

A phone, smashed to pieces, lying against the drain. Dodging traffic, he ran over to it. Was it hers? Yeah, it was, unless someone else had dropped a phone with a Middlesbrough FC casing on it. The sim card was still in it, even though the phone was in three pieces. Several cars had run over it, by the look of it. He took the card out and put it in his back pocket.

OK, so she'd dropped it into the road and it got crushed. She knew the phone was busted. That meant she knew he'd have to follow her blind. She had to have been on the right-hand pavement when she had dropped the phone, because the road was too wide for it to end up where it had been if dropped on the other side.

Narrowing his eyes, he walked along Queen Street at pace, heading east, eyes glued to the pavement. He hadn't gone far when he saw in the centre of the pavement, a streak of something in an arrow shape. Was it grease? It had darkened the paving stone a little. Getting down onto his hunkers he pushed his finger along the stem of the arrow, then sniffed it.

Vanilla.

Yes! That's what it was. It was her chap stick for her sore lips, the one he'd liked the taste of when they'd made love that morning after they'd hit the wet bar hard. It was only a small mark but she'd left it for him, probably just bending down while running and skimming the pavement. It was hard to spot but it was all she'd have time to do.

At pace he half walked, half sprinted along. There was another arrow mark pointing onwards.

He'd crossed over Frederick Street, reached the next junction and spotted one more mark when he came across another streak but this time at a right angle, pointing across the road and down Dundas Street, which dropped away down the hill quite steeply and offered a long straight view to the bottom.

There she was! Oh, god. The sweet relief. She was OK. She was just rounding the corner at the bottom of Dundas Street; he watched as she stopped and made a mark on the corner for him to spot.

She was built for endurance, so she must have been able to keep whoever she was chasing in her sights simply because the route they'd taken was so straight and clear and downhill.

Sprinting as fast as he could, he flew down Dundas Street, letting the downwards slope drive him on but being careful not to lose balance and go head over heels. As he did so, he thought it was impossible to run around Edinburgh and not feel like you were in a scene from *Trainspotting*.

He got to the bottom of the road and following her pavement mark took a left along Warriston Road. Julie was 30 yards ahead, squatting with her back to a low wall, clearly getting her breath. Nick's lungs hurt badly as he walked up to her.

'Nice work, Sherlock,' she said, reaching out to touch him, as he squatted down beside her. 'Dropped my bloody phone on the road, didn't I?' Her face was flushed pink with the exertion, sweat under her hairline.

'I got the sim card out of it.' He gasped for air and wiped streams of sweat off his forehead. 'Where did he go?'

'Next house along. Kiki Dee - presumably Charles. He was on a push bike. He came out of those offices, unlocked it from the railings and then cycled off. He was behind me and I didn't even realise he was there until the last minute when I turned around and recognised him.'

'How did you recognise her, or should I say, him? You've only seen her in the window once for a few seconds?'

'How? Because she looked just like Kiki bloody Dee.' She gave him a look.

'Christ, I hope you're right and we've not just exhausted ourselves chasing Scotland's only Kiki Dee tribute act.'

'It was her, man...or I mean him. It was.'

'I thought the bloke I chased was Charlie in his Frank guise. But it wasn't. My brain wanted it to be, just like you with Barbara in the car, so it made me believe it was. Just like Jo said it did.'

'I never even got a glimpse of him before you legged it. When I got down here, I saw the bike propped against the front wall of that house two doors down. He must be in there.'

It was a respectable, solid-looking Georgian townhouse, set into the middle of a long terrace.

'Right, so he's in there. What the hell do we do now?' said Nick.

'As I was running, I was trying to work that out. We can't report him to the police for being the murderer because of Gordon Smith being so dodgy. I didn't like him from the moment he walked up. Remember I was talking about men giving off warning signals as an abuser? He set my alarm off, right away.'

Nick took a deep breath as his heart rate began to drop. 'Why?'

'He's what we call a Dominator. You could see it from his body language. He leans in and over to you, jabs his finger, occupies your personal space. It's a way of bullying people and trying to gain power over you. Think about it. How do you talk to someone? Not like that. Add in a lot of passive aggressive behaviour and you've got a wrong 'un. He's a paedophile, if you ask me. Or at least protecting those who are and you wouldn't do that if you were at all bothered by it as a lifestyle, would you?' She wiped sweat from her pink face. 'But we've got to be careful because Charles is psychotic. He must be when you think about what he's done. A murder plot committed over years is not the work of a regular person. He's got a gun, don't forget.'

'But he doesn't know that we know he's here, does he?'

'Nope. I doubt he could even imagine we would be, even if he could remember us from last month. I wonder if he works in that office?'

'Too obvious, given the angle the photo was taken from. Smith, like us, would have sussed it out, surely. Maybe he went there to say goodbye to his accomplice who works in the building, perhaps before disappearing. Seems more likely. We'll check later.'

Nick texted Jeff to tell him where they were and why.

'Let's just cross over the road and sit at the bus stop,' he said. 'Looks less weird than squatting down here, people are giving us funny looks.'

Perching on the plastic bench set into the bus stop gave them quite a clear view of the house opposite.

Jeff rang him.

'Me and Jo are on our way down now. What's the score?'

'He's got a house down here. He's dressed as Kiki.'

'So what's the plan?'

'We're trying to work that out.'

'Don't do anything until we get there. Jo has just come up with some serious shit. Did you get her text?'

'Yeah. I think Smith is getting desperate.'

He rang off. A bus came and one person got off.

'In a way, we want to help him,' said Nick. 'We want to help him get his revenge on Sullivan and his buddies. Bring it all out into the open and make sure the victims are acknowledged. Sullivan might have had money - his victims might want to claim against that for compensation.'

'Revenge in terms of the law, yeah. But we don't want anyone else killed. You're on dodgy territory here, Nick. Really dodgy. We can't be seen to be aiding and abetting a murderer. We'll end up in jail, man. Also, he's killed everyone on the Youth Offenders Board, so does he have any more revenge to dish out?'

Nick pulled at his lip, in contemplation. 'I'm not suggesting we let him get away with it, but if they arrest him now, I won't get my story, will I? Whereas if I can get it all out of him...'

'...you still won't be able to use it until after the court case is over - it'll all be *sub judice*. By which time, it'll all have come out in court and your exclusive is knackered. You could go to him and say, I'll get your story out into the public domain. Give him a chance to tell it from his perspective before he's arrested.'

'Yeah, good idea.'

'Is it? No it's not.' She looked at him incredulously. 'He's crazy. He might just shoot you dead there and then. He's done it before. It's not worth the risk, Nick. It's not a risk I'm going to let you take. I'm not having you killed just to get a story to sell. That's bloody mad. The police are still our best bet. Even though Smith is bent, others won't be.'

'That's crazy, Jules. The police have done nothing so far. Smith's got that place locked down tight. You know that's the truth.'

She folded her arms and pulled a face. 'I don't get why Charles has got a house here and a flat up the road?'

'Don't know. It's like the flat on Howe Street is where he lives as his parents. Here must be where he lives as himself.'

'Except that he didn't, he went in dressed as Kiki Dee.'

'Maybe that *is* how he lives.'

She nodded. 'Yeah, smart thinking, that. We keep saying he's dressed up as Kiki, but maybe he isn't. Maybe that's just who he is all of the time and when we saw him as Frank and Barbara, it's then that he's dressing up.'

They went quiet. When you come into contact with people and situations that are outside of your normal experience, it's scary, simply because it's hard to understand. Most people lead simple, uncomplicated lives. They are able to live openly because they fit accepted societal definitions of what is currently thought to be 'normal'. They live under a single name and they are assumed to have been assigned a female identity at birth if they present themselves as female. However, there are people who live on the margins of society, who feel they have to hide who they are, because other people struggle to understand and accept what is outside their own experience. These people don't easily fit into such narrow definitions of 'normal'.

'Have you always felt female, Jules?' said Nick, looking up the road for Jeff.

'That's an odd question. I think so. Yeah. It's sometimes hard to know what that means, though. At least outside of the basic physiology. I was always a tomboy. I liked fixing things, I loved learning about how cars worked. I didn't mind getting dirty and sweaty and I didn't give a shit about Barbie dolls and handbags. I liked rock music, more than pop. Some would say that's more male than female.' She wiped sweat from her forehead with her fingertips.

'It's funny, that.'

'Is it? Why?'

'You know why.'

'I don't.'

Another bus pulled up and let two people off.

'You're not most people's idea of a tomboy.'

'Am I not? But I've hardly ever worn much make-up. I've never tottered around on stilettos and worn tight little mini skirts and a push-up bra. But I always felt comfortable with being female. No...not just comfortable. I bloody love it. I love being a woman.'

Nick looked up the street. Jeff and Jo seemed to be taking ages.

'So did you always feel male?' she said. 'No dressing-up tendencies?'

'I knew from an early age I wasn't an uber male lad. I don't know how you learn that, but it was obvious I wasn't a macho sort. I was always too sensitive and wrapped up in my own thoughts. But I never for a moment felt I was a woman in a man's body, or anything like that. You saying you love being a woman, I could never say that about being a man. I'm just not that convinced we're a force for good in the world. Maybe that's why most of my friends from 16 onwards were girls.'

'Really? How odd. Are you sure you're not gay?' She laughed a little.

'I think I might have missed my vocation. I do remember thinking that girls were simply nicer than boys. Not that I was naïve about it, I knew there were nasty girls, too - but just for friends to chat to and have a laugh with, girls were a much preferred option for me. By and large, anyway.'

'And you secretly hoped one of them would fall in love with you and then perform an act of physical love upon your body.'

'Obviously. That goes without saying. No straight teenage boy has girls who are friends without at least occasionally entertaining the thought that somehow you might end up accidentally naked together and she might fall on your accidentally erect penis.'

She yelped a laugh again.

'Ah, here are Jeff and Jo.'

He waved at them.

'So, which house is it?' said Jeff as they entered the bus stop.

'The second one along from the lamp post,' said Nick.

Jo was about to say something, when Julie let out a humming noise.

'Don't look now...I said don't look...just carry on chatting - Kiki Dee has just come out of the house....so we're just standing here chatting and being sociable with each other and not even looking at him.'

Julie turned her back to the house and began making gestures as though describing something.

Jo put her green baseball boot on the bus stop bench and began fiddling with the laces, casting a glance across the road as she did so.

'He's off up the street. We can't all tail him. He's never seen you before, Jeff - follow him, see where he goes. Keep in touch by text,' said Jo. She quickly took out a baseball cap from her rucksack. 'Put that on for a bit, then take it off. It'll make you look different enough to stop her thinking she's being followed.'

'Aye, aye, Captain...and she's a he, remember?'

'Maybe,' said Jo.

Jeff strode off, crossed the road, keeping a good distance behind, put his hands in his army pants pockets and strolled away nonchalantly.

'Practically a professional,' said Jo, watching him go with a quick smile.

As she spoke, Nick looked from Jeff to the house.

He saw something.

Or did he?

Were his eyes playing tricks on him? Was it like Jo's photo of the haunted house? Had his brain invented something that wasn't there? But surely, you couldn't imagine seeing something or someone move. You couldn't, could you?

218

'I've just seen someone at the window,' he said, feeling like he'd seen a ghost.

'What? At Charles's house?' said Julie, following his gaze.

'Are you sure?' said Jo. 'What did you see?'

Nick didn't want to say. It was too weird. Too scary. His mouth went dry and he felt a little sick.

'It...it was a woman.'

'Maybe he's got a wife or something,' said Julie.

'No, it wasn't his wife.'

'How do you know?' said Jo.

'Because...because...'

'Because what?' said Julie, concerned.

'...because it was his mother, Barbara,' he finally said.

'Oh, come on!' said Julie, spinning round and squatting slightly, head in her hands, then turning quickly back to him. 'You are shitting me. It was *not* his mother. She's dead!!'

Jo said nothing. Her eyes were darting from side to side as she thought through the implications.

'I know. But it was her. She looked just like when he dressed as her, but older. Same white shoulder-length hair. He looks like she does now because she's actually still alive. She's his inspiration. And before you say it was a trick of the light, I know it wasn't. I saw her looking out of the window up at the sky, as though checking the weather.'

'I'm sorry. My mind has officially melted. I don't know what the fuck is going on,' said Julie, looking at Warriston playing fields behind them. She pushed her hair off her face as the wind blew it around. 'It can't be right. We had it all sorted out. You're wrong, you must be wrong.'

'This is so fucking cool,' said Jo, almost under her breath. 'Come here, you two,' she gestured to them to gather around her beside the wrought iron gates which divided the road from the grassy expanse beyond.

She held her scarred and bruised hands out wide. 'Right. This is the deal. I've sussed this gig totally.'

'Are you sure? How?' said Julie.

'Faking shit is my gig. Messing with reality is my stock in trade, innit? This is a fucking beauty.'

'Spill it then,' said Nick. He suddenly felt exhausted by all of this. Story or no story, it was some of the deepest, most messed-up shit he'd ever come across and it didn't make him feel happy. Jo was clearly excited by it, though.

She bent her thumb back and looked from Julie to Nick and back again. 'OK, one, everything we think we know about Ma Stewart is wrong. She didn't die in 1985. Who told you she did?'

'A woman from the hospice that she'd raised money for,' said Nick.

'What have I told you about that sort of info? Question it. She wasn't trying to mislead you, but she just heard wrongly. She thinks Barbara Stewart died, but she didn't. She got mixed up or whatever.'

Nick felt stupid for not questioning the veracity of the info before now.

Jo bent back her right index finger. 'Two. The 2007 A9 crash is disinformation. Ask yourself who told you about that?'

Nick looked at her. 'It was Gordon Smith and we already know from our meeting with him that he's probably a bent, corrupt, bad guy,' said Nick, rubbing his eyes. 'He's told me lies all the way along. That PNC printout about the A9 crash, that was crap. All that shit about the photo and the CCTV camera. That was all lies. Everything he's told me is all crap.'

'You mean...you mean he's...' Jo said.

'A paedophile? Probably, yeah,' said Nick.

'So, Ma Stewart is alive and well. I love how the son is going out into the world as his own mother. Damn! That's so cool,' said Jo. She looked over to the house with real admiration. 'That house is hers. It all fits together so well. I bet she is officially dead, you know. Somehow in 1985 there was a mix-up over her death and she's been officially dead ever since. Right, well, we know what we've got to do now, don't we?'

'Do we? I don't,' said Julie. 'And there's something not right about...'

Jo interrupted her. 'We have to nail Gordon Smith and the people he's trying to protect...now, how do we do that?'

'What about Charles murdering Grayson-Thomas?' said Julie. 'He can't be allowed to get away with murder.'

'That can wait. He's not going anywhere,' said Jo.

'I don't agree. I think Smith wants to find him and dispose of him, so he can't talk. I don't think they knew who'd been doing the killings until this final shooting and I reckon it was us who have led them to Charles. We gave them Barbara's name and his name.'

'I agree, but only to a degree. What these people want more than anything is for the focus of attention on Grayson-Thomas's murder to go away. Charles showed the gun to the camera and sent the photo out into the world, so it was clearly a murder. He knew they'd try and sweep it under the carpet, unless it was as obvious as he could make it. He had that photo taken by someone, just as you said. He wanted it to be a high-profile and dramatic image. But Smith and whoever else he's working with, these people don't want anyone else sniffing around and getting wind of rumours of child abuse or a paedophile ring because it's still active. If they kill Charles, it potentially only draws more attention to it,' said Jo. 'That being said, if they snuff him out quietly and make the body disappear, that would suit them nicely.'

It was good reasoning. But was it right?

'You've forgotten one thing, though,' said Nick. 'Charles might not have finished killing people. Maybe Grayson-Thomas was just the latest in the killings,' said Nick. 'He might have others in his sights, if there's a child abuse ring up here that is, or was related to, the one on Teesside.'

'Oh, shit,' Julie put her hand over her mouth. 'I am not being party, even vicariously, to more murders. We have to stop him.'

'He might - he's killed all the members of that Youth Offenders Board now. But if there are others, do we care about that?' said Jo. 'Seriously? I care more about exposing the powerful and corrupt than I do about grassing up someone who is shooting them.'

Julie shook her head. 'Two wrongs don't make a right. I know it's a cliché but it is true. I can't be party to the murder of people, no matter how evil they are. It's for the law to decide about them, not some crazy bloke in a dress.'

Jo was indignant. 'Surely it must obvious to you that he's not a "crazy bloke in a dress". That's a terrible thing to say. Your work should have taught you that.'

Julie looked a bit sheepish and held up a hand. 'Sorry, I was out of order. It's the stress of this situation.'

'You're forgiven,' said Jo. 'Anyway, the law doesn't want to know. The irony is, Charles knew that. He knew that when he shot Sullivan, some significant people in the police would be more concerned with preserving Sullivan's current identity and not exposing him as a man with a paedophile past, than actually catching the person who shot him.'

Julie twitched her nose and chewed on her lip.

Nick's phone vibrated. A text from Jeff: '*He's walked through the Botanic Gardens, now about to head into Inverleith Park. Am in pursuit like a massive private dick.*'

'Jeff's still on his tail...look, what about this for an idea? I call Mandy Beale and tell her everything. She knows some of it, anyway. Tell her the local plod stinks. Give it to her to deal with,' said Nick. It was the only idea he had.

'Is she cool?' said Jo.

'I don't know, Jo. Maybe she's in with the evil people, but we have to trust someone,' said Nick, losing faith in the idea almost immediately.

'The chances of her being a paedophile are very small. The chances of her protecting someone in the force who is, are equally small. In 2010, it would just be very hard to do that, even if you wanted to and I don't believe she does or would,' said Julie. 'I'm sure she's a nice person. That's not a reality I'm prepared to question. Call her now.' She pointed firmly at his phone.

He texted Mandy and asked her to call him urgently. She must have just been in her office because she called him right back.

' 'Ello!' she said in her cheery, Yorkshire way. 'What've you bin up to, then? Caught me some villains?'

Nick explained where they were and as much as he could about the whole affair, up to and including the fact that they suspected Gordon Smith was a paedophile, or protecting those who were. He talked as fast as he could. She listened without saying anything, but made her odd little pops and squeaks in reaction to what he said.

'We need help, Mandy. We've got a killer on the loose, he might shoot other people. Gordon Smith might just fancy shutting both him and us up, as well. Does any of this make sense?'

'Aye, it's a proper pickle, eh. I dunno what to do - I can't just send coppers up to Edinburgh. We've not got enough down here, as it is and I couldn't even if I wanted to - well above my pay grade, that sort of thing. But but but...aye...well, we've got to do summat, 'aven't we? ' She hummed and made more little farting noises with her lips, as she contemplated a way through this. 'I'll be honest, Nick. I don't think I can help. I'd *have* to tell the local plod if we come up.'

'Why?'

'It's protocol and we're all coppers, we can't go treading on each others toes. And even if you're right about this Gordon Smith bloke, not everyone up there will be a bad guy, will they?'

'No, of course not, but we don't know which ones are and which ones aren't.'

'Alright. Leave it with me...'

'...don't say that, Mandy...that's what people say when they're going to knock it into the long grass. Don't let me down. Please...this is serious shit.'

'I know. I'm takin' it serious. Proper serious. But I'm not Mandy the maverick cop off a telly show, am I? I've got to do this right. I'll sort it but it'll take some calls, so calm down and wait to hear from me.' She spoke with the degree of mild indignation that is every Yorkshire person's birthright.

'OK, thanks.'

He rang off and told Julie and Jo what she'd said.

Jo nodded, hands in pockets. 'Owee, let's do something. I'm going for a chat with Ma Stewart.'

She didn't wait for them, but ran across the road and up to the front door of the Stewart house.

Nick sprinted after her. She'd beaten the iron lion's paw knocker before he could stop her.

'What are you doing?' said Nick.

'Making something happen,' said Jo, with a wide-eyed, confrontational, punky look.

The door opened and a frail woman stood there. Little more than a bag of bones with long white hair, she didn't look well. She was an old middle-class woman, dressed in a sensible blouse and skirt. But her left hand was remarkable. Every nail was so long that it curled under the fingertip.

'Is Charles here by any chance? We just wanted a quick word with him,' said Jo.

Barbara Stewart raised her right hand and shakily rubbed at her forehead a little. The nails on those fingers were just as long and the same grubby yellowy colour. Why would you not cut your nails? Why is that something you decide you're not going to do, but still maintain appearances in all other respects?

'Charles? Who's he? Are you friends of his?'

'Yes. I thought we saw him leaving here as we were walking around the corner,' said Nick.

Barbara looked at him, her mouth slightly open, then at Julie and back to him. It was impossible to read her. Her expression was totally blank. In that moment she looked just like his mother had on her most confused days, days when she'd almost look through you, like you were a ghost, unable to quite locate herself in her own mental landscape; so adrift that she wasn't even aware she was adrift. Nick had often felt that was a blessing, in some regard. Losing your grip and knowing you had, must be profoundly distressing. But Barbara wasn't distressed at all, it looked like it was all birdsong in her mind.

Then she came back to herself. You could see it wash in like a tide. Her eyes brightened. 'Oh, that was Shirley. She just popped in. She's very good like that.'

'Shirley? OK, is she your care visitor?' said Julie.

'I don't get out of the house,' said Barbara, who didn't really seem up to answering questions. She really wasn't quite all there, poor old girl.

Nick glanced down. She was wearing threadbare slippers and standing on a doormat which had mail on it. He bent down and picked it up. It looked like a couple of bills.

'You've got some mail, save you bending down,' he said and handed it to her. As he did so he glanced at the name and address. Edith Coulson. Not Barbara Stewart. He tipped the letters towards Jo and Julie and pointed. They clocked it.

'OK, we'll be going. We must have made a mistake. Sorry to have disturbed you,' said Nick. She stood at the door and watched them go, apparently having drifted off again.

'That's the last time I listen to either of you,' said Julie, very annoyed. 'That bloody wasn't Barbara Stewart at all. Christ, you were both totally wrong. Never bloody mind question all realities, eh. Bloody hell...' She was really cross. 'I *knew* it was rubbish. You just rushed into that like you always know what's what, but you'd just made it all up in your own head, in exactly the way you're always saying you should be aware about. Talk about physician bloody well heal thyself.' She let out a bark of indignation.

'Alright, alright. So we got it wrong,' said Jo.

'She was just a confused and unwell old lady,' said Nick. 'But I was right in one way. He is using her as an inspiration. He does dress like her when being Barbara.'

As they walked into the Botanical Gardens, Julie spread her arms out wide.

'Right, Shut up and let me settle this once and for all. This is what has happened: Barbara is dead and so is Frank. They died in the 80s. The gravestone is just someone else altogether. Right? Charles lives his life as Shirley, except when pretending to be his mother or father. He's resurrected them as real people, by getting a job as his mother and by renting a flat as his father, and he's done that in order to be able to use them as cover for his murder of the man who was once Rupert Sullivan, a man who abused him and many others. That has to be the final, 100 per cent truth,' said Julie, making a mid-air fist to emphasise the point. 'Now will everyone just shut up and not come up with any more theories? Please!'

'Let's go and find Jeff,' said Nick. This was like being insane; fact and fiction blurred.

They walked briskly through the beautiful gardens, but Nick's mind was too busy with the events of the day to really appreciate it. They had just emerged through the western gate and stood with Inverleith Park opposite them, when Jeff called.

'Where are you?'

Nick told him. 'What's going on?'

'He's heading up onto a rooftop next to the police station. This isn't looking good, man. Some very bad shit is going to go down.'

CHAPTER 13

'Where are you?'

'Opposite the police station. Go through the park, straight down and it's on your left. Big ugly brick building.' Jeff's voice was urgent and frightened. 'I think I know what he's doing. We've got to stop him. He's going to kill again. He's going to take out some coppers.'

Nick set off at high pace. 'A murder is about to happen!' he yelled and beckoned Julie and Jo to follow him.

Sprinting fast through the grassy parkland, he followed Jeff's directions, seeing the large police station; set into its own grassy grounds, it was like so many 1960s stations, built on the cheap and nasty on every level. Opposite was a secondary school, at the end of the road stood Fettes College. A huge late Victorian Gothic school for the children of rich people, it dominates views on the north side of the city. In a graphic display of inequality, how galling it must be for the kids going to the state school opposite. It was as though they were deliberately having their noses rubbed into wealth and privilege. Every time there was no money at their school for something, they must surely cast a glance over the way and wonder what they'd done so wrong to be so deprived, when others had so much. Were their lives not worth the same as the rich people's kids lives?

Jeff was standing beside the school gates as Nick came to halt, panting for breath. The big man pointed across the street.

'See that ramp across the road? It leads up to Waitrose's car park. He's gone up there and onto the roof. He's not going up there to appreciate the view, is he? He's not shopping for marsh samphire and giant ducks fed on crushed rubies, or whatever it is they sell in there.'

'Did he have a gun with him?'

'Nothing I could see, so it's nothing big. He could have a pistol but nothing else. Two options. He's got a gun nest already up there, ready to mow down the police as they come out of work. Or he's going to top himself by jumping off onto someone's head in the police car park below. Either way we've got to stop him.'

'Could he really not just be doing some shopping?' said Nick, looking up to the car park roof.

'Why didn't he go into the shop, then? Why go up to the car park on foot? It directly overlooks the police station car park.'

'We can't exactly call the police, though, can we?'

Nick looked to his right. Julie was running towards them, Jo was some distance behind, unable to keep up with her. No-one else was around. The school kids were still in class.

'Say we follow him up there. What then? If he's got a gun, we've got no way to defend ourselves,' said Nick. Julie came up, gasping.

'Is he doing a Malcolm McDowell in *If?*' she said, referring to one of their mutually favourite films.

'I reckon so, Jules,' said Nick.

'Well, let's get up there and stop him. No-one else dies. Right?'

'We've got to be careful. He must have a gun, but we don't want to alert the police, either. The minute they come out and go to their cars, he'll start picking them off. That's got to be his intention. We can't risk that,' said Nick.

Jo joined them. 'Fucking hell, I'm going to throw up with all this running.' She leaned over, hands on her legs, trying to get her breath.

'We've got the element of surprise,' said Julie. 'He doesn't know we're here and he's never even seen Jeff or Jo before.'

'Why don't I go up there and pretend to be some sort of workie gadgee? I'm fixing the roof,' said Jeff.

'And you get hold of him and then what do we do?' said Nick. 'Politely tell him not to commit any more murders and/or possibly kill himself?'

'If we don't do something soon, it'll be a moot point,' said Julie, hands on hips.

'Look, it's free parking up there. Maybe she's just parked up there for free,' said Jo.

'So he's cycled from work...' said Nick.

'...she has,' interrupted Jo.

'He or she or whatever, has cycled from Charlotte Square to visit the old woman, walks here to pick up a car and drive home? Seems very odd to me,' said Jeff.

Jo shook her head. 'Jeff man, you've really gone off on one here. What makes you think that she's going to do anything murderous?'

Jeff tugged on his beard and winced. 'Because it's next to the cop shop.'

Someone came out of the police station and walked across the large car park where a lot of squad cars were parked as well as riot vans and civilian cars.

Nick tugged at his stubble wondering what to do for the best. 'We should go up and have a look, see what he's up to. There'll be shoppers up there so surely he can't just...'

As he was speaking the man who had been approaching the parked cars seemed to fall over and out of view behind an estate car. He just dropped like the proverbial stone. Nick paused, distracted by another man in a blue gilet walking out of the back of the station, reaching for his keys in his pocket and unlocking a BMW. As he pulled the door open, he seemed to slip over and fall backwards.

The first man hadn't got up.

Then it came to Nick.

They hadn't fallen, they'd been silently shot and killed.

A painful surge of adrenalin washed into his nervous system.

'Two men have just been shot,' he hissed in a low whisper. 'Come on, let's get up there.'

'What? Are you sure?' said Julie. 'Where, who?'

'Didn't you see them?' he said, 'They both went down. Shot with a silencer. Made no noise.'

Without further thought, he ran across the road and up the ramp with Jeff right behind him. The first floor was quite empty. Maybe six cars parked up. The second floor was the roof top. Sprinting to the top of the ramp took Nick into the open air. One side of the building looked south. In the distance was Edinburgh Castle and Arthur's Seat. The police station and Fettes College lay close by to the north. He had to be shooting over the surrounding wall on that side. But there was no-one there. In fact, aside from four parked cars, there was no-one and nothing there.

'Where is he?' said Jeff, standing alongside him, breathing heavily, Julie and Jo behind him.

'Can't see him at all.'

'Maybe she's gone,' said Jo.

They stood still for a full minute, then Jeff tapped Nick on the arm and pointed to a metal step ladder.

'Those steps go down to a lower platform. He must be on there. He can't see us without standing up.'

Jo stepped forward and pointed. 'Look. She's got a camera hooked up to a mobile. Look, it's on the wall. See? She's watching the car park through that and only standing up to shoot when someone comes out. Clever. Minimum exposure.'

A small black box sat on the lip of the car park. Jo was right.

Nick turned to look down at the car park. As he did so, a familiar figure walked out of the station and strode across the car park. It was Gordon Smith, still dressed as he had been before, in his awful black slacks. In an instant there was a dull thud of the gun being discharged with a silencer on it. Charles was shooting at Smith.

But Charles missed.

The bullet hit the top of a car with ping and zing. Smith dived down and rolled behind a car.

Having missed the target, a figure stood up from the hiding place, plucked the camera off the wall, slid a pistol into an inside pocket, walked towards a red Vauxhall Corsa parked nearby, got in quickly, turned the ignition and drove past them on the edge of the ramp, without looking at them even once.

They watched Charles go. 'Never seen anyone look more like Kiki Dee,' said Jeff, almost absentmindedly, as the car passed them.

'This is a bad place to be. It's a crime scene. Let's get out of here,' said Nick, pointing to the door that led to the stairs down into the supermarket.

They hurried down as sirens blared out, with police cars roaring out of the station as the alarm was raised, presumably by Gordon Smith. Once in the foyer of the supermarket, they walked out onto the main road, crossed over and walked back through Stockbridge to the flat on Howe Street.

Sitting on the sofa, Nick put the TV on. It had already made national media. BBC News24 had reports of the shooting of two police officers. Nothing was really known, but by the look of the live footage, the whole area had been sealed off and treated as one big crime scene.

'This is very weird, you know. We're the only people who know what happened there,' said Nick. 'I feel like I should tell someone, but the very people we should tell - the police - are the very people we can't tell. God, what do we do? We witnessed two murders and a third attempted murder.'

'This is has got to stop,' said Julie. 'I feel sick. I don't care if Gordon Smith and the other two who were shot are corrupt, or are paedophiles, or anything else, I'm not having members of the public killing people. It's just wrong. We need to live by the law. I totally get that we've got to be careful what we say to whom, but we can't do or say nothing. We just can't.' Her voice was high-pitched and strained with tension. She was pale and drawn with the stress.

Nick rolled a strand of his hair around his finger. 'Yeah. I agree. Just don't know what to do, though, Jules.'

'Mandy Beale is our only hope,' said Jeff. 'We can give it all to her and she can deal with it. We're so out of our depth here. We've witnessed two murders, for fuck's sake! Two! Charles Stewart is fucking crazy. I sympathise with anyone who's been abused like he was, but that can't excuse a murderous rampage.'

'I'm glad you're seeing my way of thinking,' said Julie.

Jo was pensive and sat, her knees pulled up to her chin. 'You've got to remember that she's in a very distressed state of mind,' she said.

'Why do you keep calling him "she"?' said Nick. 'He's Charles Stewart. He's a he and very much not a she.'

'Is she? You don't know what she's going through.'

'What *he's* going through,' asserted Nick.

'No. She. She wants to be seen as and known as a woman. Think about it, Nick, we have no evidence that Charles Stewart has lived as a man since he was in his teens. She's a woman. That's how she feels about herself. And she may be 100 per cent female now. It's plain and simple. You've got to free your mind from these old-fashioned narrow ideas of gender. Just because she was born Charles, is no reason to assume that is who she *really* is. She's Shirley. Right?'

Nick wasn't sure he really understood. They had a couple more drinks. Then Nick's phone buzzed. It was Mandy.

'Hiya, Mandy.'

'Are you all still in Edinburgh?' she said without introduction.

'Aye.'

'You've got to come home. All of you. Back to Teesside.'

'What? Now?'

'Now. I can't protect you up there.'

'Protect us? I don't understand.'

'Look. You're in danger up there. You've kicked over a wasps nest and they're going to come after you. I know what's what down here. I know 'oo I can trust and 'oo I can't. When you're up there, I can't help you. So gerron the next train and come back. Right? I don't wanna 'ave to scrape you lot up off the pavement, do I?'

Nick stared at the ground. 'Is it that urgent?'

'Bloody 'ell, man. Yes, it bloody is! There's people severely unchuffed with you up there, people on the force and their powerful friends and god only knows what they might do. Desperate bloody people do desperate bloody things. It's all going to go off in that force. Big ructions. So get yer arse in gear and come back 'ome. I'll meet you at Darlo station. Watch your backs all the way. Right? If the local plod pull you in, tell them they have to call me. Ring me when you're on the train. The next one leaves in 30 minutes. No fuckin' around. Gerrit done! The longer you're there, the more danger you're in.'

'C'mon, we're offski.' said Nick, standing up. 'Mandy's orders. She reckons we're in danger up here.'

'Are we bollocks?' said Jo, flicking through the TV channels. 'Who from, like?'

'The police and other powerful people,' said Nick. 'I'm not arguing with Mandy. She's serious. Next train south is in 30 minutes. It takes 20 to walk to the station from here, so we've got to go and go now!'

Julie ran through to the bedroom, picked up their bag and toothbrushes and ran back. 'Right, I'm good to go. Are you sorted, Jeff?'

He pointed at his rucksack. 'All in here. Owee, Jo. We've got to split. Your bag's here.'

'You're over-reacting. We've had no grief off anyone.'

Nick looked at his watch. They had to go now to have a chance to get the train.

'Look, she's number two at Cleveland Police, she doesn't say stuff without good reason. If she's saying we're in danger, then we are. Jeff...pick her up, we're going.'

'Bugger off,' said Jo. Jeff ignored her and lifted her up with little effort; being a foot taller and about five stone heavier made her a light lift. He put her over his shoulder. She began kicking out and cursing him as they ran down the stairs and out onto the street. 'Alright, alright, put us down,' she yelled, as they crossed Heriot Row and walked up towards Princes Street.

'Mandy said we should watch our backs the whole way,' said Nick. 'So no stopping for any reason. Right?'

'Bloody hell, I'm bricking it,' said Julie. 'Is it Gordon Smith after us, do you reckon?'

'Got to be.'

They froze midstep as a police car siren screeched up ahead of them, and a squad car flew at speed along Queen Street.

'Fuck me. I thought that was them,' said Nick, as they hurried on.

Jeff looked around. 'There's no-one following us. We'll be alright.'

They reached Princes Street, turned left and half walked, half ran, down to Waverley Station, weaving through the crowds of tourists.

Thirteen minutes before the train left.

As they waited at the traffic lights to cross the road to reach the station, Julie grabbed Nick's arm and pointed down the street. Two unmarked police cars with blue flashing lights on top were parked up outside the entrance and four men, who were as obviously policemen as Gordon Smith was, stood on the pavement looking at people as they passed by and walked down the incline into the station.

'Shitting hell,' said Nick.

'They might not be after us,' said Jeff.

'Do you believe that?' said Nick. 'Of course they fucking are. There's no way we can get in that way.'

'There's another entrance further along Princes Street,' said Jo, sprinting between cars as they pulled up at the lights. Big crowds of tourists made for good cover as they wove through to the three levels of steps that went down into the station off Princes Street.

'No-one here,' said Jo.

'Our platform is number eight, it's right underneath here,' said Julie, looking up at a monitor of departures as they went down the steep steps.

But as they got half way down, Nick put his arms out to stop Julie and Jo and guided them into the entrance to the awful shopping mall that can be accessed from the station steps. Two more plain-clothes officers stood at the top of the escalator that led down into the station, right beside their train, which was sitting waiting to head south to King's Cross, stopping at Berwick, Newcastle and then Darlington.

'Do you reckon they're coppers? Those two in black waterproofs and black pants?' he said.

'Of course they are,' said Jeff. 'They look like every copper looks who has taken off their jacket. Ties off, black slacks, shiny black shoes. And they're checking everyone as they pass by.'

'Not just that, look, one of them has got a piece of paper...looks like a photo is printed on it. That'll be of us in Waitrose,' said Julie. 'Shit, how the hell do we get past them?'

Jeff tied his hair back tightly and stuffed it down the back of his shirt. 'Might as well get the most identifiable marker hidden. You do the same, Jules. Tie your hair up and put this cap on.' She did as she was told.

'They've got this place blocked off. We can't get past them. Train is due out in seven minutes,' said Nick, glancing at his watch. 'Anyone got any ideas?'

Jo squatted down and opened up her rucksack. 'Don't fucking shit yer knickers, kids. Jo's 'ere. I've been in tighter scrapes than this, believe me. This lot are nowt. Get ready. I'll distract them. When I go out there, you go to the far side of these stairs and walk right behind the fattest person you can see, use them as cover. Nick, put this wool hat and dark glasses on. Jules, wrap this scarf around your chin and mouth. You too Jeff, hide that feckin' beard.' She passed them each a small, tartan scarf. 'Break up. Don't go down as a group. Use the stairs to the platform, not the escalators. Quicker.'

She put something in her pockets, stood up and grinned at the three of them, not a trace of worry or stress in her sparky eyes. She was in her element. Talk about your Inner Boro. This was where she was King Tees, or maybe King Tease. 'I absolutely fuckin' love this.' Arms out wide, she jutted her jaw out at them, arrogant, cocky and full of herself. 'Am I real or am I fake? Show time! Rock and fuckin' roll.'

She turned, trotted down the flight of stairs, strode towards the two plain-clothes coppers, as though she was just another member of the public. Then, stopping a few yards from them, she sank to her knees with a groan and began clutching at her throat, as though she couldn't breathe, letting out little pants of breath and frightened yelps. A woman walking alongside her let out a scream as she fell to the ground and stared at Jo. She began coughing, as though she was choking.

'Fuck me, she's good,' said Nick, under his breath.

'She's spent all her life pretending - it comes as second nature to her,' said Jeff.

'The police might be aware she's some sort of con artist,' said Julie, 'and totally discount it.'

'Nah, they won't have a clue who she is,' said Jeff, putting the scarf on to totally hide his facial hair.

As he spoke, Jo let out a scream of, 'Oh, my god, oh my god, I'm bleeding, help!! Please help!!'

A man in his mid 40s squatted down beside her. 'Are you alright? Oh, my god...this woman is in a bad way. She's...she's had her throat cut, I think.'

Nick, Julie and Jeff stepped out from their cover, one at a time. Nick spotted someone who was obviously an American tourist; fat and waddling, with a look on his face that suggested having to walk anywhere was some sort of European insult. He walked to the far side of them, past the stricken Jo, without looking at her, to the stairs beside the escalator and legged it down them as fast as possible.

As he reached the platform, he turned to look behind him. Julie and Jeff were coming down the stairs.

Two minutes until the train left.

It was a very long train - at least 11 carriages. If there were police on the platform there was no way they could guard it all.

Nick waited for Jeff and Julie and then boarded the train. They got onto the fourth carriage and took a table seat. Nick's heart pounded hard in his chest.

'Shit, I hope Jo is OK. They'll arrest her when they realise she's just faking it,' said Julie.

Jeff shook his head. 'She's too tricky for that. She'll have worked a way out. She's been getting out of one situation or another all her life.'

'Are you sure? I'm worried about her,' said Nick, as the train lurched a little and began to move. 'She's on her own. Smith and his mob are evil bastards.'

'You underestimate her,' said Jeff, taking off his scarf. 'Everyone does. Even people who think they know her, don't know what she's capable of.'

'And you do, then?' said Julie as the train pulled out of the station and picked up speed.

'Yeah, we clicked from the start, didn't we?' He held up his hands. 'She opened up to me. I opened up to her. She's not...she's not normal.'

'So what's going on with you two?' said Julie.

He looked out of the window. 'Nothing. Not like that. I just understand where she's coming from.'

They went quiet as the adrenaline of the last half an hour began to subside. The train was busy as it traveled through the anonymous dark night, out into East Lothian and then south towards Berwick-upon-Tweed. They had to pay full price to the conductor for their tickets, which meant paying a small fortune for a journey that, if you bought the ticket in advance, was only a few quid.

God, this had been exhausting and it wasn't over yet. Nick felt so tense that his neck was knotted into a tight ball. If Mandy thought that they needed protection on Teesside, then they were still in serious trouble. Nick fully expected to see police coming through the train, looking for them, like Nazis in a war film. And you couldn't get away on a train.

There was nowhere to hide, except the toilet and frankly, being arrested by corrupt police officers was probably preferable than having to go into the toilet.

At Berwick, someone walked down the aisle between the seats, stopped and sat down in the empty seat next to Nick, opposite Julie. Nick shuffled closer to the window to make room for them, always keen to give himself and other people enough personal space. Julie was nodding, half asleep, Jeff had his eyes closed.

You don't really look at people who sit next to you on public transport. It seems rude. You can't do it subtly, anyway. It requires turning and peering into their face. A sideways glance at this person didn't reveal much. They had a beanie hat on and dark glasses. Nick wondered briefly if they were blind. Couldn't be the police though, could it? Or could it? Shit, he was boxed into the window seat now. Well, if it was, what could he do about it? Not much. What could they do now, anyway? They'd have to arrest them, drag them off at Newcastle and dispose of them, but that would be a very public thing to do. It would have a lot of witnesses. It didn't seem impossible, but it felt less likely than someone coming after them on Teesside. Some bloody psychotic Edinburgh hit man, in all probability. Smith had surely already paid two thugs to try and scare him off. If it looked like they were all going down, who knows how desperate they'd get? After all, these were powerful people, high up in society and with law enforcers to do their dirty work.

The carriage went still and quiet. There is something unique about traveling on a train at night. It's a soothing, insular experience. Everyone settled into their own space. Then again, if you got stuck next to a screaming kid, some Newcastle United fans on an away day, or a Scots-man on a 12-can bender, you'd do anything to be alone in your own car, in the silence of your own world.

Even despite the tension that gripped his whole body, he started to doze off. The warmth, the rhythm of the train and the background white noise of the rails on the track, made it impossible to stay awake. He went into that space we all have that is somewhere between being asleep and awake. It is the best of all spaces. Warm and secure and distant from the troubles of consciousness, but lacking the weird surrealism of the dream state that deep sleep inevitably delivers. It felt like a meditative state. His mind still worked on things, but was somehow at rest.

'How long is it going take for youse lot to realise who I am?'

The voice invaded his consciousness but he felt some distance from it.

'It's just as well I'm not the filth, innit?'

Nick opened his eyes and looked to his right where the voice was coming from.

He let out a little yelp of shock. Julie and Jeff opened their eyes in response to the voice.

It was Jo.

She grinned at him. She'd taken off the dark glasses and hat, sat up and seemed to reshape her body to look like herself.

'Bloody hell. What...how...err...where...?' Nick couldn't get the words out, he was so shocked to see her.

'Yes! I told you, this isn't your ordinary chick,' said Jeff, leaning forward to hi-five her. 'Never thought it was you. I did wonder, but you looked taller and broader and have different clothes on.'

'Changed in the toilet, didn't I?'

'I'm so pleased to see you, Jo. We were dead worried. How on earth did you get from bleeding on those stairs to this train?' said Julie, rubbing her eyes.

Jo locked her fingers together and cracked her knuckles. 'It *was* a bit tricky.'

'She won't tell you,' said Jeff, with an admiring grin. 'Tricks of the trade, and all that. Magic Circle code of silence.'

Julie knitted her eyebrows together. 'I just can't see how that was possible. We only just got on the train in time, you had to have been less than a minute or two behind us.'

'Well, they obviously didn't stop us,' said Jo. 'Never underestimate the general public's ability to be an unwitting accomplice to your schemes. Also never underestimate how good a cover a well-deployed thick smoke bomb is.'

'Ah, that's how you did it, eh?' said Jeff, laughing. 'Brilliant. Are there any other police on the train, do you reckon?'

She shook her head. 'I was last on at the far end, I'd have seen them get on. It was an absolute classic. Brilliant.'

'Of course, we don't know if those men who we assumed were coppers, were actually waiting for us,' said Nick.

Jo pointed at him and nodded. 'Good point. Still no proof of that. You're taking on trust what Mandy Beale said. But I've told you so many times to question all realities. She might be the one we need to be most careful of. We don't know.'

'Mandy Beale is a good woman,' said Julie, arms crossed. 'I know what you're saying, but you've also got to trust your own judgement and everything I know about the way people are, tells me she's on our side and she's totally trustworthy. For a start, Colin Harcombe wouldn't have her as his number two if she wasn't. We know Colin well and he's about as upright and moralistic as anyone could be in his job.'

Jo pointed at her and nodded. 'Good. I like it. I know it narks you, but all I'm getting you to do is to question why you think something. That's all.'

Darlington station used to be a grand and bustling place. Now, despite its important location on the East Coast mainline, it was almost unrecognisable as the station of Nick's youth. It was all but deserted at night, but at least it still had a roof and had kept its basic structure in place, which could hardly be said for any other stations on Teesside, especially Stockton's, which for no good reason had been all but abandoned, despite being the actual birthplace of the railways. The fact the once-wonderful station had been deconstructed and was nothing more than two crumbling platforms these days, was something which amazed almost everyone on Teesside. Why such a unique asset had never been exploited as a tourist or historical attraction was very puzzling. Most places dress up the slightest historically significant aspect of the town as more important than it really was, but Stockton did the exact opposite. Then again, there was something quite typically Teesside about that.

As the train pulled in, Nick caught sight of Mandy Beale standing on the platform dressed in a black anorak. There was no other obvious police presence.

' 'Ello, you lot,' she said, with a nod, as they disembarked. 'You made it down here, alright then. Good.'

'Yeah, we had a bit of a scare at Edinburgh station, but Jo got us out of that,' said Nick.

'We've not met. 'Ello, Jo. Nick told me about your show. I never got to see it while I were up there. We could use a magician in the force, sometimes. Ha. Come on...'

'Where are we going, Mandy?' said Julie.

'My office at the station. I know you must be knackered, but I'd rather do this now, than wait.'

Nick's stomach turned over with nerves. How had this happened? The journey from seeing Barbara Stewart for a minute on the stairwell that day, through to the murder and all the strange twists and turns in identifying Charles as the shooter and the child abuse ring that had been his target, had been so long and complex that he felt quite bewildered.

'Are we in serious danger?' said Nick as she drove them back to Stockton police station.

'That's an unknown quantity, but I was told in confidence by a mate I've got on the force up there, that the shit is about to hit the fan. The bent coppers up there are going to be gutted and filleted. One thing this job 'as taught me, though, like I said to you on the phone, is that desperate people do increasingly desperate things. And when that 'appens, all bets are off. That Smith lad, he's a proper bad 'un, my mate reckons.'

Nick shuddered at what that might mean. To think he'd been sitting so close to a man who...well...who knows what heinous things he'd seen and done, over the years.

'Takes the police a long time to build a case against one of its own and 'e's a smart one, this Smith, but by the sounds of it, 'e's going to feel the force of the bloody law, sooner rather than later.'

The station was quiet. A sergeant on the desk looked up as they trooped in.

'No crimes around, Alfie? What's going on?'

The man shrugged. 'Maybe crime is out of fashion, Mand. We've had nowt through the door all night.'

'Enjoy it while it lasts, mate, some scumbags will be here soon enough,' said Mandy, pushing open her office door, adding, 'they'd better be or my arrest numbers will look bloody rubbish and I'll have to go and bust Hair Bear just to make us look good. And no-one wants that.'

It was soulless box of a room with a cheap desk, plaster walls covered in various sheets of A4 paper, a white board with names on it and a desktop PC whirring away.

She pulled out some chairs from around the walls for the four of them to sit down facing each other.

'Right. I did some digging, well, I say that, but Smith's records are far from complete and have obviously, to my mind, been doctored and messed with.' She leaned over and took a sheet of paper from her desk, then pointed at it with a thick index finger. 'He's from Edinburgh, but he started his career 26 years ago in North Yorkshire...'

'...I found that out, as well,' said Jo. 'Just by doing a search on the Harrogate *Advertiser* archives. He's mentioned as attending various police functions and in court reports from Northallerton and Ripon.'

'So that's where he's come into contact with Sullivan and the rest of them,' said Nick.

'Aye, seems more than likely, that. He wasn't on that Youth Offenders Board, according to his record, but he might have had that taken off, somehow. It's not unknown. But he worked all over the area and got transferred up to Edinburgh a few years back. His boss up there, for most of the time, was Francis Driscoll. Fat Franny. Even I'd heard of him. Met him once at some conference, years ago. One of these ruddy-cheeked sorts who comes on like he's a big teddy bear...'

'...but in reality he's the exact opposite?' said Julie.

'Aye. Exactly. Hands all over the place. One of them sorts. 'orrible. He was retired 18 months ago aged 59. Same age as Smith. Now, I'm guessing about this, but I reckon someone's 'ad a word and told him to get out before what he's been up to comes out.' She took out some papers from a folder and shuffled them, tapping them into line on her lap. 'Y'see, Fat Franny worked with Grayson-Thomas for a younger offenders charity in Edinburgh...well, you know what that probably bloody means, don't you, given what we know?'

'Is Driscoll still alive, then? Charles hasn't shot him?' said Jeff.

'Not yet. I reckon that's 'cos he weren't part of the ring of abusers that attacked Charles all them years ago. He's only gone after them, until now, but the two coppers you saw get shot are two detectives that work with Smith. 'E's targeted them, so maybe he's widening his range.'

'So they're going to arrest Smith?' said Julie, stifling a yawn, emotionally and physically drained by the day.

'Aye, by all accounts, they've been keeping tabs on him for a while, now. These sorts of things take ages to sort out. A clever copper can get away with a lot over a long period of time, if they're careful enough.' She puffed out her capacious pink cheeks. 'Like I said on the phone, I can do more to protect you here, better than up there, if he comes down or sends someone down to sort you out.'

'Bloody hell. What's he got to gain by doing that?' said Jeff.

'A lot. My guess is he doesn't know where this Charles Stewart is and he'll reckon you do and he'll want to get that out of you, won't 'e? He might even think you're working with him, especially as you'd gone up to Edinburgh on the day he gets shot at. He might even think you were the shooter. The fact that he nearly took a bullet is likely to concentrate his mind. The noose is tightening around his neck. My guess is he'll be ready to do a runner.'

'Both times I've met him, he's been really stressed and intense. He was making stuff up but was obviously struggling to keep up with all his own lies,' said Nick. 'And he definitely wanted to know where Charles was, didn't he, Jules?' She nodded.

Jo had been quiet, her long, pointy fingers locked together on her lap. She looked up. 'Charles doesn't exist. He hasn't existed since the 80s.'

'You reckon, Jo?' said Mandy, pushing her raggy hair off her forehead. 'What are you talking about?'

'I think she's Shirley and has been for a long time. It's Shirley who dresses up as Frank and Barbara, not Charles.'

Julie rested her chin on her hand and nodded. 'I get that totally. So is she transgender?'

Jo nodded.

'Sorry, I don't know what that means,' said Mandy. 'I know I should, but I'm an old bird 'oo spends her days nicking smack heads for stealing razor blades. Sorry if I don't dress this up in the right language, but does that mean he were a bloke but he's had 'is old lad lopped off and is now a woman?'

'She may have undergone sex reassignment surgery, yes,' said Jo. 'Or she might not. She might just know she's been born into the wrong body and lives as a woman.'

Mandy pulled a face. 'God, that'd be bloody horrible, that; feeling like you're in the wrong body. Poor sod. So does that mean, like...err...you're a bloke physically, but inside you're a woman, so you end up fancying blokes, but 'cos you're a bloke that makes you seem gay, but really you're just in the wrong body?'

'That's one possible scenario,' said Jo.

'Bloody hell, that must be sodding confusing,' said Mandy.

'We sometimes deal with transgender people at work,' said Julie.

'Christ on a bike, I bet that's why Sullivan picked on him all them years ago. He's likely to 'ave been proper messed up about who he was,' said Mandy. 'Twats like Sullivan spot vulnerable or mixed-up kids and go after 'em. The bastard.' She said it with a look of unrefined disgust on her face.

'But it's important to make the point that the abuse she suffered was *because* of who she was; it didn't make her who she was,' said Jo.

'If the stories I've read about Sullivan are typical of what happened to Charles, and we've no reason to presume otherwise, he will have been absolutely brutalised in every heinous, violent and sexual way you can imagine,' said Nick.

'Poor bugger. Am I right in thinking that you've never actually met him being *him*, as it were,' said Mandy.

Nick shook his head. 'No, I met him...or rather, her...when she was pretending to be her father and mother. I think Jo's right. She isn't ever Charles, she's Shirley. The old lady she visited only knew her as Shirley.'

Mandy crossed her arms over her big bosom and looked at some more papers. 'I looked him up. Charles was born in 64, but after being taken out of Northdean in 1980, he drops right off the radar. No breaking the law, can't even find a National Insurance number for him, which all suggests you're right, Jo. Clever lass, you.'

'Yeah, cleverer than most,' said Jo, her natural self-confidence never far below the surface.

'Bingo. Aye. We're cracking along 'ere. Top work. That flat in Edinburgh is rented in his, I mean her, father's name, as are the utilities. I tell you what, she's been a right clever bugger. She's used all the documents she's got about her mam and dad to pretend they're alive.'

'Easy to do. Once you've got one bit of ID you can use it to get loads more. She probably just updated her parent's passports. Dressed as them for the photo; if she looks vaguely similar, she'd easily get away with that,' said Jo. 'Maybe she's probably spent time as her parents, on and off, for the last 25 years.'

Nick rubbed his stubble. 'That means she could literally be anywhere now.'

'She'll disappear now. She'll change appearance again. Perhaps change identity altogether once more and live in a different part of the country, or even go abroad. I think it's been really well planned over a long period of time,' said Julie. 'I mean, she should obviously be arrested for murder, but how are you going to catch her?'

Mandy pulled a rubbery face. 'Frankly luv, if she goes abroad we just won't. She's obviously good at creating identities for himself, or herself, I should say. I keep forgetting what to call 'er.'

Jeff yawned and that set off everyone else. 'Can we go home, Mandy? I'm almost asleep here,' he said.

She nodded. 'Yeah, I'm out on my feet as well. You get off home. Where are you staying, Jo?'

Jo looked at Jeff and jerked a thumb at him. 'With the big man, if that's OK, Jeff.'

241

Jeff put his thumbs up.

'I can't give you round-the-clock protection, but just on the off chance that Smith and his cronies turn up on your doorstep, put this mobile number in your phones - only use it if you're in trouble or an emergency. You don't have to speak, just let it ring and I'll put me white 'at on and ride over to save you - if I can - which is by no means guaranteed. That's as much as I can do - but it's a lot more than you'd have got up in Edinburgh.' She pushed a number across the desk on a piece of paper. They all saved it into their phones.

Nick woke up just after 7am. He hated staying in bed once he was awake, so he got up and began writing notes about Charles Stewart and everything they'd learned about him - or Shirley, as Nick now understood. It was an amazing story in many ways, and as he looked over it, he realised, as long as he couched the accusations about her being a murderer to keep on the right side of the law, he could sell the story. He'd have to be careful what was said about the police but it was all do-able. A paper would run it past their lawyers, anyway.

He went for a shower and thought about what to do for the best. In whose interest was it for this story to be made public, apart from his financial gain? It exposed corruption at the highest levels of the police, it would give a voice to the abused people and acknowledge they had been terribly served by the law. But then it would expose Shirley's private life to some degree. It might even get her arrested if someone who knew her saw the story. What would it feel like to see some aspects of your life laid out for public consumption, for, effectively, entertainment? Not good. And also, he still didn't feel that what Shirley had done was so wrong.

It just didn't feel right. He got out of the shower and stood in front of their long, narrow bathroom mirror, looking at himself. A bead of water rolled down his chest and belly, over his pubic hair and down the length of his penis, halting for a moment and then dripping onto the towel on the floor. He watched it go. Another fell off his hair and made the journey south again.

Although in hindsight, he'd been depressed, to one degree or another, off and on, for most of his adult life and for some of his teenage years, too, he couldn't help but feel like he'd had it lucky compared to poor Charles. To suffer that kind of abuse at an early age must affect how you feel about yourself to an almost incomprehensible degree. It's OK being told to not be weighed down or defined by it but that must surely be almost impossible. There are some things in life you can't cut yourself free from, no matter how much you want to. Even changing your identity in the most profound way possible surely wouldn't make it go away, but then maybe it would allow you to live a life separate from it, especially if Charles/Shirley perhaps had been targeted because of how she felt herself to be.

'Like what you see in the mirror, do you?' Julie came into the bathroom and sat down on the toilet. 'It's alright, it's just a wee.'

She looked up at him with bleary eyes and pushed a strand of hair off her face.

'I was just thinking about Charles as a boy. I'm standing here looking at my naked body and while I'm not exactly full of self-love or admiration, what I see doesn't make me think of bad things that happened to me as a kid. I'm not at ease in my own skin because I know what goes on inside my head but even so, physically, I had a clean, safe passage through childhood. Apart from Mickey Smith twatting me in the face at the 4th-year school disco for no good reason at all, it was violence free. There was no dirty old fucker abusing me at the end of the day. When someone has ruined your life like that, it doesn't surprise me that you'd want to splatter their brains all over an office wall.' He made a low growl in his throat, finding the cruelty of humans to each other very hard to accept or to take.

She flushed the toilet and washed her hands, looking at him while she did so. 'I see women most weeks who have been raped, abused, assaulted or...or whatever...often since they were kids and not once, or a few times, but repeatedly and, darlin', you know...people do find a way to deal with it. They find a way to put the hurt and pain in a box, lock it away, and get on with living without it being the whole thing about them. It doesn't go away. It's not like it didn't happen and they need help to do it, that's why we're there, but it *can* be done. I'm not saying it doesn't leave its mark - of course it does - but you don't have to slaughter your way out of the hurt. What Shirley did was wrong, plain and simple, and I won't have it any other way. She should have gathered the evidence and prosecuted Sullivan. Someone would have listened, eventually. Mandy would have.'

'I'm sure she tried that and got nowhere. Then what? Let the fucker get away with it? You don't believe that. You'd take matters into your own hands. You know you would.'

'Would I? Would I? Really?!' She stood hands on hips and stared at him, a quick anger in her tone. If there was one thing she hated, it was being told what she would or wouldn't think or feel or do.

'Yeah, you were brought up to look after yourself. You're a Hardwick lass. If you were abused, you'd take matters into your own hands, one way or another.'

She turned away from him and looked at the floor. 'Not necessarily. No, I wouldn't.'

'You would.' He insisted.

She went quiet and then looked up at him as he dried his hair.

'No. I *didn't*.'

The change of tense was profound.

He stood in silence.

'Didn't?' he said, softly.

She nodded. 'Didn't.'

He let the word soak into him, feeling its meaning.

Even when you love someone, when you're as close, when you're as intimate as it's possible to be with someone, connected together physically and spiritually, we still trick ourselves into feeling and believing we know the other person: that we really *know* them. But really, ultimately, we don't. Not totally. Ultimately we're all on our own. We all walk alone in our own skin through life. People know of us, they know our typical reactions and emotions. But *know* us? Really knowing? How could they? Do we even really know ourselves? Every person is, by the nature of existence itself, an isolated island of emotion, intelligence and experience. We talk about ourselves and how we feel, we recount our experiences, we open up to our loved ones and we placate our loneliness by doing so, but at the end of it all, we're still alone with our own secrets and lies and truths.

'But you always said that you hadn't been...' he began his sentence but stopped, understanding that she had lied to him. Of course she had. Why wouldn't she? It was her way to deal with it. Of course. Even to him. He took a deep breath and reached out to her.

She cleared her throat.

He took her hand and rubbed his thumb up and down the back of hers. She narrowed her eyes a little.

'That man who I said had a poet's eyes? It was him. And no, I didn't report him for raping me. Nor did I exact any sort of revenge. Like millions of women, I took it as my lot in life. I was 25. I even blamed myself, for a while. Wrongly, obviously, but that's what I did. But now, I don't want to talk about it. I've dealt with it. OK? I know about this stuff. There are other things in my past, as well. Right? So don't tell me what I would or wouldn't do. You don't know. Right?' She spoke briefly in her original, unrefined Teesside accent. The one that, perhaps underneath everything, was really her.

He nodded. He didn't want to know any more. It was hers. A private thing. What right do any of us have to intrude on even our closest lover's, friend's or family member's pain? None. Until it is willingly externalised, it should be private to the life that lived it. We all get through life any bloody way we can and god knows, it hurts more often than it should.

Nick got dressed in clean, smart, dark blue jeans and a fitted black t-shirt. He sat on the edge of their bed pulling on his socks when she came in and started getting clean clothes for her work day.

'Don't go dwelling on things,' she said, ruffling his hair.

'Dwelling on things? Me? Never.' He said it with the self-deprecation that only anyone who had spent their life dwelling on things, could manage.

'I'll tell you about it all when I'm ready,' she said taking a white blouse off a hanger. She didn't seem upset.

'Don't feel obliged. Someone once said life is a shit cartoon from which death is a blessed relief. And I agree with that.'

'Someone? You, you mean?' she said and looked so lovely when she said it, he could feel tears well behind his eyes, because she understood him and understanding in life is more rare than it should be.

'Yeah. Busted.' He pushed his tears back down.

She smiled at him, all blue-eyed, tough womanliness. He'd never felt less equal to her. He had his troubles, but she'd experienced the tough times that so many women do and yet almost take for granted as the nature of being female: the discrimination, physical and mental oppression that is all too often woman's lot in a world built by men for men.

'Remember, "I'm forever yours. Faithfully",' he said, singing the line from the song at her, arms out wide as though in a show.

She smiled again and stuck out her bottom lip a little. 'Quoting Journey at me, are you? What a bloody puff.' She finished getting ready for work. 'You look nice in that t-shirt,' she said, with a little stroke to his chest.

In such moments is life lived. Experience understood. Quiet love given. And then you've just got to get on with it, because if you don't, what the hell are you going to do? Life will crush you if you just don't swallow it all down and deal with the shit, sometime-maybe-never.

She finished a coffee and checked her hair in the mirror by the door, the way we all do, flicked the door catch and left with a wave. He watched her go with silent admiration. Walk a mile in my shoes. Yeah, well, maybe if we all could, we'd stop our headbanger monkey ways. The fact seems to be, we can't and maybe that's because when it comes down to it, we're all islands of pain.

He went to the music room and took out Robin Trower's *Twice Removed from Yesterday*, dropping the needle on 'Daydream', a ballad which had always spoken to him about how he felt about Julie, both lyrically and musically, put the headphones on and got on with writing his pieces for websites and newspapers.

When wrapped up inside the music, he could quickly get into writing mode because it focused his mind and took away everyday realities. Plus, the inspirational music just seemed to make his creative juices flow. Time passes in a different way when you're absorbed in something. After an hour's work, he got up to go to the toilet and noticed his phone had rung while he was under the headphones, but he'd been unable to hear it. That was another advantage. It was from Jeff. There was a text from him, too.

'*Am on my way round. Got something brilliant to show you.*'

He'd sent it three minutes ago. Soon, the buzzer went and Nick let him in. Jeff appeared at the door with a record in one hand.

'Now, then. Sorry I missed your call, I was under headphones,' said Nick, as Jeff stepped into the hallway.

'I thought as much. Couldn't wait to show you this. Now, before I show you it, gird your collector's loins.'

'What is it?'

'Before I show you, you should know that it came in two boxes from a house clearance. The rest of it was all *Sound of Music*, *The King and I*, *West Side Story* and Jim Reeves.'

'Ever was it thus, with house clearances.'

'Indeed, but in the middle of it all was this.' He held up the record, dancing on his toes as he did so. The cover was a black and white drawing. Along the middle it said 'Forever Amber' with *The Love Cycle* underneath. In the bottom right corner was a record label logo which said 'Advance'. Nick froze, unable to believe it. It was a progressive rock legendary rare album; it was worth thousands of pounds, as only 99 were rumoured to have been pressed in 1969. My god. You heard about these records and you saw them in *Record Collector*, but to hold one in real life was absolutely amazing.

He took it from him, a huge smile on his face. 'Bloody hell, Jeff, it's in really good condition, as well. Whoo hoo!! This will sell for a fortune.'

The big man looked pleased. 'I know. I've got Emily listing it already. I've seen them go for up to five grand. What's more, as it just came in with the weekly auction room stuff for my default bid of £30, I don't even feel guilty for conning someone out of it.'

'Perfect. Wow. My hands are actually shaking. I've only seen this online, never in reality. I'm sure we never even saw a copy when we were kids, did we?'

'No. Deffo not. It was a private pressing. I don't think it even went into a shop. This has been sitting in someone's stereogram for 40 years, untouched and unplayed. Anyway, it'll make some collector very happy and it'll pay for the electrics at the club. It's a cash injection I really needed.' He beamed at Nick. 'Jo was well chuffed. Not that she'd heard of it, obviously.'

'Well, she's a civilian when it comes to record collecting. No civilian has heard of Forever Amber. Where is she?'

'At the shop with Emily, Matty and the Argmeister.'

'She's not cut off a limb this morning, then?' said Nick, his back to the front door, handing the rare record back to the big man. Jeff slipped it out of its sleeve again and tilted it to the light, admiring it once more.

'Nope. All hands are intact. I've told her to make all the Cliff Richard records disappear, but she's struggling with that. There are some things that magic cannot help with, it seems.'

Nick laughed. 'So pleased about that record, though. Amazing to see it. See, sometimes good things happen to good people.'

'Aye, must be some good karma coming back to me in return for buying all those wristbands for various charities, even though I'd never wear a wristband and am vaguely contemptuous of anyone who does.'

Someone knocked at the door. No buzzer. Must be someone else in the building.

In football, it's often said that you are at your most vulnerable when you have just scored a goal. Your concentration slips because you're so pleased with your success. It's a human instinct to want to enjoy the moment of triumph for a little longer and as a result, you stop focusing on the game, the opposition take advantage of your lapse, go up the other end and score. As in football, so in life. Nick and Jeff were so distracted by the rare record, so pleased to see it, on so many levels, that Nick didn't even think to pause for a moment before he turned and opened the door.

It was a mistake.

A big, big mistake.

CHAPTER 14

He had only just pulled it open by perhaps six inches when the door was forced back with power, knocking Nick backwards, making him fall over onto his back, colliding with Jeff as he went down. He knew in an instant what was happening, but it was already too late.

Four men burst in. One of them was Gordon Smith, his black eyes burning with anger as he stared down at Nick, while another man came through the door and leapt on him, pinning Nick to the floor. Another two got hold of Jeff, grabbed the record from his hands, threw it against the wall and pulled his arm up his back. It was all over in an instant.

'Hey...what the fuck are you doing?!' said Jeff, struggling. 'Leave the fucking record alone, man, eh!'

Smith said nothing but bent over and picked it up, cast a glance at it and then broke it over his knee, while staring Jeff down.

That single act of wanton destruction enraged both Nick and Jeff. Incandescent with fury at seeing such a lovely, rare and valuable thing destroyed just like that, Jeff used all of his 6-foot 3-inch, 15-stone power to wrestle loose from the two men who had gripped him, hitting one on the neck with an elbow and then swinging wildly at the other, connecting with a haymaker to the man's cheek, pole axing him stone cold unconscious. The man fell backwards on his heels, like a cartoon character who has been hit with a flying anvil. It must have been like getting hit by George Foreman at his peak and it was a punch the like of which Nick could never have hoped to throw - what's more, Jeff was roaring like an angry bear as he threw it.

Nick pushed up at the man who pinned him to the floor by the shoulders; getting a hand free, he gripped the man around the neck. He was bigger and stronger by far and though in a vulnerable position, soon began to prevent the man from breathing. He went a bright pink colour and had to let his grip loosen. Nick heaved him off and to one side. Jeff had grabbed the third man by the hair and rammed his head into the plaster wall. 'You fucking philistines!' he yelled, as he threw the man around like he was a rag doll, banging his head into the plaster repeatedly. As the man that had been on top of Nick was getting to his feet, Nick volleyed him in the face, right on the instep, leaping a little off the ground as he connected, the way a footballer does to volley a ball into the top corner of the net. Bam! Right in the face.

Smith stepped back and pulled a face, contemptuous of his own men's inability to overpower Nick and Jeff. Nick, panting for breath, looked around. The two men Jeff had dealt with were groggy on the floor, the third holding his bleeding face.

'Fucking hell. Can youse three stop getting the fucking shit kicked out of you by these two? Do I have to shoot some fucker?' said Smith, pulling a pistol out of his inside pocket, clipping a silencer onto it and holding it to Jeff's head, just as the big man was about to grab him, tear Smith's throat out and choke him with it.

The three men Smith had brought with him seemed as afraid of being shot as Nick and Jeff were.

'You three useless shits, stand there.' He gestured to them to gather by the coat stand. 'You two twats - there.' He pointed for Nick and Jeff to stand opposite. 'Hands on your heads. Move and I'll put a bullet in your head.'

His men were messed up, two barely conscious and a third losing blood. But they all did as they were told, panting for breath after the fight. Smith's dark, blank eyes were as hard to read now as they were when Nick had first met him. He cursed himself for not being more vigilant. Jeff cast a glance at the snapped record lying on the floor, a look of fearless determination about him. Their eyes met. Nick knew they could have all four blokes in a stand-up fight. In his fury, Jeff could probably mash them all with one hand tied behind his back. But Smith was a different matter; he meant business, he had the gun and he was a mean bastard. Like Mandy had said, he was desperate and desperate men do desperate things.

'Right, I'm not messing around with you. Where is Charles Stewart?' said Smith, jabbing the pistol into Nick's ribs. It was hard and frightening. Nick looked at it. This bloody thing could rob him of his life in a microsecond, or worse, it could just really hurt him.

Don't show fear. Be like Souness in a tackle. Stare the bastard down. Inner. Fucking. Boro.

'We haven't a clue,' said Nick, folding his arms. 'Why would we know?'

'Don't fuck me around!' he yelled and jabbed the gun into his chest. 'Tell me and I'll let you live. Don't tell me and I'll shoot your head off.'

Nick stared at him, still unflinching, scared but indignant. What Smith had said just didn't really make sense. He was panicking and not thinking straight. He'd struggled to work out a strategy to put Nick off the Grayson-Thomas trail and had, basically, botched the whole thing. Nick knew he had to be smart. They were trapped in the flat. He needed to get them outside and he needed to get enough time to hit his phone's speed dial number for Mandy.

'Alright, son. You're right. We know where he is. He's from this area. We'll bring him to you,' said Nick. 'He's probably not far away, as it happens.'

Smith smiled a horrible smile, the smile of a man used to getting his own way and exerting power over people. 'The Dominator', Jules had said. Yeah, that was so very right. 'Aye, right. I thought he would be one of your mob. His family are all from round here.'

'What are you going to do to him?'

'What am I going to do? What do you think I'm going to do?' said Smith.

'Kill him?' said Nick.

Smith just smiled at him again in a way which wasn't a smile at all. 'Make the call. Tell him to meet us in the shopping centre roof car park. That's where we parked.'

It was too easy. Smith was too desperate to think this through.

'I'll text him.' Nick took out his phone, copied Mandy and Julie into the same message: '*Smith and 3 thugs are at the flat. He's got a gun. Me and Jeff battered 3 of them. They want Charles Stewart. I'll take them to Castlegate rooftop car park. Be there.*'

'Right, I've told him to meet us in the Castlegate car park. Why do you want him, detective? What's this all about? Must be heavy for you to come down here with three goons in tow, who, by the way, are not hard enough. These three are worse than the two from the Iona bar that you paid to scare me off. I fucked them up good and proper, as well.'

The three, rather nondescript blokes in hoodies and jeans, looked a bit sheepish as well as a bit bloodied and bruised.

Smith, like a lot of proper hard men, grudgingly admired men who could dish out a beating, even if it was to his own hired thugs. 'Aye. I reckon you're right. You fuckin' missed your role in life as paid muscle, Guymer. And this fucking one, dear me, pal. You're a wild fuckin' animal, you, pal.'

'You were well out of order, breaking that record,' said Jeff, hurt in his eyes, as though Smith had killed someone in front of him.

Nick's phone vibrated. He glanced at the screen. '*Go there now, we'll be mob handed in 10 minutes.*'

'That's him,' said Nick, quickly deleting the messages he'd sent and received in case Smith took the phone off him. 'He's driving over and parking in the Castlegate centre on the top floor. It's only three minutes' walk. So what the hell do you want with him? What's this all about?'

'I'm not about to explain it to you. You already fuckin' know, pal, if I'm any judge. Right, we're out of here, you lead the way. I've got this in your back the whole way so don't do anything that might make you end up dead.'

It was all working well. He had Smith just where he wanted him. Smith thought he was in control but he wasn't. Just play it cool and Mandy's mob would move in and collar the lot of them.

But Jeff thought differently.

With one last glance at the broken record, he looked at Smith with withering contempt and, regardless of the fact he was holding a gun at him, just battered the fucker in the face. Wham! One. Wham! Two. Wham! Three. Right full in the face. Two right crosses followed up with a left. Smith staggered back against the wall, dazed and confused by the full frontal assault. It was as quick as Nick had ever seen Jeff move. Hell hath no fury like a record store owner who loses a rare record. Before the three other thugs could do anything, Jeff had smashed Smith into the middle of next week. It was a thing of peculiar beauty but it was really bloody dangerous because Smith still held his gun.

The three hired muscle types moved to help their boss. Nick didn't know what to do. He'd wanted them arrested at the car park. Jeff's intervention had screwed things up.

Two of them leapt on Jeff's back. Nick gave them both a heavy dig in the kidneys which made them lose their grip and then chinned the third one, following up the punch with a knee in the balls. He was the one whose face he ruined earlier. He'd better be getting good money for this because bits of him were falling off.

'Son, this isn't going well for you and your mob. You're getting a fucking kicking, again,' said Jeff, about to hit Smith into an unconscious state.

But Smith wasn't having it. He looked up at Jeff and shot him. Just like that. Shot him.

Just raised the gun and squeezed the trigger.

Nick screamed at the top of his voice. 'Nooooo!!!'

Jeff looked down at where the bullet had hit him, leaned over and hit Smith again in the face, smashing his cheek bone into pieces as Smith turned his head away to try and protect himself from the punch.

Nick leapt through the air at Smith before he could fire again, grabbing his right hand and forcing it upwards. He squeezed the trigger again and sent another silenced bullet into the plaster ceiling.

'Nice of you to try and kill the mice in the roof, Smith, you fucking prick,' said Nick, gripping him by the wrist. How to get him to drop the gun? He bit him hard right where the artery goes into the hand. Smith screamed and let the gun go, unable to hold onto anything when in so much pain.

But unluckily, it bounced on its barrel off a small table where they put their keys and landed in front of the thugs.

'I've got the gun, boss,' said one of them, picking it up. 'Shall I fuckin' kill him?'

Smith struggled to his feet, clutching his broken face.

'Jeff! Are you alright?' said Nick, looking at him just standing there, patting at himself.

'Aye, I think so. Somehow, the prick missed me.'

'You think it's your fucking lucky day, pal? You're fuckin' wrong. Fuck me, my fucking face. I will take great pleasure in knee capping you for doing that to me.' Smith reached for the gun.

Nick had to think fast.

'You can't do that. You need both of us in the car park. I told Charles me and Jeff would be there. He's super paranoid, if only one of us turns up he'll know something is wrong. He'll leg it and you'll never see him again.'

Smith looked at him. He was drunkenly dazed, the clear whites of his eyes now full of burst blood vessels. His nose was dislodged from its moorings, drifting to the right and swelling up. His cheek was already a strange strawberry colour, as tissue and bone blended into one large, angry haematoma. His face was a total mess and must have hurt like hell. But Nick's words had worked. Smith couldn't risk putting who he thought was Charles Stewart off, so he put the gun into his pocket, pushed at Jeff like a furious teenager and then, holding onto his bloody nose, pointed to the door. One of his men opened it. 'Stand back, I'll keep them covered,' he said.

'Why don't we cuff them, boss?' said Jim.

'Yeah, good fuckin' idea. Jim, do it.'

Jim produced two sets of metal handcuffs and proceeded to grab both Nick's and Jeff's hands and fasten them behind their backs.

They were pushed out of the door. 'Are you sure you're OK?' said Nick to Jeff.

'Aye. It must have gone under my armpit. Can't believe what he did to *The Love Cycle.* That was wrong, man.'

'Stop going on about the fucking record, for fuck's sake. You fucking people do my head in,' said Gordon Smith, angry and in pain, as they walked down the stairs and out into Green Dragon Yard. Drinkers outside of the Green Dragon who were having a fag gave them a cursory glance, but the gun must have been hidden and seeing people who have recently been hit in the face is not an uncommon thing in Stockton town centre. You don't ask. You're just glad it's not you. With hands behind their backs, they looked like they were being arrested. Again, a not-uncommon sight.

They walked in silence along to the ugly Castlegate shopping centre and went up the stairs to the car park on the top. It was an ugly concrete place, every corner piss-stained. As they emerged onto the roof top parking space, panting for breath from the exertion, the stiff northeasterly blowing in their hair, they were met by a familiar face.

'Let them go,' said Jo King, standing square on to Smith and the three thugs at the top of the car park steps. They just laughed at her.

'Aye, right, darlin', said Smith, bitterly, his face swollen. 'Do you want to fight us all together or one at a time, eh?'

The other three laughed and pushed Nick and Jeff towards an estate car. A stiff wind blew over the top of the car park.

'Don't do anything daft, Jo,' Jeff said.

'Are you alright?' she said.

'We're fine,' said Jeff.

'Aye, just be a good little girl, eh, whoever the fuck you are,' said one of Smith's men.

'Fuck you!' yelled Jo, and pulled the knife she used on stage from somewhere in her jacket. 'See this? It's very sharp. It could cut your throat with just one move.' She mimed it across her own throat.

Smith produced his gun and pointed at her. Nick was sure he was going to shoot her dead. 'No! Don't shoot her. Jo, get away from here. These men are dangerous.'

'Are they? Well, I'm fucking dangerous as well,' she said, in her cocky way, tapping the tip of the knife on the palm of her right hand. She really did have some fucking Inner Boro, this one, but he was so scared that Smith would pull that trigger.

'Fuckin' take another step and I'll kill ye,' said Smith. He would. He really bloody would. Thankfully, Jo didn't take another step. She stared him down, the point of the knife on her wrist. You couldn't tell it wasn't a real hand.

'There's a good girl, now deal with her, Jim,' said Smith, pointing the gun at Nick and Jeff and pushing them towards the open back door of the estate car, a big Mercedes.

Jim moved towards her. 'Put the knife down, darlin' or I'll fuckin' hurt ye,' he said.

'You will, will you?' said Jo, fearlessly.

'You've got balls, you, I'll give ye that,' said one of the other men, also moving towards her.

Smith pushed Nick and Jeff into the back of the large car, but as he did so, there was a piercing scream.

Nick knew what he'd see when he looked over to Jo. She was leaning forward, hacking at her right wrist with the knife held in her left hand. A big squirt of blood fired up into the air and hit one of Smith's men full in the face as he was walking towards her.

'Fucking hell. What the fuck...?' said Smith, seeing what she was doing. All the colour fell from his swollen face and he turned away from the car.

The three thugs were not just shocked by the sight of Jo hacking off her hand and by the blood - they were scared witless. And rightly so. It was absolutely bloody terrifying because it looked 100 per cent real and as she severed it right off, screaming wild and terrified as she did so, it gave Nick and Jeff a chance to get out of the car.

'It's just a fucking stunt, you pricks!' shouted Smith as he moved towards Jo, but realising too late. Nick and Jeff sprinted away from the car, running in erratic lines to try and make themselves difficult targets, hands behind their backs, trying not to fall over.

Smith fired. Nick felt the bullet whistle past his head. A puff of concrete dust exploded when the shell hit the wall. They both dived down behind parked cars for protection.

A red-faced Mandy Beale came running up the steps from the market hall, with six other policemen in tow and Julie hot on their heels. There was a screech of tyres from the ramp and three police cars emerged onto the roof top.

'He's got a gun, Mandy!' shouted Nick. 'Jules, get down, get out of the way!' She ducked down behind a Range Rover. Mandy stood, hands on hips.

' 'As he, now? We'll see about that. I don't bloody like bloody perverts coming onto my patch. Larry, get these lads' cuffs off.' She pointed to

Nick and Jeff squatting down beside the cars.

She marched over to Smith's henchmen, who were looking around themselves in a panic as their way out was blocked. The one called Jim tried to sprint for the ramp to get away, but with the expertise of an old school defender, Mandy stuck out a big left leg and tripped him up, sending him sprawling. 'I don't think so, do you?' she said, with magnificent contempt. 'Collar 'im, George.' She directed her men like a traffic cop, waving and pointing at them, 'Mal, Kev - take the other two in the hoodies. Is one of them Gordon Smith, Nick?'

'No.'

'Well, where is he?' said Mandy.

In the confusion of Mandy and her men arriving, after firing the shot at Nick, Smith had disappeared. He couldn't have got away. All his exits were blocked, so he had to be in hiding.

Nick and Jeff stood up and looked around.

'Wherever he is, he's got a gun, Mandy.'

'No 'e 'asn't,' said Mandy, pointing at the black pistol lying on the tarmac. He must have dropped it, or maybe it was out of bullets. 'Tommy, bag that gun up.' She gestured to her man to get the gun, then she called out in her flat Yorkshire voice. 'Gordon Smith - there's no way out of here, wherever you're hiding, you might as well come out and give yourself up. I'm going to nick you one way or another, you know it and I know it. You're absolutely banged to rights. The only 'ope you've got is to co-operate with us, so come on, let's be 'avin you!' She stood, hands on her big hips, looking around, absolutely in command of the situation: totally bossing it.

They all stood still and looked around for movement.

Nothing.

Then Nick saw him. He was quick as he crawled out from under a car and clambered up the perimeter wall, the back of his calves resting against a perimeter metal pole. There he stood for literally one second, framed against the grey Teesside sky that was about to dispense heavy rain, then outstretched his arms and with a final dark-eyed look straight at Nick, still expressionless, he leaned back into the void, disappeared from view and fell to his death.

Seconds later, there were screams from below on the High Street.

Mandy walked to where he'd been and looked over. Smith was lying dead, his body twisted at an odd angle and bleeding copiously from the head.

'Well, a couple of Ibuprofen won't fix that headache,' she said, almost under her breath.

It was over.

CHAPTER 15

When they all left the police station later that day, after hours of statements, they adjourned to the Royal Oak for a bloody big drink.

Nick bought three glasses of white wine, and a tonic water for himself.

'Cheers, people. I'm just glad you're still alive, Jeff. When Smith fired his gun at you, almost point blank, I thought that was you gone,' he said.

Jeff made a face at him and held an index finger aloft. 'See, this is the advantage of wearing big baggy clothes - no-one knows where they start and your body ends. It went right under my armpit.' He held out the loose checked fabric. A hole was clearly visible. 'Mind, we made a mess of your flat by the door. There's bullets in the wall and roof and I smashed that fella's head into the plaster a few times.'

'There's blood off his broken face on the walls,' said Julie. 'Shall we move out soon, Nick? I feel like it's got a bad vibe in there.'

'Yeah, maybe we should,' said Nick, who thought it sounded like a great idea.

'Do you think they'll ever find Shirley?' said Jeff, rubbing at his sore wrists from where the cuffs had dug into him.

'No chance,' said Jo with her customary certainty.

'Why are you so sure?' asked Julie.

Jo swilled her drink around in her glass. 'Because she planned all of this rigorously and when you rigorously plan something, when you've got everything in place, when you know exactly what you're doing, then you can get away with almost anything. It's like doing a show. I think she'll have had all sorts of back-up plans in place and was prepared for any eventuality. She was brilliant at muddying the waters and she understood just how Smith would operate. If you think about it, she was like a puppet master, controlling all of our perceptions of the crime. She shaped the reality for us. She'd created her parents as real people. Brought them back to life, in a way. To have rented a flat in her dad's name, and to work for a year as your own mother - man, that is serious psycho shit. It was a brilliant thing to do: creating real people with real lives in order to use them as cover to murder someone and have a photo of yourself taken doing it, in the knowledge that it will bring down the people involved in your own historic abuse. Then you can just put them to bed, and walk away forever. As long as she doesn't do something stupid, like tell someone what she's done, or the friend who took the photo from the office in Charlotte Square doesn't shop her, she'll melt back into society. I can't see how the police will find who took that photo because anyone could walk up those stairs and take a picture from that window. They might work there or they might not. Like I say, it's brilliant, really,' said Jo.

'It was just as Josh said, being invisible *was* the best way to get away with something. I should've realised when I met her dressed as Frank, what was going on. "Frank" was so certain that I hadn't met Barbara - and obviously she'd know whether I had or not, as she was her,' said Nick.

'Smith was out-thought by Shirley, every step of the way,' said Jeff. 'I'll tell you what I'd love to know. Frank Stewart fell downstairs and was found dead by Barbara. Is it possible she pushed him? Did she kill him because Frank was a paedophile, too? Maybe Frank abused young Charles and she killed him.'

Jo sucked in air and blew it out of her nose. 'That had crossed my mind, but I don't think so.'

'Why not, Jo?' asked Julie.

'Because she wouldn't have dressed as him. It'd be too painful to play that role. But we'll never know, will we? Not for sure, anyway.'

Jeff nodded. 'I must say, I've never been so glad that a bloke is dead as I am that Smith took the big leap. What a wrong 'un he was. And to break that Forever Amber album was a crime.'

Nick put his fingers together. 'Yeah, I don't think anyone will be sorry he's leaking crimson onto the High Street. He was having to walk an impossible line. Obviously, he knew that Grayson-Thomas was Sullivan. He also knew why he'd been killed and that he was the last of the Young Offenders Board to be murdered, but he couldn't let that into the public domain. He was protecting his own back, protecting Fat Franny, his ex-boss and the paedophile ring that he was involved in, but all the while trying to look like he was investigating a murder properly and trying to find out the identity of the person who did it, so he could kill them and close them down.'

'That was all too much for him,' said Jo. 'He couldn't square the circle of having to find his killer for his own needs, whilst hiding who it was from everyone else.'

Nick nodded and took a drink. 'No wonder he messed up, really. There was no way he could keep on top of it all. It was too many plates on sticks to keep spinning and he's obviously drawn attention to himself, because they were going to bust him, by what Mandy said. I suspect the police that came to see us at the flat that night reported what we'd said back to him, and he just made the info disappear. But I bet when we said it was Barbara Stewart, he would have found out she was dead, and knew it couldn't be her. Even if he guessed it was likely to be the Stewarts' only child doing the killing, he just didn't know how to find "him" - for the same reasons we couldn't find "him". He had no idea he was Shirley Someone. He was stuck and he certainly didn't want the press sniffing around in case they got a whiff of child abuse - hence he paid those two idiots to attack me to scare me off after seeing me with Wally, a journo he already knew. He thought uh-oh, the press are digging into this.'

'Those coppers who came to the flat *were* genuine, then?' said Jeff.

'Yeah, I think they were just asking around to try and find out who she was. Just doing their job. Smith couldn't suppress the photo because Shirley had sent it to the police and the media all at the same time,' said Nick. 'That was the masterstroke because it meant Smith couldn't stop it being in the public domain.'

'It was Smith who came to see me after my show,' said Jo. 'Lucky for me he didn't see the show or I might not have had the element of surprise on him in that car park. He obviously wanted to know if I was in any way a threat to him.'

Jeff stroked his beard. 'You know how you're always saying that your act relies on shaping the audience's perceptions and expectations, Jo?'

'Aye. That's the big thing.' she said.

'Well, weirdly, Gordon Smith was really trying to do the same thing to Nick. Faking that PNC printout and trying to create a web of lies to throw you off the scent.'

'Yeah. This whole thing has been about misdirection,' said Julie.

'Good word, Jules,' said Jo, with a grin.

'Just a pity I went off on one about seeing Barbara in Bedale. Eee, god, I was so sure it was her. One thing that this whole business has taught me is that your brain plays tricks on you and you can see things just because you want to, or have been prompted to believe them.'

Nick took a drink and let out a long sigh. 'Yeah, right down to the Barbara Stewart gravestone. For Shirley to have found that and had it in her mind to refer to, off the cuff, that's detailed research, man. It showed how well constructed her story was. She had it all in place.'

'Impressive, really,' said Jeff. 'I think she must have written it all out, almost like a film script, and prepared for any eventuality, so that no matter what happened, she had a route through it. But why do you think that even after Shirley killed Sullivan, in her Barbara guise, she was still going about as Frank? Wouldn't it have made more sense to make Frank disappear at the same time as Barbara?'

Nick pulled on his bottom lip. 'It *was* a risk. The Frank I met was scared, really scared when I said hello. I think it's simply that she had to clear the flat up. She was done there now that the shooting had happened. That part of the plot was complete. She had to do that as Frank. If she'd done it as Barbara, she might have been recognised from the newspaper. And she couldn't do it as the person we've called Kiki Dee, which we now know is just Shirley, because that would potentially connect her real identity to the woman who did the murder. She went there at night when I was staying over and again, she shit herself when I opened that door. She must have thought I was out to get her. As Frank she'd put two bin bags into the car. Maybe that was the last of the stuff moved out but then she came back under cover of night to get something else.'

Julie tapped on the table with a fingertip. 'You know, when we met "Barbara" neither of us thought she looked old. You even said that in bed one night, didn't you?' she said, looking at Nick. 'And that was obviously because she wasn't. That was another clue we should have picked up on.'

'Yeah, but we're not conditioned to expect the people we meet to be someone they're not, if you get what I mean,' said Jeff.

Nick nodded. 'Do you think it's harder for a man to be a woman than it is the other way round? I think I do,' said Nick.

But Jeff raised his bushy eyebrows at that. 'And what makes you think that, O wise one?'

Nick said, 'Blokes don't have hips. We're straight up and down. Hips are a uniquely female thing.'

'Some women don't have curvy hips,' said Julie. 'You see women all the time who are also straight up and down.'

'I know what you mean, but they do still have hips and that makes you walk a bit different. Even when a bloke is a convincing *looking* woman, the walk gives it away. You'd have to learn to walk like a woman.'

Jeff folded his arms across his chest. 'Is that right? I never knew you were such an expert in human physiology.' He laughed a little.

Jo leaned forward and took a big drink. 'Well, let me tell you this, Nick Guymer, *I* didn't have to learn to walk like a woman,' she said, her narrow eyebrows raised.

'Eh? But you are a woman, so obviously, you didn't have to learn,' said Nick. He looked at her. She looked back at him.

'You might want to think a bit harder about that. My show isn't called

King Tees for nothing. You were on the money when you asked if it was King Tease,' said Jo, her eyebrows still raised. Jeff made a low rumbling laugh.

Julie let out a small yelp and put her hand over her mouth. Nick stared at her in blankly. What was he missing here?

'What did I tell you all along to do?' said Jo, taking a big drink.

'To question all realities,' said Julie, immediately.

'Exactly. And that applied to me as well. I'm no less physically a man than you are in that photo you sent Julie, Nick, give or take an inch or three.' She grinned at him and then at Julie and Jeff. Julie yelped in shock again and gave Nick a slack-jawed, wide-eyed look.

Nick looked at her. Jo was a man? What? Was she just trying to mess with his head?

'Fizzin' hell, you've not seen that photo, have you?' said Julie, peeping out from behind her fingers and wincing. 'How embarrassing.'

'Oh, yeah, I'm not surprised you're always smiling, Jules,' said Jo, laughing.

'Ha, that's what Mandy Beale said as well,' said Nick, rubbing his face with the palms of his hands.

Julie howled a laugh and punched him on the arm. 'How has she seen it?! Have you been showing off? Silly question, of course you haven't. That'd be the last thing you'd do.'

'It was just an accident that she saw it,' said Nick, sheepishly. 'She thought it was funny as well.'

Julie was rocking forwards and backwards now, still laughing.

'You shouldn't leave your phone lying around,' said Jo, 'or nosy people like me will look at it.'

'That's literally the only time in my life I've taken a picture like that and it'll be the last, I can tell you that,' he said.

'I've not seen the photo and I never, ever want to,' said Jeff. 'I fear the male anatomy, especially my own.'

Nick cleared his throat. 'Can we stop talking about that bloody photo? I'm going to delete it. So, Jo, you're telling me that you're a man. That you're male?' said Nick, looking Jo in the eyes.

She was solid and clear. 'Yes. Or rather, I was born physically male, but I've known I was female since I was a kid.'

He could scarcely believe it. She didn't look male at all in his eyes. It was just another layer of illusion. Jules had said when they first met her that she was a funny little rooster. How true that was.

'But you haven't got an Adam's Apple.'

'Hormones, darling. Hormones. All part of the treatment to make me physically into who I really am.'

Nick stared at her. Was she joking? No, she was Jo King. He felt a bit numb. Jeff was grinning.

'Why aren't you shocked, Jeff?' said Nick, seeing his expression.

'Because I've known all along, or at least after the first night Jo stayed at mine, but she swore me to secrecy. Sorry, man. It's very cool, though, isn't it?'

Nick felt the scales drop from his eyes. He and Julie had said there was nothing sexual between Jeff and Jo. That was obviously why. They were friends, not lovers.

'You're a little bundle of surprises, you, lass,' Julie said, raising her eyebrows and smiling.

Jo nodded. 'Maybe I should have told you two earlier, but it does freak some people out. It's pretty simple. Probably, like Charles Stewart, I'm just a woman who's got a bloke's body. Not for too much longer, though, thankfully. It took me a long time to work it all out, but I'm in a good place about it all now. Got a lot of help from a Women's Aid group in London. The hormones have kicked in big style. They've made my arse massive, but you can't have everything. My voice is lighter now and I'll start surgery early next year. I don't make a habit of telling people, except for the big man here and I thought he'd be cool about it, after talking to you, Jules, when were in the Masham.' She gave him a big, wonky-toothed smile and squeezed his arm.

Jeff grinned and saluted her. 'Mind you, I am notoriously appealing to the transgender community,' he said, nodding and pulling a smug face. 'Largely because I am actually a woman called Bernard...err...I think.' He looked down his shirt, inspecting his breasts and then jiggling them. 'Yeah, Bernard, that's right.'

They all laughed.

Jeff went on. 'But it's all rock 'n' roll, isn't it? I shall look forward to the new installation, Jo. Genitals 2.0, as it were, like.' He stroked her on the back of the head with his big hand.

'Well, I hope they make a good job of it. I want a premium-quality vagina.'

'It's major shit, is that. I think you're so brave, man,' said Jeff, an arm around her shoulder.

'I wouldn't worry, Jo, most blokes don't spend much time looking down there,' said Julie. 'For half of them, it's all a mysterious and complicated world of flaps 'n' gaps. If you gave them a diagram and magnifying glass most of them still couldn't find your clitoris, trust me.'

Nick put his hand in the air. 'Please miss, I know where your clitoris is.'

Julie laughed. 'Yeah, but I had to give you a guided tour and comprehensive notes, first.'

'True. But I found the powerpoint presentation very useful and the homework involving a pencil very enjoyable.'

Jeff saluted. 'At least if you made a mistake you could always use a rubber! Boom! Come on, Big Fish would pay 50 quid for that joke. Vaginas rule!'

'Well, there are certainly plenty of twats in the government!' said Julie, with her best innocent look. 'If you'll pardon my French.'

That made them all laugh, again.

Nick ran his fingers through his hair and looked at Jo, this new friend, this quirky, confident, funny and original person. She was grinning with bright eyes, clearly at ease with herself and with who she was, however difficult that journey had been. And maybe that's all any of us really want out of life; to be allowed to be who we really are, because if we're not comfortable in our own skin, we'll never be truly happy.

He felt quite envious of her. She was on the way towards being outwardly, what she knew she was inwardly. But Nick was pretty sure he'd often struggle with being who he was, for all of his life, but then, that was *his* thing, be it a blessing or a curse. Maybe, like Jo, he just had to embrace who he was a lot more and fight it a lot less.

And after all, he always had that secret Teesside weapon to help him: his Inner Boro.

THE END

Books in the Nick Guymer Series
Published by HEAD PUBLISHING

Kindle/Paperback

http://www.johnnicholsonwriter.co.uk

About John Nicholson

John is a well-known football writer whose work is read by tens of thousands of people every week. He's a columnist for Football365.com and has worked for the Daily Record, The Mirror, Sky and many other publications over the last 14 years.

Books in the Archie Taylor Series
Published by HEAD PUBLISHING

1. The Girl Can't Help It (2014)
2. Sugar Mama (2016)

Kindle/Paperback

http://www.johnnicholsonwriter.co.uk

Other John Nicholson Books
published by Biteback Publishing

We Ate All The Pies -
How Football Swallowed Britain Whole (2010)

The Meat Fix -
How 26 Years of Healthy Eating Nearly Killed Me (2012)